Meg Hutchinson

Meg Hutchinson left school at fifteen and didn't return to education until she was thirty-three, when she entered Teacher Training College and studied for her degree in the evenings. Ever since she was a child, she has loved telling stories and writing 'compositions'. She lived for sixty years in Wednesbury, where her parents and grandparents spent all their lives, but now has a quiet little cottage in Shropshire where she can indulge her passion for storytelling.

Meg Hutchinson's previous novels, *Abel's Daughter*, *For the Sake of Her Child*, *A Handful of Silver* and *No Place of Angels* are also available from Coronet.

Also by Meg Hutchinson

Abel's Daughter
For the Sake of her Child
A Handful of Silver
No Place of Angels

A Promise Given

Meg Hutchinson

CORONET BOOKS
Hodder and Stoughton

Copyright © 1998 Meg Hutchinson

First published in 1998 by Hodder and Stoughton
First published in paperback in 1999 by Hodder and Stoughton
A division of Hodder Headline PLC
A Coronet paperback

The right of Meg Hutchinson to be identified as the Author of
the Work has been asserted by her in accordance with the
Copyright, Designs and Patents Act 1988.

10 9 8 7 6 5 4 3 2 1

A CIP catalogue record for this title
is available from the British Library.

ISBN 0 340 69684 2

Printed and bound in Great Britain by
Clays Ltd, St Ives plc

Hodder and Stoughton
A division of Hodder Headline PLC
338 Euston Road
London NW1 3BH

For my grandchildren, Matthew, Esther, Carys and Liam, who must be heartily weary of that time-worn phrase: 'When I was a little girl . . .'

Chapter One

'You killed him. You killed my son!'

Hannah Cade glared fixedly at her step-daughter.

'You drowned my child . . . my baby. You killed him!'

'The wench wouldn't do that, Hannah Cade. Her wouldn't do the lad harm.'

Hannah swung round, eyes rapidly surveying the faces of the crowd that had gathered, the gleam of madness deepening as they settled on the stick-thin figure of Ginny Marshall.

'No, p'raps her wouldn't, not without help from another.' Hannah's voice rose to a screech. 'Maybe that other one be you, Ginny Marshall! We all know you be partial to Richie Cade's daughter, like we all knows you be partial to anything female. What did her give you, Ginny? What did her give you for helping her to kill my son . . . what did Rachel Cade let you do to her?'

'I never helped her.' Ginny's crow-bright eyes met her accuser's squarely but already the seeds of suspicion had sprouted. The listening women sensed a lynching in the offing and were ripe for the entertainment. 'I never helped her 'cos her didn't do it. Rachel loved the lad, ain't nobody 'ere can say other. As for what you say, 'tis a lie, Hannah Cade. I never killed for no woman!'

'Mebbe not.' A second voice rose from the centre of the crowd. 'But you've fumbled more than a few.'

1

'That be true, the dirty bastard!'

'Wenches don't be safe where her be!'

'Chuck her in the lock – it be the best place for the likes of her.'

The cries came from all sides now, feeding on each other, threats flying thick and fast.

'Throw her in. P'raps the cut will wash the filth from her black soul!'

The latest cry adding fuel to the flames, the group of women closed tighter about Ginny and the terrified girl.

'And her!' Hannah Cade's body twitched and jigged to the tune of madness playing within her, her crazed eyes gleaming and her finger pointing at her step-daughter. 'Let that one feel the water an' all. Let her know the touch of it in her nostrils, let it fill her lungs as it filled my babby's, let it fill her mouth while it carries her deep. Do to her what was done to my son!'

'Yes, do it, do what the madness inside Hannah Cade be wanting you to do.' Ginny Marshall stepped to the side of the young girl. 'C'mon,' she goaded. 'Where be your spirit? Which of you will be the first to cross Ginny Marshall?'

Almost as one the advancing women halted as Ginny, her clothes hanging like rags on her skinny frame, lifted a warning hand. 'You all know the things Ginny Marshall can do. All but two or three of you 'as sought her out to shift an unwanted child from the womb. If that be the fumbling you speak of then, yes, I fumbled you, but it was of your own asking. And how many of you 'ave come for potions? Like you come, Hannah Cade.' Her glance, black and piercing, swung to her accuser. 'You came to seek a potion that would bring Richie Cade to your bed when your own plain face and scrawny body could not. You got what you asked – but you forgot to ask for one that would hold him there. He came to you once only and when you told him the result of his lying with you, he married you. But never since that one night has he slept beside you, never but that one time has his body covered your own, and *that* be your bitterness, *that* be the root of the jealousy and spite that grows like hemlock inside you, sending its poison into your veins, nourishing its fruit of bitterness and deceit.'

'That be lies!' Hannah's demented scream rang out over the heads of the now silent women. 'Richie Cade loves me. He married me out of love.'

'Did he?' Ginny's thin face held a mocking sneer. 'Ask *them*. Ask who believes it was love and not Ginny Marshall's potion brought him to your bed?'

The watching women shuffled uneasily and their glances fell before Ginny's fierce stare.

'Richie Cade lives in the same house as you for one reason only, and she be standing 'ere beside me. It be his daughter. The child you loathe with all the strength that be in you – a hatred born of jealousy for the love he holds for her and the one who birthed her, a love you know he never had for you nor never will. That be the canker that be eating you away, Hannah Cade, the rot that will see you in your grave.'

'My grave waits for me same as yours waits for you.' Hannah stared at the silent onlookers, eyes rolling like a terrified horse's. 'Will you go to it in peace knowing the murder of a five-year-old boy went unavenged? Will your spirit lie quiet in the knowledge you let a murderer go unpunished, left her free to roam God's earth, maybe to commit the same foulness, again and again? Who knows how many more mothers' children that girl will kill?'

'Ar, your graves be waiting on you.' Ginny lifted her head, her thin hair blowing like dust before the breeze. ''Ow many of you will go to them with blood on your hands? The blood of a young wench, guilty of no more than loving a half-brother, and 'ow many be willing to risk the words of Ginny Marshall? For I tell you this: any woman who lays hands on the daughter of Richie Cade will know *my* vengeance. Any woman raising her hand against this wench raises it against me and in the raising condemns her own, for no child of her body will live. Each, whether 'tis born or yet to come, will go before her into the ground.'

'Your words hold no fear for me.' Hannah's manic laughter rang out. 'My child was taken from the canal, the life already gone from him, and my body will carry no more. But my spirit will lie in peace, the peace of knowing I repaid the death of my boy, knowing I took the life of her that robbed him of his.'

Before anyone could move, she grabbed a brick that had fallen from the half-demolished wall at her back, lunging with it towards the trembling girl.

'Your words won't save her, Ginny Marshall, you shan't keep me from paying her out. You shan't keep me from killing her!'

The words screaming from her Hannah threw herself forward, the brick raised in her hand.

'Her has to die, as my lad has died.'

Swinging the brick in an arc about her head, she brought it slashing downward as Ginny stepped in front of the girl. The same instant the brick caught her full in the face, smashing her skull instantly.

Rachel Cade opened her mouth but there was no scream, only blackness as her body crumpled to the ground.

'You are charged with murder.'

The sound of Isaiah Bedworth's voice echoed in the high-ceilinged upstairs room of The Jolly Collier.

'You are accused of deliberately throwing a five-year-old boy into the canal at Toll End Locks. How do you plead, guilty or not guilty?'

'I didn't.' Rachel's mouth trembled. 'I would never hurt Robbie, he was my brother and I loved him.'

'That is no answer!' The magistrate brought his fist down hard on the table before him. 'How do you plead, guilty or not guilty?'

Her fingers twisting tightly together, her voice little more than a whisper, Rachel gave her reply. 'Not guilty.'

Isaiah looked closer at the girl the constable had brought before him. Hair the colour of wild wheat framed a face that already held a remarkable beauty before tumbling over breasts that looked firm and pert beneath the simple brown dress. Beneath the cover of the table he felt a stiffening in his groin. This girl was pretty, very pretty. He had not had one like her for a long time.

''Tis a lie! 'Er killed him, 'er killed my Robbie!'

Hannah's wild cry rang through the room of the tavern that served the small community of Horseley as courtroom, interrupting Isaiah's anticipation of what he was sure was to come.

'Silence!' He slapped the palm of his hand against the table as he glanced at Hannah. 'I recognise the pain you are suffering, but this room is now a court of law and will be observed as such. Any disturbance and I will have the constable remove the lot of you.'

Turning his attention once more to Rachel, the constable standing at her side, Isaiah quenched the lust that flared in him.

'Now,' he said, small eyes roving over her, 'tell me exactly what happened?'

'We . . . we were out for a walk.' Rachel's quiet voice trembled as much as her mouth. 'I . . . I always took him out for a walk on the heath when . . . whenever my stepmother allowed.'

'And you took him on the heath this morning?' Isaiah fingered the generous moustache that spread over his cheeks joining bushy sideburns, effectively framing the upper half of his podgy face.

Rachel looked over to where her father sat, his head in his hands, among the folk crowded into the room to watch the spectacle. Someone had fetched him from the mine and he had come running just as Ginny Marshall had fallen dead, her face smashed in. He had held Robbie a long time, cradling the small body in his arms while tears marked long white channels through the black coal dust that covered his face. Then, after laying the small form on the kitchen table, he had kissed his son and come to see his daughter brought before the magistrate.

'Yes, sir.' Rachel tried to stem her own tears but they refused to be stopped. 'Hannah . . . my stepmother . . . wanted groceries from Tipton Green and when Robbie begged to go with me, she said he could. We were on the way home when Robbie asked to see the barges that tie up in the basin at Workhouse Lane. I . . . I know I should have said no,' she glanced up at the magistrate, her wide violet eyes swimming with tears, 'but I never could refuse Robbie anything. I loved him . . . I loved him.'

Glancing sternly towards the murmuring villagers the magistrate waited a few moments, allowing Rachel's sobs to subside, then asked: 'Did you take your half-brother to the basin at Workhouse Lane?'

Wiping away tears with her fingers, she nodded. 'Yes,' she whispered. 'We didn't stay very long. I knew his mother would be angry if we were late.'

'And what happened then?' Isaiah asked, her tears affecting his groin more than his mind.

'We made our way home, following the heath along the canal. Robbie was hoping to see a barge being towed. He liked to stroke the horses and the bargees were always very kind. They would lift him on to a horse's back and let him ride a little way along the towpath, or sometimes they even let him ride on the barge. We were about to branch off across the heath back to Horseley when he shouted that the lock was being filled. He darted away before I could prevent him. I ran after him but the basket of groceries was heavy. I saw him jumping up and down on the edge of the lock, and then he . . . he was gone.'

'Are you saying the child fell in?'

'Yes.'

''Tis lies!' Hannah screeched, drowning Rachel's whispered response. 'He didn't fall in, her pushed him in! Her pushed my Robbie in the lock.'

'Hannah Cade!' The magistrate's eyes glared from between bushy eyebrows and encompassing whiskers. 'You also are under indictment and will in turn answer to this court. Until then you will remain silent or be taken to a place of security until you are called.' Turning back to Rachel he asked in a milder tone, mindful of more pleasurable events to come, 'Go on, tell us what happened then.'

Glancing first towards her father, Rachel saw he had not lifted his head but sat slumped as he had from the moment of her being brought into this room, the constable's hand about her elbow.

'I shouted for Robbie to step away from the edge but he called out there was a barge being lifted. He . . . he half turned towards me. I saw his face, full of excitement, and then he began to lean over the lock. He . . . he seemed to hang in the air, and then he fell in.'

Somewhere among the people she had known from childhood, Rachel heard her stepmother's keening stifled as a sympathetic hand was clapped over her mouth. In the murmurings that accompanied the action she heard no sympathy for herself. It was as if the folk of Horseley had already condemned her.

'I ran to the edge of the lock but there was no sign of Robbie. All I could see was the barge with the water churning around it.'

'Was there anyone on the barge at the time?' The magistrate's question was aimed at the constable.

'Just a lad, your worship.'

'Just a lad! Do you mean that barge was being handled by a boy?'

'It be usual practice, your worship. Ain't much a bargee can do while the boat be in the lock, 'cept wait. It be usual for 'im to turn the horse loose to graze and take 'isself into the nearest hostelry, leaving a lad or a wife with the barge.'

'And in this case?'

'A ten-year-old lad was with the barge, your worship, while his father was in The Navigation – that be a public house set near the wharf. There weren't no wife.'

'I see.' The plump face enveloped in iron grey whiskers turned back to the young girl whose fingers twisted incessantly, but the next question was still directed at the constable. 'Did this boy make any attempt to save the child?'

'Weren't no chance o' that, sir.' The constable shook his head solemnly. 'Lock be just big enough to take a barge. Ain't but a few inches between the boat and the sides. Anything that gets sucked under a boat once it be shut inside of a lock has no chance of surfacing till the operation be over. Weren't nobody could have gone in after that child.'

'O' course not!' Hannah struggled free of the hands that held her, madness born of grief lending her strength, propelling her towards the table. 'O' course nobody could have got him out. Locks be twenty-foot deep and their sides be covered in slime. There be little chance of saving a body when no barge be in there, but given it holds a boat, that chance be gone – and 'er knowed that!' She turned a wild glance on Rachel. ''Er knowed my little babby would drown. 'Er knowed it . . . 'er knowed it!'

Picking up the wooden gavel that had lain unused on the table, the magistrate brought it down with a bang.

'Remove that woman from the court,' he ordered. 'She will be heard tomorrow.'

''Er was always jealous!' Hannah screamed as two of the watching men grabbed her arms and began to haul her from the room. ''Er were jealous of her father's marrying me, her were resentful right from the start.' Twisting her head to the side, she sank her teeth into a hand that restrained her. As the man released her, yelping from the sting of her teeth, she pointed to Rachel. 'You killed my babby,' she said, voice now low with hatred. 'You killed him and you'll pay. If I 'ave to dance with the devil for all eternity because of it, I'll see you pay!'

Tibbington workhouse smelled powerfully of soda, carbolic and misery.

'You will be lodged at the workhouse until this day week.'

The magistrate's closing words had turned Rachel's blood to ice in her veins. The workhouse! A week there would seem an eternity. She had passed the low, dark, tiny paned building with its heavy wooden doors many times when going along Church or Workhouse Lane, and each time had felt a sense of foreboding. Once in there, the women of the village said, you only got to come out in a wooden box.

Now a grim-faced woman escorted her inside. Dressed in heavy grey serge, unrelieved by anything other than a bunch of keys to the left side of a black leather belt and a short thick-ended truncheon on the right, the wardress was a fearsome sight.

'You be treated special.' She grinned, showing several blackened stumps among yellow teeth. 'You be given this nice room all to yourself. Magistrate said you was to be made comfortable until you was sent for, and that's what you'll be – if you know what's good for you!' The woman's large hand fondled the stick at her side, the meaning behind her words made clearer by the threat in her cold eyes. 'Now, you got two minutes to change into that nightgown and get yourself to bed.'

Dazed by the swiftness of it all, Rachel glanced about the tiny room. Light from the single candle flickered over brick walls painted brown. Against one, a table not much bigger than a stool held a plain jug and bowl, a square of rough calico draped over its edge. Beyond this the room held nothing but a narrow iron-framed bed.

'Well, what you waiting for!' The wardress's hand tapped against the stick. 'P'raps you be wanting me to help you?'

'No!' Rachel's hands flew to the buttons at her throat, remembering the feel of the woman's rough hands propelling her through the dimly lit corridors of the workhouse.

Trembling beneath the cold gaze, pressing dry sobs back in her throat, she removed dress and petticoats, folding each garment before laying it on the foot of the bed.

'And the rest!'

The order was sharp as Rachel reached for the calico nightgown.

'I . . .' She felt the word catch in her throat as she looked at the wardress. 'I would like to be left alone.'

'Oh, you would like to be left alone!' The woman's harsh laughter rang against the painted walls seeking a way of escape from the nauseating enclosure of the tiny room. 'And just who do you think you are? Lady muck!' She stepped forward, her hard face half lit by the candle flame bore a menacing gleam. 'Just you get one thing clear,' she hissed, 'you ain't in no fancy house and you ain't no honoured guest – you be in the workhouse. You be here until you goes to the gibbet for child murder, and while you am here you'll do as Sadie Buckley tells you. Now I be telling you to strip or else you'll be going back to face the magistrate in naught but your skin, and that marked nicely with a "P".'

'Marked!' The fear already clouding Rachel's violet eyes deepened.

'O' course.' Pleasure at instilling terror into another person throbbed in Sadie Buckley's voice. This was her one consolation in working as wardress where she had once thought to be governess. Thought to be until that cow upstairs had smarmed like butter over the Appointments Board! 'Like I said, you be in the workhouse, and like everybody else who eats at the expense of the parish, you'll be branded.'

In a sudden swift movement she lunged forward, knocking Rachel's hands free of her throat and at the same time snatching at her thin cotton chemise, ripping it open to the waist.

'I wonder where you'll feel the iron?' She smiled sadistically, eyes roving over the trembling girl. 'Here?' She touched one shoulder. 'Or maybe here.' The smile widened as she touched a finger to the pale brow. 'Though it be my bet the brand will go here.' Cold eyes glittering like those of a serpent, Sadie Buckley trailed her hand slowly down Rachel's face, then over her neck and throat, down to the soft flesh of her breast.

'Yes!' She breathed faster, the noise of it rasping in the silence. 'That be the spot the brander likes best to press the iron. He likes to leave his mark on a woman's tits, 'specially young tits like these.'

The cry she had tried so desperately to hold back burst from Rachel as she shrank away from the hand fondling her breast.

'Don't touch me!' she gasped. 'Don't touch me.'

Sadie's hand dropped but the malicious smile remained. 'There'll be time enough for me to stroke them. I prefers to do it while the flesh be festering from the iron – you squirms even more that way. Think on that while you be waiting for morning to come.'

Swaying in the blackness she felt descending upon her, Rachel heard the slam of the door and the rasp of a bolt being shot into place.

Branded! The word rang in her brain. She would be branded with the mark of the workhouse. But wasn't she already branded with a far worse mark? Wasn't she branded her brother's killer?

Humiliation and revulsion at the wardress's treatment mixing with the fear already potent within her, she sank to the bed.

'I did not kill Robbie,' she sobbed into the darkness. 'I did not kill my brother.'

* * *

A small square of light played on the wall above the jug and basin, telling her it was morning. Rachel pushed herself from the bed, her body stiff with cold. Somewhere in the silent building a door banged. Grabbing her clothes, she struggled into them, anxiety making her fingers clumsy as she raced to be dressed before the odious wardress made an appearance. Having no comb, she smoothed her hair with her hands, dropping them as the bolt on her door scraped back.

She had passed no one when Sadie Buckley had escorted her last night but now, as they entered a room at the end of a corridor, Rachel saw three long trestle tables, the benches to either side of them filled with women, each wearing the same dun-coloured uniform, each head cropped to within an inch of the scalp.

Following the wardress's barked instructions, Rachel collected a tin bowl and spoon from a table alongside the door, taking it to a crop-headed woman standing behind a second table at the farther side of the room. On the stone flags stood a large two-handled pan from which she served porridge.

Following a brief nod of direction Rachel seated herself on the nearest bench, but no head lifted towards her and no one spoke.

'Room one will be in the wash house.' Sadie Buckley's strident voice overrode the rattle of spoons against bowls. 'Room two, in the kitchen. Three, the corridors and stairs. Four, the floors. And you . . .' She poked a sharp finger between Rachel's shoulder blades. '*You* will take the privies.'

'Why has her put you doin' the privies?'

A thin stringy woman, her scalp showing pink through her close cropped mousy hair, whispered to Rachel as she led the way from the dining hall to the yard behind the workhouse.

'Did you hit her? God, I 'ope you fetched the bastard a

wallop that knocked her senseless! Though by the look of you, I doubt you have the strength.'

'No, I did not strike her,' Rachel whispered back, feeling the wardress's eyes following them as she stood in the doorway that gave on to the huge wash house.

'Pity!' The thin woman stopped before a pile of large rectangular metal trays, each about a foot deep, and beside them several short-handled shovels. 'I only be waiting for the chance to have another go at the hard-faced bitch, I swear I'll do for her then. But if you ain't tried landing her one, 'ow come you be put cleaning out privies?'

'Is it unusual?' Rachel took the tray and shovel handed to her.

'Ar.' Taking a second tray and shovel, the woman set off in the direction of a row of low-roofed narrow buildings, each barely faced with a narrow door that left a wide gap to top and bottom. 'I be the only one for six month or more been put to shovelling shit. It be her way of paying me out.'

'Paying you out for what?' Rachel glanced back across her shoulder to where the wardress still stood watching them.

'For hitting her in the face with a jug!' Kicking open the first of the doors, the woman glanced at Rachel, a smile creasing her thin face. 'It weren't so much the breaking of the governess's platter jug that bastard minded, as all the women laughing to see the gravy it held running down 'er face. Ever since then 'er's had me emptying the privies. So what did you do to upset her?'

'I . . . I haven't done anything.'

'I see.' The woman's smile slipped away. 'That be another of Sadie Buckley's dislikes. 'Er don't like a woman as don't respond to her petting, and that be what you done, ain't it?'

'I . . . I did not care for her watching me undress.'

'Nor for where 'er put her hands?' the woman said,

seeing the colour rise high in the girl's pale face. 'One of these days that woman will have no hands with which to maul a wench. One day 'er will find them chopped off!'

'Cleaning privies not fit work for you this morning, Paget? Is it the bending and scraping you dislike . . . or perhaps the smell is not to your liking? Maybe we should sprinkle a little cologne in each privy so as not to offend your delicate nose.' The wardress's smile was vicious as she crossed the yard to them.

Squatting on her haunches in the first privy, the thin woman drew out a metal tray from beneath a bench-like seat with a hole in it. Bringing it out into the yard, she stood with it resting against the hessian apron that covered her down to her feet.

Rachel stepped away, stomach heaving at the sight of the evil-smelling mass that filled the tray.

'It ain't the smell of the privies be offending my nose,' Paget said, staring into the wardress's mocking eyes, 'it be the smell of a shit hawk – the stink of *you*, Sadie Buckley. You've had shit in your mouth ever since you learned to speak, now see 'ow it feels to swallow it!'

Lifting the tray she had taken from the privy, she heaved it full in the face of the wardress. Then, snatching off the hessian apron, she was over the surrounding wall and gone.

In the bath house Rachel had scrubbed her whole body until the skin burned but still the smell of the privies remained thick in her nostrils. All around the giggles of the women bore testimony to a delight that had lightened their soul-weary day: the delight of seeing Sadie Buckley covered from head to toe in excrement.

'Be Rachel Cade in here?'

Rachel stiffened as she heard her name called.

'You be Rachel Cade?'

A wardress she had not previously seen marched into the cubicle that housed one of the tin baths, and suddenly Rachel felt cold.

'Hurry up and get dressed,' the wardress continued as the girl nodded. 'You be wanted. There be a man waiting to see you.'

She had wondered when he would come. Now he was here, and it was to be done. She was to be branded.

Chapter Two

Where would the mark be made? Her whole body trembling, Rachel followed the wardress up bare stone steps and long dismal brown-painted corridors.

'You ready, Cade?'

Paralysed with fear, Rachel felt the woman's hand against the small of her back, propelling her through the door she had opened.

'Well, good evening, my dear.'

The voice was soft, almost sibilant, but if it was meant to calm the terror that rooted her to the spot, it failed. How could they do this? How could they burn a mark into her flesh? She was not a pauper, dependent for her keep upon the parish, nor was she a condemned criminal. The magistrate had adjourned her hearing for a week, of which as yet only one day had passed. She had not been judged.

'Come in, you will be much more comfortable here beside the fire.'

Comfortable, before a fire that would leave her marked for life? Rachel felt her stomach heave and her knees buckle.

'Come, take a chair.'

Suddenly a man's arm was about her, supporting her as she was led to a seat and gently lowered into it.

'A little faintness, my dear. That is to be understood,' the voice beside her crooned. 'This place is not as desirable as one would wish a young woman to be housed in.'

'Please . . .' Rachel made her plea through gritted teeth. 'Just do it.'

'Do what, my dear?'

'Is it not enough for you to burn a woman with your branding iron?' Sobs she prayed would stay locked inside her caused her voice to shake. 'Must you torment her as well?'

'Brand? Is that what has you trembling? My dear, we no longer use a branding iron on those the parish supports. That practice has been abandoned in Tipton, though should you be sent to Bilston or to Birmingham to be tried by a court there then the outcome would be very different. The policy in those places is not so lenient as here. They still affix a brass letter "P" to the clothing of offenders. But we *can* be most lenient – provided, of course, we are convinced of the innocence of the accused.'

'But I *am* innocent!'

She was not to be branded! Some of the fear she had felt since thinking herself threatened with the branding iron left her and for the first time since being propelled into the room, Rachel looked about her. It was lit by gas lamps instead of candles but the single lamp placed on each of three walls did not entirely light the room, but left puddles of shadow in which a small table and cupboard lurked like crouched animals, and as her eyes grew accustomed to the consumptive yellow glow she saw in the deepest pool of all a bed.

'That is not the opinion of the people of Horseley. They see you as a murderer, the murderer of a child, and intend to see you pay the penalty for such a crime.'

'But the bargee . . . the boy on the boat . . . they saw what happened. They will tell you Robbie ran away from me, that I was still some distance from him when he fell over the edge of the lock!'

'The bargee might have told us that, but he did not come forward when you were brought into court. Without his evidence, and that of the boy, it is your word against that of your accusers, and they are very willing to testify . . . against you!'

He moved from her side as he spoke, coming to stand in front of her, his back to the fire burning in the grate, and Rachel looked up into the face of Isaiah Bedworth. This was the magistrate before whom she had been dragged, snatched from her father as he had tried to protect her, followed by the very women she had thought her friends, each of them claiming that she had killed her own brother. Each except for Ginny.

'But Ginny Marshall!' Rachel exclaimed. 'She knows I would never harm Robbie, she will tell you . . .'

'Ginny Marshall will tell me nothing.' Above bushy grey whiskers, small eyes glittered, catching the gaslight like pieces of cold glass. 'Ginny Marshall is dead.'

Her stepmother! Rachel caught her breath as memories of that scene in the village street came rushing back. Hannah screaming that Richie Cade's daughter had drowned her half-brother; the shouts of the quickly gathered women; Ginny Marshall defending her; and last of all Hannah's arm swinging towards her, a brick clasped in her hand. But it had struck Ginny. The blow was meant for Rachel, it was her that Hannah had wanted to kill, but instead it had struck Ginny and now the woman was dead.

'But I didn't do it!'

It was a cry of desperation. Rachel instinctively raised her hands towards the man looking down at her.

'I am sure you did not, my dear.' Isaiah caught the hands lifted towards him, holding them in his own. 'But I need to be . . . shall we say . . . convinced absolutely of your innocence.'

'But how can I do that? I have already told you all that happened.'

'A little wine?' Releasing her hands Isaiah turned to a table set to one side of the fireplace. Pouring two glasses from the carafe set there, he handed one to Rachel. 'Drink that, my dear, and then we can talk.'

'But there is nothing more I *can* tell you.'

'Then we must find another way for you to convince me, must we not?'

His eyes still on her face, the magistrate drained his glass, swallowing the wine in one gulp before refilling the glass and carrying it across to the deeply shadowed alcove where he set it down on a small cabinet beside the bed.

'I am not hard to convince.'

He had returned to stand behind her chair and one hand had dropped to her shoulder.

'A girl as pretty as you should have no difficulty doing that.'

The hand slid slowly down, closing over one breast, squeezing the softness beneath the dun-coloured dress. Her mouth dry, Rachel tried not to pull away. She had heard women talk of this man and the things he did to get what he wanted. But she was accused of murder, and with Ginny Marshall dead there was none who would speak for her.

Her hand trembled so much it sent droplets of wine spilling on to her skirts. She stood up, taking the glass and placing it back beside the carafe.

Isaiah Bedworth's eyes gleamed as he watched her, at the promise of her slim young body beneath his own. He often sent the younger, prettier women who were brought before him to the workhouse before sentence. There they could be held securely whilst awaiting transportation to prison he told the Board of Management, of which he was an officer. In reality it was for explaining to them the benefit, or otherwise, of agreeing to his suggestions for reducing the sentence he would pass, and their payment for his leniency.

'Let me tell you what could be in store for you, my dear.' He smiled, moustaches lifting, fleshy cheeks enfolding his eyes in layers of fat. 'First you could be found guilty of murder, in which case you would be taken to a place of execution and there hanged by the neck until you are dead.'

He came to stand before her once more, again taking her hands, a smile still curling his mouth.

'Secondly, you could be found guilty of manslaughter, in which case you would not hang but would be sent to prison. There you would be branded and remain, serving a term of hard labour that would last for the rest of your natural . . . or some might say highly unnatural . . . life. Either option, I am sure you will agree, is hardly desirable. So, you see,' he pulled her closer his eyes glittering in the waxy light, 'it is in your own best interests to do as I advise. In other words, convince me it would be wrong to pass either of those sentences upon you. You do agree, don't you?'

Oh God! What had happened to her? Rachel shuddered. Only yesterday afternoon she had laughed with Robbie as they walked home from Tipton Green, trying to answer his hundred and one questions about the things that caught his ready curiosity, then on the way home had held the wild flowers he had gathered on the heath while he looked for more and now she was being held in the workhouse awaiting trial for murder!

'You could already be in prison in Birmingham or Wolver-hampton,' Isaiah began again. 'With an accusation as serious as that brought against you, I could already have sent you there. But I had no wish to see you locked in a cell with five or six other women, with no privacy for even the most intimate human functions. Prisons are not pleasant places, my dear. I would say they are places to be avoided at all costs.'

At all costs . . . Rachel wanted to scream. And what was the cost to be for her? What payment would this man extract for his leniency, what price must she pay to escape the gallows?

'Think about it,' he said softly. 'You have only been in this institution for a night and a day but already you must have some knowledge of the harshness of life here. How much more harsh and savage prison life is cannot be imagined, but it can be lived, and *will* be lived by you unless you act sensibly.'

Rachel's blood seemed to freeze beneath that glittering gaze. 'What must I do?' she whispered.

Slowly, still holding on to her hands, he backed across the room, stopping beside the bed.

'Please me.' The words were thick in his throat as he twisted her round so she stood with her back to the bed. 'Just please me.'

She had to do this, Rachel thought, sinking on to the bed, she had to do what he wanted if she were to live. It would be over soon. Just this one night and then he would give her her freedom; just a few hours and she could forget.

Concentrating her mind on not screaming aloud, she sat hardly registering the removal of his clothes, her eyes empty as she watched them drop away, item by item.

His breathing rapid and heavy as he flung away the last garment, he took her hands again, this time grabbing them roughly, the pressure of his own biting into them.

'Now!' he almost moaned. 'Kiss me.'

You have to do it, you have to do it! The thought throbbing in her brain, eyes closed against the sight of his flabby body, its skin almost yellow in the gaslight, Rachel forced herself to lift her face for a kiss.

'Not there, my dear.'

Above her upturned face the magistrate's voice sounded harsh, almost strangled.

'Not there, here . . . kiss me here!'

With that last word he pushed her hands into his groin, pressing them against hard, pumping flesh.

'No!'

The touch of his moist flesh too much to bear, Rachel snatched her hands away, knocking him backward as she jumped to her feet.

'Don't touch me!' she gasped. 'Don't touch me!'

Staggering back against the cabinet, Isaiah glared as the glass of wine fell to the floor, shattering into a thousand glistening fragments.

'You little fool!' he hissed. 'Do you realise what I can do to you?'

'I realise what you were about to do to me,' she sobbed. 'The talk I heard about you in Tipton wasn't all lies – the talk of how you treat a woman prisoner.'

Grabbing his shirt, Isaiah held it against a groin that had suddenly lost the throbbing urgency of seconds ago.

'Did the women of Tipton tell you what Isaiah Bedworth does to those who do not take the mercy he offers?' he grated. 'No, they did not, because none of them refused. None of them was stupid enough to choose the lash followed by a prison term. Is that what you want? Is that preferable – to spend the rest of your life in the stinking hell of a prison rather than spend one night in bed with me?'

'Yes!' Her whole body shaking, Rachel turned from the sight of him. 'I would rather rot in hell than lie with you!'

'Oh, you won't rot in hell.'

Movement behind her told Rachel he was replacing his clothes. 'You are not going to stay in any prison.' Isaiah Bedworth's voice throbbed with unmasked vengeance. 'You are going to hang! You are going to feel the drag of the rope against your skin as it tightens about your neck, feel the trapdoor give beneath your feet as you wait in fear and trembling. And until it does you can think on this: I had no intention of finding you not guilty. I would have taken all that tight little body of yours had to offer, and not just for tonight but for every night until sentence was passed, the sentence I fully intend to give, that sentence being death.'

'That be her! That be the one as chucked a babby in the lock.'

'No need to take her in there, constable, we all knows 'twas her done it. Ain't no need for Isaiah Bedworth to say what's to be done. We know 'ow to deal with them as kills innocent children. Just you 'and her over to us, we'll see 'er gets what be coming to her.'

From among the crowd gathered around The Jolly Collier to watch Rachel brought back before the magistrate, women shouted accusations and threats. From the edge of the assembly Richard Cade came forward, taking his daughter in his arms as she stepped from the wagon that had brought her, from the workhouse and Tibbington.

'Rachel. Oh, Rachel, my little wench!'

'I did not kill him, Father.' She clung to him, whispering her innocence against his shoulder. 'I did not kill Robbie.'

'I know, my wench. I know.' Richard Cade's voice caught in his throat. 'Have no fear, the magistrate will see you be telling no lie. He won't let you be sent to no prison.'

'*You are not going to stay in any prison. You are going to hang.*' Isaiah Bedworth's words of the night before rang in Rachel's mind. Her father was right in his supposition: the magistrate would not allow her to be sent to prison. He was sending her to the gallows.

'Now then, Richie, there can be no talking to the prisoner.' The constable gently eased her father's arms from around her, ignoring the jibes of the women who crowded after him into the upstairs room.

Seated before the table that served as judge's bench, Rachel could not bring herself to look into the face of the man who had thought to use her and now sat in judgement over her. She kept her eyes downcast as first one woman of the village and then another spoke against her. Were they doing so in order to gain themselves a moment of glory in an otherwise drab existence or had they been paid to speak as they did? Such an action would hardly be alien to the man whose eyes had silently mocked her as she was brought before him.

It could only have been half an hour but to Rachel it seemed she sat in that room for a lifetime before the gavel was brought down, its noise silencing the murmurs of the onlookers.

'We have heard the evidence of witnesses for the prosecution.' Beneath their bushy eyebrows Isaiah Bedworth's eyes glared at the listening public, his whole attitude daring one of them to cross him.

'And yesterday we heard the evidence of Hannah Cade, mother of that innocent boy, her only child, taken from her and cruelly murdered.'

Directing his stare towards Rachel, he smiled inwardly. It was a pity the girl had refused to submit. He would have enjoyed having her kiss his penis, having her do so many of the other little practices he enjoyed, just as he was going to enjoy sentencing her to death . . . but not yet. Not until he had heightened the blood lust of the people in this room; not until his words had tortured her still more. He should not, of course, use emotive terms such as he had just employed, deliberately leading the listening court. As a magistrate he should be impartial. That thought amused him and he found it hard not to give a smile. After all, who in Tipton would dare oppose him?

'We heard Hannah Cade describe how, since her marriage to Richard Cade, the accused had displayed constant jealousy. How with the birth of Hannah's son that jealousy not only increased but became centred upon the boy. We have heard how the father refused to hear the truth of his wife's words. How on each and every occasion she spoke to him of the girl's jealousy, he said it was only imagination on the part of his wife, that his daughter was not of a jealous nature; and when Hannah Cade told him she had become fearful for the child's safety, he said his daughter would not harm a fly, much less her own brother. Sadly, as this court has seen, how wrong he was. We have heard how three days ago the accused took her brother on an errand from which he did not return. So why did Hannah Cade allow her son to accompany his half-sister to the market at Tipton Green?'

Isaiah lifted his eyes to gaze solemnly at the faces about him, drawing the strings of his net tighter about the silent girl.

'For the benefit of those not present in the court to hear

Hannah Cade's own witness, I will tell you. That poor woman had prayed constantly that her step-daughter would come to return the deep love Hannah held for her – prayed almost every hour that Rachel would come to love, if not her, then the second child of her father, her own half-brother. And when Rachel Cade offered to take the boy with her to the market, Hannah thanked God – thanked Him that at last her prayers seemed answered. Poor deluded woman.'

Breaking off he shook his head, again almost smiling at the sound of sobs from the listening women and short embarrassed coughs from the men. After this they would welcome the death sentence. There would be no reprieve for Rachel Cade.

'Poor misguided Hannah Cade.' Isaiah timed the continuation of his speech with the ease of an expert. He had the crowd in the palm of his hand, all he need do now was deliver his verdict. 'To be so cruelly deceived, so heart-broken that in its mercy this court excused her from further testament, for she will spend the rest of her unhappy life feeling the pain that only a mother can feel: the pain of losing an only child, a child murdered by a jealous and heartless girl. It is that same mercy that now asks, is there any among you will speak in defence of the accused? Will anyone speak for Rachel Cade?'

'I do.' Richard Cade jumped to his feet. 'I say my wench would never have done what her be accused of. Her would never lift a finger against the boy ... it be all lies, cruel wicked lies!'

'You too have been heard by this court.' Isaiah glared at this interruption. 'As the father of the accused you cannot truly be blamed for remaining blind to her guilt – in fact, you are to be commended for your loyalty. But the court cannot be blind, cannot turn its eyes from the obvious. It has a duty not only to protect the innocent but to punish the guilty. And in the knowledge that when giving judgement it, as every being on earth, stands in the sight of God, it humbly asks His mercy for what it now must do.'

Waiting a full minute, Isaiah savoured the silence. Then, taking up the gavel, he began to speak the words that would send Rachel Cade to the gallows.

'Don't know why the girl wasn't sent to the Assize at Birmingham.'

The keeper of The Navigation tavern set a glass of porter before his only customer. It was still early in the day, but men often called in for a drink or a bite when travelling to and fro between the brickworks or coalmines and the canal wharf at nearby Tipton Green.

'Should rightly 'ave sent the wench there, to my way of thinking, what with the charge being so serious.'

'Serious?' Jared Lytton was only half listening to the inn-keeper's gossip, his mind on the chain he must get to the dockyards at Portsmouth.

'Ain't nothing more serious, sir.' The man whipped a cloth from the pocket of a long brown apron tied about his waist, wiping the top of a nearby table, clearly intent on utilising this opportunity to air his latest story. 'Murder be the most serious crime of all, especially when it be an innocent babe as were the victim.'

'Murder, you say?' Jared's brown eyes flickered with momentary interest. He would drink his porter and be on his way, and that damn' barge better be at Toll End wharf or there might well be a second murder for the Assize to try.

'Ar.' The table wiped and cloth flipped back into his pocket, the innkeeper nodded. 'It happened last time you was here in The Navigation, only a few days since. You remembers, Mr Lytton? We heard a wench scream and we ran outside.'

Jared's fine brows drew together in a frown.

'Surely you remembers?' the innkeeper urged. 'Was me and yourself, just like it be now. Were no other customers except for a bargee, it being the time of day when the brickyards and such be going full blast. I remembers you saying you was off to hire a barge for some delivery down Portsmouth way.'

'Which I am about to do again.' Jared tossed back his porter, the flicker of interest already faded. 'Damn' boat never turned up.'

'Be it important cargo, Mr Lytton?'

'Important enough to me. If I don't get that load to the docks I could well be out of the chain business, and that could be disastrous for more than a few families in Tipton.'

'Which wharf be that barge supposed to pull into, if you don't mind my asking, sir?'

Picking up a short-handled riding crop from the table, Jared handed the man a coin.

'Toll End,' he answered.

Taking the coin, the innkeeper followed the tall broad-shouldered man out into the warm morning air.

'Begging your pardon, Mr Lytton . . .' He watched the easy swing that carried the younger man into the saddle of a coal black stallion, its hooves already restlessly pawing the ground. 'But if it be that the barge you speak of ain't at the wharf, then maybe you might take the boat my wife's brother has out at the basin along of Workhouse Lane? It be a sound boat and old Jem be trustworthy. You wouldn't find a better bloke to take your cargo, whatever it be.'

'You say this barge is in the basin now?'

'Pulled in last evening. He'll be looking for a new cargo.'

Holding the reins short, curbing the impatient stallion, Jared gave a brief smile. 'Then if your brother-in-law is still lying in that basin, he has himself a cargo.'

'Jem'll be right glad. The day be a good one for him.' Shading his eyes against a sudden bright gleam of sunlight, the landlord of The Navigation looked towards the canal that ran just a few yards away. 'Not like that poor wench.'

Swinging the horse about, Jared glanced at the man. 'What poor wench will that be?'

'The one I were telling you about but a moment ago. The

one they be trying for murder this afternoon, up at Horseley. The one they says chucked her young half-brother in the cut, right there.' He pointed towards the lock. 'But to my mind her didn't throw the lad in, he tumbled over the edge while watching a barge being raised. Least that be my reckoning of it.'

'Of course I remember!' Jared glanced towards the canal. 'We heard a scream and came out of the inn as a girl was running towards the lock. A girl in a brown dress . . .'

'That be the one, sir. Be Richie Cade's daughter if talk be true. Though if it is, I'll be more'n surprised. That one be a fine wench, always well-mannered. I never heard no man speak against her, tho' I'll not say the same for Richie Cade's wife.'

'The girl's mother?' Jared's arm jerked and his fingers tightened as the horse fought for its head.

'Stepmother, sir,' the landlord corrected. 'And a right spiteful bugger to that girl, so my missis tells me. But I reckon her won't have the chance to vent her spite on the wench again, for it be my bet that girl will swing. Old Isaiah Bedworth be one for giving maximum sentence. He'd hang a bloke for breathing if he could. I reckon that daughter of Richie Cade's will be hanged afore the month be out.'

'But how can the charge be murder? What happened was an accident. The boy on the barge must have seen exactly what happened. Surely he has testified?'

'Barge carried on up the cut no sooner it were out of the lock.' The landlord stepped back out of reach of the prancing hooves. 'The lad and the bargee ain't been back since. They could be anywhere in the country by now, and Magistrate Bedworth ain't one to wait till they be found. No, 'tis my bet he will send that wench to the gallows.'

'But you saw what happened!' Jared held the horse with ease. 'Surely you have testified?'

'Begging your pardon, Mr Lytton, I didn't *see* what actually happened. Like yourself, I only seen the girl running towards the lock. I didn't see the lad – not till he were dredged up anyway – so it could be argued that my evidence has no real evidence at all. Besides, Isaiah Bedworth don't be one to forget easy. It be sounder for a man to stay clear of him – that be any man who has to earn his living.'

So no one had spoken for the girl, thought Jared, guiding his mount across Horseley heath. The landlord of The Navigation could not really be blamed for avoiding a clash with Isaiah Bedworth. Jared knew too well the nature of the man.

Tethering his stallion he walked a few yards along Horseley village's single street before entering The Jolly Collier. This, he guessed, was the building where any matter involving the village would be discussed, and it was here, away from the more discerning, that Isaiah Bedworth would be likely to conduct the hearing against the daughter of Richie Cade.

In the upstairs room women whispered among themselves, eyes fastened on the girl sitting before a table behind which the magistrate held a wooden gavel in his plump fist.

'Rachel Cade . . .' The gavel rose.

'you are charged with murder. This court has heard the witnesses brought against you.' The gavel hovered.

'I have listened to the evidence . . .'

'So you have.' From the back of the room Jared's voice rang loud and clear. 'But you have not heard mine!'

Chapter Three

'Thank you. Thank you, sir.'

Arms around his daughter, Richie Cade turned a grateful glance to the man who had followed them from the public house.

'I thought my girl was a goner. Seemed nobody in the world was prepared to stand up for her.'

'But you believed in her?'

'Ar, I did. I know my daughter. Her loved that little lad, loved him true. And in spite of what folk hereabouts have said, her would never have lifted a finger against him.'

'You wasn't there, Richie Cade!' a woman shouted from among the onlookers who even now were reluctant to forego an entertainment they might never see again. 'You didn't see *what* happened.'

Turning towards the muttering crowd, Jared Lytton swept them with a forbidding look. How many of them would be there had the cause been anything but trial for a murder? How many had spoken against the girl now safe in her father's arms? How many would be prepared to forget? Or would her life here be one of torment, constantly accused of something she had not done?

'No, you didn't see what that daughter of yourn done, you weren't there.'

'Were you?' His face clearly showing anger as well as contempt, Jared turned on the crowd. 'Were any of you there beside that lock? Did any of you *see* this girl throw her brother into the water? The answer is no. No you did not, yet you were ready to see her hang, to see a young girl die.'

''Er did kill my Robbie.' Eyes red and swollen, hair escaping in tufts from the pins that held it, Hannah Cade pushed free from her neighbour's arms, stepping in front of Jared. ''Er killed my boy and 'er should have hanged.'

'Ar, 'er should have hanged. 'Er should die like that babby. I say chuck 'er in the cut, let her drown like 'e did.'

'You won in there, Lytton.' Behind Jared the magistrate's low voice was spiced with venom. 'Inside that room you argued with the law but out here there is no law. What will you do against mob rule? It will take more than a ready tongue to dissuade this lot from stringing the girl up here and now . . . and what could one constable and a magistrate do against so many?'

'Ar, let 'er drown!' The call flashed from mouth to mouth. 'Chuck 'er in the cut.'

Raising his crop above his head, Jared faced them, Isaiah Bedworth's soft laughter reaching him beneath the cries of the crowd.

'Keep back!' The warning in his voice was clear, the light in his eyes deadly. 'The first one to lay hands on this girl will regret it!'

'Who do you think you be, coming 'ere to Horseley and telling folk what to do?'

Jared's mouth curved in a cold smile but his glance did not seek the woman who had shouted.

'I can see some among you who know very well who I am, and who know well what I can do to this village. You women . . .' he glanced around the hostile faces glaring out from beneath woollen shawls '. . . how many of you have husbands and sons who work in Lytton mines? How many labour in Lytton brickworks, and how many make chain at Blowers Green or in their own outhouse workshop? Chain bought by Lytton. I see by your faces there are many. And you men . . .' The cold stare was directed to the few men dotted among the women, those who had taken advantage of a late shift to view the spectacle and take a drink at The Jolly Collier. 'Take off your trousers and give them to the women! Do it now, for I am left in no doubt as to who rules in your households. And after that you may collect your tins for any man who can allow such tormenting of a young girl has no place with Jared Lytton.'

'We beg your pardon, Mr Lytton, sir, but we thought it were widely known. We thought . . . we were told Cade's wench had been seen to push that lad into the canal.'

'I said . . .'

'You says too much!' The man who had called out to Jared turned on the woman who had spoken by his side, his face dark with anger. 'Say one more word and you'll have my fist about your face! Get yourself off home and stay there. And you lot . . .' He glared at the women round about him. 'Keep yourselves and your lying tongues out of my house. If I catch you anywhere near mine, I'll throw *you* in the bloody cut. Ar, and any man who tries to stop me!'

The few remaining men glanced anxiously at Jared, at the person who with one word could take away their livelihood.

'Please.' Rachel stepped free from her father's arms. 'Please don't take away the jobs of these men. I have been acquitted and no harm has been done.'

'No harm done?' Jared grated. 'I think there has been a great deal of harm done.'

'Then do not do any more. Do not take away the jobs of these men.'

For a moment he could only stare at the girl whose eyes met his pleadingly. Isaiah Bedworth had had her locked away in Tibbington workhouse instead of sending her to a Birmingham prison – that much he had learned from listening to the murmurs in that upstairs room. And for what reason? He knew of the man's reputation, of his eye for women – especially young, pretty women – and though he had no proof, he did not doubt what rumour held to be true of his dealings with female prisoners. Had such use been made of Rachel Cade? Had she been forced to accept Isaiah Bedworth's 'leniency'? The thought suddenly wrenching his gut, Jared swung back to face the waiting men.

'You have this girl to thank for your jobs and homes – be sure your wives remember that. Should any of them raise a hand against her, you will be gone from Horseley and any other place where I have influence. And remember they are many. You and your families will have to travel very far to escape the influence of Jared Lytton.'

'Ain't everybody depends on Lytton for their living.' A hard-faced man with a cap pulled low over grey hair, ragged black trousers skimming his heavy boots, stared defiantly back at Jared. 'Ain't everybody in Horseley be beholden to you. I say that wench you be defending best look to herself. You won't be in Horseley every night, Mr Jared Lytton. You won't be 'ere when darkness covers the moon. You won't be able to stop justice being done, not for long you won't.'

'He's right, Lytton,' said Isaiah softly. 'You might have protected the girl today but what of tomorrow and the days after that? You won't be able to stand between her and women like these for long. Sooner or later they will have the sport they want – the sport you cheated them of.'

'And what of *your* sport, Bedworth?' Jared's eyes glinted like polished bronze. 'Have I cheated you as well? Denied you what you enjoy so much – having a pretty girl helpless in your hands. Or should that be your bed?'

'Maybe, Lytton.' Within their frame of whiskers, the magistrate's eyes mocked him. 'But then, you'll never know, will you? You could try the girl yourself, but if the way be already open you won't know whether the doing of it be mine or another man's.'

His hand tightening about the short whip, Jared stared at

the man to whom justice was entrusted and for a moment toyed with the notion of meting out justice of his own. Then he turned his glance back to Richie Cade, his arms about his daughter once more.

'Is Magistrate Bedworth correct in assuming the matter of your daughter will not be left here?'

'Too bloody sure he be right!' Came a voice from the crowd. 'Murder will be paid for, and if Isaiah Bedworth don't take payment, there be them as will. It'll take more than the high-falutin' Jared Lytton to prevent that.'

Half facing the crowd Jared saw that the shout had come from the same man who had made a threat some moments before.

'Get yourself and your interfering ways out of Horseley,' the man snarled. Bending, he picked up a stone and hurled it at Jared, striking him on the side of the head. 'Leave we to look after our own.'

Jared's mouth tightened with fury and his eyes blazed. With the whip gripped so fast his knuckles stood out from his hand, he strode over to the man who had thrown the stone, shouldering his way through the crowd, pushing men and women aside as though he did not see them.

'Why, you bastard!' he hissed. Then pulling back the hand that was ready to strike, gave an icy smile. 'No, that way would be too easy for me, and too short for you. You are not going to look after anyone except yourself for a very long time, my friend.' The words were hissed between his clenched teeth. 'And that will require much more thought and expertise than throwing any stone,' he continued. 'You are going to have to watch yourself every minute of the day and night. You will be afraid to close your eyes, never knowing if they will open again.

'You have just made the most serious mistake of your life and now it is your turn to pay. And, believe me, you *will* pay – hard and long. You are going down the line, for as long as Jared Lytton's lawyers can keep you there.'

The swift gasps of the women and the low mutterings of the men not yet dispersed hung like insects on the afternoon air.

'Constable!'

Jared kept his eyes on the man staring murderously at him, recognising him for one he had dismissed a month ago for turning out poorly forged chain.

'Mr Lytton, sir?' The constable stepped forward, lifting his hand in a salute.

Jared's face set into harsh lines. 'I accuse this man of verbal assault and with physical injury to my person. I request that you take him in charge.' Turning to the magistrate, he added: 'Perhaps you will acquaint me with the date of this man's hearing? This time *I* would like to be present to witness your leniency.'

'He was just angry.' Once again Rachel stepped free from her father's arms. 'He did not mean to do you an injury, I'm sure of it.'

'Are you, Miss Cade?'

The same softness touched her face and the same pleading shone in her eyes, but this time to no effect.

'Are you? Unfortunately for him, I am not. Your pleading will meet with no reward this time. He will go to prison, and for a very long time. And now . . .' he directed his glance over the muttering crowd '. . . I suggest you all go home before others among you come to regret this day.'

'You'll not come into the house again.' Hannah Cade had stood in silence as the constable left with his prisoner but now she glared at Rachel. 'You will never set foot inside my door. And you!' Eyes holding the glint of madness were lifted to Jared. 'You have saved *her* but you won't save yourself. My curse be upon you, Jared Lytton. You will feel the pain I feel, yours will be the agony of losing one you love, you will tread the path of sorrow and eat from the dish of bitter herbs, and you will remember, you will always remember, the words of Hannah Cade!'

*   *   *

'I have to go, Father. I can't stay here.'

Rachel looked down at the tattered remnants of her Sunday dress and the fragments of slashed petticoats lying outside the house where she had been born. Hannah had run from them as they had left The Jolly Collier, and now behind the closed door of the house her crazed laughter was audible.

'But this is your home.' Richie Cade's face, still showing traces of the good looks that had once had the girls of Horseley vying for his attention, creased with worry.

'It is also *your* home, Father,' she said gently. 'As it is Hannah's. She is your wife, Father. She needs you.'

'She never needed me.' Richie looked deep into the eyes of his daughter. 'She only wanted me – wanted to own me, body and soul. But I could not love her. I could not love any woman after your mother – perhaps one day you will understand that. I gave Hannah Cade my name and, God help me, my son, but my love was never hers. Now my son is gone and soon you will be also. And at that moment I will be free of her lying tongue and her endless complaints, for when you leave, I leave.'

'No, Father.' Throwing her arms about him, Rachel pressed her face against his shoulder, the cloth of his jacket rough against her skin. 'You can't leave Hannah. Losing first Robbie and then you will be too much for her to bear. I've seen the unhappiness on your face, I know life has not been easy for you – but then, it has not been easy for Hannah either. She must know your true feelings and that is a heavy burden she has carried. Now the death of her son has increased that burden a hundredfold. You can't give her more to bear, Father. You can't leave her now.'

Richie stroked the pale golden hair, so like the hair of the love of his heart. He had thought never to marry again when his wife had died of the brain fever, and just why he had only the hosts of heaven could tell for afterwards he never could understand it. Hannah had brought nothing but spite and jealousy to his house, and now she was driving away his only happiness. But he *had* married her, and his daughter was right. He could not leave her now; she was his wife, his responsibility. *Till death do us part.* He had repeated the words of the preacher, and only death would free him from his vow.

'I must be the one to go, Father,' Rachel whispered against his shoulder. 'It is the only way. Just remember I love you, and that I loved Robbie. I vow to you, I did not kill him.' Pulling free, she looked up into her father's face, her eyes brimming with tears. 'No matter what others have said, I did not kill your son.'

'I knew that from the first.' Richie Cade's voice caught on the tears in his throat. 'You would have given your own life sooner than see that boy harmed in any way at all. 'Twere an accident and the whole of Horseley knows it – there just be a few as enjoys a spectacle, no matter who be the one paying for it. And 'tis the two of us will be doing the paying, you and me. I only pray the Almighty will see fit to ease your burden soon. I love you, my little Rachel, I love you.'

Turning quickly, tears almost blinding her, she began to run: out of the village of Horseley, out of her father's life.

The scream of a steam-whistle bringing her to a stop, she looked about her. The heath had given way to buildings. Tall brick store houses and warehouses lined a basin partly filled with barges around which men were busy unloading cargo while others were engaged in lining up new ones ready to fill every empty space. To her left the sound of hymn-singing filtered into the purpling dusk as the mission room service for barge people was brought to an end. A short distance ahead a lad led a horse across Five Bricks bridge, no doubt on his way to the smithy that stood close to the railway cutting.

Which way should she go? It made little difference: a bed under the hedge would be the same anywhere. Pulling her shawl closer about her, Rachel walked on, passing the group of houses huddled at the corner of Hurst Lane, before turning right at the junction with the road that a carter had once told her led to Woodsetton. How long would it take her to walk there? It must be miles away from Tipton Green. She glanced again at the sky, its colour already changing to grey; whether it be many miles or few, she would not reach it before dark.

'If you be thinkin' o' following that road, you would do better to think otherwise.'

Rachel looked at the boy who had stopped to speak to her. No more than ten years old, the trousers he wore were too short and his over-large coat was ragged, revealing boots several sizes too big for him. He wiped a hand beneath his nostrils.

'Ain't nuthin' out that way fer miles. I know 'cos I come that way wi' me dad. You go out there an' you'll spend the night on the 'eath.'

'I have nowhere else to spend it, but thank you for the warning.'

'You means, you ain't got nowhere to sleep?'

Rachel looked at the face beneath the flat cap, its pale flesh streaked with dirt – a young face with an adult expression.

'Not yet.'

'Maddie Bartrum runs a good place.' He jerked his head in a quick sideways motion. 'The rooms be cheap and the ale be good.'

Rachel's glance followed the direction he had indicated, seeing a wooden board painted with a picture of a man working a furnace, the lettering proclaiming: The Fiery Holes.

'I'm sure she does,' answered Rachel, 'but I will be pressing on.'

'You ain't got no money, 'ave yer?' The face at her shoulder regarded her solemnly.

'No.' Rachel tried to smile but couldn't. 'I don't have any money.'

'That why be you going to Woodsetton?' Once more

the boy wiped a hand beneath his nostrils. ''Ave you got folk there?'

Pulling her shawl closer about her shoulders, Rachel shivered as the cold fingers of night settled upon her. She should be getting on if she were to find a place to sleep before darkness settled.

'I have no kin at Woodsetton,' she said, tugging the shawl more securely about her bare arms.

'Then why be you going there?' The enquiry was bold, the boy seeing no reason not to ask questions. 'Ain't nothin' it'll bring you 'cept sore feet and a hungry belly. Seems to me you might just as well stop 'ere in Tipton. You won't find work any easier in 'Setton than you'll find it 'ere, 'cos there ain't none. That be why me and my dad come to this place – so 'e could find work.'

'And did he?' Rachel knew she should move on but somehow felt herself drawn to the boy who regarded her with eyes that seemed to hold all the knowledge of the world.

'Oh, ar.' The lad nodded, sniffing a wet droplet from the end of his nose. 'He found a job working in a mine until there was a cave in at the face. 'E didn't work after that.'

'Why?' She felt a surge of pity. She well knew what rock falls underground meant to the men who dug for coal. 'Was your father badly hurt?'

Wiping the offending droplet on his sleeve the boy shook his head. 'No, me dad weren't 'urt. 'E were killed.'

For a moment there was silence between them, then the lad smiled. 'I 'ave a place you can sleep, if you wants to take advantage of it? Though it ain't no room at Maddie Bartrum's.'

Despite her own unhappiness, Rachel could not resist a smile in answer to the boy's grin.

'You'll be all right there,' he assured her as she hesitated. 'Nobody don't usually come ferretin' around after dark. Y'see, the place belongs to old Samuel Potter. 'E's so tight-fisted 'e would skin a fart for a farthing! He lets the place to three of the pit bank wenches and they lets me bunk in with them for free – though if Sam Potter knowed I was sleeping there 'e would up the rent quicker than a ferret down a rabbit hole.'

'I don't think I should.' Rachel shivered again, the night promised to be a cold one. 'The women you share with might not be too pleased at my turning up, especially as I have no money to pay for my night's lodging.'

'C'mon!' The boy caught her hand, pulling her along as he began to walk back the way she had come, past the huddle of houses grouped along the narrow street. 'Like I said afore, there be no shelter along the road to Woodsetton and without money you'll get no lodging in Tipton. Charity in this town be harder to come by than a cold bath in hell.'

Still smiling, Rachel allowed herself to be pulled along. 'In that case, I accept. But to whom do I owe my thanks?'

'My name is Bartholomew.' He skipped adroitly between a horse-drawn cart and a wagon piled high with sacks of grain. 'Me mother named me after some saint or other, but folk 'ave always called me Bart.'

'And does your mother stay with you at Mr Potter's place?'

Passing the last of the houses he headed for what looked like a much older house set some way back. The windows of its upper storey were closed with wooden shutters, and a beam and pulley that once had been used for raising sacks of grain loomed from the building above their heads.

'Me mother be in the cemetery at 'Setton. 'Er went soon after I was born. There were just me and me dad together after that. Least we was till 'e were flattened in that mine.'

Rachel felt a surge of pity. How could a boy so young endure the misery this lad had lived through and still face up to life? How could he be so young in years and yet so old in experience?

'Have you no other relative?' she asked.

'None.' He sniffed. 'And afore you asks why it is I ain't gone to the parish, I'll tell you. Bart Jevons ain't being put in no workhouse, and neither is he being rented out to no iron master, nor any other kind of master. 'E will find work for himself and eat food paid for by himself.' He glanced up at her, a roguish smile twisting his mouth. 'Even if 'e does sleep rent-free,' he finished, as if guessing what her next thought might be.

'This be it.' He stopped before a narrow wooden door set beside a pair of large ones that must once have allowed farm wagons to pass. 'This be where I sleeps. It looks a mite ancient but it ain't too bad inside. The pit bank don't pay the wenches who work it a great deal but these ones 'ave managed to fix this place with beds, an' that be about all they need, seeing as they be out all day working.'

'Pit bank wenches?' Rachel's tone was questioning as he pushed open the single narrow door.

'Ar, you knows. They pick bits of coal from the spoil heaps, the waste that be dumped from the mines, then they sells it to the jagger. Sometimes they gets fourpence for 'alf a hundredweight, but that ain't very often. Usually it be threepence – depends on the size of the pieces.'

'I've heard the people of . . .' Rachel hesitated, not wanting to say the name of her home village, not wanting to remember what had happened there or those hours in Tibbington workhouse. Did Bart too have recollections of a workhouse somewhere? Was he familiar with the hospitality of another parish? Was that the real reason he hadn't asked for shelter here in Tipton? 'I've heard people talk of a coal jagger. He sells the coal the women pick, doesn't he?'

'Ar.' The boy sniffed loudly as the warmer air of the house set his nose running again. 'And at a nice profit an' all. Some of the lah-di-dah houses pays him ninepence a bag, but they likes to keep it quiet that they buys from a jagger, seeing as 'ow coal picking don't be legal. Tansy has been down the line once for picking on the Bloomfield heaps – done six months in Digbeth gaol.'

'Shut that bloody door, Bart! How many more times do

you need telling? The place be hard enough to keep warm without you standing there with your arse to the wind.'

Bart glanced quickly at Rachel, breaking into a smile. 'That be Tansy. Her sounds hard but her ain't. Don't let her cussing put you off.'

Rachel held back, using the shadows of the doorway to mask her presence, not altogether convinced by Bart's words.

'Evenin'.'

The boy's airy greeting brought no reply but as he drew Rachel forward into the light of the several candles burning about the room the three women stopped what they were doing and turned to her, eyes hard and suspicious.

'What you brought her here for?'

The question was Tansy's, asked as the ladle she held in her left hand was raised threateningly.

'It's all right.' Bart wiped his nose on his sleeve. ''Er ain't no stoolie, 'er ain't snooping for Potter.'

'Oh . . . I suppose you knows *all* of Potter's stool pigeons, do you?' Tansy accused. 'A proper little Mr Know-all you be, don't you? If her ain't been sent by Potter, what's her doing here?'

'I brought 'er.' Bart took Rachel's hand again, his own warm against her cold fingers, pulling her into the light. ''Er don't 'ave nowhere to sleep.'

'There be plenty of room at Maddie Bartrum's.' Tansy stared at Rachel, her eyes hostile.

''Er ain't got the money Maddie Bartrum asks.'

'Oh, I see.' Tansy lowered the ladle but did not put it down. 'Her don't have the money to pay for a room so 'er reckons to come here and doss down for nothing? A body can save quite a lot playing that game. "I ain't got no money, please can I stay with you?" Well, Tansy Croft be too old a hand to fall for *that*. One free lodger be enough for this 'ouse.'

'I'm sorry to have disturbed you.' Rachel pulled her hand from the boy's. 'I should not have come, I'll leave at

43

once.' She glanced at Bart. 'Thank you for wanting to help me.'

'Hold up!' Tansy's voice was sharp as Rachel turned towards the door. 'I ain't told you you 'as to go – not yet I ain't anyway. You can bide an hour, get warm against going out into the night.'

'Thank you, but I won't. I have no wish to cause you and your friends any worry. It was foolish and thoughtless of me to have come here without invitation.'

'I invited you!' Bart piped up, sniffing yet another drip from the end of his nose.

Tansy looked at the girl facing her by the weak glow of the candles. Her body was thin beneath a brown dress that looked as if it would never survive another wash. Wherever she had come from they had not been over generous in feeding her. But beneath the shawl Tansy could see hair that shone from regular washing, and the lovely face was well scrubbed. She obviously kept herself clean, not like Potter's regular women.

'Seems you did.' Tansy turned, dipping the ladle into a large pot that hung over the glowing fire. 'So you best sit yourself down and take a bowl of mutton broth. And you . . .' she said as Bart grinned '. . . find that handkercha I give you this mornin' and use it, or you can find your own supper somewhere outside this 'ouse.'

'Let's have your shawl.' One of the other two women, who up to this point had remained silent, moved across to Rachel. 'Now sit you there by the table while I gets another bowl and spoon.'

'Bart said he asked you to come here but he did not tell us your name?'

Rachel glanced over to the third woman. Her voice was less harsh than the others and her mode of speech held more than a hint of refinement.

Watching as the third member of the trio advanced into the light, Rachel was surprised to see she was much younger than her companions and though not pretty, her looks were pleasant with brown hair dressed neatly into a bun at the back of her head.

'I am Ellen.' The girl who now stood in the candlelight seemed to be little more than twenty. She smiled at Rachel. 'Ellen Walker. And this . . .' she turned her smile to an older, grey-haired woman now setting a white platter bowl in front of Rachel '. . . this is Cora.'

'Cora – what a pretty name.' Rachel smiled at the woman now placing a spoon beside the bowl.

'Ar, the name be pretty enough.' The woman returned her smile, faded eyes reflecting the yellow gleam of the candle set in the middle of the bare wooden table. 'Me mother named me Coralie. Her must have thought a pretty name would ensure a pretty daughter, but her was wrong. I finished up with a face as plain as a pikestaff so it were shortened to Cora.'

'Your nature still belongs to a Coralie,' the girl named Ellen said gently. 'For there couldn't be a prettier one anywhere.'

'When you 'ave finished doling out praise, you might pass that there bowl so we can give the wench some supper.'

'No, thank you.' Rachel spoke quickly, rising from the table as Cora picked up the bowl. 'I will not take any supper when I have no means of paying for it. I am pleased to have made your acquaintance but now I must go.'

'To where?' Tansy turned from stirring the large pot, its base and sides blackened by soot from many fires. 'Bart says you told him as you ain't got nowhere to go?'

'Her was about to set off for Woodsetton when I met 'er along of the 'ouses below Five Bricks bridge.' Bart made a display of wiping his nose on the newly discovered rag Tansy had given him to use as a handkerchief.

'Oh, ar!' She regarded them both with shrewd eyes. 'What does there be for you in 'Setton?'

'Nothing.' Rachel reached for her shawl, taking it from the peg set on the back of the door where Cora had hung it.

'Then why go there? 'Tis a sight of a long way to go if there be nothing at the end of it.'

'The farther away the better.' Slipping the shawl over her head, Rachel twisted the ends into a knot, pulling it tight beneath her breasts.

'Oh!' Tansy's face closed with suspicion. 'Why be that, I wonder?'

'That be nowt to do wi' you, Tansy Croft!' Cora's voice was sharp. 'We can give a wench a meal without puttin' her through no inquisition. We might be pit bank wenches but we ain't sunk so low as to turn on one of our own.'

'If 'er be one of our own!' But Tansy took the bowl, filling it with a generous quantity of mutton broth.

'I tells you, Tansy, her ain't no snoop for Samuel Potter.' Bart settled on to a chair pulled close into the table.

'And you ain't getting anything at this table until them hands and face be washed, Bart Jevons. Pit bank wenches we might be, but cleanliness we will have in this house. And that includes washing as well as using a handkercha.'

'Mrs Croft . . .'

'Tansy!' The woman's glance swept to Rachel. 'I be called plain Tansy.'

'Tansy,' she began again, 'I assure you, I do not have any dealings with a man called Samuel Potter. I know only what Bart has told me: that he is a coal jagger, and that he pays you for the coal you pick and then sells it in the town.'

'Pays? Pah!' Tansy set the bowl on the table, taking up the one set in Bart's place. 'Steals, that be what he does. A few pennies for a bag of coal it can take a full day to pick, and that be cut in 'alf if the bag don't be full or if he says it be half bats.'

'Surely he must know you would not put such in with coal?' Rachel answered, recognising the local colloquialism for black slate.

'Oh, he knows that well enough.' Tansy placed a steaming bowl on the table, snatching off Bart's flat cap as he hurried back to his chair and throwing it across the room. 'But that be a way of bringing down the price. He knows if we don't sell it to him we like as not won't get a sale for it any place else. Either that or he might tell the mine owner we be picking on his land, and that would bring the bobbies down on our necks. He knows what he be about does Samuel Potter. He be sly in more ways than a duck has feathers – and one of them ways be to set folk to spy on us wenches.'

'Well, I am no spy for Mr Potter, nor for any other man.' Rachel pulled the edges of her shawl closer around her face. 'Goodnight, Bart.' She smiled at the lad busily spooning broth into his mouth. 'Maybe we will see each other again.'

'Might be best to wait till morning,' Tansy said as Rachel turned to leave. 'Promises to be a cold night out there and you won't find it pleasant sleeping under a hedge.'

'Stay here with us.' Ellen came up to her, placing a hand on her arm. 'Whatever has happened to put you on to the streets it can only look better after a hot meal and a night's sleep. Who knows? Maybe you will feel like going home tomorrow. I am sure your mother must be praying that you will.'

But there was no mother praying for her return. Rachel felt warm tears clog her throat. Hannah Cade wanted her dead, as did many in Horseley. They saw her as a cold-blooded killer, a girl who had murdered her own brother. No, she would not be returning home in the morning. The question was, where could Rachel Cade go? How far would it have to be to evade the finger of suspicion?

Chapter Four

'The *Flower of England*, you says, sir?'

'Yes.' Jared Lytton turned his glance over the narrow boats lying at their moorings in the canal basin at the bend where Owen Street merged into Workhouse Lane.

'That one be Jem Mathews's boat.' The manager of the basin pointed to one. ''E were away about three this afternoon – loaded chain no sooner it were delivered in the late morning. It were you yourself give him his cargo if I remembers aright, and I ain't been known to forget yet, Mr Lytton.'

'I was not questioning your ability as basin manager nor your memory.' Jared glanced in the direction the man had pointed. 'I merely wished to ensure the load had left and that the bargee had not decided to spend the evening in the tavern and begin his journey tomorrow.'

'There be many as would do that, Mr Lytton, but Jem Mathews don't be among 'em. Gives his word and sticks to it he does, 'e be one of the most trustworthy blokes as works the cut. You need have no fears, that chain of yourn be well on its way by this time.'

'That's as well.' Jared's shoulders relaxed and a smile flickered about his mouth. 'Her Majesty's Navy does not like to be kept waiting for its anchor chain.'

'Well, sir,' the manager laughed, 'the days of locking folk away in the Bloody Tower be over.'

'But not the days of locking them away in Digbeth gaol. Besides, a contract is a contract, and the ones I make, I like to keep.'

'Well, that one will be kept, sir. Like I says, Jem be a first-rate bargeman and 'e sticks to his word. And I will pledge mine that he will be back in this basin in less than two weeks.'

'We could do with more like him,' said Jared, turning towards the manager's small brick-built office. 'The wheels of commerce would grind more easily could a man be sure his goods were delivered on time.'

'It don't be many of the cutmen you can't trust, sir.' The manager followed behind him. 'They mostly 'ave wives and little 'uns to keep, and the only way of doing that is to do their job proper. But you gets a rogue one every now and again, and it seems you hit on one of them to deliver some of your goods.'

'It seems I did.' Taking his mount's halter from the post, to which he had attached it, Jared swung into the saddle. He preferred to ride whenever he could, finding a carriage restricting. 'But from now on, perhaps I may depend upon your guidance in the matter of choosing who to transport my goods?' Taking a sovereign from the pocket of his waistcoat, he passed it to the keeper of the basin.

'My judgement you can trust, sir, along with my integrity.' The man held out the sovereign. 'There be no need to pay me.'

'I apologise if my action was misunderstood,' Jared said, the smile gone from his mouth. 'I did not intend any slight. Allow me to say what I ought to have said a moment since. It is this. If you can find time, in addition to your other duties here at this basin, to ensure the timely loading and departure of all Lytton goods, the arrival back at the wharf of any barges hired by me, and to keep a log of all my business here, then you will be paid two sovereigns weekly as an employee of Lytton's.'

'Two sovereigns a week!' the man gasped. ''Tis as good as done, Mr Lytton, sir. 'Tis as good as done.'

Holding the restless horse in check, Jared looked down at the beaming man. 'Mind, there is to be no preference given to my business over any other man's. All I ask is that my business be given only to those you see as reliable, those you think most likely to stick to the bargain they strike.'

'I understand, Mr Lytton. You can rely on me, sir, it shall be as you say.'

Why had he not thought to do that before? Jared guided his horse along the towpath that ran parallel with Owen Street. It was more peaceful along the canal, the more so once he had passed beyond the houses of the colliers and brick workers that were tightly knit along Neptune Street and the older Chapel and Hall Streets. Since the building of the canals to service the coal mines and the limestone workings of the nearby town of Dudley, the villages around Tipton had grown, the terraces of drab grey houses stretching over what once had been fields and heath; canalside warehouses rising where in his grandfather's day tall oaks had reached towards the sky.

But had change brought improvement? Had industry given men and their families any real benefit? Had exchanging life on farms and in the countryside to work deep underground mining coal or limestone, spending their days in almost total darkness, been all that men had thought it would be?

Raising his riding crop in answer to a greeting from a passing narrow boat, Jared knew the answer to his questions, just as he knew the land would not support all these men, just as he knew there would always be those who from necessity would toil their lives away in the bowels of the earth. But at least those who worked in the Lytton mines would receive a fair wage.

All around him the darkening sky was filled with the song of birds settling in to roost among the trees that patched the heath now the sprawl of Tipton Green lay behind him. Jared listened to the melody, thankful for the peaceful sound of it after the bustle of Dudley Port and the flurry of the boats entering and leaving the canal wharfs that gave it its name.

Touching a heel to the animal's flank, Jared moved on. Ahead, set back from the towpath, he could see The Navigation. A mug of ale before finishing his journey home would be a pleasant break after the day's business.

'Evenin', Mr Lytton, sir.'

Ordering ale, Jared glanced about him. The room seemed to waver and flicker about him in the smoke-drenched light of the fire glowing in the hearth, helped by a motley collection of candle holders each supporting a slim column of wax.

'A seat beside the fire, sir?' The innkeeper, a pewter tankard in his hand, hesitated as Jared continued to sweep the room with his glance, acknowledging the nods of several men he knew to be employees, sitting now with cutmen from narrow boats moored alongside the towpath.

'No, thank you.' Handing the innkeeper a coin, Jared carried the mug towards the far end of the small bar room, with a shake of his head as the landlord opened a door he knew gave on to a more select drinking room. Jared was not of a mood to take his ale alone and guessed the snug would be empty; not many genteel customers frequented the canal towpath beer houses.

'Did you find old Jem, sir?'

Jared glanced at the innkeeper who had followed him to his seat in the corner. 'I found him and we did business together. I'm grateful to you for your mention of him.'

'Ar, he be a good cutman, do Jem, you'll have no problems of his making.'

'I am relieved to hear it.' Jared took a long swallow, feeling the cool liquid wash down his throat. 'I can find enough of those all around me without adding to them.'

'Speaking of which, sir, you remembers what it was we was talking of when you was 'ere this morning?'

'Should I?' Lifting the tankard, Jared swallowed again. 'Was it important?'

'Mebbe not to you and me.' The tavern keeper spoke quickly as he caught Jared's frown. 'But it were important enough to Richie Cade's girl.'

'To who?' Jared's attention was given more to the occupants of the smoke-filled bar than its landlord.

'You remembers, sir – the wench from along Horseley way, the one who was accused of pushing her young brother into the lock there? Seems hers been run out of the village.'

'What!' Jared brought the tankard crashing down on the table in front of him. They had dared to go against him, dared to run the girl off after all he had said to them! Pushing his way clear of both table and landlord, he strode from the inn, ignoring the polite goodnights of his workmen and the covert glances of the others.

Snatching the reins free from the wooden rail that stood to one side of the inn, he swung himself into the saddle. The people of Horseley had heard his evidence, heard him tell of seeing the child fall into the lock while his sister was still yards away. It had not been the truth but it had saved a young woman's life, saved a girl he had instinctively felt could never commit such a crime; and he had told them that turning her out of her home would be to invoke his wrath. That advice they had chosen to ignore. Jerking the reins, he turned the horse, sending it galloping in the direction of home.

Tomorrow the people of Horseley would learn to regret their action. Tomorrow they would discover just how harsh was the wrath of Jared Lytton.

'So you be from Horseley way?'

Tansy joined the group sitting around the table, now cleared of everything save the candle burning in a jam jar.

'Yes.' The warmth of the fire slowly chasing the chill from her bones together with the meal of mutton broth had made

Rachel drowsy, but at Tansy's question she roused herself. It was time to leave.

'Must have been somethin' pretty bad happened to bring you away when you had no place else to go?' Tansy's eyes glistened in the pale light. 'So bad you don't even tell a body your name.'

'Leave the wench be, Tansy.' Cora sprang to Rachel's defence. 'Since when does a woman have to give her name to us?'

'Coming into anybody's house be the usual time,' Tansy went on, taking little notice of Cora's reprimand. 'But seems her don't cotton to custom. Or could it be her don't want it known who her be?'

'I have no wish to keep my name from you,' Rachel said wearily. Today she had carried as many accusations and as much innuendo as she could shoulder. It might well be cold sleeping beneath a hedge but at least it would free her, if only for a few hours, from what seemed to be an everlasting stream of questions. She pushed herself back from the table. 'My name is Rachel Cade, and the reason for my leaving Horseley was that I was accused of the murder of my brother.'

The eyes of the three women and Bart were instantly fastened on her face.

'Rachel . . . you . . . you didn't!' Ellen's blue gaze was filled more with concern than horror, almost as if she knew the accusation to be false.

'No.' Rachel's reply to the half-spoken question was almost inaudible. 'I did not kill my brother. He died as the result of an accident.'

'Oh, Rachel, how terrible.' Ellen rose from her place at the table, coming to where Rachel stood and putting an arm about her shoulders. 'I am so very sorry.'

'Was you there when this accident took place?'

'No more questions, Tansy,' Cora interjected. 'Anybody can see this wench has had enough questions for one day.'

'I was there.' Rachel looked at Tansy through a film of tears. 'I saw ... I saw Robbie run to the edge of the lock, I was too far away to restrain him. He wanted to see the lock fill with water – he loved watching the barges lift – but he got so excited he lost his footing and fell into the lock. There was nothing anyone could do.'

'Oh, you poor wench.' Cora too went to stand beside the girl whose eyes now swam with tears. 'No wonder you wants to be away. But how could they accuse you of his killing?'

Rachel realised the question had not been intended as such but now the explanations had begun she found herself wanting to tell these women all that had happened.

'It was less than a week ago.' She fumbled in the pocket of her skirt, taking out a handkerchief and dabbing it against the tears spilling down her cheeks. 'I had taken Robbie with me to Tipton Green on an errand for my stepmother. She did not often allow me to take him so far from Horseley. Robbie was her only child and she thought I was jealous of him for replacing me in my father's affections.'

'Oh, Rachel, that cannot be true, surely?'

Dabbing her tears, she shook her head. 'I wasn't jealous of Robbie nor of Hannah, my stepmother, though she was convinced I was. My father had the same love for both his children. When ... when Robbie's body was carried home, Hannah accused me of causing his death and there were others only too ready to support her accusation. Only Ginny Marshall, a friend of my mother's, spoke up for me but Hannah became so incensed she smashed Ginny's skull with a brick. Then I was taken before Magistrate Bedworth ...'

'Oh my God!' Tansy dropped one hand heavily on the table while Cora's flew to her throat. 'Not you an' all? Not that swine! He don't give women justice, he just takes his pleasure of 'em two ways. First he takes his pleasure of their bodies and then he takes it again, by sending them down the line.'

'It was Magistrate Bedworth who sentenced Tansy,' Ellen

said. 'He gave her six months in prison for picking coal on the Ravensworth spoil heaps.'

''Ow come you didn't go to prison, Rachel?' Bart's voice, which had not yet broken, piped up in the ensuing quiet.

'Bed!' Tansy's head whipped round, an angry glare lighting her eyes. 'And keep your questions to yourself. You best learn when to keep a still tongue, my lad, and sharp, afore it lands you in trouble.'

'I only asked . . .'

'I knows what you only asked!' Tansy snapped. 'You only asks far too often, especially when it be something not meant for the ears of a lad. Now get yourself off to bed or you'll feel my boot against your arse!'

Bart pushed back his chair, the sound of it harsh against the stone flags. 'I only wondered,' he mumbled, low enough to avoid fanning Tansy's anger to even greater heights. 'Six months for coal picking and nowt for murder. Summat wrong there somewhere. Ain't like old Bedworth, ain't that.'

'Too old for his years be that one.' Tansy watched as Bart left through a door in the far end of the room. 'That tongue of his will land him on the gibbet one of these days.'

'He meant no hurt to you, Rachel.' Ellen gently squeezed her shoulder.

'He be nobbut a lad,' Cora supported her. 'Bart doesn't mean any harm. Sit you down, girl, at least till that trembling be stilled. You be like to fall down if you tries walking while you be shaking like that.'

Rachel had not realised she was trembling; her mind had been so full of the horror of what Isaiah Bedworth had tried to make her do that she was unaware of Tansy's sharp exchange with Bart.

'I'll make some tea.' Ellen settled Rachel back on a chair then crossed to the fireplace, swinging the hook that held a smoke-blackened kettle over the glowing coals.

'God, how I hate that bastard!' Tansy closed her eyes, pressing the lids tight on to her eyeballs as though to squeeze away what she saw printed on them. 'If ever a man deserved to die that one does, and the more painfully the better.'

'Magistrate Bedworth had them give Tansy six strokes of the cat as well as her gaol sentence.' Reaching across the table, Cora pressed a hand over that of her friend.

'Oh, Tansy!' Rachel's own memories paled immediately against the horror of such a punishment. 'The cat-o'-nine-tails . . . but why? Surely picking coal is not so dreadful a crime?'

Opening her eyes, Tansy flashed a brief smile as Ellen brought a brown earthenware teapot to the table. ''Tweren't no coal picking I were lashed for, 'twas for telling him what he could do with his dick . . . I told him to stick it up his arse for a jug handle!' She looked at Cora with a gleam of humour lurking in the depths of her green eyes. 'He might have done that an' all, the dirty old bugger, except it weren't big enough.'

The women burst out laughing even Ellen's mouth curving into a smile as she fetched thick platter cups from a cupboard set beside the door through which Bart had gone, returning for milk and sugar.

'Wants somebody to chop it off, he does.' Tansy lifted the hem of her black skirt, revealing cotton petticoats as she dabbed it to her eyes. 'And I swear by Him above, should I ever be fetched up afore that lecher again, then I'll be the one as will do the chopping.'

'He ordered you to be given six strokes of the cat-o'-nine-tails.' Rachel looked at her hard. 'He was going to give me the death sentence.'

'But not fer murder, I reckon.' The gleam of humour faded from Tansy's eyes, leaving them cold and hard. 'My bet be you did the same as me, only you might not have told him to stick his dick up his arse. He send you to the workhouse, did he?'

'Tibbington,' Rachel nodded. 'He came to me there and promised a lenient sentence if I did what he wanted.'

'That being shoving his podgy tool in your mouth?'

Rachel nodded again.

Accepting the tea that Ellen handed her, Tansy let out a long breath. 'And I wondered if you were one of we!'

'When I refused, he told me he would have used me not once but every night until he passed sentence on me – and that his ruling then would still be that I should hang for murder.'

'That sounds like the bastard!' Tansy said through gritted teeth. 'That be just what he would do.'

'But you were not sentenced to death?' Ellen placed a cup of steaming tea before Rachel.

'No thanks to Isaiah Bedworth, I'll be bound,' Cora guessed.

'No, no thanks to him.' Rachel glanced at her. 'He was about to pronounce sentence when someone at the back of the room called out that he was an eye witness to what had happened.'

'An eye witness?' Ellen sounded relieved. 'That was fortunate for you, Rachel.'

'Fortunate be a poor description.' Tansy swallowed some of the hot liquid. 'Miracle be a better one. Takes a brave body to speak out before Isaiah Bedworth. He be too well known for getting his own back on any who snatch his pleasure from beneath his nose.'

'Was it your father spoke for you, Rachel?' Cora asked. 'Or p'raps somebody from the village?'

'My father was at work in the mine when Robbie fell into the lock.' Rachel stared at her untouched cup as if seeing the accident all over again in its milky depth. 'So he could not claim to have seen what occurred, though he told the magistrate I would never have harmed my brother, I loved him too much for that; and as for anyone of Horseley speaking for me that proved not to be except for Ginny, the rest were too keen on seeing the spectacle of a murder trial.'

'Then who did speak for you?'

Rachel met Ellen's soft blue eyes, seeing the compassion

in them, noting how differently she was heard by this girl she had known little more than an hour from the way she had been by women she had known all her life.

'I do not know who he was,' she replied, 'I had never seen him before that moment, but Magistrate Bedworth seemed to recognise him for His face turned thunderous when the man came forward.'

'Did this man see the accident? Did he really see what happened?'

'I cannot be sure.' Her brows knitting together, Rachel searched her memory, seeing again the figure who strode through the upper room in The Jolly Collier. 'I cannot remember seeing anything or anyone other than Robbie falling into the lock.'

'Ain't hardly likely he would make up a story to save the neck of a wench he'd never met.' Tansy finished her tea. 'That be too far-fetched to be real.'

'Well, made up or not, it put paid to Bedworth's plans,' Cora said, her tone revealing the satisfaction she felt.

'He saved my life. He was a total stranger but he saved my life.' Bemused, as if waking from some awful nightmare, Rachel spoke the words softly, almost holding them to herself. 'He saved my life.'

'So who was this man? Did he say his name?'

'Not until we were outside The Collier.' Pulling her thoughts together, Rachel answered Tansy's question. 'A man threw a stone at him, cutting him on the side of his face. It was then he said his name. He told the man he would go to gaol for as long as Jared Lytton's lawyers could keep him there.'

'Lytton!' Cora's glance flew to the others.

'Do you know him?'

'Not exactly.' Cora shook her head. 'But we knows *of* him. He be a fair man to them as treats him proper, but cross him and you find yourself at odds with the devil himself.'

'Lytton be quite a name hereabouts,' Tansy took up the explanation. 'Owns coal mines up along Rounds Hill as well as Tibbington and the Foxyards. Then there be the brick works along of Bloomfield and right here in Tipton Green, to say nothing of the limestone workings he owns out Dudley way. Ar, Lytton be a name to reckon with. No wonder old Bedworth's face dropped when he saw who it was spoke out for you. That one wouldn't be frightened off.'

'If only it had been his land you had been on when you were caught, Tansy.' Compassion filled Ellen's soft blue gaze. 'Then maybe you would not have gone to prison.'

'Maybe,' Tansy replied, 'but what's done be done and there be no undoing of it.'

'Thank the good God he was there for you, though.' Cora drained her own cup before setting it on the table. 'Without his help you would have had less chance than an aynuk in a harem.'

'I think you mean a eunuch, Cora.' A smile lit Ellen's eyes, replacing the compassion.

'Ar, well, as long as what you says means a man with no balls!'

Colour rising in her cheeks, Ellen swept up the empty cups, taking Rachel's untouched one with her into the scullery.

'What I don't understand is . . .' Cora paused as if searching for the right words. 'What I means is, if Jared Lytton got you off, how come you be here? What I'm saying is . . .'

'What you be wanting to say but be going all around the Wrekin to say it is: if you was found not guilty and set free, 'ow come you be running from home? 'Cos truth be told, that's what you be doing.'

Tansy's voice carried easily to the scullery where Ellen listened for the reply.

'Yes, that is what I am doing.'

The reply was soft, and to Ellen, drying her hands on a piece of well-scrubbed huckaback, it sounded slurred, one word running into another. Taking up the freshly washed cups, she carried them back into the other room and began to replace them in the cupboard.

'Don't make no sense to me,' Tansy said flatly.

Going across to the fireplace, Cora took up the iron poker laid in the hearth and began to rake ash from beneath the glowing embers, banging the poker several times on the bars before putting it down again.

'That be 'cos you don't know the all of it, Tansy Croft.'

'No, and I ain't asking neither.' She pushed herself to her feet, picking up the small blue basin half filled with sugar and passing it to Ellen to return to the cupboard. 'Seems the wench has already told us enough of her private business.'

'That be a swift turnabout!' Cora's answer was tart and as she swung to face the other woman her mouth was drawn into a tight offended line. 'First off you wanted to know the top and bottom of old Meg's arse and now you be saying we should mind our own business!'

'I says what I says!' Tansy flashed. 'I don't have to ask you, Cora Perry, and I say the wench has told us enough.'

Dropping the latch on the cupboard, Ellen caught the slight movement of the door beside it. Keeping her body between it and the rest of the room, she stepped up to it, seeing a slice of Bart's face pressed to an opening a few inches wide. Her own face showing what she hoped was a frown, Ellen despaired of the smile she felt take control of her mouth as the lad grinned at her, and she closed the door quietly.

'I think you should hear the rest,' Rachel said as Ellen joined them, taking the chairs from around the table and grouping them about the fireplace.

'I was found not guilty but my stepmother was unhappy with the verdict and barred me from ever entering my home again.'

From the corner of her eye she saw Ellen's slight shoulders stiffen and her knuckles whiten as she gripped her hands tightly together in her lap.

'After the trial she cursed the man who had saved me then ran from us. When my father and I reached home, my clothes were in shreds in the street. I knew I could never live in the same house as her after that, so I left.'

In the hush that followed her words Rachel turned to the door, drawing her shawl further on to her brow. Outside the air was crisp with the bite of a late-spring frost and above her head the moon wore a halo, its pale luminescence the promise of a cold night.

Shivering against the shock of its sudden icy touch, she stepped into the darkness.

Chapter Five

'Well, wench, you have the choice.' Tansy finished wrapping a thick slice of bread and a much smaller wedge of cheese in a scrap of cloth, placing it in a carpet bag alongside the bottle she had filled with sweet milky tea, the neck wedged with a screw of newspaper.

'It be better than going on to Woodsetton and likely finding nothing there for you when you gets there.'

'You mind your own business, Bart Jevons!' Tansy's hand flew out, catching the lad a cuff about his ear. 'I've told you afore what sticking your nose in other people's business will bring. Now get you off out of here and find business that will buy your supper. And mind . . .' she added as he scrambled out of reach of her ever-ready hand '. . . take a handkercha with you!'

'You calls this a handkerchief?' Waving the scrap of clean rag, he grinned cheekily.

'It be more than you had when you first come here, you cheeky little bugger.' Tansy's laughter was just below the surface. 'You would have been wiping your nose on the tail of your shirt but for the fact you didn't *have* a shirt.'

'One day I'll have a dozen shirts, and every one silk, I'll dress like a king, I will.'

'Oh, ar.' Tansy's laughter broke out. 'Well, remember me when you come into your kingdom.'

Rachel smiled as the lad doffed his grimy flat cap, sweeping Tansy a low bow before darting away.

'That one will do all right,' she said with more than a little affection in her tone. 'That is, if the devil don't get him first. Now you, wench, what be your decision?'

Rachel had thought long into the night. Ellen had come after her almost immediately she had left, drawing her back into the warmth where the three of them had offered her a place with them, giving her a choice of working alone to earn her keep or joining with them in picking coal on the pit banks. What else could she do? The long hours of darkness had brought no alternative schemes for employment, and who was there would offer a girl as yet not eighteen a post as housekeeper.

'I would prefer to work alongside the three of you,' she said shyly.

'That be settled then.' Tansy fastened the strings of her own bonnet beneath her chin then reached for her heavy maroon wool shawl that hung on the back of the door. 'Not like some as picks alone. Working on your own means that often you can't fill a bag and that means not getting a fair payment for the coal you've picked. We find that by mucking in together we gets at least one full bag every day, and most days we can fill two. The money we get paid is shared out equal and each woman pays so much into the pot for food and rent, together with what else be needed. If it should be as a monthly proves too painful for working one or two days, then the others cover. We find that way we manages well enough. Be that satisfactory to you?'

'Very satisfactory,' Rachel nodded, fastening her own shawl in a knot beneath her breasts.

'Stay beside me.' Ellen smiled, handing Rachel a cloth-wrapped slice of bread and cheese. 'The banks will have your back aching and your fingers sore but you get used to it . . . eventually!'

With the two elder women leading and Rachel walking

behind beside Ellen, they passed along Owen Street, crossing a small area of open ground before coming into Neptune Street with its few huddled houses that rapidly gave on to heathland.

'Tansy thought to try picking over at the Foxyards colliery. It's a longer walk but we don't stand the same chance of being bothered there.'

'Bothered?' Rachel glanced sideways at the girl whose sherry-brown hair escaped her shawl, sending curling wisps over her pale cheeks. Ellen was not what might be described as beautiful, her straight nose a little too large while her mouth was small, but eyes of a wonderful deep blue, the exact shade of cornflowers, more than made up for her otherwise plain features. And as for her nature . . . Rachel had already decided Ellen Walker had a gentleness and kindness of heart that went beyond beauty.

'By the constable,' she explained. 'The owner of the pits out along the Foxyards makes no complaint to the magistrates about people picking over his waste heaps. Not like some.' She glanced at Tansy, walking ahead.

'Are there many like her? Have many been put in prison for picking coal from the heaps?'

'Enough.' Ellen caught Rachel's elbow, holding her back and pointing to a gaping hole in the ground only inches from the path worn into the heath. 'And many a child has fallen into the like of that. Gin pits are sunk all over Tipton then left open when the diggers can't go any deeper. Once you've fallen in it's as good as the end.'

'But are the miners not made to cover them or fill them in once they are finished working them?'

'The law is one thing.' Releasing her elbow, Ellen followed Cora and Tansy once more. 'Even if there was such a law, and I'm not sure that there is, catching the men who sink these shafts is something else. The land they work usually belongs to another so they do not advertise their presence. A couple of weeks extracting surface coal and then they're off to sink a new shaft elsewhere. It's a fly-by-night method of mining.'

'We'll take that over there.' Tansy looked back over her shoulder then pointed to her left where a pile of pit waste rose like a black hill, looming over the heath.

Rachel felt the tears rise in her throat, the scene was so evocative of Horseley: the heath about the village dominated by pit heaps rising all around, the older ones just beginning to don a thin cover of grass.

'Here, give me that.' Following their two friends to a spot a little apart from the half dozen or so women already gathered on the banks, Ellen held out a hand for Rachel's bread and cheese. 'I'll put it with mine. We'll eat together about one, or at least when we guess it to be that time for we will hear no church bell this far out.' Putting Rachel's food with her own in a carpet bag similar to the one Tansy had carried, she wrapped it in her shawl before placing it on the ground.

'Let's start over there.' Ellen pointed as Rachel removed her own shawl, shivering in the cool morning. 'You can recognise which is coal and which is slate?'

Rachel nodded, following suit as Ellen sank to her knees, thankful she had accepted the offer of a hessian sack to kneel on.

'We fill the buckets then transfer the coal to the sack Cora brought. Later they are picked up by a jagger. You have to be watchful when dealing with those men, Rachel, they're apt to cheat. Either by bringing a bag that holds more than half a hundredweight or by claiming your pickings hold more slate than coal.'

Damp from the ground quickly soaked the hessian sack, she knelt on, seeping through Rachel's petticoats then the skirts of her thin brown dress, and the sharp spring breeze pulled at her hair, whipping it loose of its pins. Scrabbling among the gritty black waste, prising out small lumps of coal, she was soon wincing with pain as the sharp edges ripped into her skin, coating gouged flesh with soggy black coal dust.

At last Ellen called a break, handing Rachel a slice of cheese and bread, saying nothing when it was refused. Only her blue eyes said she knew the pain and misery the other girl was suffering.

Accepting the offer of a drink, Rachel swallowed a mouthful of cold sweet tea, wincing as her bleeding fingers closed about the bottle. Was this to be her life from now on? She turned her head, facing out over the pocked heath, shielding her face from Ellen. Was this all there was for her now, to spend her days kneeling on the damp earth, scratching out tiny lumps of coal with fingers that marked every piece with blood? Was this to be her sentence?

But I didn't do it! she cried in her heart. I did not kill Robbie.

'Where is the house of Richard Cade?'

Jared Lytton stared coldly at the woman to whom he had called his question.

'It be that one.' She jerked her head in a backward motion. 'The one at the end beside the wall that be half tumbling down, you can hardly miss it. Though if it be any of the Cades you be looking to see, then you won't.'

'Why not?'

''Cos there don't none of them be there.' The woman's answer was as simple as Jared's question had been terse.

'Where will I find them?'

'The youngest you'll find in the churchyard. He be dead, drowned more than a week gone.'

Irritation prickling his skin, Jared glared about him. There would be other women in this Godforsaken place, but doubtless they would not show themselves to him; they would prefer to watch from behind curtains and half closed doors.

'Where will I find Richard Cade?'

The woman had already begun to move off along the street, her black skirts sweeping the dusty ground.

It seemed for several moments that she would ignore the question as she walked on, the short veil that hung from the back of her small black velvet bonnet waving like a mourning flag. Then she stopped, turning her head as she answered.

'Richie Cade be at his work, like any able-bodied man should be – instead of bothering a body who has her own work to do.'

Jared's jaw clenched in irritation. 'And his wife and daughter?'

From a few feet away the woman squinted at him, her eyes playing over his face. 'You be Cyrus Lytton's lad?' she asked, recognition flitting like a cloud across her face.

Jared nodded.

'Mmm, it shows.' The woman revealed no trace of worry that her reply might have given offence. 'They tells me you was there when Magistrate Bedworth gave his ruling – that it was you got Richie Cade's wench off when her seemed likely to hang?'

'I was there.' Jared clung on to his patience.

'Then you should know as 'er left Horseley the same day.'

He allowed his mouth to tighten but otherwise gave no sign that that much at least he did know.

'Hannah Cade was fetched up in front of Magistrate Bedworth the following morning.' The woman hitched the basket she was carrying from one arm to the other. 'You'll not be seeing that one in these parts again, nor any place else. Life was what old Bedworth dished out to 'er – life in Digbeth asylum. Would have been the hangman's noose for sure but he said as he reckoned 'er were nigh on insane. Life!' She turned away, her last words floating back. 'Poor bugger! 'Er would have been better off with the hangman.'

Watching the woman disappear among the crowded

houses, Jared tapped his riding crop against his boot. Hannah Cade was in prison and Richard Cade at his place of work. He sent a glance along the narrow street, looking in turn at each of the tiny houses leaning drunkenly together, the spent mines they were built over slowly subsiding beneath their weight. The one at the end, the old woman had told him. He began to walk towards it then halted. The woman had also said there was no one there. He glanced again at the houses, each door firmly shut, no twitch of a curtain to bely the fact that at least some were occupied.

He brought the crop down several times against his riding boot, the slap of leather on leather echoing back from the crumbling brickwork. Irritation slowly mounted to anger. He had ridden here to find the reason the girl had left her home, to ascertain who was responsible, just who it was had chosen to ignore his ultimatum – and find out he would. Then the whole of Horseley village would know what it meant to go against Jared Lytton!

Richie Cade had left Horseley.

Jared's hand lay easy on the reins, allowing his mount to follow its own path across the heath.

He had gone to The Jolly Collier after his fruitless encounter with the woman in Horseley village. He supposed, upon reflection, he would have done better going to the public house in the first place. If anyone would be in possession of all of the facts, it would be the local inn-keeper.

But why did he want all the facts? Why go to Horseley at all? Was it out of interest in a supposed child murder or because of injured pride? Was it merely pique that his threat was being ignored that had taken him back there?

The questions turned over in his mind like leaves before the wind, tumbling and turning. There was, of course, no other reason. He looked up, following the flight of a lark, its song filling the sky as it rose vertically from a nest hidden somewhere among the grass of the heath. He had gone to that courtroom to prevent a young girl being sentenced to death, and having done so had given his word that should she be harmed, the Lytton mines and chain shops would be closed to the people of Horseley. The thought of their choosing to disregard his warning and drive Richard Cade's daughter out of the village had been the driving force behind his second visit.

Above his head, swathed in sunlight, the tiny bird sang loud and long.

Or had there been some other reason?

He had gone to The Jolly Collier with vengeance on his mind, determined to show he meant all he had said that day. But the landlord had declared the girl had left of her own choice, that no neighbour had forced her from her home. Then, if no neighbour, who? A young girl does not just up and leave, Jared had pressed his point.

'When the wench and her father reached home, they found everything she had ripped to pieces and lying in the street.'

Now the words circled his mind, closing out the song of the lark.

'Hannah had got there afore them. She was like a crazed woman, said the girl would never enter the house again.'

'And the father, Richard Cade?'

'He was set to leave . . .'

Jared watched the bird swoop to earth, disappearing into the tall grass.

'. . . thought his going might ease the jealousy Hannah held for his daughter. But the girl wouldn't hear of that. She said that Hannah needed him now more than ever and he should stay; she would be the one to leave Horseley.'

Jared touched a heel to his mount, still listening to the voice in his head.

'Girl run off then, afore anybody could stop her. Constable caught up with Hannah and carted her off to the cell at the police station. Then in the morning of the day following, the constable fetched Hannah up before the magistrate and he passed a sentence of life. I saw Richie turn from the bench, and if I live to be a thousand I will never forget the look on his face. He was a tortured man. He seemed to have suffered more in them few days than any criminal in a gaol. I offered him a tankard of ale. If any man needed one it were him, but he walked straight past me, that terrible look on his face and his eyes all sort of empty. "There's nothing left," were all the words he spoke. "Both my children gone . . . there's nothing left." He walked out of the Collier and out of Horseley and ain't nobody seen him since.'

Jared had left then. There had been no outlet for the vengeance that had boiled within him. He need take no action against the people of the village. Yet some emotion still seethed within him, something he could not define, a feeling that was with him when he woke and with him still when he slept.

Ahead of him, along the path worn across the heath, a cart pulled by a huge shire horse rumbled towards Tipton Green. Jared lifted his crop, acknowledging the jagger's greeting as the cart lumbered past him.

His enquiries at each of the coal mines and brickworks owned by him, as well as some that were not, had brought him no news of Richie Cade or his daughter.

But why had he enquired of her? She was not the object or cause of the feelings that lurked in him.

Beside the towpath of the canal that carried barges into Dudley Port, and from there to almost every part of England, he caught the faint pale, almost silvery, gleam of the first early buttercups. The girl had had hair that colour, the colour of wild wheat . . .

Annoyed at the sudden tightening sensation within him,

he pulled on the reins, sending the horse into a gallop. He must forget what had happened at Horseley.

The sudden drum of the horse's hooves on the hardened earth of the towpath sent a fresh flurry of movement among the grasses of the adjacent heathland and several larks rose into the air, their protestations loud on the soft spring air. Jared did not check the horse's speed but let it run until the sight of another, being led by a man, forced him to a standstill. Knowing there was room enough on the towpath for one animal only, Jared guided his own mount to a spot a few yards into the rough heathland.

'Will you pass now, sir?' the man leading the horse called as he neared Jared. 'I 'ave to unhitch old Tiger 'ere and take him over yonder bridge for there be no towpath going under that one.'

Jared glanced in the direction of the man's outstretched hand. He had forgotten Gospel Bridge. He smiled inwardly, remembering his grandfather telling him of the Methodist preacher standing on the bridge while trying to convert the people of Rounds Hill and Bloomfield to his beliefs, and the summary justice he had received at their hands.

They had frogmarched him from the place, his grandfather had said: 'No ifs or buts, just ran the fellow off.'

Just as Jared was set to do with the folk of Horseley. It would appear he had inherited more than Foxley House or the Foxyards; he also, it seemed, had his share of the Tipton temper.

'I am in no hurry,' he called to the man who stood watching him. 'Take your horse over, I will wait.'

'Hold up there, Tiger.'

The bargee was dressed in heavy boots, black trousers shiny from wear tied beneath the knee with string. A worn jacket covered a collarless shirt, into the neck of which had been thrust the ends of a once white muffler, while the inevitable flat cap covered tousled brown hair. He halted the horse, beginning the process of unhitching the rope by which the barge was towed.

Jared smiled to hear the horse's name, guessing the horse to be as docile as a newly dropped lamb.

'That one be tasting his oats.' The bargee smiled towards Jared as his mount gave a high-pitched whinny. 'But he be on a loser if he's a fancy for old Tiger. Her be long past the age of wanting to play his sort of game.'

'You can't blame him for trying.' Jared returned the smile.

'That you can't!' the man laughed as the line fell loose from the harness. 'I just hopes he finds more fortune in the trying than a man on a Saturday night.'

'Possibly a man should try the oats more and the ale less,' Jared answered, smile turning to a laugh.

'Ar, possibly.' The bargee jumped aboard the gaily painted narrow boat with an agile motion, one hand already banging on the roof of the small cabin Jared knew to be the living quarters. 'But meself, I'll take the ale.'

His hand loose on his own mount's rein, the animal content to investigate the heath in search of grass, Jared sat watching as a woman emerged from below. Her long skirt was caught up into its waistband, displaying high button boots, a red fringed shawl crossing her breasts, two long dark plaits caught together at the back of her neck. As he watched she jumped easily to the towpath. Catching Tiger by the bridle, she spoke to him softly and immediately the horse began to plod obediently up the small rise that carried the path alongside the bridge, taking it back down the other side.

Jared had watched the same operation since boyhood but it never failed to hold his interest, and he sat now as he had years ago, his eyes on the bargee as the man climbed on to the cabin roof, lying on his back then placing both feet on the wall of the small tunnel that ran below the bridge. Slowly, one foot passing over the other with a sideways motion, the sole of his boots always placed flat and firm on the wall, the man began to propel the narrow boat forward, legging it through the tunnel, bringing it through to where the woman and the horse waited on the far side.

Watching while Tiger was once more hitched to the tow rope and pulled the boat until it disappeared around a curve of the canal, Jared shortened the reins on his own mount, setting it to a walk in the direction of home. The boat had been carrying coal, and he knew from the boldly painted name, *Staffordshire Knot*, and the looped rope design beneath, that it was one that carried coal from his own Foxyards Colliery to the iron foundry at Bloomfield as well as supplying the newly built gasworks at Tipton Green.

Tipton Green . . . His thoughts shifted at once to the locks that abounded in the area, enabling boats to be lifted or lowered to follow the level of the many canals, and to one lock in particular. That boy had drowned in Toll End lock – pushed, it was claimed, by his sister, a girl Jared had lied to save.

But why? What in God's name had driven him to do such a thing? It wasn't as if he even knew her.

From across the heath laughter drifted towards him and Jared raised his eyes. Women were picking on the coal heaps, scratching what they could to make a living. He watched idly for a moment, making no move towards them. They had his permission to pick on any of his spoil heaps; so long as they didn't approach the pit head there would be no action taken against them. He had no quarrel with the pit bank wenches, unlike many pit owners who demanded the full penalty of the law should descend on any woman caught. Stealing, it was called, taking away the property of its lawful owner without due permission. His breath was released in a short sardonic hiss. But why prosecute a woman for taking that for which there was no other use?

The laughter rang out again, catching his attention. He saw a shawl being lifted and held momentarily to the rising breeze to open its folds before it was lowered over a head of silver-gold hair. He had seen hair just that colour days ago. Silver-gold curls tumbling about the face of a girl, wisps of silk which she smoothed away from eyes the colour of wood violets.

Again he felt that tug at his stomach. What was it about the girl that had him running back to Horseley, and sent his innards churning at the sight of a fair head? Jared tugged at the reins, almost welcoming the irritation that returned with the thought.

He must forget the girl with the golden hair.

Chapter Six

'Ellen, get a bowl of water and bathe Rachel's hands, the kettle will still be hot. Cora and meself will see to a meal.'

'I'll help.' Rachel tried unfastening the knot of her shawl but winced at the pain.

'You'll do as you'm bid, wench!' Her own shawl already hung behind the door, Tansy turned to the grate, poking out grey ash before adding fresh coals to the glowing embers. 'Them hands of yours need to be cleaned and dressed afore an infection sets in. You get blood poisoning and it'll be more than the fingertips the surgeon will be removing.'

'Tansy is right, Rachel.' Ellen swiftly released the knot, slipping the shawl from the girl's shoulders. 'Sit here beside the fire while I get some water.'

'Make sure and put plenty of salt in it,' Tansy called as Ellen disappeared into the scullery, then to Rachel, 'It'll make you wet your drawers with the bite of it but it will kill off any badness – help the flesh heal clean.'

Her fingers still oozing blood from the lacerations caused by the jagged edges of the coal she had scraped from the banks, Rachel stared at the blue edged flames licking greedily at the freshly added fuel. It had been two days since she had left Horseley; since she had run from home rather than see her father leave his own house. Two days since last seeing his smile or feeling his gentle kiss on her cheek. It was pointless to wonder if he missed her as she did him, she knew he would. And Hannah . . . what of Hannah? She was to be brought to trial for the killing of Ginny Marshall. Would the magistrate be lenient? Would he take into consideration the fact that the loss of her only child had driven her half mad, making her not responsible for her actions that day? Rachel hoped it would be so; she felt nothing but pity for her stepmother despite the woman's dislike of her.

'Here we are.' Ellen placed a small enamel bowl on the table then fetched the kettle from the hob, pouring the hot water over the mound of salt in the bowl. Testing the steaming liquid with the tip of her finger, she shook her head. 'Don't put your hands in yet, I'll get a jug of cold water to cool the bowl a little.'

'Don't go making it too cold.' Tansy looked up from the potatoes she was peeling. 'Won't do no good if it's cold!'

Ellen's eyes held an encouraging smile as they met Rachel's. 'This is going to hurt.' She nodded, satisfied with the temperature of the water in the bowl. 'You can cry out if it helps, none of us will mind. It's something each of us has done before.'

'Get them in, Rachel.' Cora laid thick strips of belly pork in a roasting pan and set it in the oven. 'The sooner they be in, the sooner they can come out.'

Holding her hands over the basin, Rachel hesitated, the steam stinging like fire where it curled about her bleeding fingers.

'Go on, Rachel,' Ellen urged gently. 'Be brave.'

Her mouth fixed in a strangled gasp as the sting of the salt water bit into her cut fingers, she forced herself to hold her hands in the warm water.

'There!' Tansy nodded approvingly. 'Now keep them there and later we'll bind them up.'

The initial shock of pain over, Rachel felt her body relax, the water soaking the pain from her hands, the warmth of the revived fire soothing the aches from her body. She had worked beside Ellen the whole day, kneeling or squatting on the damp waste heaps, and had not once stopped pulling and scratching, digging her fingers into the sharp black rubble, but even so she had not managed to fill two buckets before the jagger had come to collect the day's pickings. She glanced down at the mud drying grey on her skirts. Could she really go on like this, cold and dirty day after day, her body aching and her hands cut and bleeding?

Rachel closed her eyes, forbidding the tears to pass her throat. It was not a question of could she, she *had* to if she wanted to survive. Like Bart, she would never go to the parish; one day in Tibbington workhouse had been enough. If becoming a pit bank wench was what it took to keep her from that place, then that was what she would be.

'Old Potter were asking about you lot earlier today.' Bart breezed into the room, the street door banging behind him.

'Oh, ar?' Tansy looked up from testing the potatoes with a long-handled fork. 'What did he want?'

'Ooh, them looks sore.' Bart grimaced, coming to look at Rachel's hands. 'You won't be picking your nose wi' them for a week or two.' Then, glancing to where Tansy stood, he added: 'Potter asked why you wasn't picking on the Britannia ground?'

'What did you tell him?' Cora fetched plates from the dresser, setting them on the table.

'I said you was feeling like a change.'

'I'd like a permanent change from him.' Tansy laid the fork aside. 'That man be not only a robber, paying the lowest penny he can for the coal a woman picks, but he be sly with it. One day, God willing, he will get his comeuppance.'

'Did you get a better deal today?' Bart placed a paper-wrapped parcel on the table. '*I* did. I got this from the butcher along Owen Street for running an errand for his wife. Seems her ordered a bonnet from Kate Barnett but the ribbons on it were pink and her had ordered cerise.'

'Ordered what?' Tansy ignored his question about the amount the jagger paid for their day's work.

'Cerise. Least that's what I think her said.'

'Hmmph, that woman be getting ideas above her head.'

'No.' Bart's mischievous grin flashed again. 'It be a bonnet her be getting for her head.'

'Let's have less of your lip, Mister Smart Arse.' Tansy glared at him, delving into a pocket of her voluminous black skirts and drawing out a silver threepenny piece which she handed to the boy. 'Get you round to Longmore's and fetch a tin of Indian Cereate. Them fingers of Rachel's need an ointment. And, mind, I expects a penny change.'

'You mean, I don't get a penny for going?'

'You'll be getting a fourpenny one about your ears, me lad, if you try my patience any further.'

She couldn't help a smile from breaking about her lips. But as Tansy lifted Rachel's hands gently from the water, it faded as she saw the raw flesh.

'This be my fault!' She reached for a cloth hanging from a line strung above the fireplace. 'I should have seen, you ain't never picked coal in your life.'

'You wasn't to know,' Cora defended her friend as the other woman patted Rachel's hands dry.

'I *would* have known had I taken the trouble to look, but I was too suspicious, too ready to judge.'

'That's only to be expected, Tansy, after what happened.'

'Mebbe.' She sat on the stool from which Ellen lifted the basin, inspecting each hand in turn. 'But that don't ease the pain of this girl any.'

'Shall I get something to bind Rachel's hands with?' Ellen returned from emptying the bowl, wincing at the sight of the red, angry-looking fingers.

'There be a length of white calico in the chest alongside my bed. Bring it here.'

Tansy picked up the small round tin Bart had placed on a corner of the table, the penny he was given in change conspicuously placed on its lid, and twisted it open.

'This will have them fingers healed in no time.' Touching

one corner of the calico into the creamy white paste, she proceeded to smear the ointment on to the cuts. 'They'll take a few days for the skin to heal over,' she said, taking more of the calico torn into strips and binding Rachel's hands. 'Then we will see about hardening your skin. That way your fingers won't cut so readily.'

'I expect you feel ready for a cup of tea?' Cora smiled, already handing out steaming mugs. 'A drop of tea soon has a body feeling better.'

'Thank you.' Rachel held the mug awkwardly between her bandaged hands. Her mother had always relied on a cup of tea whenever things became difficult. But it would take more than that to put Rachel Cade's life back together again.

'What did Cora mean when she said it was not surprising that Tansy should be suspicious of me?'

Standing in the bedroom she shared with Ellen, Rachel lifted her arms into the nightgown the other girl guided over her head. Ellen had given her a change of underwear as well as the nightgown, saying they were old and ready to be thrown away, but Rachel knew that was not the truth. Ellen had given her clothing she could barely spare.

'It was a woman who reported Tansy for picking coal.' Ellen tied the thin cotton ribbons at the neck of the gown, then reached for a comb that lay on a shelf above a table whose surface was just large enough to hold the jug and bowl the girls used for washing.

'You mean, one of the pit bank girls told on her?'

'Yes.' Ellen pulled the comb through long strands of Rachel's pale silken hair. 'Except she was not truly a pit bank girl, she had been sent to spy on Tansy.'

'But why?'

Tying Rachel's hair with a ribbon, Ellen folded back the bedclothes. After waiting for the girl to settle, she tucked the blanket over her.

'Tansy was turned out of her home after her husband

died in a rock fall. He was a miner in the limestone quarries somewhere in the area of Dudley Castle, I believe. Anyway, the mine owner said he wanted Tansy's house for a man and his family. She had no choice but to leave. She came here to Tipton Green several years ago and found a place with the pickers on the coal heaps. Samuel Potter offered to buy the coal she picked.' Ellen braided her own hair, tying off the two long plaits with a length of ribbon, the fellow to that she had fastened in Rachel's. 'Potter offered a price, but he wanted more than coal. Such as was scratched from the pit waste was difficult to sell, he told her. The money he paid her for it was more than it was worth, but if she made up for it in other ways . . .'

Ellen broke off, turning her back on Rachel, who lay propped on a pillow, the brass-framed bedstead gleaming in the muted light of the solitary candle.

Other ways! Rachel's mind was filled with the picture of that other dimly lit room, of a man who'd promised her leniency provided she paid in other ways; a man who had used his position to prey on women. Magistrate Bedworth and Samuel Potter, so different in social class, so alike in their carnal desires.

'. . . When Tansy refused him,' Ellen went on, her voice so soft as to be barely audible, 'he sent one of his women to work beside her, then once she was sure of the areas in which Tansy picked, she reported her to the constable and Tansy was arrested. The woman testified and Magistrate Bedworth sent Tansy to prison for six months. It was the woman who reported and testified against her, and when it was over she openly boasted of the money Potter paid her for doing his dirty work.'

That was the meaning behind Tansy's words that first night, when she had exclaimed, 'Not you an' all' and 'I wondered if you were one of we'. Samuel Potter and Isaiah Bedworth. Both had tried to force Tansy to lie with them and both had taken their revenge when she refused, just as Isaiah

Bedworth had been prepared to take revenge on Rachel by ordering her death!

Crossing to the little shelf over the wash stand, Ellen replaced the comb then blew out the candle, waiting until the grey light of night filtered through the small window to temper the blackness of the room.

'Why did Tansy come back to Tipton Green?' Rachel asked once Ellen had slipped into the bed they shared.

'Cora once told me that Tansy returned from prison a different character. She was no longer the gentle person her friends once knew but a hard, bitter woman who distrusted almost everyone she came into contact with. But that is a defence, a shield she has placed about herself so as not to be hurt again. Once she lets you inside you will find the same gentle, thoughtful woman she's always been.'

But to come back at all, Rachel thought, wondering how long she herself would remain in Tipton, so close to Toll End lock, the place where Robbie had died.

'I think Tansy came back to take revenge on Samuel Potter,' Ellen went on. 'I see it in her face every time he comes to take the coal we have picked. Every time that sneering smile crosses his face.'

Staring at the ceiling which was lost in shadow, Rachel felt the girl beside her shudder as she mentioned the coal jagger.

'I think Tansy would kill him,' Ellen murmured, 'especially if she knew . . .'

'Knew what?'

It was almost as if Ellen had invited the question, as if she held some secret she sought to share.

'She's not the only woman in this house to have been a victim of Samuel Potter's.'

A deep sigh racked the girl's body and Rachel felt her own tauten. Not Ellen, not this gentle, kindly girl? No man would be swine enough . . .

'I came here to Tipton Green two years ago.'

From the softness of Ellen's voice Rachel knew she was reliving a part of her past, one that caused her great pain. 'My home had been in Wallbrook – Bayton Hall. I was my parents' only child. To be brief, I fell in love with the son of one of my father's estate workers, but when we asked permission to marry it was refused. My father was furious and threatened Tom with prison should he not leave Wallbrook at once. I told my father he could not have Tom gaoled simply for asking to marry me but he was adamant. He told us both it would not be simply an unwarranted proposal Tom would be accused of, that his lawyers would come up with something far more serious, so Tom should leave while he still had the chance. I was determined that if Tom went, I too would leave Wallbrook.'

'It might have been better if you'd stayed.'

'I couldn't,' Ellen answered. 'You see, I was expecting a child. There was no way my father would forgive that.'

'But your mother . . .'

'My mother did as she was told, Rachel.' Ellen's voice trembled on a swallowed sob, 'My father loved us both but his was the only voice that was heard in the house. I never once recall hearing my mother question a decision of his. He had decided I should not marry Tom, had even threatened him with prison for daring to ask me. Heaven only knows what he would have done if he had learned I already carried Tom's child!'

Her gaze still fixed on the shadows shrouding the ceiling, Rachel remained silent, yet every part of her was aware of the other girl's grief.

'When Tom left, I went with him,' she continued. 'He could find no work, my father saw to that. We were desperate, so much so that Tom signed on with the army. He was to go to India where I would be allowed to join him after our child was born. We were married three days before he was due to sail. But Tom never got to India. He took the fever just days out of harbour. They buried him at sea.'

'You were married!' Rachel felt the girl's trembling, heard the stifled sobs. 'I did not realise.'

'How could you when I wear no wedding ring?' The quiet explanation went on, interspersed with small silences as tears choked her. 'My time was almost on me. I knew I would not be given shelter at Bayton Hall and was making my way towards the workhouse at Tibbington. I could think of no other place that would shelter my baby. Then I met Tansy and she brought me here. She and Cora were so kind. Two days later my son was born. Such a beautiful child, with hair so fair it seemed spun from sunlight while his eyes were the colour of sapphires . . .'

Beyond the house the bells of St Michael's church chimed ten.

'. . . he died that same night.'

Rachel felt her heart stop. She had thought her own sorrow unbearable but it was nothing compared to what the girl beside her must be feeling.

'The next day Cora brought back a box given to her by the owner of the shop on the corner of Owen Street, and she and Tansy laid my little boy in it. He looked so tiny and so very beautiful. Tansy said she would take the box round to the gravedigger's house because we had not the money to pay for a funeral. She said he often did such a service for the poor of the parish, and that for tuppence he would put the baby in with a burial and that way he would lie in consecrated ground. Before . . . before she set the lid in place, I threaded my wedding ring on a string and fastened it about my child's neck. It was all I could give him, all he would ever have of his mother and father.

'I do not know how long it was after that day that Samuel Potter came here to the house. I was alone. Tansy had insisted I work only three days a week at the coal picking until my strength built up, Potter saw me with her and Cora when he came to buy our pickings. He must have guessed that on the days I was not with them on the pit banks, I would be in the house.

'He said I must pay if I wanted to stay, that the property belonged to him. It was when I said I would pay what addition he made to the rent that he told me what that payment would be: I must lie with him.'

At her sides Rachel's hands curled into tight fists, anger churning in her stomach.

'I refused.' If Ellen felt the slight movement beside her she gave no sign. 'Then he said either I lay with him or I must leave. This house belonged to him and he would say who could or could not live in it. So I told him I would leave.'

'And he left you?'

Ellen turned on her side, her back to Rachel, the pillow half obliterating her reply. 'Yes, he left, but not before he raped me.'

'I know how you feel, I felt the same way when they had me do it.' Ellen's eyes held a sympathetic gleam as they held Rachel's.

'I can't.' Rachel closed her own eyes, shuddering at the thought of what she had been told to do.

'You can, Rachel, and believe me it does work. Don't ask me how, I only know it does. Soaking your hands in it will toughen the skin and make coal picking far less painful.'

'No!' Opening her eyes, Rachel shot a glance towards the scullery. She had been told to soak her hands, that it was the most effective way of hardening the skin, but still she held back. The cuts on her palms and fingers had healed in the couple of weeks she had spent in the house and she dreaded having to go out onto the coal heaps again; but she could not go on living off the charity of these three women, not to mention Bart. But to put her hands in that!

'Ain't you got your hands in there yet!' Tansy's voice was sharp as she came to stand in the doorway. 'Waving them over the top of it won't do no good, you ain't no magician.'

'I can't, Tansy. Really, I can't.'

'Don't talk so crackpotical!' Tansy bustled across to where Rachel sat on a low wooden stool, a flowered china pot on a second stool set in front of her. 'It be something we've all had to do and you be no different. Salt water hurt your hands, this hurts your pride; it'll hurt no more than that.'

'But . . .' Rachel's cheeks flamed. 'But it . . . it's . . .'

'Piddle,' Tansy said bluntly, hands on her hips. 'There be nothing like it for hardening the skin. You ask any packman. Soak hands or feet in the chamber pot for a seven day and you'll have no more soreness.'

'C'mon, Rachel. Do what I did. Pretend you're Cleopatra, and you're holding your hands in a bowl of scented ass's milk.'

'Her can pretend to be the Queen of Sheba if her likes, just so long as her puts her hands in that chamber pot.' Tansy stood by determinedly.

Seeing there was no way out other than to hurt Tansy by openly refusing what she saw as help, Rachel took a long breath and, teeth clenched, plunged her hands into the urine.

'They got you paddling your 'ands in the pee pot?'

Bart's head appeared round the scullery door, his face creased in a cheeky grin. 'I guessed they might 'ave, so I brought you this.'

His oversized boots clumping on the stone quarries that Ellen had scrubbed less than an hour before, he came to stand beside Rachel. Dipping a hand into the pocket of his jacket, he drew out a metal container not dissimilar to the one that had held the Indian Cereate ointment. 'I got this from old Simkins, the chemist along Dudley Port.'

Despite her embarrassment, Rachel smiled at the lad. Would he ever meet anyone he would not refer to as old?

'Old Simkins said as it be one of the better quality scents.' He held the small round tin on the palm of one outstretched hand. 'What he means by quality I ain't sure. A smell be a smell, don't it? Though I hopes it smells a bit more pleasant than that there pee pot.' He grinned again, half turning towards the kitchen as Tansy called for him to wash his hands if he hoped for his supper.

'You open it.' He thrust the container into Ellen's hands. 'I get some of that on me and folk will think I be turning queer.'

Twisting off the prettily painted lid, she held the tin of delicately scented cream towards Rachel. 'I think it does smell more pleasant than the brand you are using at the moment, madam.'

'He is a kind lad, and always smiling.' Rachel's eyes misted over as her mind sped to that other, much younger boy whose smile had always enchanted her. Robbie had been such a happy child . . .

'I'll fetch the hot water.' Seeing tears shimmer on Rachel's lashes, Ellen placed the tin of perfumed hand cream on the edge of the brownstone sink that commanded a complete wall of the tiny scullery.

Why had it all happened? Silent tears she could not wipe away coursing down her cheeks, Rachel let the thoughts she tried so desperately to keep at bay roam free in her mind. Why had Hannah hated her so? She could not truly have believed Rachel hated her half-brother, or that Richie Cade loved one of his children more than the other. What then? What was it that drove the woman to accuse her step-daughter of murder? What madness lurked in Hannah Cade that would stay with her until the day she died?

Chapter Seven

Her hands free from bandages, Rachel wiped a duster over the small dresser against the farther end of the room for the second time that morning. Tansy had declared that she should not go on to the coal heaps for another couple of days, though her hands were now completely healed.

No more soaking in the chamber pot either. The older woman had clucked disgustedly at her use of hand cream, scented or otherwise. 'What be the use of trying to harden off them hands if you be going to soften them up again by using that stuff?' she had demanded.

Rachel smiled. After their soaking she had made her hands almost as sore as the coal picking had, scrubbing them again and again in hot water laced with carbolic. But the cream Bart had bought for her had soothed them, even if it did not entirely mask the smell of carbolic.

Bart . . . Her thoughts turned to the lad who had brought her to this house. He had come back at lunchtime every day while she had been alone in the house, always with a meat pie or fresh bread and a quarter of cheese he insisted she share with him. Robbie would have grown to be like Bart; he would have had the same kind nature, the same caring attitude.

'I thought I would find you here.'

Rachel wheeled round at the sound of the voice. She had not heard the door open.

A man stood framed in the doorway. He was dressed in dark trousers that bagged at the knee from long wear, a great buckle showing where the jacket he wore over a collarless shirt was stretched apart over a paunch of a stomach. Eyes framed by heavy brows, white side-whiskers joining a bushy beard, he let his gaze travel over her.

'I'm sorry.' Rachel swallowed nervously 'I did not hear your knock.'

'That be because I gave none.' He stepped into the room, letting the door to the street close behind him. 'I need no permission to enter my own premises.'

'Your premises?' Rachel glanced over to where the window gave on to the street; something about the man, about the way he looked at her, was awakening memories of Isaiah Bedworth and that room in Tibbington workhouse.

'Ar, my premises.' He took off the black bowler hat perched on his greying head. 'I rents this house to Tansy Croft.'

Samuel Potter. Rachel felt her stomach lurch. This was the man who had tried to seduce Tansy then had her sent to gaol when she refused.

'I saw you picking beside her on the banks a couple of weeks ago and guessed you would be living here along of the others, even though that sprite of a lad, Jevons, wouldn't admit to it.'

Rachel glanced again towards the window then the door, still blocked by the man's stocky frame.

'Ain't no need for you to be feared.' Potter smiled, interpreting her glance. '*He* only comes for *his* rent.'

'I . . .' Rachel hesitated. She did not know if it were usual for this man to call and collect rent or whether Tansy took it to him. He had not called since she had lived here, but that did not necessarily mean it was not his custom; he could come to collect on a monthly basis, that way she would not have seen him previously.

'I'm sorry but Tansy . . . Mrs Croft . . . has not left the rent money with me, and I have none. Perhaps you could call back this evening, when the others are at home?'

'Well now, I could . . .'

Rachel backed away as he advanced further into the room. 'But seeing as it don't be the others I've come to see, that would be a waste of my time.'

'Perhaps Bart will know about paying the rent . . .' She heard the clink of crockery as her back came up against the small dresser. 'He comes home every lunchtime. He . . . he'll be here any minute.'

'Not today he won't.' Samuel Potter's eyes took in the pretty face and promise of pert breasts, constricted now by a brown dress that must have been bought for her several years ago. And then there was that glorious hair, almost like liquid gold. How would it feel, loose and flowing, cascading over his stomach, the soft curls folding about his penis . . . 'Bart Jevons be doing the round for me,' he said, voice thick, eyes lifting to hers, hot and urgent. 'He won't finish much afore seven tonight. About the same time as the women.'

'Then that is the time I suggest you return.' Rachel tried to expunge the fear from her voice but the words sounded strained as they left her lips.

'I already told you once, that will be a waste of my time.' He stepped in front of her, movements rapid for a man of his stature. 'It don't be none of them I've called to see, it be you.'

His breath hot in her face, Rachel turned her head sideways, prevented by his arm from stepping away from him.

'I don't pay the rent, Mr Potter, at least not to you directly.'

'And that be what I'm here about.' He let his body lean forward, pressing against hers. 'You *don't* pay rent. My little visit today is to rectify that. You see, I must increase payment.'

'You had no need to call.' Rachel tried to push her way clear, the touch of his body making her want to scream. 'You could have informed Tansy of any increase to be paid for my living here and I would have given it to her to be passed on to you.'

'Tansy can't pass on the payment I require.' The arm that had rested alongside her, preventing her from moving, now circled her back, his free hand closing about her breast. 'This be a due you must pay yourself, direct as you might say.'

'Mr Potter, please . . .'

He laughed, her struggle obviously heightening his pleasure. 'You don't have to say please.' His voice was thicker now, breath coming in short hot gasps against her face. 'Samuel Potter be the one to be pleased – pleased to take payment from a pretty girl like you.'

'Don't!' Rachel tried to push him away, panic making her voice rise to a scream. 'I will pay you . . .'

'Of course you will, my dear, and that payment I will take . . . right now!'

Grabbing her arm, he stepped back and swung her round to face him. Disregarding the clatter of crockery shaken by the sudden violent movement, he forced her down, using his weight to bear her to the floor.

'No . . . please . . . no!' Rachel's cries were lost as his mouth closed over hers, remaining clamped there as his hand pushed her skirts about her waist then snatched at her cotton drawers, tearing them away.

'I didn't come here to listen to you say no.' He released her mouth but held her pinioned beneath him as he struggled to release the belt about his waist, then push away his trousers.

'No . . . go away . . . leave me alone!' she screamed again, feeling the throbbing of his flesh against her thigh as he heaved himself over her, one knee forcing her legs apart.

'Leave her be, you dirty old bastard!'

'What the bloody hell . . .' Potter rolled sideways, mouth hanging open.

With his weight removed Rachel scrambled to her feet,

the torn drawers about her ankles hampering her dash for the stairs.

'I thought as 'ow I would find you 'ere.' An iron bar in his hand, Bart glared at the coal jagger. 'You asked a few too many questions about the girl with golden hair – like where had she got to, and why wasn't her on the heaps with the others? I guessed what was in your mind. That be why I come 'ome, and I see I weren't wrong.'

'You'll be sorry for this, you bloody little guttersnipe!' Grabbing at his trousers, Potter struggled to his feet.

'Ar, well, mebbe I will and mebbe I won't.' Bart lifted the bar of metal menacingly, eyes never leaving the other man's face.

'There be no mebbe about it.' Potter snatched at his belt, fastening it about his waist. 'I'll have them women out of this house before the week be out. And you . . .' He glared at Bart, eyes darkening with threat. 'There'll be something special for you, me lad. Samuel Potter don't care to be interfered with, not by anybody, much less a snotty-nosed kid. So remember, something special.'

Bart circled around, keeping the table between himself and the jagger. 'Whatever you do will be no surprise, though I doubt it will be as easy to spot as your coal wagon be right now.'

Pausing as he swept his bowler from the table where he had dropped it before closing in on Rachel, Samuel Potter's face started to drain of colour.

'What you done!' he gasped. 'What you done with it?'

The iron bar still prominent, Bart grinned. 'It ain't what *I've* done with it. I collected the pickings from the wenches, and paid them the money you gave me. Then I got to thinking of you, paying a call on Rachel . . . That was when I left the wagon in Old Cross Street.'

'You left my wagon in that thieves' nest?' Potter's face lost its remaining colour.

'I told you, didn't I?' Bart's reply was terse, the grin fading from his mouth. 'You should get yourself along there sharp like, Mr Potter. That be if you want to find your wagon in one piece. As for the coal that was on it, well, I reckon that be long gone.'

Eyes narrowing, Samuel Potter glared furiously. 'Remember!' he hissed. 'There'll be something special for you!'

'Rachel, what's wrong?' Ellen reached into her cloth bag, drawing out the bottle of cold tea and removing the twist of newspaper that served as a cork. 'There is something. I saw the colour drain from your face when Potter came to collect the pickings.'

She shook her head, refusing the offer of a drink. She had said nothing of the jagger's visit to the house, knowing Tansy would want revenge and as terrified of the course that revenge might take, and its consequences to a woman who had shown her nothing but kindness, as she had been of rape.

'I . . . I'm just tired. I will get used to the picking, I only need time.'

Ellen glanced over to where Tansy and Cora sat a few yards from them, their lunch of cheese and bread on their laps.

'It's not the coal picking, is it?' Ellen returned the twist of paper to the neck of the bottle, tucking it upright in the bag. 'You had fear written all over you when we returned three nights ago. You made a good enough job of hiding it but I knew something had happened and so, I'm sure, did Tansy. But she won't ask, she'll wait until she's told by you . . . or by Bart.' Ellen's hands moved deftly, wrapping what remained of the cheese and bread then repacking it into the bag beside the bottle. 'Is it something Bart has done or said to you?' She looked up. 'He can be cheeky sometimes but he would mean no harm.'

'No, it isn't Bart . . .' The words came quickly, the sudden high tone drawing Tansy's glance. 'Bart came back just in time.'

'Oh, my God!' Ellen sat back on her heels. 'Potter . . . oh, Rachel, not you too!'

'He came that morning.' Twisting so her face was hidden from Tansy and Cora, Rachel let the episode spill from her. 'He said the rent had to be increased because I was there. I told him I would pay the increase to Tansy, who would pass it to him. But that wasn't the way he wanted it.'

'No,' Ellen breathed. 'No, it wouldn't be.'

Hands clenched in her lap, Rachel stared out over the black mounds of coal waste, stretching away like dark clothed hills.

'He said my payment had to be made direct to him and then he threw me to the floor, tearing at my clothes. If . . . if Bart had not come at that moment . . .'

'Thank God he did! I know it is sinful to wish evil on another person, Rachel, but I wish with all my heart that Potter were dead. This world holds enough sorrow for such as we without men like him battening upon us.'

'I don't want the others to know. Bart promised to say nothing of what happened, will you promise the same?'

'If that is what you really want. I felt the same when he raped me. But you must not blame yourself – the fault does not lie with you but with that beast. How many more women will he force himself upon? That is a question I find myself asking more and more: how many other women will suffer because of him?' Picking up the cloth bag that held the remains of their lunch, Ellen returned the wave of Tansy's hand that signalled the return to work. 'The more I think of him getting away with what he has done, and is likely to do again, the more I think I should report him to the justice.'

'With what proof?' Rachel got stiffly to her knees. 'I was alone in the house, as you were. There is no one to say what Samuel Potter did except for Bart, and I will not have him implicated. Besides . . .' Jagged pieces of coal digging into the worn soles of her boots, Rachel picked her way towards the spot where they were working. 'The justice here in Tipton is Isaiah Bedworth. How far do you think we would get with him? A man out of the same mould as Potter.'

'So we have six of one and half a dozen of the other.' Ellen slipped off her shawl, wrapping it around the bag before placing it on the ground, and sinking to her knees beside it. 'Lord, how I wish them in hell!'

'Who's that you be wishing in hell?' Tansy's sharp ears caught the last of her words.

'Coal jaggers and magistrates.'

'Amen to that,' Tansy breathed, scraping a nugget of coal free with her fingers and tossing it into the bucket. 'Amen to that.'

'It be ninepence a bag, you know that well enough.'

Samuel Potter glared at the small girl, her dress torn at the hem, a scrap of cloth tied shawl-like about her thin shoulders, her hair uncombed.

'But I ain't got ninepence.' The child held out a grubby palm, displaying a clutch of pennies.

'Then you don't get no coal.' Raising the crop he held in one hand, he struck the girl's hand, sending the coins flying into the gutter. 'Now bugger off out of it!'

Taking a brass bell from beneath the driving seat of the wagon, he felt a fresh surge of the anger that had been with him for over a week now. That snipe-nosed brat had not only robbed him of his pleasure but lost him a wagonload of coal and a brass bell. But he would pay, oh, yes, that lad would pay.

'Coal!' His cry, accompanied by the ringing of his new bell, rang down the narrow alley that separated the lines of narrow houses, most of which leaned against their neighbours, the whole street seemingly ready to collapse.

'Please, Mr Potter, me dad said to tell you he would see to it you get the rest on Monday only we needs the coal now. Me mother be awful bad.'

'Oh, your dad said that, did he?' Potter watched the girl run a finger over the coins she had retrieved, checking she had them all. 'So what have you left to pawn? Your father will have to think up a better tale than that to fool me. If you had anything the pawnshop would take it would be in there now and you might have enough money for coal, though I doubt you lot ever owned anything worth ninepence.'

'Me dad weren't getting the money from the pawnshop. He's got a job, in the limestone.'

'Oh, ar!' Potter jeered. 'And who would be daft enough to give him a job? Anybody can see he has the consumption, same as your mother.'

'He *has* got a job.' The girl ran along beside the wagon. 'He's working in the quarries along Dudley way.'

'Well, tell him Samuel Potter says there will be coal when he has the money to pay for it and not until then.'

'Hold up!'

The call came from a woman emerging from the mouth of an entry that served a clutch of houses and set Potter pulling on the reins, bringing the wagon to a halt.

''Ave you a quarter hundredweight?'

'They be half hundredweight.' The reply was made from the driving seat, Samuel not bothering to climb down.

'Do it still be ninepence a bag?'

'That be the price.'

'The last bag I had from you weren't worth tuppence.' The woman squinted at him against the daylight. 'It were mostly bats. Spit at you like gunfire every time you made the fire up. Not worth tuppence!'

'Then don't buy any more, get your coal from the yard.' Samuel clucked to his horse.

'You know full well we can't go paying coal yard prices,' the woman called. 'If we could, you'd have had your arse kicked out of Tipton Green long ago, Potter.'

'Well then, you pay the price I ask or go without altogether.' He smirked, watching the woman glance at the coins she drew from her apron pocket.

'I can't be giving you what I don't have.' Her hand closing over the bronze coins, the woman looked up. 'And I don't have ninepence. Couldn't you halve a bag? I could pay for a quarter of a hundredweight.'

'That be a deal of work for no extra profit . . .'

'Don't you make enough profit, Sam Potter!' she cut in fiercely. 'You buys the stuff for next to nothing and sells it for the most you can squeeze from a body.'

'It be ninepence, take it or leave it!' Picking up the reins, he clucked again to the horse.

'Wait on, Mr Potter.' The girl sprang to the horse's head, laying a hand on the bridle. Then turning to the woman, she said: 'You have the money for a half sack and I got enough for a half sack. We could buy one and share it between the two. That way both of us get coal, and I'll do the work of it while you watch. What do you say?'

'I say count out your fourpence halfpenny. And you, Sam Potter, get down off your arse and carry that sack of coal up the entry.'

Climbing back on to the wagon, he felt his foot catch against the new brass bell. That Jevons kid had thought to better Samuel Potter . . . He pulled on the reins, guiding the horse to the left, out from the warren of Canal Street into the busier Owen Street. He was halfway along, the wagon stationary, waiting until the dray cart had been emptied of barrels, each painstakingly rolled from the cart into the cellar of The Albion public house, when his eye caught sight of a slight figure dressed in an overlarge coat, a flat cap pulled low on to its head, feet shoved into boots several sizes too big.

Bart Jevons! Potter's hand tightened on the reins. The figure walking away in the direction of Toll End lock was definitely Bart Jevons.

The last barrel rolled clear, the draymen signalled the way ahead. His eyes still fastened on Bart, Potter urged the horse forward, at the same time swivelling the crop that had been specially made for him, bringing the end that carried a thin blade to the fore.

Ahead of him Bart Jevons stepped into the road at the very moment a steam-whistle screamed from the direction of Howl Colliery. Quick as a flash Samuel Potter leaned forward, jabbing the point of the blade into the rear of the horse. The animal's startled whinny joining the screech of the whistle, it darted forward, dragging the wagon after it like a toy.

Across the street a woman screamed but it was too late. The shoulder of the bolting horse caught Bart, sending him tumbling to the ground. Seconds later the heavy iron-bound wheels of the wagon rolled over him.

'It were an accident.'

A man touched Samuel's shoulder as he stood, face hidden in his hands, while others lifted Bart from beneath the wheels.

'You weren't to know the horse would bolt.' The man glanced at the quickly gathering crowd. ''Ow many times have we folk said them steam-whistles should be banned, frightening kids and setting horses to flight? Well, now p'raps something *will* be done about it, now a lad has been killed.'

'Lad ain't dead,' one of the men gently lifting Bart answered. 'Though by the look of him, he don't be far from it. Do any of you know who he is?'

'I've seen him before.' A woman in a black bonnet clutched her basket tightly. 'He's often to be seen about here, but as for kin or where he lives ... .' She broke off, melting back into the crowd.

'Best get the bobby.' It was a second woman who spoke. 'He'll know what to do. We can't just leave the lad lying here.'

'He ... he needs a doctor.' Samuel dropped his hands. A policeman was the last person he wanted called. 'If you put him in the wagon, I'll take him to the Guest.'

'Ar, that be the best place.' The black bonnet bobbed as its owner nodded agreement. 'Dudley Guest be a good hospital, they'll look after him there.'

'I'll call at the police station when I get back.' Samuel climbed quickly into the driving seat. 'The constable will be likely to know the lad and his parents. I will go to see them and tell them what happened.'

'Poor little sod.' One of the men who had lifted Bart into the back of the wagon placed the flat cap on the boy's chest. 'He don't look like he's got much.'

'I'll see he's taken care of.'

'Now don't you go worrying, mate.' The man who had picked up the cap walked to the front of the wagon. 'We all seen what happened and it weren't your fault, can't no blame be set on your shoulders; horse bolted and the lad were knocked down.' He shook his head slowly. 'It happens.'

Watched by the assembled crowd, Samuel drove the wagon along Owen Street, but once clear turned into Canal Street. 'I told you there would be something special for you, Jevons,' he muttered under his breath, 'and it don't be a trip to Dudley Guest.'

Bringing the horse to a halt, he jumped from the wagon. Going around to the back, he covered the still form with empty sacks. He wanted no eyes to see what the wagon carried besides coal.

Following the narrower streets and back alleys, he finally brought the wagon to a halt outside the double doors of the building that adjoined the house let to Tansy. Taking a key from the pocket of his waistcoat, he unlocked the doors, swinging them wide before leading horse and wagon inside.

No one had used the old malt house for years. He had intended to sell it but the opportunity had never arisen. Throwing aside the coal, he heaved the unconscious boy from the wagon, letting him fall to the ground.

'I promised you something special,' he grunted as a moan escaped Bart's lips. 'But you've only had the half. Now you be going to get the rest of it.'

Going to the horse's head, he took the halter straps in one hand, resting the other on the animal's neck.

'Back,' he ordered. 'Back, boy, back.'

Obediently the horse backed up, rolling the wagon wheels once more over the body of the boy.

Chapter Eight

It was my fault. It was my fault.

Following the line of a path showing like a ribbon in the light of a rising moon, Rachel walked on, the same words churning endlessly in her brain.

They had not worried overmuch when Bart did not return to the house by the time a meal had been cooked; he would be running an errand for someone, one that would most likely be paying an extra penny because of its late hour. But then the clock of St Michael's church had struck ten and Tansy had reached for her shawl.

'I'll have a look around,' she had said, refusing Cora's offer of company. 'He's probably hanging around outside The Fiery Holes. Maddie Bartrum often has a customer who will pay a few coppers for somebody to see them home, saves them falling into the cut.'

But Bart had not been outside The Fiery Holes, nor any other of his favourite stamping grounds. Tansy had been back some minutes when Cora had suggested the old malt house. The house had once been the living quarters that adjoined a barn, now no longer used, and the door at the end of the living room gave straight onto it.

'He often gets himself into there, you know, when he wants to be by himself. Mebbe he went in afore we got back and then dropped off to sleep,' Cora said again.

Ellen had reached for a candle, lighting it from the one

standing in the centre of the table. Shielding it with her hand, she led the way into the malt house.

The walls of the building stretched upward into a darkness the candle was powerless to penetrate, while in the loft and roof space birds twittered, made nervous by the disturbance.

Cora had called Bart's name several times, agitating the roosting birds still further, and among the shadows covering the floor the rustling of mice told the same story.

'He ain't in here.' Tansy had half turned to leave when Ellen's foot kicked against something on the floor. Startled, she screamed, and only Cora's quick movement saved the candle from falling.

'It be only sacks, you silly fool.' Cora held the flickering flame close to the ground. It was then they saw the boots, the overlarge jacket, and the dark stains spread across it. Then the cap, not on the tousled head but half across the pale face, as if thrown by a careless hand.

Ellen had screamed again, stopping only when Tansy's hand caught her face in a sharp slap.

Now, her foot catching against a stone, Rachel stumbled on, seeing nothing but the pictures in her mind.

Shoving the candle into her hand, Cora had helped Tansy lift the boy, their boots shuffling on the floor of the malt house as they carried him back to the living room.

He did not try to cry out as they laid him on his narrow truckle bed which Ellen pulled from beneath the sofa, but his lips moved silently all the time Tansy wiped the blood from his face with a cloth, shaking her head at Ellen's suggestion of calling a doctor.

'Ain't no doctor can mend the lad.' Tansy's voice had cracked with emotion. 'There don't be a bone in him as ain't broken.'

Rachel remembered wanting to scream, remembered pushing her fist hard against her teeth to hold it back.

'But how?' Cora had asked. 'How do you reckon this happened? What was it broke him to pieces?'

'How it happened I don't be sure of, but I reckon it were a wagon, a heavy wagon, what run over him. Ain't nothing else would have caused this.'

'But the lad were in the malt house!' Cora continued as she gently eased away his boots. 'Don't be no wagons in there, not any more. Do you reckon he walked back there after an accident?'

'He didn't walk.' Tansy put out her hand as Cora made to remove Bart's jacket. 'Somebody had to bring him there, somebody as knowed where he lived!'

'Rachel . . .'

A long sob shuddering through her, she seemed to hear again the faint voice call her name.

'Rachel.' Bart's lids had flickered open but already his eyes held a far away look.

She dropped to her knees beside him, holding his blood-stained hand in one of her own, the other touching his brow.

'I didn't let 'im hurt you, did I, Rachel?' he murmured. 'I didn't let him . . .'

He did not finish the sentence. The breath sighing from him, his eyes glazed and his head fell against her arm.

Folding her own arms about him, resting her cheek on his, Rachel caught Tansy's quiet whisper: 'Remember me when you come into your kingdom.'

In the long hours that followed, Rachel had known with certainty what the others could only guess.

The doctor issued a death certificate confirming Bart's injuries as having been caused by a wagon rolling over him. She knew it had been that belonging to Samuel Potter.

'I didn't let 'im hurt you, did I, Rachel?'

The whispered words had returned to her again and again. Bart had caught Potter trying to rape her. Bart had prevented it. Bart had not let him hurt her . . . The words themselves told her the boy's death was no accident, but the result of Potter's vengeance.

And it *was* her fault. If she had not stayed in Tipton Green, Bart would still be alive; just as if she had not taken Robbie to see the boats in the lock, *he* would still be alive.

Two lives. Rachel stumbled on. Two lives gone, and both times it had been her fault.

It was Tansy who had prepared the body for burial, dressing it in a suit she bought, not from the pawnshop but brand new from Jackson the tailor's. She had allowed no handkerchief to tie up the boy's jaw, nor pennies to rest on his tongue or eyelids.

'Hold your head up high, lad,' she had said softly, placing the beloved flat cap beside his right hand. 'Hold it proud. Go into your kingdom like a true king.'

Together they had sat through the long hours of the night, each keeping her own silent vigil over the still form. In the days the house stood silent, the grate cold and empty of fire, the light dimmed by close-drawn curtains.

Then they had come.

Five tall men, each of them dressed in black; tall hats with purple silk ribbons hanging from the back, their hands encased in black cotton gloves.

It was time, the first of the five had told them, his voice lowered as if afraid the slightest vibration would bring the house down about them. If they had any last goodbyes . . .

Rachel had stood beside the coffin, resting there on the table in that tiny living room to which Bart had brought her such a short time ago. His face was so pale, the lips a faint purple, the eyelids fine as butterfly wings, criss-crossed with minute blue veins.

The touch of a man's hand at her elbow said it was the final moment and she had bent to kiss that cold face, the skin turned to marble by the hand of death; then she held a sobbing Ellen in her arms as the lid was screwed on to the plain deal coffin. She had watched the pall bearers lift it on to their shoulders and, led by the eldest of the five, carry it to the horse-drawn hearse. Half supporting a sobbing Ellen, they walked behind to the Church of St Michael.

The words of the priest had echoed in the cold church, floating to the high roof, circling the empty pews in search of listening ears, but her own were closed to all except her own unspoken ones. It was my fault . . . it was my fault.

Outside, the sun poured warmth over the little churchyard – a warmth she had not felt as she watched the men slowly lower the coffin into the ground, withdrawing the guiding tapes before standing silently aside.

'Ashes to ashes, dust to dust . . .'

His surplice crisp and white against a black clerical robe, an embroidered stole about his neck, the priest intoned the last words of the burial service as he threw a handful of soil into the grave.

Beside Rachel the three women each took a handful from a small box held out to them by the lead bearer, their quiet sobs adding their own plea that for Bart there would be truth in the words of the priest: '. . . *in the true and certain knowledge of the resurrection.*' But as the box of earth was held to her, Rachel had turned away.

That last act had been too terrible for her to perform. She could not throw soil into that yawning pit, she could not cover that laughing, cheeky lad with earth, it was too much like goodbye. She never wanted to say goodbye to Bart, never wanted to think of him lying beneath the cold earth.

Tears streaming down her cheeks, she had turned, feet stumbling on the coarse, hillocky grass as she walked away.

Afterwards their days had returned to normal. Except they were not normal. They picked coal during the day, cooked a meal and cleaned the house in the evening. On Saturday afternoons three of them did the weekly wash whilst the other shopped. But the happy atmosphere was gone. Conversation in the house was patchy, each of them seeming to lose interest quickly, and Rachel often found herself staring at the door beside the dresser, the door that led to the malt house, reminding her of their discovery of that poor broken body.

But somehow she had gone on. The days had melted into night and night paled to dawn. Now she understood the pain that had consumed her stepmother, the agony that had driven her to accuse her husband's daughter of murder, the wretched, desolating torment of losing a beloved child – a torment and a pain that could only have been greater than the one tearing her own heart apart.

'Robbie! Bart!' Her broken cry floated into the night, finding no answer in the darkness.

Then there had been Samuel Potter.

In the silence that engulfed her, Rachel felt her nerves start violently at the memory of yesterday.

They had been working up along Soaphouse Walk. The demolition of the Excelsior Soapworks had revealed a seam of surface coal and the pit bank wenches had descended upon it, their cotton bonnets bobbing like cabbage whites as they worked to retrieve the coal before the owners of the site moved them on.

In the impetus of the work she had not noticed the growing gap between herself and the rest of the women, most of them chatting and laughing, their work unexpectedly easy due to the ground-clearing of the builders. Only when that thick voice had spoken her name had she realised she was virtually alone.

'There could be better things for you than grubbing in the dirt.' His eyes had roved over her, staying on her breasts pressing against her dress, the tip of his tongue flicking over his mouth.

'I'm not interested in better things.' She had jumped to her feet, trying to cover her breasts without touching her mud-caked hands to her dress.

'That be 'cause you ain't never had any of them.' Samuel Potter had stepped closer. 'Get that tasty little body of yours in silk petticoats and a fine taffeta frock and could be you would feel different.'

'No!' Rachel had stepped away, her foot catching against the bucket she was filling, sending it rolling down a gentle incline. 'I would not feel differently.'

'You ain't worked a winter on the banks yet.' The flabby lips stretched into a confident smile. 'Frozen fingers slashed by prising coal from frozen ground will soon have you changing your tune.'

'And dancing to whose, Potter? To yours? Be that what you be hoping on?' Tansy had seen the jagger from where she was working and come to stand behind him in time to hear his words. 'You'll be hoping a long time.'

'Will I?'

From the shadowed horror of her thoughts, Rachel remembered the menacing, animal gleam of his small eyes as he swung again to her.

'You come to my house tonight . . . that is, if you want payment for the coal you women have picked.'

'We'll take payment now, same as always,' Tansy had answered. Potter's eyes had lingered on the bodice of Rachel's dress as if his stare could in some way strip it from her.

'I have no more money with me,' he answered Tansy, but his eyes remained on Rachel. 'The picking has been heavy today, but there's money at the house. My wife will pay what is owed.'

'And you'll be there to take what isn't owed. We all know the payment you want, Potter, but you must seek it somewhere else. You won't play your dirty games with this wench.'

'If her don't call to the house then you don't get your money!' This time his eyes swung to Tansy. 'Either the wench comes to collect or you does without. Like I said, the picking has been heavy. There'll be no other jagger anxious to buy yours. And, remember, if the money for the house isn't on the table when it's due then you're out, the lot of you. Try thinking that over, Tansy Croft!'

She had turned away without a word. Rachel had watched her black-skirted figure, the shawl pulled tight about her head and shoulders, walk back to her place on the bank and sink to her knees on the clay.

'You be at my house at nine o' clock this evening,' Potter smirked, reaching out to touch Rachel's breast. 'This time there'll be no bloody kid to interrupt.'

She had felt the tension that had held her like steel, drain from her body as he left her. Heedless then of the smears of clay and coal dust on her dress, she had rubbed at her chest where his eyes had lingered; where his paw of a hand had descended.

This would happen every time he came to collect their pickings. Retrieving the fallen bucket, she carried it to the nearby canal, standing it on the towpath while she knelt to wash her hands in the water.

'I didn't let 'im hurt you, did I?'

The words seemed to rise up from the green depths. But following them came others.

'This time there'll be no bloody kid to interrupt.'

It would go on and on, Potter's treatment of her. Go on until he got what he wanted. And when he did, what would Tansy's reaction be? Whatever it was could only lead to more unhappiness.

Water dripping from her fingers, Rachel had stood up and turned to stare across to where her friends bent over the black earth.

They had done enough for her. Suffered enough because of her. It was time for her to leave.

Her heart spilling tears her eyes no longer could, she had told them quietly that she was leaving, saying only that she could no longer bear to live so close to the lock where Robbie had drowned, in the house where Bart had died.

Then she had simply walked away, their protests lost in

the misery pressing in on her, walked from the town, out beyond the last of the houses, out on to the heath, oblivious of its danger in the coming darkness, oblivious of the coal shafts – many of them disused and abandoned, their entrances lying like gaping black mouths, deep clefts in the earth half hidden by bracken and gorse, their depths concealing black, oily bottomless waters. But she had walked on, her mind giving no warning of where she was, repeating only those terrible words: It was my fault. Only when she stumbled into a large rock did she halt, the sharp sting of it against her hands jerking her back to the present.

How far had she walked? Rachel stared about her, the pain in her hands forgotten as she realised she was alone in the middle of nowhere. Where was she walking to? All around her, painted silver by the high sailing moon, the heath lay empty; no landmark, no building of any kind to give an indication of where she might be.

It was then she became aware of the sound. A low drumming in the distance behind her. Hoof beats. A carriage. She turned, straining her eyes towards the shadowed horizon. Perhaps whoever rode in it would help her, tell her of a place, if only a barn or a byre, where she might spend the night? But was there a carriage? A twinge of fear riding her nerves, Rachel listened. Would she not hear the rumble of carriage wheels? What if it were a lone rider, someone not disposed to help her? What if . . . She tugged the shawl more closely beneath her breasts as if the cloth somehow afforded her protection. Was it someone looking for her? The breath catching in her throat, she strained towards the approaching sound. Was it him . . . was it Samuel Potter . . . was he not content with one attempt at raping her?

She must get off the heathland path, she must not be seen. But the coal shafts! She could not risk the heath. But neither could she risk rape.

The drumming of hooves grew stronger. In moments it would be level with her. But there was no shelter, no hiding place . . . except for the rock. Perhaps if she crouched low to the ground its shadow would conceal her and the rider would pass in the darkness.

Sinking low on her haunches, she hid her face in the folds of her shawl. It would take only seconds for a horse to pass. Drawing in her breath as the sound of hooves filled her ears, she held it, waiting for the drumming to die away, then loosed it in a gasp as the animal whinnied loudly and a dull thud sounded beside her.

'What in heaven's name . . .'

A figure was on its feet in an instant, etched tall and menacing against the moonlight.

'What the bloody hell do you reckon you're about, skulking in the dark waiting to rob a man! I'm going to knock your worthless brain right out of your head.'

Most of her breath stolen by fear of being seen, the rest snatched from her as she was hauled to her feet, Rachel loosed her shawl, hearing a swift intake of breath as her hair tumbled in a swirl of silver about her shoulders.

'A woman!'

The hand grasping her shoulder swung her about.

'My God, a woman!'

'Yes, a woman.' Rachel squirmed but the grasp stayed firm. 'And I was not skulking in the dark waiting to rob you.'

'No?' The hand held her as easily as it would a wriggling puppy, the voice was hard. 'Then what do you call crouching on the ground by the side of the road? It's hardly a normal activity for a woman – unless, of course, your accomplice is nearby. Though I warn you, he will not find me an easy target.'

'I . . . I was not skulking.' Rachel pulled away, leaving her shawl in the man's hand. 'And I have no accomplice. I . . . I was trying to hide, though not in order to rob you.'

'Then for what other reason?'

Rachel noticed he did not look about him. If he anticipated an attack, he was supremely indifferent to it.

'I . . . I was afraid of . . . of . . .'

'Of being molested? And so you should be! So why are you here? I know why you are not at home in Horseley, Miss Rachel Cade, but I am at a loss to know what brings you to the middle of the heath at this time of night.'

'How do you know my name?' She peered at the man but the moon at his back threw his face into shadow.

'I recognised your voice. We have met before. I have not forgotten so soon as it seems you have. I am Jared Lytton. But what are you doing here, you are surely not alone?'

'I am going to Woodsetton.' She said the first words to jump into her mind.

'At this time of night?' Jared whistled softly and the horse trotted to him, snuffling into the palm of his hand.

'What's so important in Woodsetton that it cannot wait until morning?'

'That, Mr Lytton, is my business.' Relieved that the man regarding her by moonlight was not Samuel Potter, Rachel felt a little of her courage return.

'So it is, Miss Cade. It was impertinent of me to ask. As soon as your father rejoins you, I will wish you both goodnight.'

Rachel caught at her shawl. 'There is no need for you to wait, my father will only be a moment.'

'Then I will wait only a moment.' Jared let the shawl slide slowly through his fingers as if reluctant to part from it.

'No,' Rachel said quickly. 'I . . . I must not detain you. I apologise for startling your horse.'

As he turned to catch at the reins she saw his face, the strong contours of a clean-shaven jaw and straight nose, but it was his eyes that caught at her soul: deep, dark, endless pools that gleamed in the pale light.

Swinging into the saddle, he looked down at her. 'Well, that is a start. And now you have apologised for getting me thrown from my horse, maybe you will apologise for lying to me.'

'Lying to you!' Throwing the shawl about her shoulders,

crossing the ends beneath her breasts, Rachel shivered, not so much from the keen air blowing across the heath as from the coldness of his tone.

'Yes, girl! Lying to me. Had your father, or anyone else, been here with you they would have shown themselves by now. Isn't it true to say you're out here alone? My God, what are you thinking of! Don't you know the whole area is pitted with mine shafts?'

'Yes, I know.' Rachel's chin came up. This man had helped her on the day when the magistrate had been prepared to pass sentence of death upon her, but that did not give him the right to speak to her in that tone. 'I have lived in the village of Horseley all my life, I am well acquainted with the fact that coal pits abound all over Tipton.'

'Then if you know it, why in the name of all that is holy are you stumbling about here at night?'

The agony of her brother's drowning, Isaiah Bedworth's forcing of himself upon her, Samuel Potter's attempt to rape her and the death of Bart, suddenly coalesced in a consuming anger. 'I am not stumbling!' she blasted, eyes ablaze with fury. 'I'm on my way to Woodsetton, and why and with whom have nothing at all to do with you!'

'They drove you out, didn't they?' Clouds passing over the moon masked the look of anger that spread across his face but did not temper that in his voice. 'Regardless of what I was told in Horseley, I believe they drove you away. Well, they will be sorry. I will have them all out, every last damned man . . .'

'No!' Rachel's exclamation rang on the silent heath, causing the horse to shy. 'They did not drive me out. I wanted to leave. I have wanted to leave for some time.'

'You plead much better than you lie, Miss Cade,' he said, calming the horse. 'But we can leave that for the moment. However, you seem to be leaving what lodging you found and again I feel it might not be purely from choice or you would not have chosen to travel by night. Neither,

I'm thinking, would you voluntarily leave without taking at least one change of clothing with you. Don't bother to deny it.' Above her, his face was dark in the moonlight. 'Let's just get you home.'

'I will not go back! I will not return to Horseley, nor to Tipton Green!'

'Who said anything about Horseley? I'm taking you to Foxley.'

Rachel took a step back. 'I have never heard of a town called Foxley. And anyway, I can't go anywhere with you.'

'Foxley is not a town, it's my home, and I can't go there while you're out here alone.' An edge of impatience tinged his voice. 'Now get up behind me and let's get on. The heath is hardly the most pleasant place to be at night.'

'I can't . . .'

'Oh, for God's sake, girl!'

The answer exploding from him, he leaned down, hauling her unceremoniously in front of him, at the same time touching the crop to the animal's flanks.

Wind rushing past her face snatched away Rachel's protest, leaving it to be swallowed by the silence of the heath. Where was Foxley, and why should Jared Lytton take her there?

The answer jangled in her mind.

His purpose must be the same as Isaiah Bedworth's had been in placing her in Tibbington workhouse.

He intended making her his whore!

Chapter Nine

The moon had climbed halfway into the sky as Jared Lytton rode past a cluster of houses then turned into a cobbled yard.

'We will get something warm inside you before we go on,' he said, lifting her easily from the back of the horse.

'Where is this place?' Rachel pulled the shawl over her wind-blown hair.

'The whole area goes by the name of the Foxyards.' Jared handed over the horse to an ostler who appeared from a side building. 'This is the local inn, The Fox.'

Giving no further explanation, he caught her arm, bustling her into the inn.

'Evening, Mr Lytton sir. Be a bit late for you, ain't it?'

Jared returned the greeting with a nod. 'I was delayed in Tipton Green. There were a couple of barges in the basin there without cargo. I hired them to deliver anchor chain to Chatham. I needed to get it down there before the end of the week, so I stayed to see them loaded then called back in the early evening just to make sure they had left.'

'Will you be wanting a meal, sir?'

Rachel pulled the shawl closer about her, painfully aware of the stares of men seated about a fire burning at one end of a low-ceilinged room, its dark beams hung with dusty brasses.

'Not tonight, but something warm to drink for the young lady.'

'Right away, Mr Lytton. A tankard of ale that's had the poker in it? Or perhaps a glass of mulled wine?'

'Wine.' Jared glanced at the men, acknowledging their greetings with a smile.

'Not for me, thank you.' Blushing beneath the stares of the occupants of the bar room and the enquiring look of the landlord, Rachel turned back towards the door. Never in all her years had she been in a public house, her father would be furious if he knew where she was now. But her father would not know. Tears rose, stinging her eyes. Her father would probably never see her again.

'I will wait outside,' she said, forcing back the tears.

'No!' Jared caught her arm as he had when lifting her on to the horse. 'I don't fancy scouring the heath in the dark looking for a girl who has no more sense than to go running off by herself.' He glanced at the landlord who now wore a look of enquiry on his face as openly as his customers did. 'Something hot, and we will take it in the bar parlour.'

'Why are you doing this?'

Her face burning with embarrassment at the landlord's knowing smile, Rachel sat on the edge of a chair in the empty bar parlour.

'If by "this" you mean bringing you into a public house, then I would have thought the answer was plain. You are half frozen from traipsing near across the county. It seems only sensible to get you warmed through before continuing on to Foxley.'

'I will not go with you to Foxley!' Rachel stared evenly into brown eyes that suddenly grew cloudy with anger.

'Then where will you go?' The question was snapped at her.

'I don't know . . . somewhere.'

'You don't know . . . somewhere.' He broke off as the landlord entered the room, putting two steaming mugs of mulled wine on the table. 'Somewhere!' Jared said again as the door closed, leaving them alone in the room. 'You have never been further than Tipton Green in your life, have you? Have you?'

Rachel dropped her glance before the anger in his, then shook her head.

'Then how the hell do you expect to survive? You don't know a soul beyond Horseley, you have nothing to your name, not even a petticoat, and it's a safe bet you have no money. My God! What was your father thinking of, allowing you to leave home like this!'

Rachel's head shot up and now her own eyes were angry. 'My father did not want me to leave, it was my choice, and as for money, he gave me enough.' Her heart tripped as she spoke the lie but it did not deter her. 'So you see, Mr Lytton, I can manage very well for myself. I thank you for your help but I do not require your further assistance.'

Picking up one of the pewter mugs, Jared swallowed some of the hot wine, watching the flash of her violet eyes, the silken sheen of hair the colour of wild wheat escaping from the confines of her shawl. She was beautiful. Isaiah Bedworth had taste at least.

'So you can manage.' He replaced the mug on the table. 'Doing what?'

'It may come as something of a shock to you, Mr Lytton, but I am not the helpless child you appear to think me. I am healthy and strong, I can find work.'

'Is that why you were going to Woodsetton?'

The nod was her second lie. She had no idea of her own reason for going to that place, except for the fact that the road led away from Tipton.

'There will be work for you at Foxley.' He took another swallow from his mug.

'Of what sort, Mr Lytton?' Rachel's eyes flashed again. 'The sort Magistrate Bedworth would have had me do? If you think to take me to your house in order to warm your bed, you can think again.'

'I could sit and think of such a pleasant prospect all night.'

He smiled, showing strong white teeth. 'But I was never one to indulge myself too soon. I will leave that particular delight a while longer. For now I need to get home. Drink up.'

Rachel followed his movement with a defiant stare as he stood up, throwing a coin on to the table.

'I have told you before, I will not go with you.'

'Then to hell with you!'

His reply was sudden, and not really expected. It took the defiance from her stare, leaving Rachel with a strange feeling of being abandoned.

'I offer you my help and you accuse me of wanting to make you my mistress! Well, before I tell you that my help is no longer on offer, let me tell you this. Had I wanted a mistress, I would not choose the half-starved, rag bag daughter of a Horseley pitman!'

Rachel sat staring into the fire that warmed the little parlour. Neither Jared Lytton's outburst nor his choice of words surprised her. In an area where every meal was hard earned, she had early in life become used to hearing far worse. No, it was not his anger that had left her feeling so shaken, so what was it?

She did not want to go with him. She had not wanted his help. She in no way wanted anything to do with Jared Lytton. So why did his going leave her with the same feeling of desolation that parting from her father had brought? The unhappiness she had felt then was understandable, she'd loved her father, but there was no explaining the feeling that filled her now. Jared Lytton was an almost total stranger to her, she had only met him once before, so why did she feel her life had gone with him through that door?

She had refused his help. Rachel rose, pulling the shawl tight about her shoulders. Refused an offer that would have found her work and a place to sleep.

Crossing the room, she stepped out into the public bar feeling the eyes of the men drinking there turn towards her, following her into the night.

*   *   *

Jared had left enough money to pay for her lodging at The Fox for several weeks.

Rachel pulled the shawl about her shoulders, trying to ward off the nip in the early-morning air.

The landlord's wife had followed her out into the darkness the night before, pointing out to her the foolishness of trying to find somewhere else to spend the night, reiterating what Rachel already knew: the heath, with its myriad gin pits, was no place to wander in the darkness. That it would be best to accept Jared Lytton's kindness and stay at The Fox.

But what the landlord's wife saw as kindness Rachel looked on as charity, and she wanted no man's charity. Somehow, sometime, she would pay back what he had given; pay back with interest what it had cost to keep her for one night at that inn; for one night was all she would accept. From this day Rachel Cade would make her own way in the world.

But where, and doing what?

Cresting a small rise, she gazed out over rough heathland, on a landscape bare and empty in every direction to the horizon. She had no idea how far it still was to the cottage set below Ox Leasowes bridge or what it would hold when she got there. Were there no more than two cottages huddling together or was there a village, built around a mine as Horseley was? What would there be there for a young woman on her own to do?

The landlord's wife had told her of a woman, a Widow Thomas, who had been left to care for a weak-minded son. She might be of a mind to take on help. But further than that she had not ventured, her husband's shout recalling her to the inn.

But what sort of help would be wanted?

Doubt beginning to creep into her mind, Rachel continued to stare out over the heath. Maybe she should have accepted Jared Lytton's offer of work at his home. Maybe she should have remained in her father's house at Horseley and tried to ignore the feelings rife against her . . . or at least have stayed in Tipton Green.

There would have been no peace of mind there, but would there be any with Widow Thomas?

Taking care to follow the thread-like path, one of many spreading like narrow veins over the heath, trodden by miners who'd worked long-dead pits, Rachel followed the directions given by the landlord's wife.

'You can't miss 'em,' the woman had assured her. 'There be two of 'em built alongside one another. One cottage holds Widow Thomas and her lad, t'other be empty so I be told. Look out for the bridge crossing the canal, you'll not miss 'em.'

But there were many bridges, each spanning the canal at some point, which was Ox Leasowes bridge? Was she even going the right way?

Her father would have known.

Rachel's heart twisted at the thought. He had taken a great pride in knowing the name of every bridge, often taking her on Sunday afternoon walks along the canalside, pointing out and naming each one they came to, teaching her to recite them like a poem:

> Horseley bridge is broad and wide,
> Across Summer Hill bridge a man might ride,
> Parker bridge is narrow and stony,
> Quarry bridge has crossing for a pony,
> Factory bridge leads men to Tipton main,
> While Five Bricks leads them home again . . .

She had been so happy then. Her father had tried to make all things pleasant for her, even more so after her mother's death. Then with his marriage to Hannah she had seen him change, seen the unhappiness in his face; but never when he was with her and Robbie.

Even before he learned to walk, Robbie wanted to be with

her. Rachel swallowed hard, memories rising like tears. He would hold out his tiny arms, his baby cries demanding her attention, a wonderful smile spreading across his little face when she went to him. And later, when he was older, he would follow her about the house like a shadow, except Robbie was never silent. His favourite word had been 'Why'. Robbie had wanted to know everything, demanding she tell him the names of animals, trees, flowers, and even canal barges. His favourite place to stand and watch the narrow boats drawn along the canal behind the huge Shire horses was 'Aggie duck' bridge.

'Rachel, can we go see Aggie duck? Please can we?'

Rachel remembered the frown settling over her step-mother's face whenever the child asked to be taken out, wanting him always with her. But if their father was home he would ignore Hannah's frown, taking them both along to 'Aggie duck'. He had kept the secret, allowing his wife to think the boy had asked to see a favourite bird in some outlying farm; he had never revealed the boy's baby name for Aqueduct bridge.

Hannah had seemed to have an innate fear of the canals. Rachel had thought that strange in a woman born and bred in the Black Country, an area criss-crossed with waterways. Looking back, it appeared as if she knew they wanted to rob her, to take away the most cherished thing in her life.

And for that she had blamed Rachel.

'But I didn't do it!' The words broke into the silence unheard by any but a goshawk hovering above a clump of yellow-flowered gorse. 'Oh, God! I didn't kill Robbie.'

Tears stinging her eyes again she walked on, keeping the canal always in sight. The cottages were built close to a bridge and that bridge spanned a canal, so sooner or later she would come to them, or at least to a place where she could ask further directions.

*   *   *

The woman had seen Rachel long before she reached the cottages, one standing an acre away from the other.

'Ar, I be her.'

A pan of corn in her hands, a white apron reaching to the hem of her long black skirts, the woman's sallow face peered out from beneath a cotton poke bonnet.

'I'm Beulah Thomas, and who might you be?'

'My name is Rachel Cade.' She swallowed nervously sensing the woman's suspicion. 'The landlady of the Fox Inn told me you might be thinking of taking on help?'

'Oh, her did, did her!'

Berry-bright eyes swept over Rachel, taking in the mud stains on her dress, glancing at hands which carried the marks of the pit banks. She had seen the type before, dissatisfied with one life and looking for another, always searching for one that was easier than the last.

'. . . well, her were wrong. Mary Tindall be too free with her telling what other folk be needing. That woman would be well served to mind her own business, 'stead of poking her nose into that of others. I ain't wanting help, I don't . . .'

The pan of corn tilted, spilling on to the ground as the woman's face blanched, one hand going to her midriff.

'Are you not feeling well? Can I . . . ?'

Rachel's question was cut off as the woman pulled herself upright, only her eyes showing pain.

'I told you, I needs no help, and I don't be no charity either. You be on your way for you'll find nothing here.'

'I did not come looking for charity, Mrs Thomas.' Rachel quelled the despair rising in her. The woman did not want to take on help, the landlord's wife had been mistaken, so where next? 'And I am sure Mary Tindall meant no harm in advising me to come here. I think her intention was to do us both a good turn, but sometimes the best of intentions are misconstrued. Forgive me for having interrupted your work.'

Beulah Thomas watched the girl turn around. There was a pride about her, in the way in which she held herself, her body straight and her head lifted. She had not begged, she had asked for nothing; neither had there been any animosity in her reply to Beulah's sharp words, only a quiet apology.

'There be a tankard of lemonade should you feel the need of a drink.'

Already beyond the hedge that enfolded a small garden filled with the colours of early summer, Rachel shook her head, denying the dryness of her throat. 'I have taken enough of your time, Mrs Thomas. But I thank you for the offer.'

'Well, I be ready for one.' Beulah set aside the pan. 'And I would take it kindly if you would join me in a sup.'

There was no smile on the sallow, sharp-boned face and the brightness still burned in the berry eyes, but the suspicion had gone from her voice.

'I would like that.' Rachel turned back. 'Perhaps I could feed the hens while you fetch it?'

'No need.' Beulah led the way to a door half hidden by a sprawling purple clematis. 'They'll be seen to.'

In a kitchen that boasted a fire despite the promised warmth of the day, Rachel felt a familiar lump fill her throat. This was so like the kitchen of her father's house in Horseley: the range blackleaded to a silvery shine, a kettle slung from a hook steaming above it, a fat earthenware teapot standing on a trivet on the hob, and before it on the bright scrubbed quarry tiles a pegged rug, its diamond-patterned centre a blaze of blue. How many times had she tumbled Robbie on just such a rug?

'Sit you there, wench.' Beulah pointed to a spindle-back chair, its legs sawn comfortably short. 'Lemonade be in the brew house.'

Waiting while the woman fetched the drink, Rachel resumed her scrutiny of the kitchen that smelled of fresh-baked bread. It boasted a dresser filled with a mosaic of crockery. Beneath the one small-paned window, a wooden settle claimed almost the whole length of the wall, leaving barely enough space for a stool on which stood what Rachel guessed to be a sewing box. It was obvious that Beulah Thomas, like all the women Rachel knew, had turned her kitchen into a kind of sitting room, keeping any other downstairs room as a front parlour. A parlour to hold treasures and dreams.

Rachel watched as the woman returned then took a third tankard from the tray, carrying it outside and leaving it somewhere beyond the door. Mary Tindall had said she had a weak-minded boy. Was the third tankard for him, and if so why not give it to the child here with them?

'What brought you to The Fox?' Beulah asked after taking a drink from her tankard. 'Does your home be in Foxyards?'

Rachel drank some of the cool liquid, savouring the taste of fresh lemons on her tongue. 'My home was in Horseley Field, Mrs Thomas.'

'Horseley?' Beulah repeated the name. 'Can't say I've heard mention of it, but then that don't be surprising with my never venturing further than The Fox. The carter brings anything I be needing to that place and I picks it up when next I be there.'

'Horseley is a very small village,' Rachel found herself volunteering. 'A baker's shop and a butcher's and The Jolly Collier.' Her voice dropped on the last words and her glance fell to the pewter tankard in her hands.

'I take it that be a public house?'

'Yes.' Rachel nodded. 'It also serves as the Magistrates Court.'

'Be your parents still there?' Beulah queried, the change of tone not lost on her.

'My father is. My stepmother . . . my stepmother . . .'

'Don't be saying anything more.' Beulah returned her tankard to the wooden tray she had set on the large scrubbed table. 'I don't thank folk for asking my business and I want to hear none of yours. There be a day's work here for you if you have a mind to take it. It will pay a midday meal and the price of a supper and a bed you may buy somewhere along your way. Be the offer taken?'

'Yes.' Rachel smiled, feeling relief flood through her. One day at a time, that was all she asked, one day at a time.

'I think you must mean Rachel – Rachel Cade.'

Ellen pushed a strand of hair from her face, squinting against the sunlight as she looked at the man seated on horseback. She had noticed him on several occasions, his gaze searching the faces of the women working the waste heaps. At first she had taken him to be someone sent to remove the pickers but Tansy had said he was Jared Lytton, owner of several of the mines whose spoil heaps they worked.

'I seem to recall that was the name I was given.' He kept his tone deliberately offhand. 'The girl had a head of pale hair, silver-gold, and her eyes were a shade of deep violet. I thought I saw a girl with such hair among you some weeks ago.'

'Rachel had the colouring you describe, sir.' Ellen glanced beyond him to where Tansy and Cora watched.

'This girl, why is she not with you today?'

Ellen turned her glance back to him, wishing Tansy would intervene. Why was Jared Lytton looking for Rachel? Was it to do with her brother's drowning? Had it been found to be Rachel's fault after all? Did he want to have her brought before the magistrate again? She hesitated, willing Tansy to join them. She would know what to say, she would be able to judge the motives behind this man's questions.

'She . . . she left,' Ellen was forced to answer when Tansy made no move.

'Left!' The sudden sharpness in his voice caused the horse to prance nervously and it was a few seconds before he asked the rest of the question. 'Why did she leave?'

Ellen's cheeks took on a tinge of pink and her eyelids dropped. She could not tell him, a stranger, what had driven Rachel away: of how Samuel Potter had once tried to rape her and once tried to lure her to his house with the obvious intention of doing so again; of how he had told the girl there would be other times.

'I . . . I don't know why she left.' The lie added to the colour in Ellen's cheeks.

'Then perhaps you can tell me where she went?'

The slightly acid tone of his voice revealing he did not believe her, Ellen looked up and this time there was no hesitation in her answer.

'No, sir, I cannot tell you that, for the simple reason she did not say where it was she intended to go. Or at least, she did not say as much in my hearing, though she might have intimated something to Tansy or Cora. You may ask them, they are working just there.'

Jared followed the line of her finger to where the two women stood watching.

'I'll do that.' He touched the riding crop to the side of his bare head. 'Thank you and good day to you.'

Keeping to the heath, Jared took the path that led to Toll End. He had come to check the progress of the narrow boats he had commissioned from the boat builder there. But why had he stopped at every spoil heap in the area, and why had he come this way every day for a week, always finding an excuse that would take him through Tipton Green?

Impatient with himself, the excuse of going again to the boat yard only serving to irritate him further, he swung the horse around, making across the heath toward Bloomfield.

Tansy had told him nothing. 'Rachel Cade stayed some time with us in Tipton Green, then she left. Could have been the coal picking was too hard for her.' The words echoed in his mind. Picking coal was a hard enough way for anyone to make a living, but somehow that being the reason for the girl leaving her home yet again did not ring entirely true. She had been terrified that night he found her on the heath. Terrified of what, or whom?

It could not be fear of Hannah Cade, that woman was locked away in some institution. Isaiah Bedworth?

Jared reined abruptly, bringing a whinny of protest from his horse.

Had Bedworth made an approach to the girl . . . was that the reason she had been halfway across the heath in the dark of night, was that what she was running away from?

Jared stared towards the distant ribbon of green water.

Where had she run to? She had stayed only one night at The Fox, so the landlord had informed him when he had stopped there next. That had been a week ago.

But why should it bother him where she had gone, or with whom for that matter? Touching a heel to the animal's flank, he moved on. He had better things to do than concern himself with a girl he barely knew.

Chapter Ten

Beulah Thomas watched from the window of the kitchen. The girl worked well and willingly, no matter what task was given her. It had been a fortnight since her arrival at the cottage, and with the passing of each day Beulah had determined that the girl would be sent on her way, yet each time the words had not been spoken.

She needed help. Beulah returned to her task of kneading the dough for the week's bread. The pain was worse every day. It would not be long, she knew that, and then what would happen to the boy? Covering the dough with a cloth, she set it in the hearth to rise. He would never be able to manage alone. She had hoped, in these years since his father had gone, prayed the boy would be able to beat the curse that held him, but that hope had never been realised. Her son was bound as tight as ever he had been.

Tipping flour into a fresh bowl, she added salt and a lump of her own churned butter.

Perhaps the girl had been sent. Plunging her fingers into the bowl, she mixed the ingredients together, rolling out the pastry with a glass bottle. Perhaps the good Lord knew of the hard days that waited not far off and had directed the girl's footsteps. Maybe she was His answer.

'There were a dozen this morning.' Rachel came into the kitchen, a wicker basket on her arm. 'They look to have double yolks.'

'Hens be laying well.' Beulah nodded approvingly. 'They've taken right well to being fed by you.'

'These were in the usual place.' Rachel held up a large egg, its shell faintly bluish against the white eggs of the hens.

'I was feared them ducks might have gone off the lay after that to do with the fox, but seems they be back on form.'

Rachel laid the eggs gently in a large earthenware bowl, carrying it into the cool of the scullery where she lifted it into a cupboard. Beulah had made no reference to her child, yet it was her son who must care for the ducks for neither Beulah nor herself looked to them. But why was he so secretive? And why did he not come into the house? She glanced through the open door, looking out on to the brew house, then beyond to the fields of barley edged by the heath. She had wondered many times why the boy had never shown himself, but had not asked. Beulah Thomas valued her privacy and Rachel respected it.

'I've been thinking . . .' Beulah did not look up as Rachel turned to the kitchen but went on firming lids on the pies she was making. 'You seem to have grown used to the work of this house . . .'

Rachel held her breath, her own eyes following the older woman's deft fingers.

'. . . and I fancy her at The Fox be right. I might be of a mind to take on help. The place be a bit much for one body on her own.'

Rachel's breath stayed locked in her throat.

'If you have a mind to stay and work along of me then stay you can.' Beulah carried the pies to the oven, pushing them one at a time into its hot depths. 'But if you've no mind then say so now.'

Rachel felt her head swim as she released the breath from her throat. She could stay here, stay in this house where she felt a security she had not felt since Hannah had come as her father's wife.

'I would very much like to work for you, Mrs Thomas,' she said, a smile of pure relief lighting her face.

''Twill pay board and keep and a florin a week atop of that, do that suit you?'

'It . . . it suits me very well, Mrs Thomas.'

Two shillings a week! Rachel could hardly believe what she had heard. Two shillings, when four women had been lucky to earn as much in a week with coal picking.

'It won't be no joyride!' Beulah took the dough rising in the hearth and tipped it on to the table where she proceeded to knock it back. ''Tis hard work running this place. It ain't just the feeding of a few hens and collecting their eggs. There be the dairy and the brew house to be seen to as well as the cleaning of the house.'

Dairying would be new to her but Rachel kept the thought to herself, afraid of Beulah's changing her mind. It could not be so difficult to learn; as for the work of the brew house, she had helped her mother and Hannah in the one behind the house in Horseley.

'I'll manage, it's pleasant work compared to the pit banks.' It was out before Rachel was aware of what she was saying.

Satisfied the dough had been kneaded enough, Beulah separated it into six equal portions, laying them aside a second time. 'We'll just let the devil rise in that lot.' She glanced across to Rachel. 'You need have no worry you've told me something I didn't know already, wench. The state of your hands told me you were a pit bank lass when first you came here, to say nothing of the state of your frock.'

Rachel felt the colour surge to her face. She sponged her dress every night. She had removed the clay from her days on the coal heaps but the water left a ragged stain that defied any attempt to remove it.

'There be no call for your cheeks to colour.' Beulah busied herself tidying away her baking, for once ignoring Rachel's simply standing still. 'Nothing wrong with the sponging of a skirt, it be far better than wearing it daubed with clay, but it won't do for Bloomfield.'

'Bloomfield?'

Bowls and glass bottle pastry roller balanced on her wooden tray, Beulah shoved it into Rachel's hands. 'That be what I said, wench, Bloomfield. I take butter and cheese to the market once a week, but the walk there and back be proving a bind to me. I shall be wanting you to take it from now on.'

Following with the tray as Beulah bustled into the scullery, Rachel placed the crockery in the shallow brownstone sink then fetched the kettle of boiling water from the kitchen.

'I've never done that before,' she felt a need to admit.

'Ar, well, there be many things we all have to learn afore this life be over,' Beulah answered, pouring cold water from a jug to mix with the hot. 'Provided you take heed of what you be told, you won't go far wrong. Now get yourself into the kitchen and look to the pies afore they scorches, then put the loaves in the bread oven. I'll wash these crocks and store them away, then we'll have ourselves a cup of tea.

'It be tomorrow I takes butter and cheese to Bloomfield.' Beulah sipped the tea Rachel poured for her. 'But you will go in my stead.'

Rachel nodded, not meeting the older woman's glance, not wanting her to see the uncertainty she knew showed in her face. How would she know where to stand? Were the women who bought Beulah's butter and cheese regular customers or would she have to shout like the people in Tipton Green market? Rachel cringed at the thought.

'You'll have no bother.' It was as if Beulah read her thoughts. 'Ask for Bessie Turner, anybody will point her out to you. Tell her you be there for me and stand alongside of her. Folk who come for your stuff know what they want and you'll have no worries as to their paying the true amount. It be the trimmers you need to watch for.'

'Trimmers?'

'Ar.' Beulah nodded, sipping tea at the same time so that she was forced to swallow hard. 'Trimmers. They takes their change and holds it out on their palm for all to see, vowing and declaring they give you half a crown and you've only given change for a florin. Then in the racket that builds up they trim a pound of butter or a wedge of cheese from your stall and it's in their pocket afore you can blink. I had many a one stole until Bessie Turner took me to stand beside her. Bessie will watch out for you, I pity them as tries it out on her.' Placing her cup on the table, Beulah fished in the pocket of her skirt then placed seven silver shillings on the table.

'That frock you be wearing is good enough for the brew house but it won't do for market. A body must be spruce if folk be going to buy butter and cheese from her.'

A cup halfway to the tray, Rachel hesitated. 'But I don't have another dress.'

'I knows that.' Going to the bread oven Beulah reached out one of the loaves, tipping it over in the cloth she took from the overhead rail, tapping the bottom with a knuckle. 'Same as I knows you washes out the one pair of drawers you owns every night and likely puts them on next morning still damp. That be why you be going to Bloomfield this morning: to get yourself another frock and a couple more pairs of drawers.'

'I can't!' Rachel placed the cup alongside the platter teapot on the tray. 'I don't have the money for a dress, I . . . I have what you have given each evening but that will not buy a dress.'

'Tuppence a night that was intended to buy a meal next day.' Beulah removed the rest of the loaves, filling the kitchen with the warm yeasty smell of newly baked bread. 'But you still be here. However, like you says that won't pay for no frock so you'll be needing the money that be on the table.'

'No . . . I can't . . .'

'It be no gift,' Beulah cut in on her protest. 'It be a loan that will be taken piece by piece from your wages till it be repaid.

Now don't stand there with your tongue flapping, go smooth your hair and we'll set you on the path for Bloomfield.'

Over the bridge and follow to the left. Rachel recalled the instructions Beulah had given. *Pass beneath the railway viaduct then keep to the towpath. It leads straight into Bloomfield and it be much easier to tread than the heath. Half an hour's walk will see you there.*

She was to stay with Beulah, to live in that house. She would not go to sleep any more with the worry of having to leave the next morning.

But what of Beulah's son? The cottage had only two bedrooms. Did he not sleep in the house at all, or had her being there meant he had been put out of the house? She had seen no sign of a boy, though the woman at the inn had said there was one; but if that were so, where did the child eat, and where did he sleep? If he existed at all, why hide him away? A feeble mind . . . was that the answer? Surely a child with such an affliction needed love and companionship. He did not deserve to be shut away alone somewhere.

Ahead of her the sun glinted on the satin smoothness of the water and the heath opened its wild flowers to the warmth. But suddenly the peace of her morning was broken.

Beulah did not appear the type of woman who would lock away her own child, but she had. There could be no other cause for him not being about the house. Beulah must have her reasons. Was it because of Rachel . . . was *she* that reason?

The questions tumbled through her mind. How could she have been so blind? Had she been so wrapped up in her own problems . . . or was it that she had not wanted to see, to own the fact that by easing Rachel's problems, Beulah had increased those of a small child?

Only a moment ago she had been so happy; her life had taken a new path, she'd felt secure. Now it was shattered.

Snatched from her as her childhood had been, as her life with Tansy and the others had been.

Turning about, she walked slowly back along the towpath.

'It were a right inferno according to what I were told, the whole place a mass of flame. Bargee who filled up this morning said as how the blaze could be seen clear from the canal.'

Richie Cade bit into the thick slice of bread. It was dry and hard from being baked a week ago, but stale bread at dinnertime meant a hot meal in the evenings. Limestone mining paid low wages, and most of what he earned went on board and lodging. He had been in Dudley some weeks now, and every evening was spent seeking news of his daughter. But it seemed she was not in this town. In a week or so he would move on. He would never stop looking, never give up searching.

'Makes you wonder 'ow these things get started.'

'Fires be unpredictable,' Richie answered the man sitting at his side, his back resting against the wall of rock. 'They can start at any time, for no particular reason.'

'Ar, that be so.' The man swigged cold tea from a beer bottle. 'Or they could be started for a particular reason.'

'Such as what?' Richie chewed on the tasteless bread.

The man at his side wiped milky droplets of tea from his lips with the back of one hand, clearing a broad swathe in the white dust that covered his face.

'Such as a body's hand setting it alight.'

'Be you saying somebody deliberately set out to burn down that asylum?'

'Well, it's been there long enough, and it ain't never burned down afore, and the folk in it do be mainly lunatics, don't they? Seems a reasonable assumption to me. One of 'em set light to the place!'

'Was anybody hurt?' Richie replaced the bread in his tin box, appetite suddenly gone.

'From what he heard from the lock keeper along of Burntwood, it seems the place went up in the middle of the night. Most of them were got out but there were a couple – women, he said – that didn't. Appears they were locked up in some special part of the building. The fire had got too fierce a hold for them to be reached. Poor sods!' The man shook his head. 'As if they didn't suffer enough by being mad, they had to be roasted alive.'

Putting aside his lunch tin, Richie followed his workmate, taking up chisel and hammer to begin the long hours that still remained of the day's work mining limestone. The insane asylum at West Bromwich had been burned down. That was the institution Hannah had been sent to, the prison that Isaiah Bedworth's mercy had assigned her in place of hanging. Two women, the bargee had said, two women, both locked in some special part of that building, two women who had died. Was Hannah one of them?

The question and the fear still haunted Richie two days later. Sunday was the one day in the week when he was not at work. There had been a time when that day had been spent with his children, walking with them on the heath, naming for them the flowers and plants that coloured it where no pits had been sunk, gouging the heart from the land. Now his Sundays were spent searching for the one child left to him. He ought not to have let her go – if only he had kept her with him. Hannah had been taken the next day, there would have been no reason then for his daughter to leave. But there would have been reason. She could not have lived with the jibes and innuendo of the village women.

On each side of him the traffic rumbled along High Street, horse-drawn carts giving way deferentially to carriages while blocking the way of humbler pushcarts; the blare of a steam-tram's horn mixed with the shouts of traders: women in black bonnets holding Sunday-scrubbed children by the hand, prayer book gripped in the other, hurrying on their way to church. Hannah had been a church goer, taking

Rachel and Robbie with her morning and evening every Sunday, and what good had the pious life done for her . . . for any of them?

Richie's clenched hands dug deeper into his pockets, bitterness filling his throat and mind. Where had Hannah's God been when Robbie had drowned? Where had he been when Rachel had been accused of murder?

Passing The Hare and Hounds public house Richie followed narrow Hallam Street that lay on the edge of the town, coming to a high-walled red-brick building, part of it blackened and razed by fire. It was here Hannah had been sent to serve out her life sentence, here she had been led away from him, screaming her hatred of his daughter. He had not returned since that day; any last vestige of feeling he might have had for the woman he had married had long since died. She had taken his life and that of his daughter, her venom and spite reducing both to ashes; he owed Hannah Cade nothing, but for the sake of what little peace of mind he might hope for in the future he must know whether or not she had survived that fire.

'I am very sorry, Mr Cade.'

A sharp-featured woman, grey hair drawn into a knot on the nape of her neck, hands crossed together over the front of severe grey skirts that fell below an unadorned white cambric blouse, looked across a leather-topped desk at him.

'Your wife had been somewhat poorly on the evening of the fire. She had been taken to the infirmary but had already been returned to one of the secure cells. The blaze spread very rapidly . . .'

The woman's fingers flexed then locked together, her only outward sign of emotion.

'. . . I assure you, every effort was made to reach your wife, but it was impossible. I am very sorry to have to tell you she died in the fire.'

The words returned to him again and again as Richie made

his way back to his lodging. He had held no love for Hannah but neither had he hated her; he had merely felt a strange kind of pity, knowing she wanted a love he could not give her. Poor Hannah! To live so fruitless a life, to die so terrible a death.

'Where was your God, Hannah?' Richie laughed, a quiet bitter laugh. 'I'll tell you, He was nowhere. All your piety and God-fearing was for nothing. There is no God . . . there is no God!'

'I should have realised earlier.' Rachel stood beside the freshly scrubbed table in the warm bread-scented kitchen. 'I should have known that my sleeping in this house meant your child was put out of it.'

'Put out of it?' Beulah continued to prepare the beans she had picked from the small plot that backed on to the house, carefully pulling long fibrous strings from the sides of each before slicing them. 'What do you mean, put out of it?'

Rachel put the five-shilling piece Beulah had given her on the table. 'Mrs Thomas, I know how kind you have been, offering me a home, but . . . but I can't accept when it means your own boy . . .'

'What about my boy?' Beulah's face showed nothing, her fingers still deftly stringing the beans.

'You do have a child?' Rachel twisted the edges of her shawl between fingers grown unaccountably clumsy. 'The woman at the Fox Inn said as much.'

Beulah tossed the last of the sliced beans into a colander, its white enamel pocked by black chip marks. 'I do have a lad, and I can guess what that woman told you concerning him, but he hasn't been put from his home and wouldn't be, not for you nor the Queen herself.'

'But he has not been seen in this house since I came here.'

'Does that mean I've thrown him out?' Beulah turned from dropping the beans into a pan swung over the fire. 'Because you have not seen him in this house?'

'But . . . but he is here.' Rachel felt nervous tension begin to get the better of her. If it had not been for the fact of having to return the money Beulah had given her to buy a dress she would have just gone on, would have left this place without having to say why. 'There was the tea you carried outside, it can't have been for anyone else . . .'

'No, it were for no one else.' Putting the colander aside, wiping her hands on the corner of her long apron, Beulah studied the face of the girl to whom she had offered a home. The distress in her lovely face was genuine; she obviously believed what she said concerning the boy was true: that she had taken his place in the home. And then there was the money on the table. How many young women in her situation would have returned it?

'That room you slept in was my son's.' Beulah smiled for the first time. 'But he hasn't been turned out of it to make room for you, and the reason you have not seen him for the first week or more was on account of his not being here. He went down to Worcester to fetch hops, for the brewing. The ones we grow hereabouts be thin and don't carry much of the humulon that be needed to get a good flavour. I know how much he dislikes being with people but there be times when it can't be helped. I can't do it all myself. When he got back you were busy in the wash house. I told him of you and he agreed you should stay on as help.'

'But why was I not introduced?'

'That be a longer story.' Beulah lowered herself to a chair and for a moment her eyes looked into a world Rachel could not share. 'Sit you down, wench, while I have the telling of it, then you must choose for yourself if you stay or go.

'William, my son, was born with a defect of the tongue. From the earliest days his words would not fall easily but pushed against each other without control. As he grew older his father would lose his temper. Joseph was never an overly patient man. His shouting unnerved the boy so his tongue would lose what little control it had until he could not speak at all. Then when we sent him to school the boys there mocked and tormented him until he could stand no more. He would run across the heath, to anywhere the taunting could not reach him. This, of course, angered his father further and he would try beating the boy, making the strap do what his shouting could not. I tried my best to shield William and to help him master his tongue, but as fast as I got him to utter a word, Joseph knocked it from him until the boy became too feared even to try. By the time his father died, it was too late for my son.'

Somewhere deep inside, Rachel felt a little of the pain Beulah's son must have felt. Though not beaten she had felt the lash of Hannah's tongue till she too had wanted to run; only her father's love had held her in a home that had lost its happiness.

'He had become too locked inside himself.' Beulah went on, words falling into the silence of the kitchen. 'He trusts few strangers, afraid they will laugh and mock his broken words like the villagers round here. That is why he has kept himself out of the way.'

'I would not mock your boy, Mrs Thomas,' Rachel answered, some of her own pain evident in her voice. 'I would not mock any child. But I still cannot stay, much as I want to. I cannot take your child's room.'

'You won't have to.' Beulah drew in a long breath, closing off that unseen world. 'The cottage, along of this one, was built for my son. Joseph built it against his being married, but that is another dream I'm like never to see come true. This house will not hold us all with a bedroom each, so he has been busy since coming up from Worcester, putting the other place in proper order. It's for you, wench, if you wants it, but yours must be the choosing.'

On the mantelpiece above the grate the squat wooden clock ticked, emphasising the breathless quiet that reigned over the house. She could still stay here with Beulah and her child. She would not be depriving the boy of his home.

'Thank you, Mrs Thomas.' Rachel's answer was no louder than the clock's ticking and for the moment she ignored the question that still lurked at the back of her mind. If the boy was so withdrawn, his tongue still so tied, how did he come to travel all the way to Worcester to fetch hops? Who was it spoke for him there? 'Thank you, and thanks to your son. I won't let you down, I promise you.'

No, this girl would not let her down. Beulah rose from her chair, returning to the pan over the fire, the hope in her eyes hidden from the smiling Rachel. She would not let her down, but would she fulfil her dream?

Chapter Eleven

Jared pushed his plate away, appetite suddenly deserting him as the man standing next to his table laughed loudly.

'You thought you could throw your weight about in that place, didn't you, Lytton? Thought to kick their arses, but they kicked yours. You would have done better to save your breath for all the notice they took of you. You would have the balls off any man who tried to run her out . . .' the laugh rang out again, coarse and derisive, causing several heads to turn in its direction '. . . and the women – what would you do to them, eh?'

'Most certainly not what you would do to them.' Jared picked up his glass, swallowing a little of the red wine, his gaze cool. 'Perhaps that is what is bothering you? I have brought no charge against them, therefore you have been denied your amusement. As you were once before when I snatched that girl from under your nose.'

'Ar, snatched her!' Within its frame of silver-grey side whiskers Isaiah Bedworth's face became florid. 'And we all know why, same as we know you 'adn't seen that so-called accident. You 'adn't seen that boy fall . . .'

'Tut, tut, Bedworth.' Jared's lips curved into the semblance of a smile but his eyes remained cold. 'Are you accusing me of perjury?'

'I'm saying you are a bloody liar!' Isaiah ignored the stares and murmurings of the diners in the small eating room. 'You no more saw what happened beside that lock than I did, and if I get proof . . .'

'You will do what?' Jared's voice was low and steady, but the edge it carried was sharp and dangerous 'Rape me as you have raped so many of the women you have sent to Tibbington workhouse, and as you no doubt tried to rape that girl? Now let me tell you what *I* will do should I ever get proof of that. I will have the balls off *you*, Bedworth, and that is not just a figure of speech!'

'Fancied that one yourself, did you?' Isaiah's small eyes glinted. 'Is that what's irking you? But you haven't had it yet and that be riling you. Oh, I know about her leaving Horseley to save that father of hers leaving the house. But didn't do any good, he went anyway. Left the next day, right after I sentenced that crazy wife of his to life imprisonment. I also know you went back there enquiring after Richie Cade. Hah! It wasn't Richie Cade you wanted to find, it were his daughter. You see, Lytton, there's not much happens in Tipton that I don't get to hear of. But the girl was gone and you didn't get what you really went for, and that's left a lump between your legs that has you walking bow-legged!'

Replacing his glass on the table, Jared stood up. But as he made to leave Isaiah stepped in front of him. 'Remember, Lytton,' he smirked, 'there's nothing happens in these parts that Isaiah Bedworth doesn't get to hear of, one way or another. Maybe I will find Cade's daughter afore you do. If that be so you'll no longer have that itch for her, I guarantee you that.'

'Maybe you will.' Jared's lips scarcely moved but his eyes told their own story. 'But should you touch her, I will see to it she's the last woman you ever touch. Not one way or another, Bedworth, but by slicing off that part of you that gives you most pleasure in the using. I guarantee you that! Good day to you.'

Elbowing the magistrate from his path, Jared smiled at the

sound of the man clumsily falling across a table occupied by irate diners.

Bedworth was a fool thought Jared, walking slowly towards his carriage. That day he had gone back to Horseley *had* been to see Richie Cade, to ask if his daughter had been driven out by others; he had not gone seeking the girl, who held no interest for him.

So why that sudden jolt inside him when Bedworth had accused him of taking a fancy to her? Climbing into the driving seat, he caught up the reins with a swift irritated movement. And why, if she held no interest for him, that stab in his stomach on hearing the other man threaten her?

Did that mean it had not been Bedworth that Cade's daughter had been running from when Jared came across her on the heath that night? He talked softly to the stallion, guiding him into the busy street. But if not the magistrate then who, and for what reason?

In a shop doorway he caught a glimpse of golden hair. What do I care? he thought, as his stomach tightened. The girl held no interest for him, Rachel Cade was just another miner's daughter, what the hell did it matter who bedded her? It was no concern of his.

And still the thought remained, lurking stubbornly beneath the rest. Why did a glimpse of golden hair cause his insides to twist? And why, everywhere he went, did his eyes search for the sight of a girl with hair like wind-blown wheat?

'You still have a frock to buy.' Beulah treated herself to a rare smile. 'You'll need to go back to Bloomfield, though it be getting late in the day. I dare say that by the time you've pithered over which colour to buy and moithered over the price, it will be dark afore you reaches home and I'm none too content at the thought of you crossing the heath by yourself.'

Home. Rachel's heart warmed at the thought. Beulah and her boy had prepared the other cottage for her, she could hardly wait to see it, but Beulah had said, 'First things first.' She must go to the town and buy a dress so she would look presentable in the market tomorrow.

'You put that money back in your pocket and this time make sure and get what you went for.' Crossing the little kitchen, Beulah looked out through the door to the yard. 'My lad takes eggs and butter to some of the big houses along of Bloomfield while I sell the rest in the market, though tomorrow be the usual day for his doing of that, but seeing as you have to go there he might as well go with you today. That way you will have company and I won't have the jaunt to Bloomfield.'

Beulah was allowing her to take the child to the town! The warm glow in Rachel's heart deepened as she watched the older woman set off across the yard. It would be like being with Robbie again. Would he ask as many questions as her brother always had? Would he demand to know the name of every plant and flower? Rachel laughed softly to herself feeling a happiness she had almost forgotten. Would the boy squeal with delight if they saw a barge on the canal? Would he beg to be given a ride on the horse . . . No! The laughter dying in her throat, she suddenly remembered he would ask none of those questions; he had an affliction of the tongue and fear held him silent – the fear of being mocked.

But no one would mock him while he was with her. The happiness of a moment ago was edged aside by the flood of fierce protectiveness that rose in her like tidal water. Beulah's son would be as safe with her as with his mother.

'Eggs and butter be ready packed in the scullery.' Beulah's long skirts swished as she bustled back into the kitchen. 'They be marked with the name of each house so there can be no mix-up.' The last of her words drifted back from the scullery. 'There be two baskets.'

She re-emerged, a large basket pulling heavily on each arm. Stepping to her, Rachel took one and reached for the other, but Beulah gave a quick shake of her head then held the basket out, her smile directed beyond Rachel. The eyes that up to now had held no joy in life were bright with the pleasure and pride of a mother in her child. 'My son will take this one.'

'But it will be far too heavy,' Rachel protested, reaching again for the large tight-packed wicker basket.

'Won't be too heavy, not for my lad, not for my William.' Beulah's face shone with love as she walked towards the kitchen door.

A child could not be expected to carry a basket that size, Rachel thought, but she would not protest again. Once they had crossed the bridge and were out of sight of the house, she would take it from him.

'Rachel.' Beulah smiled as the girl turned to follow her. 'This is William, my son.'

'Hel—' Rachel's smile froze as she looked at the figure regarding her from the open door. Almost six feet tall, his well-muscled body filling the doorway, William Thomas held out one hand.

'I . . . I'm pleased to meet you, William.' Rachel took the proffered hand, feeling the strength of it though it was immediately withdrawn. But he gave no answer, merely taking the basket from his mother and striding away.

'He'll get used to you, wench,' Beulah whispered as Rachel made to follow. 'It be that he don't know what to expect as yet. He doesn't know whether you will be like all the rest and mock his tongue. That be what they do down there at the Foxyards and up in Bloomfield.'

'I will not mock him, Mrs Thomas,' Rachel said softly, 'and neither will anyone else, ever again.'

She had thought to teach him the names of the flowers that dotted the heath, their summer colours brilliant against the varying shades of gorse and hawthorn. Stooping, Rachel picked a buttercup, smoothing the gold satin petals with a fingertip.

'I had thought to hold this under your chin, like I used to

hold it to Robbie's.' She smiled up at the man beside her. 'He was my brother, and loved to walk on the heath. He would pick one of these and ask to be told whether or not he liked butter. He would laugh when I said he did not.' She looked back at the tiny flower, hiding the tears that rose in her eyes. 'He knew I was teasing every time but always squealed with delight. He . . . he was only five.'

Feeling a touch on her arm, she glanced up. William smiled at her then craned his own head back on his strong neck.

Reaching up, Rachel held the flower beneath his chin. 'You like butter, William,' she said softly, 'and I like you.'

Carrying her basket, which he had taken from her at the door of the cottage, he turned, leading the way to the Fox Inn.

He had not answered. Rachel followed, the buttercup still in her hand. He had not spoken a single word since their meeting, but his dark blue eyes spoke words of their own: words of friendship. Rachel smiled, lifting the tiny flower to her lips. They would be friends, she and Beulah's child.

'I see Widow Thomas set you on then.'

The landlady of the Fox Inn watched the tall young man count out a dozen blue-tinged duck eggs into a bowl she had set out for them on a wide, well-scrubbed table in one corner of her kitchen.

'Seems her knows what her be about.'

'What do you mean?' Rachel watched the woman run a plump finger over the coins held on the palm of one hand.

'Widow Thomas would know what I mean.' The woman eyed her speculatively. 'You be presentable enough to look at, and her lad, well . . .' Her glance returned to Rachel. 'He ain't going to be given much of a choice, is he? Not with that tied tongue of his. I'd say that mother of his has designs.' She leaned forward, bringing her face closer to Rachel's, voice dropping to a low whisper. 'You watch out for her or before you know where you are, you'll find yourself tied neck and crop to Billy Duckegg.'

Rachel's smile faded and she took a step back from the woman, but her eyes stayed fixed on that plump malicious face.

'William Thomas might not have much choice, but I do. Were he ever to consider asking me to be his wife, I would take it as a great compliment. He is a far superior man to many I have met here and elsewhere.'

'He won't do that!' The plump face turned red with indignation. 'Any asking that might be done will have to be done by you, for his tongue will speak none. I'll tell you again, though you don't be deserving of the advice: watch out for that mother of his. It won't be no easy life married to her weak-minded son.'

Maybe the woman *had* meant well, Rachel thought later, matching her steps to William's. But if that were the kindest thing she could say then Rachel would rather she had not said it at all. Had he heard, had the woman's whisper carried across the kitchen to him? She felt a flush of embarrassment colour her cheeks. The woman had called him Billy Duckegg. Was that the name by which he was addressed? Was that an example of the mockery he had suffered all his life?

Rachel pulled her shawl tighter about her shoulders. Suddenly the afternoon had lost its warmth, the happiness had gone from her day.

'It is getting late.' They had already entered the town before she spoke again. Now she had to raise her voice as a steam-trolley clanked past. She had never ridden on a steam-trolley, and from the stories her father told her had always thought how wonderful an experience it would be, actually to sit in one and be transported through the town. Now, watching the large cumbersome machine, smoke belching from a funnel at the front, she felt another dream crumble.

'You make your deliveries,' she said as the rumble of the

trolley receded, 'while I buy my . . . buy the things I came for. We'll wait for each other there.'

She pointed to an elaborately carved stone cross set on a plinth that raised it above the cluster of market stalls in a square, hemmed in by narrow shops.

'Hey, Duckegg . . . Billy Duckegg . . . what you got in the basket, Duckegg?'

Almost immediately the calls rang out. Rachel watched the tall figure stride along the street, children prancing along behind, careful to stay clear of arms longer and more powerful than their own. But William walked calmly on, never once turning on his tormentors.

Had he always been so impervious to their calls or was his behaviour towards these people a defence? Was ignoring their ridicule the only way he knew of dealing with it? Her own heart filled with anger and pity, Rachel turned towards the shops.

This was the first time in her life she could remember shopping for herself alone. Perhaps her mother had shopped just for her but that was so long ago it was past her remembering, and Hannah had never shopped just for her. In fact, Hannah had seemed to resent buying anything at all for her. Her eyes caught by some new thing at almost every step, Rachel passed from one shop window to the next, coming to a standstill before one that held a gown of palest lavender trimmed with purple satin violets from waist to hem. Rachel stared at the dress. It was the most beautiful thing she had ever seen. Freeing her hands from her shawl, she reached out as if to touch the soft fabric. Forgotten, the shawl slipped down to her shoulders.

Driving his carriage on the opposite side of the street, Jared Lytton caught a flash of gold, so pale as to have a touch of silver. Pulling hard on the reins, he brought the vehicle to a halt, arousing the anger of a carter following close behind.

Was it her? He leaned forward, trying to see the slight figure almost obscured by people passing between them.

Had that girl been wearing a brown dress? He could not be certain, but she *had* worn a shawl. But then, every working woman and girl in the Black Country wore a shawl.

'Move away! Don't stand in front of my window staring like a mawkin at something you could never afford. You're blocking the view of those who can afford to buy a gown such as that one.'

Jared caught the words as he crossed the road, dodging between a line of delivery carts, and saw the shopkeeper waving a thin hard-knuckled hand as if warding off some troublesome insect.

'So there you are.'

Drawing level with Rachel, Jared caught her elbow, his mouth curving into a smile.

'I . . . I think there has been some mistake . . .' She broke off as she lifted her eyes to his face. This was the man from the heath, the one who had taken her to the Fox Inn and left money for her lodging there; the same man who had saved her from sentence of death.

'Nonsense, my dear.' Jared held her fast as she tried to withdraw her arm. 'That is the gown you want, isn't it?'

'No, Mr Lytton, I . . .'

'Come along, my dear.' He propelled her past the gaping shopkeeper. 'If that is the gown you wish to have then have it you shall, though in all honesty I must admit it appears tawdry to me.'

Keeping hold of Rachel's arm while the gown was taken from the window, Jared commanded everyone's obedience.

Rachel watched the delicate fabric as it was folded between layers of tissue and laid almost reverently in a white box, confusion mixing with anger. Confusion as to why this man should continually take it upon himself to interfere in her life, and anger at the knowing look in the shopkeeper's eyes.

'I suppose if this is the best this town has to offer then it will have to do, until we can get you some others of a decent quality.'

The shopkeeper's thin nostrils dilated and her lips folded in upon themselves, becoming almost non-existent, but she made no answer as Jared dropped a heap of sovereigns carelessly before her.

'How dare you!' Rachel's stunned silence was broken as he steered her towards the waiting carriage.

'I see nothing daring about buying you a gown.'

The eyes that smiled down at her had lost their coldness, their brown depths holding a touch of amusement that was lost to Rachel in her anger.

'As you see no wrong in ignorant behaviour!' she snapped, jerking her arm free from his hand.

'Ignorant behaviour?'

'Yes, ignorant.' Rachel stumbled against him as he caught her arm again, pulling her from the path of a huge dray cart, then as he freed her went on: 'I suppose you would have some other term for interfering in another person's private affairs, but then no doubt you can find words to smooth over anything you might do.'

'I am rather good at it.'

Rachel ignored the smile lurking behind brown eyes. 'Then perhaps you might find some to smooth over what that shopkeeper obviously thought.'

'That being?'

Infuriatingly the smile persisted, adding to Rachel's feeling of confusion. Why was he doing this? Why, for no reason, had he bundled her into that shop, paying what to her was a small fortune for a gown she had only looked at?

'Being that she obviously thinks I am . . . am a . . .'

'Lady of the streets!' The smile disappeared from his eyes like a candle being snuffed. 'Then she is a bigger fool than you are. She at least should realise that any woman I take as a mistress, or even for a night's entertainment, would hardly be dressed as you are.'

'Oh!' Rachel's head lifted in quiet pride, her lovely eyes scathing. 'You mean, like a ragged-arsed miner's daughter?'

His mouth tightening, showing a narrow band of white about his lips, Jared pushed the dress box into her hands. 'Yes!' he grated. 'I mean just that!'

'And I mean just this.' Lifting the box, Rachel threw it into the carriage. 'I don't want your gift, Mr Lytton. I will buy my own dress and anything else I might need. The only thing I require from you is that you mind your own business and leave me to mine. I do not need your assistance in anything, much as you seem to think otherwise. I can manage quite well for myself.'

'I see you already have.' Jared's face closed as he glanced at the tall figure who came to stand protectively at Rachel's side. 'Good day to you, Miss Cade.'

Chapter Twelve

Rachel carried the underwear and blouses she had bought into the wash house and began to fill the brick-lined copper with water, fetching each bucketful from the well just beyond the yard. The clothing she had bought had not been purchased from any ladies' outfitters but from the town's pawnshop.

Thoughts of the pretty pale lavender gown crept into her mind but were quickly forced aside. How dare he treat her like that! She might be no more than a ragged arsed miner's daughter, but she would not become one who was beholden to him.

He had bought the gown out of anger. Rachel filled the bucket, once more carrying it into the wash house and emptying it into the copper. He had been angry at the way that shopkeeper had spoken to her, but why should it be of any consequence to him?

Taking a knife and a bar of soap from a shelf on the wall, she began to peel thin slices from it, dropping each yellow flake into the copper, watching it float on the surface like petals pulled from a flower.

Like the buttercup she had held to William's throat. He had walked home beside her, his very silence shouting a question. She had tried to ignore the slight tension that had intruded on their friendship; to pretend, even to herself, that Jared Lytton's speaking to her had been a casual event, merely a man helping a woman from the path of a loaded cart. But she had known that was not the truth.

The water beginning to heat from the wood fire she had lit beneath the boiler, she replaced the soap and knife on the shelf then reached for a wooden stick which stood in a round wicker basket, one end of it bleached white from years of stirring hot soapy water.

Jared Lytton's meeting with her in Bloomfield had not been purely accidental, she felt that as deeply as if he had told her so. She stirred the water, watching the slivers of soap float and circle in the water like dancers on a stage. He had marched up to her as if he had been looking for her, taking her arm as though they had been together the whole afternoon. But why? The question had plagued her half the night. Rachel closed her eyes then opened them quickly as an image of that strong, handsome face rose again in her mind.

He had climbed into his carriage, anger darkening his face as his glance had swept William, and she had felt her spine tingle as they had walked away, the feeling of being watched almost making her steps falter.

And William? Rachel sorted the laundry into small separate heaps of personal and household linen. William had stayed locked in the silence he had long since wrapped around himself, but looking up, catching his glance, she had seen a curiosity in his intensely blue eyes, a curiosity tinged with something she could only call sadness.

The water in the copper beginning to steam, Rachel scooped several buckets into the large wooden dolly tub, then dropped bed sheets and pillow cases into the soap-clouded depths, poking them beneath the surface with the stick. She refilled the copper with several buckets more from the well.

She had tried passing off the whole incident with Jared. Tried to recapture the happy atmosphere that had accompanied their walk to the town. Rachel fetched several buckets more of water from the well, her arms aching as she refilled the boiler. But something had gone out of the afternoon. The shadow of Jared Lytton seemed to walk between them.

Lifting the heavy wooden maid into the tub, she began to pound the soaking sheets. She had picked another of the golden buttercups, intending to tell William only of her brother, but in the end she had told him everything: of the accident, of her being accused of murder, of Isaiah Bedworth's attempt to lure her into his bed, only holding back Hannah's dislike of her. Then she had told him about going to Tipton Green, tears stinging her eyes as she spoke of Bart, voice dropping to a whisper as she spoke of Samuel Potter. But she had told him all, as she had told Beulah that second morning when she had offered another day's work; and with the telling William had taken her hand in his, and she had left it there.

That was a month ago. Now, holding the wooden stick in both hands, she lifted a sheet, dragging it over the edge of the dolly tub into the bucket, hands smarting from the splashes of boiling suds as she tipped the sheet into the bubbling copper. A month in which William's smiles had become wider and more prolonged but in which he had not spoken once. A month in which the scowling face of Jared Lytton had not faded one iota from her mind.

When the sheets, together with the rest of the white wash were pegged to the clothes line strung across the bottom of the yard, Rachel dropped into the tub the maroon skirt she had bought for half a crown. It had been more than she wanted to pay, but the pawnbroker had pointed out that it was serviceable and still had years of wear left in it. In the end she bought it, together with two blouses, four cotton petticoats and four pairs of good hard-wearing bloomers.

She lifted the heavy maid, the muscles of her shoulders and back screaming their protest as she began to pound it up and down on the skirt. Beulah had admonished her for not buying herself new clothing, waving aside Rachel's reply that seven shillings was enough of a debt to be under, but the smile that had crept into the older woman's face had said she was not truly displeased.

'Forgive me, but I could find no one at home in either of the houses.'

Rachel dropped the maid, blinking as the sudden movement sent splashes of soapy water into her face.

'I did knock but it appeared no one heard . . . or at least replied.'

Rachel spun around, eyes widening at the sound of a voice too well remembered.

'Mrs Thomas is not well,' she answered, brushing a strand of sweat-soaked hair from her brow. 'She . . . she is resting upstairs.'

'I am sorry to hear that.' Jared Lytton's glance swept the steamy wash house before coming back to her. 'Perhaps you will be kind enough to give her my best wishes for a speedy return to health?'

'Yes, I . . . I will.' Rachel dried her hands on the rough apron tied about her waist, trying all the time to keep her eyes from his face. 'William is up in the fields. If you will wait in the house, I will get him for you.'

'I have not come to see him or his mother.'

Suddenly Jared's temper seemed to erupt and he slammed the riding crop he carried hard down on the edge of the tub.

'Good God, look at you, girl,' he almost shouted. 'You're half dead with weariness, and look at this place!' He threw another glance around the wash house, frowning at the smell of must and damp mixed with steam. 'What in heaven's name do you think you are doing, living in a place like this! Haven't I told you there is a place for you at Foxley? You can have a position there that won't require you to break your back over a laundry tub.'

Lifting a hand, Rachel brushed again at her hair then hastily lowered it as she saw his eyes harden further as he saw the redness of her skin. 'You did tell me I could have a position at Foxley, Mr Lytton,' she answered quietly, though every nerve was racing. 'But while I am grateful for that offer, I prefer to remain here.'

'But why?' he exploded. 'Only a fool would stay here.'

Feeling the ache in her back again, Rachel stiffened. 'Then I am a fool, Mr Lytton. A fool who, if she must be indebted to another person, would rather that person were not you.'

She did not need to glance at the crop to see it rise from his palm. His swift intake of breath told her his reaction.

'So, you will not accept my offer.' The words were heavy as stones. 'Then what offer have you accepted, Miss Cade? It won't be just board and lodging. But perhaps that is not the whole of what you want here? Perhaps you have set your sights higher – perhaps it is the house and all that goes with it you want? Is it marriage you are after? Are you going to marry this . . . this Billy Duckegg?'

Rachel felt her lips tighten and her fingers curl into her palms. Why must Jared continually torment her, and what drove him to insult another man?

'No, Mr Lytton,' she replied, her own quiet dignity countering the blaze in his deep brown eyes. 'I am not going to marry Billy Duckegg – I am going to marry William Thomas.'

The rain had fallen monotonously for almost a week. Tansy stared at it through the window, watching it bounce muddy drops before settling on the road, adding themselves to the slowly mounting tide that threatened to drown it. They had sat indoors for days, talking, knitting, preparing food, until the talk had died away and the food was almost gone.

'Rain won't stop the rent man.' She turned to Cora, bent over the fireplace, adding the last tiny pieces of coal to a fire so low in the grate it gave no heat. 'Sam Potter will be wanting his money. That one don't give no mind to where his pound of flesh comes from, just so long as he gets it.'

'But we can't pick the banks in this.' Cora dropped the

coal tongs in the hearth, dusting her hands down her sides, leaving a dusty mark on her apron.

'It's either pick the bank or pick up the clap from lying underneath a customer from over Maddie's place,' Tansy turned to face the other woman. 'And I know which I'd rather do. And one or the other *has* to be done if we are to have another meal and keep a roof above our heads.'

'But will the banks be safe with all this rain, Tansy?' Ellen asked anxiously.

'Can't be no tellin' as to that.' She shrugged. 'They don't be among the safest of places at the best of times, and after all this rain . . .'

'Well, ain't nobody forcing you to go, Cora, nor you, Ellen.' Tansy fetched a bucket and sack from the scullery. 'But we can't do without food and I ain't about to earn it any other way.'

'I'll come with you.'

'No, Ellen, you stay here, wench.' Cora held Ellen's arm. 'I'll go. I can still pick twice as much as you in half the time.' She smiled, reaching for her shawl from the nail hammered into the door. 'You make up that last bit of shin into a broth against our coming back. We'll both be glad of something hot to eat.'

Ellen watched them go, shawls pulled tight over heads bent against the rain, then turned to set about the making of a meal. Bringing the handful of potatoes and the two onions, all that remained of the vegetables stored in the scullery, she shivered as she set them down on the kitchen table. The room was cold but the goose pimples that rose on her arms were not caused by cold but by fear. She glanced at the door that gave on to the street. She hated being alone in this house, alone with the terrible memory of a boy's broken body, alone with the memory of rape, terrified that Samuel Potter might call again.

Taking the pan of stewed shin from the hook that held it above the meagre fire, she settled it directly on the coals.

They might just last long enough to cook a broth. Peeling and dicing each vegetable, spinning out her movements into a slow, deliberate, overlong process, she tried to force herself not to listen to every sound from the street, but her nerves jolted with every rumble of a wheel, every tap of hurrying feet.

Carrying the colander to the sink in the scullery, she rinsed the vegetables. Surely Tansy and Cora would not stay long at the spoil heap? They would pick only enough to keep a fire in the grate then they would come home; tomorrow the rain would have stopped and they could all work the heaps together. Tansy would realise they had at least one more meal, and Samuel Potter would not brave this weather in order to collect his rent. No, he would not come today. Samuel Potter would not undergo a drenching for three shillings.

Ellen shook the colander, draining the last few drops of water from the vegetables before carrying them back into the kitchen. He would not come today, she told herself – then screamed as a knock sounded on the door.

'If you be in there, you best come quick, wench!'

Ellen heard herself sob at the sound of a woman's voice.

'It be the bank . . . you best come.'

Ellen stood for a moment, relief flooding through her. Whoever it was banging on the door it was not Samuel Potter.

'Be you in there?' the voice shouted again, its tone high and urgent, the sound of a fist loud against the door. 'It be the pit bank!'

The pit bank! Only with the last frantic thump on the door did the words register in Ellen's understanding. Something was wrong, something at the spoil heaps.

Her fingers fumbling now with a fear as terrifying as the one that had only just drained from her, she pulled open the door.

'It be the pit banks!' Rain dripping from the ends of her shawl and the hem of her dark skirts, the woman standing on the doorstep pointed away up the street. 'They be shifting.'

'Shifting?' Ellen stared into a face drawn tight with anxiety.

'Ar, wench, shifting. If you 'ave anybody up there, you best move quick.'

'How do you mean, shifting?' Ellen's question was lost in the rain. The woman was already clattering away, her boots ringing in a suddenly empty street.

'*If you have anybody up there . . .*' The words echoed in her head. Tansy and Cora were out there on the pit bank. But which one? Snatching her shawl, leaving the door swinging on its hinges, she raced after the woman.

Reaching a place she knew to be a favourite of Tansy's, Ellen stared about her in horror. Where only days ago there had been a huge mound of pit waste, a hill of dust and coal chips compacted beneath its own weight, there was now a sea of grey, heaving mud.

'Tansy?' It was a whisper, barely clearing Ellen's lips as she stared disbelievingly at the sight that stretched away to either side of her. 'Tansy . . . Cora?'

'Did you have folks on the bank?'

Another woman spoke but Ellen, eyes glued to the expanse of mud, made no response.

'Come away, wench.' The woman put an arm about her as men from the nearby Solomon mine came running up, picks and shovels in their hands. 'We be in the way.'

But Ellen stood, staring at the gelatinous grey mass that had bled into a field of black-pitted slime.

'Was anybody picking on this heap?' one of the miners asked, pitching his voice against a rising wind.

'There were a few women out today,' the one who had fetched Ellen, called in answer.

'How many, do you know?' The man turned to look at the viscous stretch as the woman shook her head.

'Don't go trying to stand on that! It won't take your weight, it'll swallow you down afore you have a chance.'

The warning from a fellow miner halted the man's rush forward but not until both legs had sunk into the thick sludge, sucking him in to his knees.

'You should have more sense even than to try!' It took three men to drag him clear of the mud that seemed to turn into a live creature, dragging at them, trying to suck them into itself, lifting grey encompassing arms, drawing them into its eternal caress.

'He . . . he's right.' A second man sank to his haunches, drawing in breath in noisy draughts. 'It ain't the first time the heaps have slipped. You know it's a daft thing to try to get on them once the rain's got inside.'

'Ar, I do know, but there probably be women under there.'

'Ain't nothing we can do, Charlie.' The man sitting on his haunches shook his head, sending a row of glistening raindrops spinning from the peak of his flat cap. 'Ain't nothing anybody can do.'

'Black bastard! The bloody black bastard!' The man addressed as Charlie shouted his frustration as he swung his shovel, sending it hurtling up the oozing slope.

'C'mon, wench.' Her arm still about Ellen's shoulders, the woman tried to turn her away as the miners began to leave.

'Tansy!' Ellen whispered.

'Hey up, it's coming again!'

One of the departing men had turned to look at the fallen mountain that once had been the entrails of the earth.

Dropping her hand to Ellen's wrist, the woman ran, dragging the bemused girl with her, beyond the reach of the encroaching mud.

'You must have set it off, chucking your shovel!'

Across the street a carriage halted, its occupant watching with the small crowd that had gathered, men and women who despite the rain stood and witnessed the glutinous slide.

Halfway up the mud bubbled, belching and spewing

out fresh waves of pit waste turned to grey cream by the rain.

'Tansy . . .'

'Keep that woman back!' The shout rang out above the wind, but Ellen had already reached the edge of the rapidly spreading slime.

'Tansy,' she whispered again as she bent to pick up a brass-studded clog which the mud carried to her feet.

'I'll get you out.' Ellen dropped the mud-filled shoe. 'You'll be all right, both of you. I'll get you . . . I'll get you!'

'Hold her! Hang on to her, for Christ's sake!'

Shouting and running at the same time, the men raced forward but Ellen was already being sucked into the wet, grey maw of the mud.

'Get her feet!'

Throwing himself flat at the edge of the spreading waste, one of them grabbed her ankle.

'Get the other one!' he called as another man dropped beside him. 'Pull . . . for Christ's sake . . . pull!'

Together they heaved, fighting the strength of the mud, robbing it of its prize.

'Get her home, missis. Ain't nobody alive in that lot.' Handing Ellen to the woman who had stood with her, the men wiped their sleeves across their faces, smearing spots of mud into grey, tattooing stripes.

'No!' Reality breaking in on her, her screams echoing over the black slopes, Ellen sank to her knees. 'No, not again! Please God, not again! Don't take them away like you took Bart. Not them as well, please . . . please!'

'I'll take her, missis.' The one called Charlie lifted Ellen gently to her feet, his arm supporting her as he guided her across the street.

Caked head to foot in clinging mud, oozing tendrils of slime slipping from her hair and sliding down her face, Ellen struggled to turn back.

'Please,' she cried, lifting her face to the carriage as they passed. But there was no answer. The face of her father turned away from her.

Why had Jared come here today? Rachel sat in the small kitchen of the cottage that Beulah had said could be her home. He had given no reason, unless his outburst about her living here had been the reason. But why should it be . . . what difference could it possibly make to him where she lived? He had made her the offer of a place in his household and she had refused. Why could he not let the matter rest there?

'Only a fool would stay here!' The words were blazoned across her mind. Well, Jared Lytton was right, she would be a fool to stay, but he was right for the wrong reason.

She glanced slowly around the little room, so comfortable with the pretty chintz curtains Beulah had saved against her son's taking of this house; at the china ornaments on the mantelpiece flanking a quietly ticking clock; a brass oil lamp, its pretty blue glass shade spreading a gentle glow that mixed with the firelight dancing across the colourful pegged rug on the hearth.

Jared Lytton was wrong if he had thought her ill suited to this place. She had been happy here and could have gone on being happy, but now that chance had gone.

Pushing herself up from the chair, she made to fetch the bucket of sleck, the fine coal dust William had mixed into a stiff paste with water and left outside the scullery door. Then, changing her mind, she lit a candle from the mantel and turned out the lamp. There was no need to bank the fire, to hold its life until morning. Tomorrow she should leave.

She had to leave. Dressed in a nightgown Beulah had given her, Rachel stood at the window of her bedroom. A short distance away the water of the canal gleamed like a silver ribbon in the moonlight. She could have been happy, if only he had not come, if only he had not driven her to give that answer.

He had looked so angry . . . Rachel leaned her head against the cool glass, her mind showing her once more the picture it had continued to throw at her all that day; the picture of a man dressed in a tan-coloured coat, fawn breeches tucked into leather boots, shirt carelessly open at the neck. A man whose tall frame was taut with fury.

Rachel closed her eyes, trying to wipe away the memory, but it stayed with her. His eyes glowing like polished bronze, mouth curving with sarcasm as it asked again, 'Is it marriage you are after? Are you going to marry this . . . this Billy Duckegg?'

Rachel groaned at the memory of her answer. It had been such a stupid thing to say, yet she had said almost the same thing to the landlady of the Fox Inn. She had been angry then as she had been this morning, angry at the name given to William, and that anger had lost her this home.

She had told Jared Lytton she was to marry William. Suppose what she had said were to reach his ears or those of his mother? They would think she had planned such a thing from the outset, that she had pushed herself into their lives merely to find herself a husband.

'But I didn't, I didn't!' Her cry was soft but the sound seemed to crash against the silence around her.

Turning from the window, she went to the bed, pulling down its heavy white cover.

She could not face seeing the disappointment in Beulah's face at having her kindness repaid in such a way, even if there was no truth to the belief.

Slipping between the sheets, she blew out the candle. Rachel lay back on the white pillows and stared into the velvet blackness.

Why had Jared Lytton called at the house? The question which had no answer circled in her brain. He had not wanted to speak to Beulah or to William, which left only herself. Yet apart from offering her a post at Foxley, then asking if it was her intention to marry William, he had said nothing . . . asked her nothing. Yet there must have been some other purpose to his visit. He would not have come out of his way only to enquire of her marriage plans.

Yet that was all he had asked her. Through the window the leaves of an apple tree traced patterns in the moonlight.

Tomorrow she would leave, try to find some other place to live, a place where she would not be found. She would slip away quietly, not wanting to face the questions that she knew would pour from Beulah's tongue, or the silent ones in William's eyes. She would go before either of them was awake for she would not have the courage to tell them her reason, and once gone would pray that gossip would not reach them.

Rachel closed her eyes but in the darkness that handsome face stared at her.

Jared Lytton. He had saved her life only to destroy it.

Chapter Thirteen

Taking the clothes that Beulah had loaned her money to buy, Rachel wrapped them in her shawl, knotting the ends together. Outdoors it would be cool as yet. She glanced through her bedroom window at a sky splashed red-gold by the newly risen sun. It would be cold without her shawl but she had to take the change of underwear with her; she would not be indebted to someone else in order to stay clean. Seven shillings . . . She glanced around the bedroom with its wash stand in one corner and a dressing chest with its own mirror on the far wall. It was not luxury but it had become home; and now she must leave, go before William and his mother were awake. She must leave without saying goodbye, without thanking Beulah one more time for her kindness in giving her a place here. But she would not forget. Taking the bundle of clothes in her arms, Rachel walked down the stairs and out of the cottage. She would not forget anything, and somehow she would repay that seven shillings.

The air of early morning was crisp, cutting into her lungs with the sharpness of a knife. Rachel shivered, feeling the heavy dew seep through the worn soles of her boots, then suddenly she wanted to laugh. She had stared at a beautiful gown, wanting if only for a moment to know how its delicate softness would feel against her skin, she had wanted a gown that dreams were made of – when all the time her feet were almost bare against the ground!

From beyond the fence that bordered the tiny patch alive with the colour of summer flowers and already heady with their scent, she glanced at Beulah's cottage. No drift of smoke from the chimney indicated that the fire had been revived, no movement told of its occupants being awake yet. The amusement she had felt a moment ago, when she had wanted to laugh at her own foolish frivolity, died in her, to be replaced by a new feeling: one of self-reproach for leaving without finding the courage to say why.

If only she had kept her temper when Jared Lytton had made that accusation, if only she had kept her tongue between her teeth, if only . . . She turned away, her steps leading her towards the bridge that spanned the glittering band of the canal, away from Beulah and William, away from Jared Lytton.

A few steps from the bridge she stopped, fingers digging deep into the soft cloth of her bundle, breath catching in her throat as a figure stepped from behind the jutting angle of brickwork.

Bathed in a background of brilliant sunshine, the face remained hidden but the outline showed a tall, broad-shouldered figure, hair turned to brazen copper where the sun's touch reached it.

Every nerve in her body jangling, Rachel felt a sting of pain as her fingernails pressed against her palms. She could make a run for Beulah's cottage but she would not reach it before being overtaken by those long legs; she could scream but would either William or his mother hear?

Against the sun the figure stepped towards her, a dark, menacing silhouette crowned with fire. Another yard and he would be able to reach out, able to fasten strong hands about her arms, able to . . .

'No!' Rachel half gasped, half screamed as a picture of Isaiah Bedworth flashed into her mind. Dropping the shawl with its contents, she began to run. Skirts flapping against her ankles, she made for the heath, heedless of the bite of stones piercing the last vestiges of leather that held her boots together, wanting only to get away from the man whose heavy tread brought the sound and threat of him nearer with every step.

'No . . . please, no!' Her scream as his hand caught her, the weight of him dragging her to the damp ground, startled a meadow pipit, its shrill protesting cry echoing loud on the silent morning as it rose into the air.

'Get away . . . don't touch me . . . don't touch me!'

The man's arms fastened about her, holding her own close to her sides, and Rachel felt the weight of him press down on her, pushing her further back into the dew-soaked grass.

'I . . . I . . . It . . .' Above her the voice was surprisingly soft, struggling with words that seemed to stick to the tongue. 'It's . . . all . . . all right.'

Easing his weight away, but his hands retaining their strong grip, he turned her over so she could see his face.

'William!' Relief robbing her of every ounce of strength, Rachel slumped against the man who had so frightened her. 'William, I thought . . . I thought . . .'

'D . . . don't s . . . say it.' He touched a hand to the back of her head, holding it gently against his chest. 'N . . . never . . . think that. I w . . . would never hurt you.'

'I couldn't see against the sun,' Rachel sobbed. 'I did not realise it was you, William, I never expected you. I'm sorry. I thought . . . I was so terrified.'

'I . . . it was my fault.' Releasing his hold on her, William stood up, stretching out a hand to help her to her feet. 'I sh . . . shouldn't have stood th . . . there.'

'But why were you standing beneath the bridge?' Glancing across to the cottage, Rachel looked again for the tracery of smoke that followed the banked down fire being fed with coals. It was the first task every morning, but it had not been done today. Her eyes swept back to William. 'You haven't been there all night?'

'But why?' she continued as he nodded. 'Why on earth stay out the whole night?'

'I th . . . thought y . . . you would go.' His face reddening with embarrassment, William fought against the bonds that held his tongue.

'You mean, you stayed there, beneath the bridge, waiting in case I left during the night?'

He nodded again.

'Oh, William!' Rachel felt her throat thicken. 'You should not have done that.'

'I h . . . had to. I d . . . don't want you to l . . . leave. I he . . . heard what you said to Lytton, and I know you didn't mean it. I g . . . guessed you w . . . wouldn't be able to face up to it, th . . . that you would run away, so I w . . . waited for you. D . . . don't go, please. It doen't m . . . matter what you said. I kn . . . know it was only sp . . . spoken in anger. It m . . . makes no difference.'

Rachel listened to the words being forced laboriously from his lips, realising now why he had never spoken to her before. This was the infirmity of the tongue Beulah had spoken of, the reason the children of Foxley village laughed and tormented him until he ran from them, the reason his father had beaten him almost daily.

'I felt so awful after I had said it.' Pushing away from him she smiled into his eyes. She would not comment that this was the first time he had spoken to her, or that his impediment made not the slightest difference to the warm feelings she held for him. William was a friend and it would take more than a stutter to turn her from him. 'It was such a stupid thing to have said, and I didn't want your mother thinking I had come here with any such plans in mind. If I leave then she will know I speak the truth, and so will you, William.'

'But there is no c . . . call for you to leave. My mother won't ever hear it from me, and I d . . . don't care. Mother needs help, and she trusts you. Say you will stay, p . . . please, Rachel.'

His stutter was decidedly less pronounced when he spoke of his mother, Rachel thought, watching the embarrassment in his strikingly blue eyes change to a softness that told of the love and trust that existed between them. It was true, Beulah did need another pair of hands about the place; Rachel had noticed how often the woman's face blanched with a pain she would not own to, a pain that had forced her to take to her bed yesterday even though she declared it was only tiredness and that it would soon pass: but it had not passed and Rachel had carried the full burden of the dairy, the livestock, the brew house and the weekly laundry as well as making meals and caring for the sick woman.

Would Beulah see that as her reason for leaving? Would she believe Rachel thought the work of the house too much in exchange for her food and lodging? Her insides curled at the thought. But it was the first time that everything had been left to her, for William was busy with the crops, and if she persisted in being too cowardly to tell the woman the truth, what else was she to think?

Watching her face, the tell-tale play of her emotions visible upon it, William turned away, his shoulders slightly less square than a moment before, and walked over to where her bundle of clothes lay in the short grass of the heath.

'I . . . I'm sorry you can't stay, Rachel.' There was no smile in his eyes as he handed her the bundle, no criticism and no condemnation, just the same softness as when he had spoken of his mother, a softness that was tinged with sadness. 'Don't you w . . . worry any. I will tell Mother you had to go.'

He hardly faltered at all. Rachel felt a wave of pleasure sweep through her. He could talk to her as he must talk to his mother, the restriction almost gone from his tongue. Was it because he trusted her? Did William trust her as he trusted his mother? So much so he could talk with almost no stutter; apart from Beulah she could be the only person to whom he could talk freely, and now she was leaving.

Rachel glanced at his strong face. This man had known

nothing but ridicule and torment all his life; he had run from the children of the village and from his father; in all his years he had trusted himself to speak only with his mother . . . until now. Now he had trusted her, risked being laughed at yet again, and she was turning her back on him.

But I am not rejecting his trust! Rachel's eyes fell before the look in William's as her mind added the thought; but she was rejecting his word. He had said Beulah would not hear of her exchange with Jared Lytton from him, by running away she was throwing the words in his face.

But what else could she do? She could not stay. Supposing Jared Lytton were to come here again, suppose he were to accuse her in front of Beulah?

No, she could no longer stay here. There was nothing to be gained from staying; it would only turn every day into a nightmare of worry and waiting; waiting for that tall figure to turn up once more on her doorstep, worry of what he would say and the effect of it upon her friendship with Beulah.

But if there was nothing to be gained by staying, what was to be gained by her leaving without a word to a woman who had befriended her, found her a home and a way of earning her keep? Regret was all that running off in secret would bring her. Regret that she had not had the courage to face Beulah.

'Never run from responsibility.' That was something her father had taught her from a child. Face up to what you know must be done and do it.

Glancing again at the man watching her, she smiled.

'Your mother will not need to ask you why I left, William,' she said, clutching her bundle of clothes and walking towards the cottage that had been given over to her use. 'I will tell her myself.'

The girl worked hard, there was no doubt of that. Beulah sat in the tiny flower-filled space that had been her garden for almost thirty years, a colander half-filled with peas she was shelling.

Beulah smiled now, watching the two of them in the distant field, one cutting the tall golden stalks of barley with sweeping strokes of a scythe that glinted in the afternoon light; the other, her hair a glowing halo that echoed the brightness of the sun, following on behind, binding the barley into sheaves and stacking the stooks into tiny pyramids.

Beulah's hands rested on the colander. The girl's face had burned bright red as she had told of her exchange of words with Jared Lytton, embarrassment causing her to falter, but she had gone on, made a clean breast of what she saw as a confession of guilt, a betrayal of trust.

Betrayal! Beulah's tired eyes followed the movements of the slim figure. If only the girl knew! But she did not know. She had shown a courage Beulah herself did not have. She had spoken what was in her mind while Beulah had kept her own secret locked inside her, a secret she had spoken of to no one, not even her son; a dream she had held since his childhood when she had watched him run from the teasing of the villagers, run from the beatings his own father had regularly given him, watched him become more and more withdrawn, more and more distrustful of his own ability to speak. But Beulah had dreamed that one day a woman would come, one he would trust as he trusted his mother, one who would see beyond the impediment, one who would see the man.

And that girl had come, out of the blue, one afternoon. And Beulah had known then, had known immediately, this was the one who would fulfil her dream.

Now the time for secrecy was past. She raised a hand to the distant figure who paused in his scything to glance towards the cottage. She would speak of her hopes, of her longing, she would tell them of her wish that they should marry.

Heaving herself to her feet, she blanched with the pain that stabbed her chest, causing her to grasp the back of the chair, gasping as she leaned her weight against it. It came more regularly now, a pain that held her body as though in a vice, squeezing the breath from her lungs until her head swam and the whole of her seemed to hang in a black, pain-filled void.

It would be soon now. She must settle things for William. He would not speak for himself, not because of the failing of his tongue but because of shyness. Her son was a man any woman of sense would be proud to call husband, but he had spent so many years as the butt of other people's jokes he no longer saw his own virtues. Left to himself, his life would be even sadder and emptier once she was gone than it had been up to now, and God knew it had been sad enough.

The dizziness subsiding, Beulah carried the colander she was still clutching into the shadowed kitchen. There had been little happiness here. She had come to her husband as a girl of sixteen, with joy in her eyes and love in her heart, but both had died beneath the grinding burden of work that left her so tired each night she was hardly aware of him as he rode her like an animal. Then had come her son, and with him her husband's violent outbursts of temper.

Tipping the freshly shelled peas into the pot bubbling over the fire, Beulah laid the colander aside.

At first she had accepted that the beatings were the result of a father's natural desire for his son to speak well and to stand up to those who taunted or bullied him. But with the passing of the years she had come to see the actions in their true light, see the beatings for what they really were: the true bully was her husband. He beat his own child for one reason – the boy could not strike back. Joseph Thomas vented his spite on his own son, taking out on William the shame he had always felt for his own short stature. Joseph had felt that badly, keeping himself away from the village whenever he could though never allowing Beulah to go there alone, jealousy and insecurity driving him into a rage if another man so much as glanced at her.

And as William grew so did his father's rages, often leaving the boy blackened with bruises; they had cried so many times together, Beulah and her son, as she had bathed the weals left by Joseph's belt with a solution of witch hazel, and she had known that one day the father would kill the son.

Which was why she had killed her husband.

Taking a fork from the table, she pressed the prongs into a pot of boiled potatoes she had placed to one side of the fire, nodding to herself as she felt their softness.

William had been a little over eight years old. He had come home from school with a torn shirt and blood on his face. His father had come from the fields to repair the scythe in the workshop behind the brew house and had caught sight of the child before Beulah had the chance to whisk him away and clean him up. Joseph's temper, only ever just beneath the surface, had boiled over as quickly as milk on a fire and he had grabbed the boy with one hand, releasing his heavy-buckled leather belt with the other.

Beulah laid the fork back on the table, her son's screams filling her ears now as they had done all those years ago. She had tried to pull him free and had caught a swinging blow from that buckle across her shoulders. Joseph had beaten the child almost to unconsciousness before finally turning away, knocking her sideways as she made to pick up her son. Fastening the belt about his waist, he had ordered her to bring a new handle for the scythe, saying there was one in the loft of the workshop.

Eyes lifting, Beulah let them travel beyond the open kitchen door to where her son worked those same fields. Strange how only now she remembered she had not cried. No tears lay on her cheeks as she climbed that ladder to the loft; no regret was in her heart as she grasped the heavy wooden stave she knew was a scythe handle. There was only cold resolution in her mind as she called out to her husband that she could find no handle.

He had climbed that steep wooden ladder to the loft, abuse loud on his tongue, and she had waited. Standing to one side of the topmost tread, where the shadows were deepest, she had waited, breathing calmly and evenly as he came.

'Wheer the bloody hell be you looking, woman?' It had been almost a scream, the temper still a fever in his blood, rising again to the surface.

'I'm here, Joseph.' Her reply had been spoken quietly as she had swung the heavy handle, hitting him with all the force of her body on the back of the head then quickly swinging the handle again across the front of him, sending him crashing backwards from the loft to the floor below.

Afterwards she had burned the handle in this same fire-place. Beulah turned her glance to the coals glowing beneath the bubbling pot. Then she had washed the blood from her son and changed his torn clothing before scribbling a note and sending him with it to the doctor in Bloomfield.

There had been commiserations for her from the villagers but no indication of blame. No one had accused her; it was an accident, a fall, they said, it could have happened to any one of them. And she had not denied their suppositions. Joseph Thomas had got what he deserved, and if she burned in hell for all eternity for paying him his dues then she would still have no regrets.

Rachel trailed the wet flannel over her body, willing the cool water to soothe joints that screamed with tiredness. Every part of her ached. Never, even after a day of picking coals from the pit banks, had she felt so utterly weary. How could she go on like this . . . how long could she continue to do the work of the house, the dairy and the brew house, then help with harvesting the barley? But she had to go on. Beulah and William depended on her.

William! She pressed the wet flannel against her face, shedding tears of tiredness into its dampness. But were her tears only those of weariness or were they due to that other reason? One that lurked deep in her soul, hiding its truth from her mind; a reason that refused to be recognised yet whose presence filled her waking hours; a truth she knew concerned her feelings for Beulah's son, yet at the same time evaded her understanding.

Slipping her cotton nightgown over her damp body, she emptied the basin of soapy water into the bucket housed beneath the small wash stand, then taking up her hairbrush, began to brush the silken folds of her hair released from its pins.

William, she thought again. His eyes had held such a deep message as Beulah had spoken of her desire that they should wed. A message that spoke of his feelings for her but at the same time seemed to say she need feel under no obligation to agree.

He had been so kind to her. Braiding her hair with a slip of ribbon, Rachel climbed into the large double bed: one she would soon be sharing with William. His eyes told her she need not say yes unless she felt love for him, and she did love him, but was it the sort of love a woman should have for her husband?

Turning off the oil lamp that burned beside the bed, she lay staring at the window, yellowed by a high sailing moon. Tiredness throbbed in every bone but sleep refused to answer her pleas for release.

Beulah had asked if there was anyone else in Rachel's life whom she wished to marry. When Rachel said no, she had nodded. She had then gone on to say that there were worse things in life than being here, and Rachel might look long and hard and still not find a man who would hold her in the esteem in which William did. She had not mentioned love, and neither had he. Beulah had said they worked well together, that they each held a liking for the other, and that was a sound enough basis for making a life together. William would treat her well, and Rachel would have a good home.

She watched the shadows fade from the walls as cloud swallowed the moon. William would treat her well, of that she had no fear, so what was this doubt in her mind? Where was the singing joy she had always expected to feel before she was to be married?

She had thought at first that Beulah had come to learn of her conversation with Jared Lytton, learned of her saying she was to become William's wife, but Beulah had made no reference to it, speaking only of the happiness it would bring her to see Rachel and her son become man and wife.

And perhaps she would be happy as William's wife? He was kind and gentle, had treated her well ever since her arrival at his mother's house. To him she was no ragged-arsed miner's daughter.

Beyond the window the moon suddenly floated free from its mantle of cloud. But it was not this radiance that suddenly cleared her mind. It was not the light from the window that washed away the fog of doubt.

A ragged-arsed miner's daughter!

Etched against the sudden illumination of her mind, Rachel saw the proud handsome face, the brilliant copper-coloured eyes staring angrily into her own. And now she understood the reason she had felt no wild happiness on agreeing to marry William. That reason was Jared Lytton . . . she was in love with him.

But how could she be?

Rachel questioned her own sanity. How could she be in love with a man she hardly knew? A man she had only spoken to on two or three occasions. True he had shown her kindness. She stared at the ceiling, the ache in her limbs forgotten. He had saved her from the gallows that day in the courtroom in Horseley and he had taken her to the Fox Inn after finding her alone on the heath, even paying for her to stay there several weeks; he had also bought her that dress when he had come across her in Bloomfield. But on each occasion he had shown scant respect for her and certainly no trace of anything that could be seen as deeper feeling. How then could she possibly be in love with him?

And what of William, what of her life with him? Just a few hours ago she had agreed to become his wife, to join her life to his in a tie only death could break. But what of the bond that held her heart . . . what of the feelings she held for Jared Lytton?

Rachel watched the shadows on the walls, watched them flicker and change in tune with her racing thoughts. She had given her word to William, given her promise to a man who would honour and love her, who would respect her as a woman as well as a wife.

'You w . . . will be safe with me.' William's words to her as he stood with her at the gate to her cottage returned to her mind.

'I . . . I could never hurt you, Rachel.'

He had looked at her with such gentleness as he had said those words, with such deep feeling colouring his tone, and for one brief moment his hand had rested on hers.

No, William would never hurt her. Rachel closed her eyes but as sleep finally came it was not his face it brought with it but one that smiled cynically. And 'I could never hurt you' were not the words that followed her into oblivion but the brutal taunt: 'I would not choose a ragged-arsed miner's daughter!'

Chapter Fourteen

'Seems that wench you brought here has landed on her feet all right.'

Jared Lytton took a tankard of ale from the landlord of the Fox Inn, placing it on a table as he listened to the man talk.

'Her was along here yesterday with butter and cheese and a dozen or so of them duck eggs.'

Taking the cloth that was tucked into the waistband of the apron that reached to his feet he wiped it across the wooden surface of the table.

'They be tasty an' all, them eggs. That lad of Widow Thomas has kept ducks ever since bein' a little 'un, sold the eggs to help his mother in the keeping of 'em both, so I suppose he can't be all daft.'

'Daft?' Jared Lytton lifted the tankard, taking a long pull at the creamy-topped liquid before replacing it.

'Oh, ar.' The landlord settled to a gossip. 'Everybody knows that one be weak-minded, like as much knocked that way by his father. He used to near enough beat the daylights out of the kid every day.'

'For what reason?' Taking a thin cigar from a case he drew from his pocket, Jared lit one end then blew out a thin stream of smoke.

'The wife always reckoned Joe Thomas beat the lad 'cos of the way his tongue were tied, couldn't put two words together, but I hold me doubts as to that. More like he knocked hell's eyes out of the kid 'cos of his own shortcomings.'

'And what were those?'

The landlord settled his weight more squarely on his feet, obviously willing to talk for as long as Jared was willing to listen.

'Joe Thomas were no more than five foot. Stood no taller than this.' The landlord held a hand level with his own shoulder. 'Resented that did Joe, always accused us other lads of poking fun at him, though to my recollection none of us never did. Made no difference to we, the only one it bothered were Joe, but it seemed he couldn't never forget the fact that he were littlest of the bunch and turned it into the excuse for many a fight with the rest of us. I reckon he nursed that resentment long after he married that wife of his. Do you know, Mr Lytton, I've seen him punch the stuffing out of a man just for looking at her, and then there were the lad. No wonder he were weak-minded, living with that man. I stand by what I said, it were like to be Joe Thomas's beatings that sent him that way.'

'This son . . . ?'

'William,' the landlord supplied. 'His name be William.'

'This William.' Jared blew out another stream of pale grey smoke. 'Is he still weak-minded?'

'Ar, sir.' The landlord nodded. ''Tis a pity to have to say it but I reckon as 'ow he must be. You still never hear him speak a word, not even when the kids calls after him. No, a bloke would *have* to be daft to put up with the things they says to him.'

Jared watched the drift of cigar smoke spiral towards the ceiling. The girl he had snatched from the vengeance of Isaiah Bedworth then brought here to this inn, the girl who had thrown his gift of a gown back in his face, the girl who had refused to leave his thoughts from the first moment of his meeting her, was to be married to an idiot!

But William Thomas was not an idiot. Jared retracted the thought even as it formed. The way William had looked at him that day in Bloomfield, intelligent and assessing, silently warning him not to make a nuisance of himself to Rachel, had been very revealing. There was nothing wrong with the man's mind, of that Jared felt certain.

Why then had he not spoken that day? If the fault did not lie with his mind then what was it held his tongue?

'You say the man is to be married to the girl I brought here?' He asked the question lightly to hide the sinking feeling the landlord's nod in reply brought to the pit of his stomach.

'They am that,' the landlord answered readily. 'Told the missis as much yesterday when they delivered the butter and cheese, and the lad seemed brighter than I'd ever seen him when he were taking the barrels off the wagon.'

'You mean he also delivers beer here to the inn?'

'He does that,' the landlord replied after replenishing Jared's tankard at the bar. 'Widow Thomas brews all I sell here and a drop of good brew it be an' all. Men don't mind the walk it takes to get a tankard of her ale. The lad grows the barley then takes it to be malted, up along of Tipton Green somewheres, or so I believe, and the hops he brings up from Worcester way. Maybe 'tis them gives the beer its good taste, but whatever it be, I sells all I gets.'

'It is good, we take it on my estate!' Jared drank from the tankard then stood up, flinging his half-smoked cigar into the brightly burning fire. 'And I can well see the men's liking for it. Let's hope the Widow Thomas has many more brewing years ahead of her.'

'That be food for thought as well as for concern, sir.' The landlord followed his only customer into the sunlight of midday, squinting into the brightness after the gloom of the inn. 'But there be rumours.'

'Rumours?' Jared climbed into the trap, gathering the reins in his hands.

'Ar, Mr Lytton, sir. Rumours.' The landlord took a step

nearer the carriage as though his next words were for Jared alone and must not be overheard by any other, though no one else was near. 'It be said the widow woman don't be as well as her was. The missis heard the market women across at Bloomfield talking. They said as how Widow Thomas hadn't been there with her butter and cheese for some weeks, that it was that wench her had taken in had the selling of it now. It was her went every week to market along of William, and not his mother.'

'But why should that mean she is ill?' Jared held the reins, reluctant to break off a conversation he knew he was continuing only in the hope it would bring him more news of the girl who plagued his thoughts.

'Stands to reason!' The landlord hooked his thumbs into the armholes of his waistcoat, at the same time pursing his lips. 'Leastways it do to anybody as knows the widow well. Joe Thomas's wife never let any other than herself take her dairying to market. No, not even when her eyes have been near closed from that man's fists. Her never did and never would now lessen there was summat serious that forbade her doing so. And from what my wife heard it seems her has been taken bad with pains in the chest a time or two, so much so it's been feared her might die right there in the market cross. And that don't bode good, now do it?'

'I reckon,' the man went on, not wanting or waiting for an answer to his question, 'that her not turning up to sell her butter and stuff be because her ain't well enough, and if her ain't well enough for that then 'tis my opinion her ain't much longer for the brewing neither, and when that day dawns it will be a bugger, for I know no other can brew a pint that would hold a candle to that of Widow Thomas.'

'Could the son not carry on the brewing?' Jared astonished himself by asking yet another question, and was relieved to see no surprise register in the other man when he might have wondered why his customer showed so much interest.

'Hmmph!' The landlord blew out disparagingly through pursed lips. 'I doubt he has the sense. The man's mind be weak – it takes more than he's got to brew beer. Duck eggs be all he knows, though I doubt they will prove enough to keep three of 'em on. I reckon they be in for hard times once that mother of his be past earning a living.'

'Maybe by the time that happens the girl will have taken herself off to some place else. Maybe the extra work will not agree with her.' Jared felt the unfairness of his comment, and by the swift shake of the landlord's head knew the man felt the same also; but stubbornly, feeling only a strange need to strike out, he added, 'Maybe she will find some other to take her in and feed her for nothing.'

'Widow Thomas ain't doing that, Mr Lytton.' The landlord looked at him sharply. 'By all accounts of them as passes the Thomas place every day then calls in the Fox afore going on home, that wench can always be seen working at summat or other about the place. Seems yesterday her were gathering barley into sheaves and setting the stooks to dry in the sun – that be hard graft even for a man – and the wench is never a day late in fetching the butter and stuff. Nobody seems to know owt about her 'cept that you yourself fetched her to the inn, and that her refused to stop here more than that one night despite your having paid for it. Apart from that folk know only what I've just related to you, but this they do say: the wench ain't idle. Whatever her be getting from Widow Thomas, her be paying for with her labours.'

His only answer a brief nod of the head, Jared flicked the reins. And what of the son? he thought as the trap moved off. With what was she paying the son?

'Done a fair bit o' damage by what I hears. Spread right across the street, half swallerin' the shops on the other side. The place still be a bit of a shambles, I seen that for myself.'

'When did all this happen?' Beulah Thomas looked at the bargee standing beside her garden gate. The men who worked the barges often called here for water and there was always a tankard of her beer for them on leaving.

'A couple of two or three weeks since.'

Beulah nodded. The indefinite answer did not surprise her, she was well acquainted with the strange speech of the bargemen and knew the couple of two or three weeks he spoke of could be as many months or even more.

'Where was it exactly?'

'Up the cut aways. I had a cargo of coal for the Coneygree Works. It were after I off loaded that I made for Tipton Green, and while I were waiting to go through the locks there I heard of the accident and . . .' He broke off as the tankard Rachel held out to him trembled, spilling a little of the foamy contents over his outstretched hand.

'An accident . , . at Tipton Green?' Her voice was as shaky as her hand. 'What sort of accident?'

'One as could 'ave been avoided.' The bargee took a long pull at his beer then wiped his mouth with the back of one hand. 'Didn't need no engineer bloke to tell 'em that one of them waste heaps would slip. Anybody with an ounce of what it takes could tell 'em them there pit banks was too high, that one day they would move, and when they did . . .'

'Pit banks . . . at Tipton Green?' Rachel's face was chalk white. 'Has there been some sort of accident there?'

'Some sort of accident?' The bargee drank again, relishing his brew with a noisy smack of his lips before once again wiping them on his hand. 'I'll say it were some sort – a bleedin' awful sort, beggin' your pardon for me language. Spread clear across the road. Nothing didn't stand a chance, not once it were on the move.'

'Rachel, would you fill the tankard again?' Beulah's generosity had a twofold motive, her natural hospitality now matched by a desire to give the girl a chance to recover herself. Beulah understood the reason for her fear. She had heard all about the kindness of the women who had befriended

Rachel at Tipton Green as well as her reasons for leaving that place.

'Will you rest your bones while Rachel fetches two glasses of lemonade?' Beulah pointed to a rough bench constructed of stripped branches from an overhanging elder tree, giving Rachel a little more time to pull her jangling nerves to order. That the girl must hear for herself all the man had to say she accepted, but a little time to absorb the first shock would help soften any that might yet be to come.

'The pit banks,' Rachel asked immediately Beulah had taken her glass. 'What exactly happened there?'

The man buried his top lip in the creamy foam brimming his tankard, then brushed it clear before answering. 'Well, miss, seems the rain set the spoil heaps of the Brittania mine on the move, the whole lot of 'em just sliding; come clear across the road they did, burying everything in their path, shops, houses, the lot, all buried under a mass of sludge.' He took another drink before looking at Beulah. 'Anybody could 'ave told them that pit banks that high don't be safe, but folk with money don't stand no talking to, it ain't their folk as gets hurt when the lot comes tumbling down.'

'Was anyone hurt?' Rachel asked the question but her eyes seemed to beg no answer. Huge and fear-filled, they rested on the man's weather-beaten face.

'Can't rightly say anybody was hurt.'

Rachel visibly relaxed.

'No, not rightly hurt,' he reiterated, finishing his beer. 'Folk reckon they wouldn't have felt anything. Would 'ave been all over afore they knowed what was happening.'

Her knees buckling, Rachel slumped on to the bench beside the bargee, lemonade spilling from her glass.

The pit banks at Tipton Green, those were the spoil heaps most frequently worked by Tansy and the others; and there had been an accident there.

Standing up the man laid the empty tankard on the bench where he had been sitting, nodding his thanks to Beulah as he drew his cap from the side pocket of his jacket, fixing it on his head then pulling the peak further down over his brow.

'No, it would like be as I said. Them women wouldn't have known much of what was happening to them. I've seen coal sludge move afore. It be over everything afore you have chance to bat your eyes.'

'Women!' Rachel clutched at his sleeve. 'Were there women on the bank?'

'Ar, wench, more's the pity.' He glanced down at the drawn face turned up to him. 'They must have needed the money real bad to have been on the banks in that weather. It had rained nigh on a week to my remembering. Still, God be thanked, they wouldn't have felt any pain. The sludge would have suffocated them before they realised.'

Women had died on the banks! The words seemed to come from a long way away, echoing and re-echoing, forcing themselves into her mind until she wanted to scream.

'How many died?'

Rachel registered Beulah's question yet wanted to shrink from the answer. Each word came crystal clear.

'Two. Were two women picking coal that afternoon, the rest had the sense to keep away. Both of them were sucked under. They was found later when the sludge had settled enough to be carted away from the street. They ought to have had the sense not to go on to the banks with that weather. The only blessing is they wouldn't have felt anything.'

Blessing! Rachel felt an absurd desire to laugh. It was a blessing to be stifled to death in a sea of mud? Two women . . . The man had said two women . . . women desperate enough to go on to the pit banks when they must have known the danger. Were they? Her unspoken question sent the world circling about her head. Were either of those women her friends . . . was it them had died beneath the sludge, Tansy and Cora, or maybe Ellen?

'I'll be away then, missis.'

The man had gently removed her hand from his sleeve but Rachel was only dimly aware of his leaving.

'I thank you for the kindness of the use of your well, and doubly so for the tankard of ale, it be right welcome, and the more so for being gladly given. You tell that lad of yourn there'll be a bucket or three of coals along of that bridge. Good day to you. And to you, miss.'

'I have to go, Mrs Thomas.'

They were in the kitchen of Beulah's cottage where the older woman had made the inevitable pot of tea.

'I have to find out. I must know whether my friends were involved.'

'I know, wench, I know.' Beulah winced at the sharp pain tightening in her chest but refused to allow it to affect her tone or show in her face; this girl had enough to cope with for now without any added worry. 'But you be in no fit state to be going there alone. Drink your tea, it will calm your nerves, then I'll away to the fields and bring William. He will go with you to Tipton Green.'

'No.' Rachel took the proffered cup but did not drink. 'He can't leave the barley. If it rains the crop will be ruined and that will mean the brewing will be affected. I'll be all right, you need not worry.'

But Beulah *was* worried. Though the girl was trying desperately to hide her fear, it showed clearly in her eyes and in the lines that were drawn across her usually clear brow. She should not return to that town alone, yet what she had said about harvesting the barley was true; if it were spoilt by rain then their money for the year would be swallowed up in buying in supplies elsewhere. That in its turn would mean a year of hunger for them all for it was selling the beer that kept the wolf from their door. Money earned through the dairy would scarce do as much.

'I will be all right,' Rachel repeated. 'I have to go, I have to know.'

'I realise that, and I understand.' Beulah heard the despair in the young voice. 'Just take care, that's all I ask.' She watched as the girl who had won a place in her affections as well as in her home ran swiftly to her own cottage. She emerged in less than a minute, throwing a shawl across her shoulders as she returned.

'I will come back, Mrs Thomas.' Rachel hesitated at the open door just long enough to call the words. 'Tell William I'll be back, you have my word.'

'And you will keep it,' Beulah whispered as, skirts flying around her feet, Rachel ran towards the bridge over the canal. 'I would expect no less from you.'

So, the girl he had saved from the hangman's noose was to be married! Jared Lytton turned the trap out of the yard of the Fox Inn, guiding it to the right along the Sedgley Road. She was to become the daughter-in-law of the woman who had taken her in. She had done all right for herself, the landlord had said. Jared laughed suddenly, a harsh sound that was meant to hold scorn yet held something else, something he refused to recognise. Where was the benefit to her in marrying there, from the poverty of a miner's house in Horseley to the grinding drudgery of a farmhand's wife, and the man dumb into the bargain! The girl would finish up as badly burned as scalded, and serve her right too!

But why serve her right, why say that? Impatient with his own thoughts, he flicked at the reins, sending the horse into a trot. Were such thoughts a product of his own anger at her refusal of his offer of a place in his household? More to the point, why should her having refused bother him at all? But it had, and if he were honest he must own it bothered him still.

Glancing away across the open heath to where the sun stretched a ribbon of gold along the canal, he caught his breath as a slight figure, a shawl part covering her brown dress, the afternoon light glinting on silver-gold hair, caught his attention.

'Bloody woman!' he swore softly, turning his glance back to the road. She seemed to be in his brain. Everywhere he looked he imagined he saw her.

But was it a mere trick of the light . . . was his imagination playing the same old trick? Despite himself he found his glance swinging sideways, back towards the line of the canal. If he were hallucinating it was at least consistently for he saw the same figure again, one that ran and walked alternately, one that was in a hurry . . . or else terrified.

Terrified! Jared felt the blood freeze in his veins. It was the girl who had thrown that dress back at him, the girl with fire in her eyes and pride in her voice. Pulling on the reins he brought the trap to a standstill, then shading his eyes with his hand, stared out across the heath separating them.

It *was* her. He watched as again she broke into a run only to slow to a walk a few yards on as though already worn out. Why was she running . . . why had she left that house . . . and why was she so frightened? As frightened she was. Jared watched as the figure tried yet again to run but quickly lapsed into a walk. No woman behaved like that unless something had scared the wits out of her. Something, or someone?

He lowered his hand. 'By Christ, I'll kill him!' he muttered, taking up the reins and urging the horse to a gallop. 'If that bloody half-wit has so much as laid a finger on her, I'll kill him!'

She must be making for Tipton Green. Jared was aware of driving too fast but did nothing to curb the horse's speed. To risk going there, to risk meeting up with Isaiah Bedworth! Something equally as unpleasant as that man's attentions must have happened to drive the girl back to the place.

Reaching a group of some six houses, huddled together against the isolation of the heath, he guided the trap on to a narrow track leading from their small agricultural plots towards the canal. If she kept to the towpath the girl would have to pass him here, and if she turned off across the heath he would still stand a good chance of seeing which way she went.

Aware of his own breathing, ragged and harsh as a man's who had fought a heavy fight, he jumped from the trap, stopping only to attach the reins to a large spent clump of gorse before sprinting towards the towpath still some distance away. In the far distance a train screeched its approach to Tipton railway station, the blast of its steam-whistle rending the silence. Jared felt every nerve within him judder. The sound was too akin to a woman's scream. Had the girl screamed? As the track come to an abrupt end he paused. It would do no good to let his imagination get the better of him. He drew a deep breath. He would hold his temper, at least until he knew the truth, but should it transpire that she had been hurt then the devil and all his helpers would not hold him.

If she had seen him standing a little way from the towpath she did not show it. Her head bent, she would have passed by had he not stepped on to the path, blocking her way.

'Have you suffered some accident, Miss Cade?' Jared's already grim face hardened as she looked up at him, showing the marks of tears on her cheeks.

'No . . . no, I . . . please let me pass.'

'In good time.' He remained squarely in her path.

'Please!' Rachel stepped to one side but found he had matched her movement.

'Tell me why you are in such a hurry you have run yourself almost to a standstill?'

It was a demand rather than a request, and accompanied by his hand fastening on her arm.

'I . . . there is no reason.' Rachel tried to pull her arm away but his grip held.

'Don't lie to me!' That strange anger rising fresh in him,

Jared shook her. 'I know there is a reason. Now tell me before I shake it out of you!'

'There has been an accident in Tipton Green.' She thought it quicker to tell him than to argue further, though as yet it did not appear in her mind to question his reason for being here and on foot. 'It seems the pit banks . . . the heaps of coal waste . . .'

'I know what pit banks are!'

'Well, they have moved, slid down on the town and . . .'

'I heard about that.' Jared felt some of the tension slip from him. Was that all that had caused such fear on her face? Was a pit bank slippage all that was responsible for darkening her lovely eyes?

'Rain loosened the core of the pit banks, turning the whole lot to sludge,' he went on. 'Once that begins to slide, its whole weight is brought to bear and it just pushes itself downward. Nothing can prevent it. And once started, nothing can stop it; it just runs on, covering everything until it has spent itself.'

'It covered several shops and some houses.'

'So I saw. I went along there myself but there was nothing to be done. But how did you hear of it?'

'A bargee.' Rachel tried again to wrench her arm free but his grip only tightened. 'He called at Mrs Thomas's cottage, she allows them to use the well to fill their cans with fresh water, and he told us what had happened.'

'Is that what has you running like a terrified rabbit?'

Rachel looked up. Even in her own nervous state she recognised the concern in his voice, a sort of nameless fear that turned his face almost to stone. But why, for what reason? Why should this man care what it was that had her hurrying towards Tipton Green?

'I would think it would set any woman running, Mr Lytton,' she said more calmly than her feelings might have allowed. 'Any accident would, much less one of this kind occurring in Tipton Green.'

'But that mud slide happened weeks ago. Why the hurry

now?' Suddenly his eyes narrowed, showing only a faint line of bronze between the lids. 'Are you telling me the truth? Is that pit bank falling the only thing that has you running . . . are you sure there is nothing more than that?'

'Isn't that enough!' Pulling away, this time freeing her arm from his hand, Rachel snatched the shawl tighter beneath her breasts – an action performed more to take her mind off the underlying tone of his question than to ward off any breeze.

'God damn you, woman, answer me!'

His exclamation echoed across the heath, bouncing from outcrops of white limestone, sending a flurry of birds soaring for the safety of the sky.

'Is that the only reason you are running or has some man tried to . . . has some man forced himself upon you?'

Rachel felt the colour race upward into her face but her gaze remained steady and her voice low and calm as she answered. 'No, Mr Lytton, no man has approached me in the manner you seem to fear. The only reason for my leaving Mrs Thomas's home is that I must discover if the women who died beneath that mud were my friends, the ones I left the night you came upon me on the heath. That, I am sure you will agree, is reason enough for me to run.'

Jared breathed more easily. She was telling the truth. God Almighty, it had to be the truth.

Side-stepping once more, Rachel regained the towpath and this time he did not try to block her way.

'It is more than reason enough,' he said as she made to turn away, 'and more than reason for me to offer my apologies. I can only say I genuinely thought, from seeing you in the distance, that you might be in need of assistance. Which I am delighted still to offer, should you wish to accept?'

Catching her arm once more, he pointed towards the trap standing a little way off on the heath.

'My horse can get you to Tipton Green more quickly, Miss

Cade.' He smiled, feeling the awful fear of the last minutes slide away. 'He can run even faster than you.'

A few minutes later, her shawl pulled tight about her, Rachel sat beside him in the open carriage. But the warmth of the sun could do nothing to dispel the cold fear that gripped her heart. Was it Tansy or Cora who had been caught in that mud slide? Was it Ellen, or even all of them? The bargee had told of two bodies being recovered from the sludge but had given no names, only saying need must have driven them to work the banks after days of rain. And her friends had been so poor.

Rachel bit hard on her lip. Tansy would not allow them to take that risk, she would not let Cora or Ellen work the banks knowing the danger; but neither would she see them go hungry. Tansy would not let the other two risk working the banks in the rain, but she herself . . . would she have done it?

Feeling the tremor that ran through her, Jared glanced at her drawn features. He had been so filled with fear for her, he felt he could easily have killed any man who touched her. Resolutely, he turned his eyes back to the track that had branched off from the first, knowing from his usual travel on horseback it would lead into Hurst Lane and from there he could drive into Neptune Street then across to Owen Street. From there it would be easy to reach wherever it was this girl needed to be.

Why had he felt like that? Why had an anger that could so easily have run out of control taken such a hold on him? This girl was nothing to him. It had amused him that day to snatch her out of the hands of Isaiah Bedworth. That was all it was, an hour or so's amusement and nothing more; just as threatening the villagers of Horseley with what would happen should they turn her from the village had been nothing more.

Amusement! Jared called to the horse, steadying it as the wheels of the carriage caught in a rut. Was it amusement that had caused him to want to feel a man's throat in his hands? The girl was a beauty, that he could not deny, but was it that alone which stirred such a feeling in him when he could buy beauty anywhere? Or was it something else . . . something he had found nowhere before? And if so, what was that something?

Beside him she trembled again and he met the movement with a rush of feeling of his own. He had to cling tight to the reins to prevent himself from taking her in his arms.

Was that what he wanted, to take this girl in his arms. Was the reason he wanted to kill any man who touched her, because he himself wanted the same thing?

That was ridiculous. Jared dismissed the thought. She was nothing, no more than a miner's ragged-arsed daughter. Why in heaven's name should he want her?

But as they came in sight of the grey shroud of solidified mud that spread like a still lake above whose motionless surface the roofs of shops and houses protruded, and he felt that same tremor shake her again, Jared knew only that he did.

Chapter Fifteen

He had insisted on bringing her to the door of the house she had shared with Tansy and the others. Winding her shawl tight about her arms, Rachel watched the small trap drive away. It had taken some time to persuade him to leave her to enter the house alone. At last he had agreed, but only after emphasising that he would be back to collect her and see her to the Thomases' house. Why he insisted she could not fathom. He had shown her similar kindness on two other occasions yet when he had called at the cottage he had been so angry, though for what reason he had not said.

Waiting until the carriage had rounded the corner of the street, she turned towards the house. It looked exactly as it had the day she had left it. Cheap cotton lace curtains closed across the windows, shutting out the world. The door that had in some forgotten time been painted brown had long since erupted into huge blisters, their great scabs hanging in huge peeling brown flakes; and beside the house, walls joined in conjugal embrace, stood the unused barn. Rachel looked at it then quickly turned away, remembering the bloodied body they had found there. Bart's body.

Tansy and Cora had carried him into the house where they had washed him, tending his broken remains with so much love, each in turn sitting beside him through the nights until he had been carried from the house.

Had this house held other bodies . . . had others been

carried here to be washed for burial? Her heart thumping, Rachel raised her hand to the door then dropped it. She could not knock, could not face up to receiving no answer, to learning what she feared most was fact. There was still an hour or two of daylight left. She glanced at the sky, to where the sun gleamed low over the warehouses of Dudley Port. The women would still be working on the pit heaps. If the house were empty it could be that the three of them were picking, that they had not yet returned. Of course, that was where they would be, Tansy and the others. Those bodies found beneath the sludge were not theirs, they were all together, picking coal; they had not died, her fears had been groundless. Everything was exactly as it had been, the street, the house, and soon the women would be home, with Cora and Ellen making a meal while Tansy saw to putting away the buckets and sacks they had used for the day's work.

She could fill the kettle from the pump in the yard and have it boiling over the fire for when they arrived. Rachel pushed at the door that was always on the latch. Tansy said that should a burglar ever bother to call at this house he would come again the next day to bring them something, for they had nothing worth the stealing.

The memory bringing a tiny smile to her mouth, Rachel stepped into the living room. The late sun played over the one window but the curtains rejected its light, closing it off, holding the room in deep gloom. Rachel stood waiting for her eyes to become accustomed to the shadowed interior, feeling a coldness strike at her from walls that smelled of damp, a mustiness that seemed almost like a living thing. It reached out to touch her with clammy fingers, to fold itself about her, to engulf her in the stench of its embrace.

Shivering, Rachel tugged her shawl closer about her, fighting the desire to turn and run. They would be home soon . . . she would set the kettle to boil.

Only there was no kettle. Her eyes used now to the eerie half-light, she glanced at the firegrate that every Saturday evening was blackleaded until it shone silver. But now no kettle swung on its hook and no enamel teapot sat on its trivet, no embers glowed red in its heart waiting to be fed with coals. The hearth was empty of its fire irons. The whole fireplace was bare, empty, dead.

Lifting her glance to the mantelshelf, Rachel felt her heart quicken. No wooden clock stood at its centre, no cheap plaster knick-knacks, no tasselled cover with its overlay of Cora's hand-crocheted lace. The shelf was empty. Cleared of every single item as if some angry hand had swept them away. Fear returning, clutching her throat until she could scarcely breathe, she glanced about her. The cupboard that had stood at the end of the room against the door that gave on to the barn was gone; the chairs that had stood to either side of the fireplace were no longer there, and neither was the rug Tansy and Cora had pegged from clippings of worn-out clothing. And the table . . . the table where they sat to eat together, where was the table?

Coldness growing inside her, Rachel realised the room was empty, stripped of every single item. Only the cotton lace that hung at the windows remained of the place that had been home to her. Knowing she must see it all, that she could not carry half truths with her for the rest of her life, she forced herself to climb the narrow wooden stairs, allowing only her toes to touch the bare treads as if any sound would be an intrusion upon the silence.

The bedrooms were bleak. Cora's and Tansy's, the one she had shared with Ellen . . . each was bare and empty as the downstairs room. Not a single thing remained of the women who had lived and slept in them, nothing to tell of their laughter or their tears, of the hopes they had shared and the fears they had known. It was gone, leaving no trace, almost as if it had never been.

But it *had* been. Rachel stifled a sob, holding it in her mouth, afraid that if she let it go she would never be able to stop. Twice she had had everything she loved snatched away from her, Robbie and her father, then Bart; and now . . . Oh, God, no! She turned away, stumbling down the stairs, elbows hitting the walls to either side of her.

Half falling back into what had been the living room, she pressed both hands against her mouth. Had the women that mud slide buried been two of her friends after all? Were they dead? What other reason could there be for the house being empty of every last stick of furniture, every last piece of crockery? Across the room the door that gave on to the street stood as she had left it, a shaft of fading sunlight filtering in where it stood ajar. Two or three steps, that was all it would take, just two or three steps and she would be outside on the footpath, away from this house that was wrapped in death and desolation.

But there was still the scullery. No half truths! Taking a long breath that filled her lungs with the smell of decay, making her want to vomit, Rachel turned towards the scullery.

The door which led into the tiny yard was closed, shrouding the scullery in deeper shadow than that of the living room. Her fingers threaded painfully through her shawl, Rachel held it close but its warmth did little to ward off the numbness that held her almost rigid. No buckets stood beneath the shallow brownstone sink. No dolly hung in place on the wall above the place where once the wash tub had stood, no basket of pegs and laundry tongs rested on the wooden box stood beside the copper and no tin bath graced the furthermost wall. The scullery was as empty as the rest of the house.

They would not have left. They would not have given up the home they had made for themselves, not unless . . .

The sob she had held in so tightly escaped in a long drawn out cry. It bounced along the empty walls, jumping back at her from bare stone-flagged floors, sounding and resounding, building cry upon cry until it seemed a whole company of mourners was weeping, for a dead house and lost friends.

And then it died away, fading into nothingness as Rachel

fastened her hands once more over her mouth; faded into a silence more terrible than her crying.

Suddenly it was too much. Feeling as if the very silence were drawing her down, sucking her into itself, drowning her in its very intensity, Rachel wrenched open the door, tumbling into the yard where she stood retching.

Heave after dry heave wracked her, rising from the pit of her stomach, searing past her throat to leave her gasping.

'Rachel Cade!'

A hand touching her shoulder brought her spinning round, a fresh scream rising to her lips and dying on a long sob.

'Ellen . . . oh, Ellen!'

Their arms wrapped about each other, they clung together, weeping against each other's shoulders, each mumbling words the other could not hear through the emotion that drowned them.

'Oh, Ellen!' Rachel said long minutes later, but without releasing the girl she had feared dead. 'Oh, Ellen, I was so afraid. I . . . I heard . . . and the house . . . why is the house so empty? Where are Tansy and Cora?'

In her arms the other girl trembled and her voice when finally she spoke was strangled. 'They . . . they are dead, Rachel, both dead.'

She felt herself reel from the blow of those words. Her fears had proved right. The women who had been suffocated in that avalanche of mud were her friends.

Mustering the last of her strength Rachel held the other girl, using her own body to support the slight figure, waiting until Ellen's tears allowed the story to be told.

'We . . . we had not been coal picking for more than a week. The rain had come in torrents for all that time. We were down to our last meal and there was no money in the house to buy so much as a stale loaf. Samuel Potter took the last for rent and said unless we all wanted to be out on the streets we had better have the next week's money on the dot.

'It was Tansy who decided to go out on to the banks, but when I said I would go as well she refused to hear of it. Then Cora said for me to make the supper and she would go picking with Tansy. They said they would only pick long enough to fill one bucket, just enough coal to keep the fire fed; they said that food we could do without for a few days but we needed a fire. This house is so damp . . . I remember trying not to listen to the rain. We all knew what it did to the waste heaps, we knew the danger. Then, about an hour after they had gone, a woman came. She said . . . she said if I had friends on the banks, I should get there right away. I ran, Rachel . . .'

Ellen pushed free, lifting a face puffy with weeping.' I ran as fast as I could; there was sludge everywhere, a thick grey sludge, and it was moving, creeping down on the town like some terrible nightmare monster. I tried to look for them, tried to find them in that grey hell, but someone pulled me away. Then I found this.'

Taking the wooden clog from beneath her shawl, she handed it to Rachel.

'Tansy.' Rachel breathed the name softly. This was all that remained of that blustering, caring woman who had shown her the true meaning of friendship.

Still supporting the other girl she guided her to the far end of the small open yard lowering her to sit on a low wall that closed off the communal privvy shared by four other houses.

'They . . . they found them?'

'It was a week later.' Ellen held a scrap of cloth, twisting it between her fingers. 'They had to wait for most of the rainwater to drain out of the sludge before it was safe to venture on to it. They were close together, Tansy and Cora, deep under the slide. They brought them here. I . . . I washed them both then a woman from the next street came. She helped me to dress them in clean clothes, and sat with me until they were buried. I . . . I had them lie next to Bart, I thought they would have wanted that.'

'I'm sure they would.' Rachel filled the small silence as Ellen stopped speaking.

'There was nothing left to buy headstones,' she went on. 'I sold the furniture to pay for the funeral. I couldn't think of any other way, Rachel. I tried but I couldn't think of any other way of finding the money for two coffins.'

'You did the right thing,' she answered, reassuring her again. 'But how have you managed since?'

'The remaining bits and pieces went to pay the rent. Samuel Potter allows no one any leeway. Once that was gone I had to pawn anything they would take: household linen, pots, kettle, even the teapot, it all went . . . now there is nothing left.'

'You did not return to the banks?'

Ellen twisted the scrap of cloth that was her handkerchief. 'I couldn't, Rachel. I don't have the courage. I will never be able to go back to coal picking, that is why I am going with Samuel Potter.'

'No!' Rachel stood up sharply. 'Ellen, you can't! You don't know what you're saying.'

'I do, Rachel.' She averted her eyes from her friend's disbelieving stare. 'There is no other way, believe me. I have tried to get work, I have been everywhere, asked everyone. I have no money and nothing left to pawn, and today is the day the rent is due. It is either accept Samuel Potter's proposal or take to the streets. I thought at first that the streets would be preferable, and in all truth I still feel that way, but come the winter I would find myself in the workhouse and prey to Isaiah Bedworth. Only that way there would be none of the benefits.'

'Benefits!' Rachel exclaimed. 'What possible benefit can you get from Samuel Potter?'

'He will pay for a room, food and clothes.'

'In return for what?'

'You know what, Rachel. You know Samuel Potter's demands.'

'Yes, I know,' she answered, fingers clenched together.

'I know what he demands. He wants you for his mistress. But you can't do that, Ellen. You can't become that man's whore!'

'Do you think I have not thought about that?' she cried. 'Do you think I would do it if there were any other way? I loathe that man, Rachel, loathe the thought of his touching me, but there is no other way.'

'There is!' Rachel pulled her to her feet. 'There is another way. You can come with me, Ellen. Mrs Thomas won't be able to pay you but we can share what I have. There will be enough food for both and we will both have a bed. We don't need any more.'

'But I can't just turn up at another woman's home and expect her to allow me to stay.'

'Mrs Thomas will not mind.' Concerned only with the fact that her friend was about to commit herself to a life of degradation, Rachel gave little thought to the consequences of bringing her uninvited to William's mother. 'She can use another pair of hands about the house, and they'll cost her nothing but a bed.'

'And if that bed is not given, what then?'

Both young women turned together, their eyes drawn to the scullery where, framed in the open doorway, Samuel Potter stood watching them.

'What if this woman Thomas won't have her to stay, what then, eh? Do you think her might find work there, wherever it is you be 'ticing her on to go? I doubt it. And what if her does, eh! What good will it do her? None at all if you be anything to go by . . . look at you, look at the frock you be wearing. You ain't exactly dressed like a lady.'

'No.' Rachel's head lifted as she faced him squarely. 'My clothes are not those of a lady, but then they are not those of any man's mistress either.'

'Might be better for you if they were.' Potter's whiskers lifted in a sneer.

'That might well be true, Mr Potter.' Rachel managed an

icy smile. 'However, that man would not be you. You see, even a pit bank wench can be choosy about the kind of dirt she sets her hands on.'

Above the stiff white collar about his neck Samuel Potter's face turned a dull red, and beneath his heavy eyebrows his small eyes gleamed with potent rage.

'You get out of my house!' The words were squeezed out. 'And you . . .' He turned his glance towards Ellen. 'You come with me now or you won't be coming at all. Refuse and I'll make sure you never work no pit bank again, and you'll get no work of any kind, not in Tipton Green or anywheres else the name of Sam Potter be known.'

'I am sure Ellen would not want the kind of work that is in your mind.'

'And I am sure you will both want any kind of work I might offer before I be through with you, only I won't be offering to *you*, not no sort, not even lying on your back!'

'I must at least thank you for that,' Rachel answered evenly though her nerves clanged like the bell of a steam-trolley. 'Thank you for having the goodness to ignore me.'

Stepping from the doorway, his squat figure in its dark jacket and trousers rendered more menacing by the whip he held in one hand, he moved closer to the two women.

'Oh, I won't ignore you!' he breathed, raising the whip. 'I won't ignore you, but every other man will after I split that pretty face o' yourn!'

'No.' Ellen's cry filled the tiny yard as she stepped in front of Rachel. 'Please . . . I . . . I will come with you, only don't hurt Rachel.'

'Get out of the way!' Striking out with his left arm, he caught Ellen full across the side of the head, sending her sprawling against the wall. His right arm lifted, brandishing the whip.

Instinctively Rachel bent over the fallen girl but felt herself being yanked backward.

'You won't be so bloody uppity about the work you do or the bed fellows you choose, not again you won't.'

She saw the whip rise above her head.

'You refused Sam Potter once before but you won't be having the chance to do it again. You won't have the chance of refusing any man, not with a face like the one you be going to get.'

Raising the whip until it extended over the back of his shoulder he ignored the moving figure a little to the rear of him, only becoming aware of it when Ellen grabbed the whip, hanging on to it with the little strength left to her.

'Leave off, you bloody bitch!' Rage deepening in him, adding blotches of purple to the red of his face, Potter swung the whip, his power hauling Ellen round in front of him. 'Leave off, or by Christ I'll do for you an' all!'

The knuckles of his free hand clenched, he jabbed his fist hard against Ellen's mouth. Already half senseless from the first fall she loosed the whip, reeling backward once more as it came lashing down across her breasts, falling heavily against the wall.

'I warned you, you bloody bitch!' The whip rose and fell again but the form beneath its stinging lash lay unmoving. 'I warned . . .'

Samuel Potter did not finish his sentence, nor did the lash find its intended victim but clattered against the ground as it fell from his hand.

Trembling in every limb Rachel threw down the whip as she heard the door to the street bang against the latch. She had snatched it up as Potter had reeled from the blow she had struck to his head. She had felt the weight of the clog she had pushed inside her shawl when he had dragged her backward, and as he lashed Ellen she had hit out at him, all her force behind the heavy brass-studded shoe. The first blow had caused him to drop the whip, the second had him spinning to face her, the third sent him stumbling from the house, blood blinding him as he went.

Waves of sickness rising in her, Rachel stood for a moment

unable to move. She had clubbed Samuel Potter with a clog. Her eyes moved to the shoe lying on the ground, then closed against the sight of the blood that covered it. She had hit him again and again about the head and face . . . dear God, she might have killed him!

But if she had not struck him then, in his rage he might have killed Ellen. At the thought she turned to the girl lying slumped, head propped at an awkward angle against the wall.

'Ellen.' She gathered the still form gently in her arms, smoothing the matted hair back from her brow. 'Ellen,' she whispered again, her heart thumping when the girl neither moved nor answered.

Taking the scrap of handkerchief that somehow had remained clutched between Ellen's fingers, she held it under the water pump then, taking it back to the still form, wiped the tear-stained face.

'Ellen,' she whispered, voice cracking on a sob. 'Ellen, please be all right . . . please don't die . . .'

But there was no answer. Not even the merest flicker of an eyelid as the cool water-soaked cloth touched against Ellen's face.

Above her head the last of the sun seemed to tumble from the sky, leaving the yard bathed in the purple-grey of evening. Soon it would be completely dark. Rachel glanced towards the house. It held no bed nor sofa but at least it would offer some protection against the night air.

Placing her hands beneath Ellen's arms, she hauled her on to the low wall, then supporting her against her own hip dragged at the air, gulping it greedily into her lungs, trying desperately to summon the strength to drag the other girl into the house.

Rachel knelt on the cold flagstones of the scullery floor, the clammy dampness seeping through her skirts, biting into her flesh. How long she had knelt there holding Ellen's still form in her arms she could not tell but now the sky outside was black except for a faint bloom of yellow moonlight.

From the street outside she could hear the shouts of men leaving the public houses that dotted every street and corner of Tipton, and the sound brought a new coldness, the coldness of fear. Samuel Potter was a drinking man, he frequented the beer houses. What if he had gone to one tonight? What if he came here after filling himself with beer? What if he brought a few of those men with him? And he was likely to do that. He knew she and Ellen would likely stay the night in this house, he would guess that the girl he had lashed with that whip would be in no state to leave.

But if they did not leave, and now, what state would they both be in should he pay a second visit?

A roar of laughter followed a man's drunken shout and Rachel held her breath, bending protectively over Ellen until she heard the voices fade into the distance. She could not risk their staying here. Somehow she must get Ellen away, get her to the safety of the Thomases' house.

'Ellen.' She shook the other girl gently. 'Ellen, we have to leave, it's not safe here . . . Ellen, please wake up.'

'I . . . I am awake, Rachel.'

It was barely a whisper but hearing it her spirits soared. Ellen was conscious. With a little help she might be able to walk.

'Ellen, I am afraid Samuel Potter may return. We must leave. Can you walk?'

Ellen lifted a hand to Rachel's arm. 'You go, Rachel, there is no need for you to . . .'

'Stop it, Ellen!' Rachel's answer rang against the damp walls of the empty house. 'I am not going anywhere without you. Unless you want us both to become that man's mistresses, you must try to walk.'

A fresh burst of laughter from the doorway of The Fiery Holes caused Rachel to shiver. Maddie Bartum's customers were hardly famous for their elegant behaviour. One whisper of two young women alone in a house . . . She shuddered again, pushing the thought away as she pulled Ellen to her feet.

The door that gave on to the street was in full view of that public house; they would have to pass the building to reach Owen Street. It was too risky. Any man in drink might think them fair game. It was then she remembered that the privy backed on to a small lane, more of a narrow track, overgrown and rarely used. It led between an unoccupied house and some derelict canal-side store houses. It would be a longer way of reaching the Sedgeley Road than she might have wished, but it would prove safer.

Taking off her shawl, she wrapped it about Ellen, fastening it over the one the girl already wore. Then, her arm about her, supporting her, Rachel helped her friend to leave the house.

'He was there.'

At the point where the path turned back upon itself, skirting the farthest end of Owen Street, Ellen stopped and looked back.

'He was there when they pulled me from that sludge.'

'Who?' Rachel allowed herself a moment's rest. 'Who was there?'

'My father,' Ellen whispered. 'My father was there.'

Chapter Sixteen

Jared Lytton swore softly to himself. His business in Bloomfield had taken longer than he had thought. Taking his watch from the pocket of his waistcoat, he held it towards the light of a street gas lamp. It was well past eight. He had already left that girl too long in that Godforsaken house.

Handing a coin to the ostler who brought the trap to the front of the Regent Hotel, he climbed in, at once urging the horse to a trot. Twenty minutes, no more. He would be back at that house in twenty minutes.

The house was in darkness. Jumping from the carriage, Jared glanced once at windows that were wreathed in blackness, no chink of light telling she might still be inside. Lifting his hand to the door, he paused as his first knock set it swinging inward. Was it usual to leave the door swinging on its hinges . . . or had something happened?

'Miss Cade!'

His call echoed in the black stillness as he stepped inside the house.

'Miss Cade.'

He called again, wrinkling his nose against the smell of damp brick and decaying wood. Good God, had she really lived in this!

Receiving no answer to his call, he took a box of matches from his coat pocket and, striking one, held it above his head. The room was empty, not a stick of furniture, not a pot, not even an ember in the firegrate. The flame touching against his fingers, he dropped it, killing its guttering light. Was he in the right house? Had he perhaps come to the wrong one?

But he was sure he had not. He had taken particular note of his surroundings earlier when he had brought her here. Striking another of the matches, he held it up. He had not been mistaken. If ever this house had once been her home, there was no trace of it now. Using the matches one by one he checked the upper rooms, going last into the scullery. If this was the house to which he had driven Rachel Cade, then she had gone and left no sign to tell him where.

Outside, on the narrow pavement that bordered the row of faceless buildings, Jared replaced the matches in his pocket.

Bathed in the glow of lamplight spilling from the doorway and bow windows of The Fiery Holes, a man swayed uncertainly on his feet before walking towards Jared.

'Ain't no use you looking in there for a woman.' He swayed to a halt then laughed, his alcohol-laden breath sending Jared stepping backward. 'I been there already but it were a bloody fool's errand I were sent on.'

'You were sent here, to this house . . . by whom?'

The man swayed again, eyes squinting in the darkness.

'By whom!' He blew disparagingly through his teeth, spraying beer-laden spittle over the front of his greasy jacket. 'By bloody Samooal Potter, that be who.'

'Samuel Potter?' Jared repeated the name. 'For what reason did he send you here?'

'What reason do you think, mister!' The man laughed loudly. ''Tweren't for no bloody picnic, that's for sure.'

'Knowing Mr Potter, I am sure it was not. So . . . why did he send you to this house?' Jared took several coins from his pocket, jingling them promisingly in one hand.

'He said there were a couple of young women there alone. Said both of 'em was kept by him, prostitutes he kept for his own use.' The man tried to focus on the moving hand.

'Seems he wanted to take one of 'em with him and said if I fetched 'em along to The Fiery Holes, I could have the other one. Well, it ain't often a bloke gets a chance like that so I comes along of here, but there was no women. The house were bare as a monkey's arse.'

'These women.' Jared bounced the coins again. 'Did Samuel Potter say their names?'

'No.' The man swayed on his feet. 'No, he said no names. Just said as how they was prostitutes. But there was no women in the house, bloody Potter were lying.'

The man had taken the coins and immediately turned back towards the public house.

Why had Potter sent him to that house? Were the women Rachel had shared a house with prostitutes? But if they were, and kept by Potter, why was the house stripped to the brickwork? Flipping the reins, Jared set the horse to a trot.

She had not been in the house when that drunken lout had called there, thank God. He turned the carriage out of Owen Street, following the High Street that would give eventually on to the main Sedgeley Road. She would go back to the Thomases' house, back to the man she was to marry.

Taking most of Ellen's weight against her, Rachel was forced to stop often, allowing the other girl to rest and herself to get her breath. They had cleared the town without meeting anyone and now were on the road Jared Lytton had brought Rachel along. It was perhaps safer than the heath but should Ellen's strength give out altogether it would not be so comfortable for her to lie on as the springy grass. Besides which Rachel was unsure where this road would lead. Maybe it would take her near the cottages, then again it might lead her away from them. She had best get back to the canal, follow it the way she had come. The heath was treacherous at the best of times, with its half-concealed mine shafts, but she had to turn on to it if she were to reach the canal.

Deciding the risk was worth the gamble, she turned off the road, following the ribbon of track worn by men going to and returning from the myriad coal mines that dotted the area. It would eventually give on to the towpath. They would be safe walking on that besides its being easier for Ellen to negotiate, the ground trodden hard by the hooves of horses pulling barges along the canal.

'Just a little further,' Rachel urged gently as Ellen stumbled yet again. 'We're almost there. It's just the next bridge. The Thomases' cottages are close to the next bridge.'

But was it the next bridge? Were they even going in the right direction? Her arm about Ellen, holding the girl while they took a moment's rest, Rachel glanced about them. The canal traced a glittering band through a heath that was silver-washed by a high, full moon. Here and there great clumps of gorse, etched black by the moon's touch, stood like sentinels about the grey outcrops of rock; but the beauty of it was lost amid Rachel's fears. Ought she to have risked staying the night at the house? It could be that Potter had not returned or sent one of his henchmen there; Ellen could have rested until morning, she herself might possibly have slept. But it was too late now for regrets.

They walked for five minutes before Rachel saw them. Saying they should rest again, she sank beside Ellen, feeling the other girl's weariness, a sharp contrast to her own jangling nerves. Ellen had not seen them and she would not draw the other girl's attention to them, not until she had to. And then what? Ellen could not run, she hardly had the strength to walk. And if they could run, how far would they manage to get before falling head first into an overgrown pit shaft?

Shivering more from fear than the cold night air, Rachel watched the bobbing pinpoints of light. There were two of them, in the distance as yet but moving.

Who was it walking out beside the canal at night? What were they looking for? Rachel half closed her eyes, peering into a darkness she could almost feel. Could it be men Potter had sent out, men looking for them? Would the coal jagger be so incensed at her striking him that he would have her hunted down? Rachel tried telling herself the idea was ridiculous yet still the thought remained. And when whoever it was carrying those lights came up to them, found them here in the middle of the heath, what then? Would they knock her and Ellen unconscious then throw them into the canal after first . . .

She shivered again, the thought of what might be in store for them turning her blood to ice.

'Take your shawl, Rachel.' Ellen fumbled with the knot beneath her breasts. 'You are cold, I felt you shiver.'

'No, I am not cold.' Rachel rested a hand on Ellen's, stilling the girl's fingers. 'We shall be at the cottage soon anyway. You keep the shawl, it's less for me to carry if you wear it.'

Maybe Ellen smiled at the weak joke but at that moment the moon veiled her face in cloud. In the deeper darkness the twin points of light glowed like fiery gems.

'Shall we go on, Rachel?' Ellen began to rise. 'I am not as tired as I was. Just being with you has made me feel so much better.'

'No . . . not yet.' Rachel pressed her back to the ground. 'I could do with another couple of minutes.'

She was glad Ellen sank back without saying anything more. Voices carried a long way over the heath. Voices carried a long way! Rachel lifted herself on to her knees, her glance travelling along the ribbon of silvered water. Why had she not heard voices? The men who were carrying those lights, why were they keeping silence?

Eyes aching from the strain, Rachel stared into the blackness towards the tiny twin orbs gleaming like fireflies. Like fireflies! Fireflies danced, and those lights were dancing. They were moving, yes, but coming no nearer; they were dancing, very gently up and down. Dancing on the water?

Suddenly she wanted to laugh. She had lived all her life surrounded by canals, they were as familiar to her as breathing. She could not remember a day when she had not seen a narrow boat being towed along by a horse led by a bargee or his wife or child. Every day of her life . . . Rachel rose to her feet, a smile of pure relief on her mouth as the moon vacated the sheltering clouds and once more bathed the heath in soft silvery light. Every day of her life, and she had failed to recognise those lights, failed to see them for what they were: the candles every bargee set in jars fastened to each end of his narrow boat whenever he moored for the night.

There was a barge moored there, just a little further along. The bargee would be able to tell her whether or not they were headed in the direction of the Thomas place, so many of them called there for fresh water.

'Ellen.' She helped the other girl to her feet. 'There is a barge moored just along the canal. The people won't have gone to bed yet, we can ask for a drink of water.' She might have added that she would also ask for directions but did not want to add to her friend's discomfort by admitting she was uncertain where they were.

Her arm still about Ellen, they began to walk. They had covered only a few yards when from the direction of the boat a dog began to bark.

'Don't worry.' Rachel felt Ellen pause. 'It will be chained to the boat.' Hoping she was right, she pressed on, only stopping when the craft was clearly discernible in the moon-light.

'Who be out there?' The question rang out in the stillness. 'What be you about along the cut at night? You best be off afore I sets the dog loose!'

'We mean no harm. My friend and I were hoping you would give us a drink of water.'

'By Christ, it be a woman!'

Rachel heard the quiet exclamation.

'What the 'ell be you about?'

The voice rang again followed by an order rasped to the barking dog.

'Cut ain't no place for a woman at night, lessen her be from the barges, and I ain't seen no barge moored along this stretch.'

'We are not from a barge.'

'Then where do you be from?' The man shouted almost before the sentence was finished. 'More to the point, why be you here at all? I warn you, old Toby here along of me be a bull terrier. Once he gets his teeth into you, Old Nick himself couldn't prise him away, so if you be up to no good then I advises you to think again.'

In the gloom Rachel saw the figure of the man bend towards a short squat animal, the chain about its neck rattling as it fell to the wooden deck.

'I apologise for having disturbed you.' Rachel trembled at the thought of the dog. She knew how ferocious a bull terrier could be. Many of the miners of Horseley had bred them for fighting, and she knew that they would fight until they killed or were themselves killed. 'My friend and I are on our way to the Thomas place. Could you tell me if we are following the right path?'

The man barked another curt order as a low growl issued from the dog's throat. 'Your friend?' he called, suspicion heavy in the question. 'I warn you again, Toby will have his throat out afore you can bat an eye, and I'll do for you with this here stave, so you and the bloke with you best look for somebody else to rob.'

'My friend is not a man, and we are not here to rob you. I told you the truth when I said we are on our way to the Thomases' cottage. It was late when we set off from Tipton Green and in the darkness we may have taken the wrong track across the heath.'

'Who be it, Charlie?' a woman's voice called from the cramped cabin that was the boat's living quarters.

'Reckon they be two women. Says they be from Tipton Green on their way to the Thomas place.'

A woman emerged from the cabin to stand beside the man,

adding her own curt command to his as the dog growled yet again.

'Did you say you be looking for the Thomases?' she called, then as Rachel answered yes, called again: 'Be that the Widow Thomas as lives up along of Leasowes bridge?'

'Yes,' Rachel answered again. 'Mrs Thomas has a son named William, who does not speak, and some months ago she took in a young woman who helps with the dairying.' Hoping this small amount of information would convince the woman that she had spoken the truth to the man, Rachel waited for her answer. If the woman refused to believe her, what else could she do?

'Charlie, fetch a lantern. Go on, I'll be all right with Toby loose the side of me. You two . . .' she snapped. 'You stand right still till he be back. Try comin' aboard and you'll pay dear.'

Returning with the lantern, Charlie swung it out over the edge of the boat.

'Step you forward.' The woman's hand dropped to the dog's neck. 'Come you into the light where a body can see you.'

Ellen close beside her, Rachel stepped forward from the shadow to where light from the lantern spilled on to the towpath. It played over her face, gleaming on her silver-gold hair.

'You be her!' The woman stepped to the very edge of the boat, craning forward to peer at Rachel. 'You be the lady with the fairy's hair – that be what my babby called you. Hers got a book with pictures in it, pictures of fairies and the little folk. Her said you had fairy's hair that day you brought eggs and butter and milk to the boat. You remember, Charlie?' The woman glanced at the man then back to the women on the bank. 'The babby were fair middlin' that time we moored up against Leasowes bridge. I was feared her had taken the chicken pox, it were rife in Brummagem when we passed through. Her were running a fever, but Widow Thomas gave me a potion of fenugreek and a bottle of barley water her had added a touch of lemon and sugar to. Did the little 'un a power of good. You said so yourself, Charlie. Her fever were gone within a day or so, and the eggs and milk the wench fetched along, they helped to feed the babby up. It were a kindness I'll not forget, not in a long while I won't, and lessen I be badly mistook that there one was the young woman as brought 'em.'

'The hair be the same colour.' Charlie swung the lantern closer.

'Your little girl is the only child you have,' Rachel said quietly. 'Or at least you had no other child with you those two days you were moored beside Leasowes bridge. The child was about five years old. She had brown hair that held a distinct trace of red and her eyes were brown as toffee apples. You called her Mariann. Said the name was given for your mother, Mary Ann.'

'You do be that wench from the Thomas place! See.'

She held out a hand to Rachel. 'Step on to the boat, wench. Here, let me steady you. And, Charlie, you fasten the dog to the chain.'

The inside of the cabin was cramped, with barely six feet between its two sides, but it smelled clean and its prettily painted pots and kettle gleamed in the light of the lantern Charlie hung from a hook set in the roof.

'Is your daughter well now?' Rachel asked, taking the seat offered her beside Ellen.

'Oh, ar.' The woman glanced towards a bunk bed set in the aft of the cabin. 'Her be bright and cheerful again. Widow Thomas be good with herbs and the like. We don't be the first whose child be healed by her, 'tis only a pity her skills didn't stretch to the curing of her own lad. Must pain her dreadful to see him walk through life with such an affliction he can't even answer to her words.'

Rachel could have told her that William was not dumb, that he could and did speak, but she kept that information to herself.

'How come you be out so late, and no man with you neither?' The woman poured boiling water into a teapot rampant with pink roses painted on its black lacquered body.

'We were visiting friends in Tipton Green.' Rachel caught Ellen's glance. 'I lived in that town before going to live with the Thomases. I'm afraid we talked a little too long. I know now we should have taken our friends' advice and stayed the night with them, but I was afraid Mrs Thomas might worry if we did not return. The heath is not the safest of places, and especially so at night.'

'That be the truth an' all.' The woman picked up the teapot, swirling its contents to quicken the infusion of the tea leaves. Then she poured the liquid into four white enamelled mugs. 'Besides which it seems that one be just about all in.'

'Ellen is very tired.' Rachel accepted the tea, sipping it gratefully. 'She is recovering from a heavy cold.'

'The influenza.' The bargee's wife nodded knowingly. 'It can be awful lowering. I know, my mother took it some years back and it took her an age to shake it off.'

'I am quite recovered.' Ellen smiled as she accepted her own tea. 'I am just a little tired, but not enough to worry over.'

'The influenza always be summat to be worried over.' The woman passed a mug of tea to her husband who sat on the topmost of the three stairs that led down to the cabin from the deck. 'If you asks me I reckon them there doctors ain't got no notion to the cause of it, and it be certain they ain't got the curing of it. You take care, you shouldn't ought to be outdoors at night, not so long as you feels the least bit weak.'

'We should not have far to go now.' Rachel turned to look at Charlie. 'How far are we from Leasowes bridge?'

'Not too far if walked by daylight.' He blew into his mug, cooling the liquid before drinking. 'But in the dark . . .' He hesitated. 'You needs to take it slower. A wrong step and you could find yourself in the cut. Could be some time afore you reaches home.'

'That wench shouldn't be out in the night air,' his wife repeated, glancing keenly at Ellen. 'It be treacherous after taking the influenza. I say you be better to bide with us tonight. You can set off early in the morning, Widow Thomas won't mind once her hears what happened. Her will agree with me, the barge be the best place for the pair of you till the morning.'

'We can't impose upon you and your husband.' Ellen's face was pale beneath her shawl. 'We thank you for the tea, it was most welcome, but we can't put you out any more.'

'Put me out!' The bargee's wife laughed. 'You ain't putting me out none, me wench. Repay a kindness with a kindness, and never let the chance pass you by lest you come to need another. That was the creed my mother lived by and taught me to live by the same. That girl . . .' she nodded towards Rachel '. . . did me a kindness when my babby were poorly. Now it be my chance to do her one. Won't be no bother. We have blankets plenty and to spare, ain't that so Charlie.'

He nodded, still blowing on his tea.

'Won't take no time to make up a bed, so long as you don't mind sharing the cabin with me. Charlie can take a blanket up on deck.'

'No.' Ellen laid her mug on the table. 'I will not have your husband sleep on deck on my account.'

'Don't be on account of you, wench.' The woman smiled broadly. 'He often has a blanket on the roof of the cabin in the summer months – most bargemen do. As a matter of fact, he has bedded down on that roof each night for a week or more. Ain't that so, Charlie?'

'Ar.' He handed the empty mug to his wife. 'And that be where I aims to lie tonight.'

'You see. You ain't putting me or Charlie out none. So you finish up that tea and we'll have you wrapped up snug for the night.'

From the road that ran adjacent to the heath, Jared Lytton

stared across the open stretch of land that rolled away in all directions, relieved by clumps of gorse and skirted to one side by a branch of the Birmingham Canal.

He had followed this road home last night after being told of Potter's sending that drunk to the house where Jared had left Rachel Cade. He had thought, on returning and finding her gone, that she would have taken this way back to the Thomases' house, but though after reaching the Sedgeley Road he had walked his horse to the point where it became necessary to branch across the heath to reach that house, he had seen no sign of her.

Letting his glance wander to the brilliant stripe of sun-kissed water he scanned the length of it in both directions. She would not have gone that way last night, alone and in the dark . . . but she had done just that once before! Who was to say she would not do so again?

Squinting against the brightness of the day he watched a barge sail slowly past, the rope that attached it to the horse that drew it trailing in the water.

He could ride across to that barge, ask if a girl in a brown dress and with hair the colour of pale sunlight had passed by on the towpath.

Touching the animal's flank lightly with his crop, he moved on. He could ask, but he would not. His interest in Rachel Cade, whatever it had been, was finished.

Skirting Tipton Green he rode immediately to the Britannia coal mine, one of several he owned in this area. His interest in Rachel Cade was finished but his business with Samuel Potter was not.

Calling for the overseer of the mine, he strode into the small brick building that served as mine office.

'You wanted to see me, Mr Lytton?'

A few minutes later a man of medium height, white collar shining above his dark suit, appeared smoothing one hand anxiously over his final few strands of grey hair.

'Yes, Enoch, I do.'

'I'll get the books, sir.'

The overseer turned toward a glass-fronted cupboard, rows of neatly bound ledgers visible through its dusty panes.

'I have not called to see the ledgers.'

A small frown appearing between eyebrows that seemed more plentifully endowed with hair than his head, Enoch Porter turned again to face his employer.

'Enoch, the women who pick coal on the waste heaps from this mine . . .'

'There do be women as picks the heaps, Mr Lytton,' the overseer cut in, voice holding more than a hint of anxiety. His was a good place, here in the Britannia, he had no desire to lose it. 'But I thought as how you had given permission like? Least you didn't say as your father's practice was to be changed when you took over as owner. But I will see to it, if that be what you want. There'll be no more picking on these banks. I'll have the women turned off now, right away.'

Jared held the man's eyes. 'It is not the women I want barred!' he said curtly. 'Tell me, to whom do they sell the coal they pick?'

Enoch raised a hand to his balding head, stroking it, the movement as filled with nervous anxiety as his eyes. 'Why, I reckon there be a couple of jaggers calls at the banks.'

'You reckon?' Jared's tone held a cold edge.

'I *knows*, sir,' the overseer corrected himself quickly. Lytton had not taken the chair that stood behind the table that doubled as a desk, he did not want to see the books, but something was niggling at him and if that something were not the women, then what the hell was it?

'There be two jaggers. What one don't take off the women, the other does. They come daily, late afternoon most often, after they have done the rounds of the town selling the coal they bought the day before.'

'Their names?' He tapped the riding crop he carried, the slap sounding loud against the soft leather palm of his glove.

'One be Killer Price . . .'

'Killer?' Jared raised an eyebrow.

'Ar, sir.' Enoch nodded, balding head shining in the light trying hard to finger its way through the film of black dust that hung against the window. 'That be the name he's called by, here and in the town, given him 'cos he's always threatening to kill anybody that upsets him. But he's careful never to pick an argument with any except the women. Though I tell you, Mr Lytton, he has to pick and choose *real* careful among that lot, for there are some among the pit bank wenches would pull his tongue out and stick it where he could lick his own arse.'

'I've no doubt.' Jared allowed a smile to creep over his lips. 'Many of them look the sort to take no nonsense from any man, no matter who he is.'

'You be right there, sir. Many is the time I've seen them fight, and a tigress wouldn't be in the piece. It ain't always been woman to woman either. Any man who badmouths one of them would have to be a fool or the Tipton Slasher himself.'

'Now there *is* a man anyone would have to be insane to take on,' Jared replied. 'I've seen that man fight, and he's a pugilist to be reckoned with.'

Enoch nodded. 'When some of these women see red, they don't stop to reckon. They just flies in with hands and feet. Ar, and anything else they 'ave an' all.'

'The other jagger,' Jared returned to the business in hand, 'what is he named?'

'Any man at the Britannia would tell you what he *should* be named.' The overseer made a derisive sound in his throat. 'Cunning bastard is what they would say, and truth to tell I would call him the same and make no apology for it. Though he were christened Samuel – Samuel Potter.'

Samuel Potter! Jared's mouth set. It was the same man, just as he'd thought. Samuel Potter had sent that drunk to the house where Rachel had once lived, and given the man carte blanche to rape her.

'This man Potter.' Jared kept his voice free from emotion but his eyes gleamed with unexpressed anger. 'He is not to be allowed on Britannia ground again, and neither is he to be allowed to buy from any woman who has picked from these heaps. Have the women informed that should they be found to have sold coals to Potter, they will no longer be allowed to pick the banks on this or any other mine that belongs to me. Tell them also that the few in this area that do not are owned mostly by friends of mine, friends who would not hesitate to agree to my request that their pit banks also be cleared of women. Make it *very* clear, Enoch. I will brook no exception. Sell to Potter and they are barred from every Lytton mine.'

Watching Jared ride away, Enoch once again stroked a hand across his head, heaving a sigh of relief. He'd been right in his assumption that somebody had upset his employer, and felt relieved that the culprit was not him. Jared Lytton could come down on a man as hard as his father had before him. Young he still was but the man knew his business, especially when that business was revenge.

Chapter Seventeen

'Right, that be the last.'

Hoisting the sack of malted barley on to the low-sided wagon, Ernest Leech stepped back. The man he had hired a week ago might not be much to look at but he worked well. He had harboured his doubts at first: the man's build had seemed too slight for the work of lifting sacks of grain. But his strength was surprising; not once had he flagged or shirked the lifting, and there had been no complaints from him. In fact, there had been hardly any talk from him at all.

Ernest watched now as the man gathered up the reins then flicked them across the flanks of the shire. No, there was hardly a word out of him. He came to the malt house promptly at six in the morning, neither early nor late. He did his day's work and left at seven at night, and in between he kept himself to himself. But that was to the good; a man who talked too much, worked too little, and though his malting business had grown, Ernest Leech could carry no idler.

Turning back to the malt house he made a record of the number of sacks of grain that had gone out, entering the particulars in a thick ledger. This was one of the special deliveries made to Widow Thomas's place. Mighty particular about her barley was Widow Thomas. Only took back what she brought in, wouldn't have it mixed with barley from another farm. To most barley was barley, but not to Widow Thomas or her lad; they knew their own and would take no other, nor mixings neither. The Thomases' barley must be kept apart from any other, the Widow insisted, and kept apart it was; even on its delivery back to them, no sacks of anyone else's grain went in the same dispatch.

But for how much longer would the woman be brewing? He lifted his cap only to settle it back immediately in place, a habit he didn't know he had. Last he had heard the Widow was middlin', fair poorly sometimes, by all accounts. And if it came to the push, who would see to the brewing if brewing there was?

'Strewth!' Ernest muttered under his breath. 'I hopes to God Widow Thomas ain't by herself when her claps eyes on that delivery chap. Sight of his face could 'ave her in her box afore night!'

The man's face was a dreadful sight. Ernest dislodged his cap only to settle it again. It had given him a start when he had first seen it: a puckered hole where the left eye should have been, and a jagged scar lined with black dots where the flesh had been crudely stitched together, running from the line of thin, mouse-coloured hair line down the brow and cheek to the jaw. One side of the man's face was reduced to a living ruin, a vivid purple weal taking the place of healthy flesh. And the throat . . . he had glimpsed it once when the man's muffler had fallen open. A red line, obviously fading now but nevertheless there, circled his neck, and his voice was croaky and hoarse. Put together they spoke of attempted strangulation. Old Ben Newley up along Gospel Oak had talked like that after he had sided with the preacher John Wesley and the people of his village had been so incensed they had strung him to a tree, almost throttling him.

Ernest nodded his head, agreeing with his own unspoken thoughts. Somewhere, and not too long ago, the man he had hired had been either part strangled or almost hanged.

Standing beside the barn that held the barley he had threshed only the day before, William Thomas watched the wagon roll into the yard. Ernest Leech was never late with his deliveries, in fact there had been no fault in either that or his malting in the many years his malt house had handled the Thomases' barley. Leech let the grains soak for no more than forty-eight hours, changing the water four or perhaps five times before spreading the soaked grain out on the malting floor, taking care it did not dry out before seeing the growing shoot, acrospire, Leech called it, showing as a bulge halfway up the husk. Then it was on the trays and in the ovens to roast gently for twelve hours. Yes, Ernest Leech knew his trade. There was no other maltster of his calibre in Tipton or out of it, not for William Thomas.

But this bloke was not Ernest Leech.

William glanced at the face of the man driving the wagon, at the scar that would not be hidden by cap or turned-up coat collar, and felt a wrench of pity. What devil-spawned cause lay behind a disfigurement such as that?

Acknowledging the man's touch of the cap with a nod of his own head, William pointed towards the brew house. Then, grabbing one of the sacks from the wagon, he helped carry them inside.

The man said no word. All through the carrying in of the malted barley, and the loading of the cart with newly threshed grain, he kept his silence, merely touching his cap in farewell as he drove from the yard.

Clearing Leasowes bridge, following the track that once beyond sight of the two houses branched into a fork, one side following the canal towpath, the other leading towards the road to Tipton Green, the driver glanced about him. The world was empty, not even a rabbit disturbed the stillness of the heath and no bird paid its tribute of a song.

It had not been like this in that other place. Even in the dark reaches of the night there had been no silence. Always someone cried out in the misery of a soul left to rot.

Then his eye caught a movement. There on the towpath, just turning the bend. Two figures. One in grey skirts, head draped in a shawl. The other in a brown dress, hair the colour of sun on spindrift falling loose about her shoulders.

He drew a long breath. Not often in a lifetime did you see hair of such a colour. Watching from the height of the wagon as the women passed by, a long breath slid silently through the twisted deformed mouth. Not often in any lifetime did you see a beauty like that.

Jared Lytton had closed his spoil heaps to him. Samuel Potter was to have no more dealings with the wenches who worked the Lytton banks; if they sold to him then they too were barred and that they would not risk.

Potter sent a savage stroke of the whip across the flanks of his horse, sending it into a gallop that had his cart careering wildly towards Tibbington. Lytton had closed the Britannia to him and it was a safe bet the rest of the Lytton properties would carry the same ban.

'Damn his eyes!' Potter cursed beneath his breath. Lytton had even gone so far as to have a man employed to patrol the banks, seeing that his order was enforced. 'But there are other mines, Lytton,' he muttered, 'other pit banks that don't be yours. Samuel Potter can buy from there. You think by taking that business from me you'll finish me? And why? Because that drunken fool told you of me sending him for them two women . . . be that the reason? Be you so high-minded, so holier than the next man, that you don't hold with prostitutes? Or be there some other reason?'

And how was it that house had been empty when his henchman had gone there? That wench Ellen Walker had been ready to come with him. The days of keeping herself in food and paying for the roof over her head had taken everything she had left after paying for the burial of the women who'd shared the house; not that there was much to sell or even to pawn, only a few paltry knick-knacks. Yes, the wench had seen that to become the mistress of Samuel Potter was her best course. And he would have seen her all right, she would have had a room and food, a frock or two; yes, Samuel Potter would have looked to her welfare . . . at least until he tired of her.

But now the wench had gone . . . Hitting a rut in the road, he dragged on the reins, slowing the horse to a less dangerous pace. To the workhouse? He doubted that. The wench was poor as a church mouse but would be a dead church mouse before admitting herself to the workhouse. No, it had to be that other one, that Cade girl. Where had she come from, sticking her nose in? And more to the point, where had she gone? And had Ellen Walker gone with her?

Directing the horse first to one mine and then another, only to find Jared Lytton's influence had closed them all against him, Samuel Potter finally hitched his wagon behind the Fountain Inn at one end of Owen Street, and went inside.

Several men were already grouped in the smoke-filled room, some from the barges moored on the nearby stretch of canal and others the adjacent colliery. Calling for a tankard of Old Best, Potter carried it to a round-table set in one corner and dropped heavily on to a stool set beside it.

Drawing a stick of shag tobacco from his pocket, he shaved several slices from it with a penknife. 'Damn that bloody Lytton!' he mumbled, stuffing the shavings of tobacco into the bowl of a long-stemmed white clay pipe. 'May the Lord strike him dead!'

'Be that the Lytton as owns most of the industry in Tipton?'

A man had moved from the end of the bar, coming to sit beside Samuel Potter.

''Cos if it be then I joins my wish for him to yours. May the Lord strike him dead.'

'Ar, he be the Lytton all right.' Samuel took a long pull at his tankard before putting a match to his pipe.

'Seems you have something against him?'

'You ain't spoke wrong.' Samuel puffed, then held the match to the bowl of the pipe once more. 'So would you if you was the one being put out of business.'

'Be that what he's done to you?'

Flicking the match towards the fireplace, Samuel sucked several times on the pipe before answering. 'It be what he's trying to do. He won't have the pit bank wenches sell their pickings to me, Christ alone knows why!'

Hitching his stool nearer to the table, the man who had joined him uninvited leaned nearer to Potter.

'Seems it might be in your interests if this Lytton were suddenly . . . shall we say . . . removed?'

Samuel's eyes narrowed. 'Might be.'

'Could be done.' The man glanced quickly around the room. No one was close enough to hear. 'Could be I'm the man to see to the doing of it, if you be willing to pay?'

Draining his tankard, Samuel set it on the table and eyed the other man. His tongue carried the Tipton drawl and his clothes were those of a miner but that was all that was recognisable about him. His face evoked no glimmer of recollection in Samuel's mind.

'Why should you?' He drew on his pipe. 'Why set yourself the task? Could it be you holds your own grudge against Lytton?'

The man darted another glance about the room, then satisfied they were not the object of any attention, went on. 'I holds a grudge against him, there be no denying that.'

Samuel squinted through the smoke curling from his pipe. 'In that case, why should I pay you for getting rid of him? How come you don't do it for yourself?'

'Could be as I will, could be as I won't,' the man drawled. 'Only you won't know which way or when. You pay me five pounds and you'll be sure.'

'Five pounds!' The exclamation was followed by a short laugh. 'Why should I pay five pounds?'

''Cos that way you'll be in no doubt,' the man answered. 'We both have a grudge, we both want Lytton dead, therefore we should both put something into it, not just me alone. I do the dispatching, you do the paying.'

'Five pounds be too much,' Samuel hedged. 'How do I know you won't just pocket the money and bugger off?'

'You want him out of it and so do I. There's nothing for me in Tipton once he knows I be back.'

'Back?' Potter blew a stream of smoke from a corner of his mouth.

Again the other man nodded. 'Ar, back. Lytton had me sent down, put away for six months, and once he claps eyes on me I might as well be back down the line for there'll be none as will give me work. So what do you say? Do you pay your stake or don't you?'

'Five pounds be a lot of money. I be taking a risk . . .'

'Taking a man's life be a bloody risk!' The other slapped his hand on the table. 'If I get caught it will be more than five quid I'll be paying. Once it be done I shall need money to get me away from here, far away. Five pounds be cheap for what you'll be getting.'

Five pounds! Samuel thought. Pay this man the money and he was like as not throwing money into the fire. He would probably pocket it and be off. Besides which, did he truly want Lytton dead . . . or had his words been a figure of speech, an outburst of temper at what the man was doing to him? The thought acted on Samuel like a spur. Lytton was closing him down, that's what he was doing. He and his cronies had closed ranks against Samuel, barred him from buying the coal the wenches picked. There was no other mine save that of Isaiah Bedworth and he allowed no jagger on his land.

The other man sat silent. The colour mounting in Potter's face and the working of the clay pipe between his teeth told him of the debate raging in the man's mind.

Only Samuel Potter, of all the jaggers that plied the coal tips, was not to be allowed to buy from the pit bank wenches. And why . . . for what reason? It could only be that business of them two women. God strike Lytton! He would see a man go under, take his living from him, and all on account of two bloody doxies! Well, p'raps the Lord were too forgiving, but Sam Potter were not. P'raps the Lord would not strike him down, but Sam Potter would.

Signalling the landlord, he waited until his tankard had been refilled. He drank, eyes taking in the face of every man in the smoky inn. This was not his usual haunt, he generally took his ale in The Fiery Holes down at the other end of the street. Here in the Fountain Inn, he could see none that he knew or who was likely to know him other than as a coal jagger.

Placing the tankard in front of him, he replaced the clay pipe in his mouth. 'You'll do for Lytton ... really do for him?'

Across the table the other man's eyes glittered in the smoky light. He nodded.

'Five pounds, you said?'

Another nod.

Samuel reached a hand into his jacket, taking out a few carefully folded bank notes. Selecting three he replaced the remainder, hiding the three by screwing them into his palm. 'Half now, half when job be done,' he said, casually placing his closed fist on the table between them.

'All of it now!' The glitter in his companion's eyes was feverish. 'I won't be able to hang about once it be done, I'll need to be away.'

'And I need to know what you say will be done, *will* be done. I ain't no bloody charity, I don't go giving money away. Things be done my way or I leave now, with my money. So ... do it be two pound ten now and two pound ten when it be done, or do we part and forget the business altogether?'

'Be it as you say!'

Quickly taking the money that slid unseen from Samuel's hand to his, the man shoved it into the pocket of his jacket.

'When will it be?' Samuel asked over his tankard.

'Soon.' The man pushed himself to his feet. 'Very soon.'

'When?'

The glittering stare was fastened on Samuel.

'I told you – soon. And before you asks where, that be my business. I'll find you when it be time to pay the rest of the money. A coal jagger on the streets of Tipton don't take much finding.'

Would he do what he had promised? Samuel watched the tall spare frame disappear through the door to the street. Would the man rid him of Lytton . . . or had he just let himself be conned out of two pound ten? But you get nowt for nowt. The thought giving him a fragment of consolation, Samuel took up the tankard. And if the job were done, what then? Who would inherit the Lytton properties, and would they open up the coal banks to Samuel Potter?

'We're almost there.' Rachel glanced at the young woman walking beside her. Ellen looked so much better after their night spent aboard the barge. Perhaps it was knowing she was safe, that Samuel Potter would not be taking her for his mistress after all – that and the breakfast of bacon and bread the bargee's wife had insisted they eat before leaving.

The woman and her husband had been so kind. For the first time since running from Beulah's house Rachel felt a flutter of apprehension. She had said that Beulah would welcome Ellen, give her a home as she had done to Rachel, but what if the opposite proved to be true? What if Beulah did not welcome Ellen . . . what if she did not want another woman about the place . . . what if she refused to let Ellen stay in Rachel's cottage?

She pulled on the shawl Ellen had insisted on returning to her. If that was the case they would both move on. She would not let Ellen return to that man Potter, nor leave her to fend for herself in another town. If Beulah would not let Ellen stay, then Rachel would not stay either.

But where would they go? What sort of living could they hope for? Rachel glanced again at the woman beside her.

One of the women who had not weighed the pro's and con's before accepting her into their home, a woman who had shared the very bed she slept in with a girl Bart had brought in from the street. What was in her mind to do was no more than Ellen would have done for her. Rachel set her lips firmly. Whatever Beulah Thomas's decision, Ellen and she would stay together.

Reaching Leasowes bridge, she glanced across to the barley fields beyond the house. William was working with the scythe. William! She paused, keeping her glance on the stooping figure. She was promised to him, she was to be his wife, but what would happen should his mother refuse Ellen a home?

Straightening to ease his back that had probably been bent from early morning, he caught sight of the pale golden hair that glistened in the sunlight, and smiled. Rachel had said she would be back and she had kept her word.

But who was the woman beside her? He watched the two figures cross the bridge, descending on to the path leading to his mother's house. Was it someone she had met on the towpath, someone from a narrow boat who was calling to get fresh water? Maybe, but no barge had gone past today.

Resting the tip of the curved blade on the ground, he leaned both hands on the handle. His mother had sat past her usual bedtime last night. She had talked for a long time about Rachel and the way she worked hard without complaint, doing all of Beulah's chores as well as her own, even trying to learn the brewing. Rachel was a woman honest as the day was long, his mother had said, there was never so much as a farthing short in the money she got for the cheese and butter either from the Fox Inn or the market. She had spoken openly about her life before coming to this house and to Beulah's mind no blame should be attached to her for anything that had gone before. The Lord moved in mysterious ways, his mother had pronounced, crossing herself at the use of His name. He had seen fit to send a woman worthy of her son, a woman who paid no mind to his halting tongue, one who would work alongside him and with a little more of the Lord's help, give him a family.

William picked up the scythe and turned back to the barley. Maybe the mysterious way of the Lord had brought Rachel to him, and his mother had been instrumental in settling things between them, but would she have been so quick to do it had Jared Lytton never come to this house?

Swinging the scythe with a regular motion, he watched the tall stems with their heavy heads of grain fall to the ground. Rachel had never spoken of the visit, not to his mother nor to him, but he knew it had left her shaken, and neither he nor his mother had asked.

Behind him, on the towpath, Rachel smiled as she pointed to the first of the two cottages. 'William and his mother live there.'

'William is the man you are to marry?' Ellen glanced sideways to the figure bent over a scythe.

'Yes.' Rachel followed Ellen's glance with her own. Strange how the sight of him brought no wild surge to her heart, no pounding of blood to her veins.

'When?'

'Oh, not for a while yet.' Rachel suddenly realised she had given no thought to a date; in fact, the thought of marriage had made no real impression on her mind. 'There is the rest of the barley to be harvested, and Beulah ... that is William's mother ... is not too well right now and it means everyone is a little too busy to have discussed things properly yet.'

They walked on in silence, Ellen thinking that a girl in love, a girl promised to the man of her choice could surely never be so busy as not to have time to talk about her wedding. A girl in love ...

She came to a standstill, eyes anxious as they probed Rachel's, searching for the secrets hidden behind those violet depths, seeking the truth of the soul. 'Rachel.' She reached out, her hands fastening over her friend's. 'You do love William? You have promised to be his wife only because you love him, not for any other reason?'

'Of course not. I . . . I do love William, why else would I consent to marry him?'

The answer was given with a smile, but it had been given too late. Ellen watched the play of emotions flicker across her friend's face, the shadows that darkened her lovely eyes. The answer had come too late, she had felt the uncertainty behind the pause. No girl whose heart was filled with love for a man would sound like that.

'Be sure, Rachel,' Ellen warned softly. 'Be very sure. There are right and wrong reasons for marrying. You must be sure that what you feel for William is not simply gratitude. A woman's heart has room for many kinds of love but it has space for just one man. Make sure you have the right one Rachel, for once the bond is made it cannot be broken. The only thing that will be is your heart.'

'I . . . I am sure, Ellen.'

But was she? Rachel walked on, leading the way along the narrow path. She did love William, but not with a love that threatened to burst her heart, not with a desire that reached to the very core of her being, not with a passion that left her trembling with need for him. Not with any of the emotions that had raced through her, and flooded her still, when she thought of Jared Lytton.

But that was a fantasy, Rachel reprimanded herself. It was a childish fancy of which she should be ashamed. Jared Lytton had been kind to her, had helped her that night he had come across her on the heath, and her mind had turned the episode into something it was not. Life was not a fairy tale, there would be no knight on horseback to carry her away; life was here with William, to be lived one day at a time. *This* was all her dream.

Almost at the gate she caught sight of Beulah sitting in her chair in the garden beside the open door of the cottage, a blue enamelled bowl nestling in her lap. Smiling, Rachel raised her hand in greeting.

But the hand resting on the edge of the bowl did not move.

Rachel's heart jolted. Had Beulah guessed the reason for Ellen's presence here? Had she already rejected the possibility of her staying before even hearing the reason?

Rachel waved again, smiling despite her worry. But the hand touching the bowl remained as still as before and the gaze Beulah had settled on her son stayed with him.

Rachel would not have thought Beulah a woman to reject another out of hand. She would have sworn that William's mother would at least have heard them out; had not thought it her nature to turn her back without hearing a word.

'It would be better if I went.' Ellen had seen Rachel's wave and the lack of acknowledgement. 'It was unwise of me to come.'

'Nonsense!' Rachel grabbed Ellen's hand, pulling her along.

Pushing open the gate, she pulled Ellen through behind her, forcing a smile back to her face as she did so. Halfway along the flower-bordered path she called hello.

Beside the doorway William's mother made no reply. Her hand remained still on the edge of the blue bowl and her gaze stayed on her son.

'Rachel, I don't want to go any further.' Ellen dug in her heels. 'It is obvious Mrs Thomas does not want me here. I will not embarrass her by continuing to stay.'

Rachel stared at the woman who only yesterday was so kind to her. How could she now adopt such an attitude? At least she might speak to them, tell them in words that Ellen was not welcome. Instead she was acting in a way Rachel could not believe. Had something happened in the time she had been in Tipton Green? If so why had William not ignored her as his mother was now? He had returned her wave.

'Stay here, Ellen.' Rachel released the other girl's hand.

'Don't leave ... not yet. I wish to speak to Mrs Thomas, then you and I will leave together.'

'No, Rachel!' Ellen spoke quickly. 'You have a home here, you can't leave it for me.'

'I *had* a home here,' Rachel replied, 'but if it is a home where you are not welcome then it is no home at all. Wait for me, Ellen. I will not leave without giving Mrs Thomas my reason. She deserves that courtesy even though it seems I do not.'

Getting Ellen's agreement to wait, Rachel stepped forward alone.

'Mrs Thomas,' she began, 'I apologise for bringing Ellen with me to your home. I would of course have liked to ask your permission first but circumstances were such I was too afraid to leave her alone.'

Half way up the bowl peas gleamed green against the blue. In the hand that rested on its rim, Beulah held a half open pod. Yet still she did not move, nor did she make any answer.

'Mrs Thomas, I have apologised and I can do no more. But Ellen is my friend. Together with Tansy and Cora she found me a home when I had nothing and I will not turn my back on her now. Ellen will leave and I will go with her. If I have your permission to go into the cottage I will collect my clothes. I do have some money saved toward that you were kind enough to lend me to buy them, I will give that to you before I go, and the rest I will send as soon as I can earn it, on that you have my solemn promise.'

Turning on her heel Rachel stifled the tears that rose to her throat. She had been so sure, so sure William's mother would understand what she had done, so sure she would welcome Ellen.

Refusing to enter Rachel's cottage, Ellen waited in the tiny garden. It was such a pretty spot. The two small white houses robed in honeysuckle and roses and backed by fields of golden barley edged by the dark greens and browns of the heath, while to the front of them the canal gleamed like a roadway of beaten gold. This was Rachel's home, she was to marry the man now working in those fields. Ellen turned back towards the house outside which Beulah sat unmoving.

She would give the woman her own apologies for causing any embarrassment, then ask her to explain to Rachel why she had left after promising not to.

'Ellen!'

The call came before Ellen had reached Beulah's gate and she waited as Rachel ran up to her, hastily gathered clothes scooped into a bundle wrapped around by her shawl.

'You promised you would not leave.'

'I do not want you to give up what you have here.' Ellen did not deny what she had intended. 'I was going to offer my apologies to Mrs Thomas.'

'You will do no such thing!' Rachel was emphatic. 'You owe her no apology, what has been done was done by me and my apology has been given. It remains only for me to give her this.' Opening her hand Rachel showed the money she had been paid over the weeks she had worked for Beulah; shillings that had been saved to pay her debt to the woman.

Leaving Ellen at the gateway, Rachel walked up to the figure that still did not acknowledge her presence.

Rachel looked down at Beulah: at the hair faded to pale sand, to the deeply veined hands, one resting against the rim of the bowl, the other on the white apron that covered her voluminous black skirts.

Beulah neither spoke nor moved.

'Mrs Thomas, please, won't you at least say goodbye?'

Her feelings threatening to overwhelm her when no answer was given, Rachel leaned forward and gently touched the woman's arm. The hand that rested on the rim of the bowl fell inside it, fingers pale against the bright green of the peas.

'Mrs Thomas!' Rachel dropped to her knees in order to look into the eyes still trained on William.

'Mrs Thomas,' she said, softly as before. But William's mother did not speak. She would never speak again.

Beulah Thomas was dead.

Chapter Eighteen

Lowering the heavy basket to the ground, Rachel stretched her aching back. It seemed that every week more and more butter and cheese were required to satisfy their customers in town. But she could not refuse, though the extra work, added to that of the brew house and alongside William in the fields, meant she was busy from early morning, working until late into the night to see to the cleaning of the cottages.

She stretched again, feeling the tug through every muscle and bone, feeling her soul cry out in weariness. It had been a month since she had found Beulah dead. A month in which she had not ceased from blaming herself for doubting the woman, for accusing her mentally of refusing to accept Ellen, when all the time . . .

Tears of tiredness and loss rose in her throat as she bent to pick up the basket. What was happening in her life? Why was the hand of heaven turned against her?

Oblivious to the sounds of the heath, she trudged on. Why was everyone she loved being taken from her? Was it retribution for something she had done? Was it because of something she had not done?

Tears trickled down her cheeks but Rachel wearily ignored them. She had never missed saying her prayers, nor ever harmed a living thing, other than hitting Samuel Potter with that clog. Would that have been against the laws of heaven?

Would her striking that man be so abhorrent to God he would punish her by taking those she loved?

Swinging the basket in front of her, she transferred it to the other hand and walked on, body angled sharply sideways to counteract the weight. No, that could not be the case, her thoughts ran on. Things had begun to go wrong before the evening she had struck Potter. First she had lost the brother she adored, then had come the parting from the father she loved; after them it had been Bart – cheeky, quick-tongued, lovable Bart.

A sob squeezed from her and resounded on the balmy late-summer air. She had thought then that heaven could hold no more heartbreak for her; that finding that twisted, battered little body was the ultimate sorrow. But she had been wrong. There were horrors still to come. Her cup had not yet been filled.

'Why? Why do this to me ... what have I done to deserve it?'

The words rang across the heath, sending a covey of startled birds darting into the sky.

But heaven's revenge was not complete. Its rod of retribution still pointed at Rachel Cade.

It had been Tansy and Cora who had been taken next. Closing her eyes, Rachel lifted her face to the sky, mouth opening in a long anguished cry that refused to leave her throat. Tansy and Cora, two women who had taken her into their home and their hearts; two women who had shown her a love that her father's wife had never felt for her; two women, each of whom she'd loved as a mother, stifled to death beneath a sea of mud.

Oh God, it was my fault ... my fault! The silent cries went on, pulling at the depths of her, tearing at her very soul. If only I had stayed, if only I had not left, then it could have been me on the banks. Why wasn't it me? Oh, God, why couldn't it have been me!

But that way her torment would have been ended, and

that fate would not allow. It held more sorrow yet for the object of its hatred. Rachel Cade was to taste further of the dish of bitter herbs. And fate *had* struck again, and quickly. It had taken William's mother.

William . . . Rachel brushed wearily at the tears that coursed down her cheeks. His mother's death had been such a shock to him. Beulah had hidden her pain from her son, mentioned no word of the illness Rachel had known to be worsening. It must have resulted in the heart attack that had killed her yet, like William, Rachel blamed herself.

Reaching the outskirts of Bloomfield, she paused to wipe her face on her handkerchief. She wanted no trace of the misery within her to show. There was gossip enough about her in this town and in Foxley without giving folk more to talk on.

Picking up the basket, she walked along the street in which stalls were already being set with meat and fish, poultry and bread, children's clothing and hardware – every commodity a household might need. And at every stall a woman's eyes turned to follow her.

The smiles had gone from the faces of these women who no longer greeted her with a friendly word. She was an unmarried girl living in the same house as a man who was no relative to her.

Heaving the basket on to a stall set beneath the Butter Cross, Rachel almost smiled at the irony of the situation. No one had asked about her accommodation. They knew only that Beulah Thomas was dead, and the girl she had taken under her roof was still there, that she was living with that woman's son, unwed and against the laws of the church.

Lining packages of cheese and butter neatly on the stall, Rachel tasted the bitterness on her tongue. They had not asked. They had judged her and found she fell short of their morals. Though that did not stop them from buying her butter and cheese, she thought as a bulky woman, a basket on her arm, bought two pounds of each. From somewhere deep in her memory Rachel recalled the words her father had once comforted her with after a woman in Horseley had complained about the way Rachel had performed some errand: 'They want jam both sides of their bread.'

'Do you be living with Billy Duckegg?'

Her wares sold, Rachel was walking between the rapidly emptying stalls, following the street that would lead her from the town.

'My mother says you be living with a bloke as you ain't married to.'

Rachel walked on in silence, but the taunts of the children grouped about her had the colour rising in her face.

'Hey!' A lad a little bolder than the rest snatched at the empty basket, jerking Rachel's arm. 'Be that right? Be you living with Billy Duckegg?'

Across the street two women halted their conversation long enough to watch her pass by, but made no attempt to intervene. This was a woman living in sin, it was no more than she deserved.

'Billy Duckegg be daft in the 'ead.' A second boy, his clothes as poor as her own, danced in front of her. 'What's it like, missis, living with somebody that's daft in the 'ead?'

'Don't call 'er missis.' The one who had snatched at the basket joined his fellow, prancing backward a few steps ahead of Rachel, a grin spreading across his face. 'That be the wrong thing to call 'er. 'Cos 'er ain't married. The name to call 'er by be whore.'

'What's a whore?' The high-pitched tones of a girl of about eight caught the attention of a man who tutted loudly then shouted that Rachel should keep a better check on the language of her brood.

'You shouldn't say words like that!' A boy whose carrot-coloured hair and freckled appearance was so like that of the girl he could only be her brother, grabbed the child roughly. 'You get yourself off home, we don't want you trailing everywhere we go. Gerroff afore I thump you!' He pushed her, sending her falling into the gutter where she sat crying loudly.

'I'll tell mother on you, our Alfie, I'll tell her what you said . . . I'll tell her you said whore!'

Regretfully the carrot-headed lad dropped behind to minister to the crying girl, but the others continued to follow Rachel, enjoying the sport they had found for themselves.

'You be no better than you should be.'

The first boy stepped sideways, and as Rachel passed he stuck out his foot, catching her across the ankles, laughing loudly as she stumbled.

'What does that mean?' His companion joined in the laughter. 'No better than her should be?'

'Don't you know nothing!' The elder of the two looked at the other disparagingly. 'It means . . .'

'Never mind what it means!'

A hand fastened on the boy's collar, lifting him bodily and shaking him before letting him drop. 'Get yourselves away before I take a bar of soap to your mouth. And should I catch you at your games again it will be more than a bar of soap I will take to you!'

'Right, mister . . . sorry, mister.'

The boys scuttled away and Rachel turned to thank the man who had come to her aid.

'You!' Her cheeks, still scarlet from the boys' taunts, glowed a deeper red.

'Good afternoon, Miss Cade.' Jared Lytton inclined his head, the movement so slight as to be almost invisible. 'Are you in Bloomfield alone?'

He had heard the taunts those boys had thrown at her, heard the words they had shouted!

'Is your fiance not with you?'

Whether she imagined the hint of cynicism in his voice or whether it were truly present, Rachel did not know. She lifted her head defiantly.

'No, Mr Lytton, William is not with me. He is busy in the fields.'

The bitter smile that touched his mouth at her answer this time left her in no doubt as to his feeling. 'So busy he leaves you to face this town alone!'

Though her cheeks still glowed with embarrassment at what he must have heard, her eyes blazed with sudden anger. 'In this town or any other, Mr Lytton, I am perfectly capable of handling the demands of the market.'

'Demands of the market, yes!' he spat. 'But what of scenes like the one I have just witnessed, and what if next time it should be men and not boys? How would you handle that?'

'I . . . I . . .' Rachel stumbled, unable to find an answer.

'Precisely! You could *not* handle it. But such a situation is almost bound to arise and you would get precious little help and no sympathy from the women of this town so long as you remain living with a man without benefit of his name. My advice to you is to get yourself married, Miss Cade, and soon.'

So he thought as they all did. He too had judged her out of hand, drawn his conclusions without asking for her side of things. Rachel drew a deep breath. Inside her embarrassment turned to cold hard resentment, tempered by resolve. So he too thought her to be living in the same house as William, to be sharing his life, living as his wife? Well, let him continue to think that way, she would not enlighten him.

'I thank you for coming to my assistance, Mr Lytton.' Violet eyes that a moment ago had blazed with anger were now impenetrable. 'You mistakenly thought I needed it. As for your advice, however, that I do *not* need. The way I choose to live my life, and with whom I choose to live it, is not your affair. Were I a man, I doubt you would take such liberties!'

'Were you a man I should be tempted to take a whip to you. As it is, I . . .' Anger getting the better of him, Jared broke off. A long breath restored some of his self-control though it eased none of the fury from his face. When he spoke it was in a voice as thick as before. 'My horse and trap are over in the yard behind the railway station. You will allow me to return you to your . . . your home?'

Catching the momentary pause, Rachel could have smiled. Instead she continued to stare coldly at him. 'No, Mr Lytton, I will not allow you to return me to my home. Your assistance of a few moments ago, though not necessary, was appreciated . . .'

'It was no more than I would have given any woman in that situation.'

No more than he would have given any woman! Despite her resentment, Rachel could not quell the tug at her heart. She was no more to him than any passing woman in the streets.

'That is to your credit, Mr Lytton. As for my returning home, I can do so without your help. Your company is not agreeable to me.'

For a moment Rachel thought he might strike her. The blood drained from his face and his eyes burned.

'Then I will not press it any further upon you. Good day, Miss Cade!'

Giving the faintest nod of his head, he turned and walked away. Seeing the height of him, the natural ease of his body beneath his grey coat and trousers, his hair bronzed by the lowering sun, Rachel felt an almost overpowering sense of loss, a force within her that drove up from the lowest pit of her stomach, gathering itself into her chest, robbing her of her breath. Jared Lytton would never speak to her again, he would cut her out of his mind, but he would always carry her heart.

'Rachel, why didn't you tell him?' Ellen watched across the table as the other girl picked at the meal she had prepared, eating none of it. 'Why did you not say that you shared this house with me while William lived in the other?'

'It would have made little difference.' She did not look up from her plate, knowing the unhappiness she felt still showed in her eyes. 'He had already made up his mind I was what those boys called me.'

'But you could have told him the truth.'

'The truth!' Rachel's laughter held all the bitterness of the afternoon, and buried beneath it the heartache of hopeless love. 'Jared Lytton does not want to hear the truth. He knows all he wants to know. To him I am William's mistress, a whore. He wants to know no more than that.'

'Now who is doing the judging?'

The question stinging, Rachel pushed herself to her feet. 'Let's get these dishes washed and then you can tell me how your day has gone.'

Helping to gather plates and cutlery, Ellen followed her into the scullery. It was no use raking over old ashes, that only caused fresh misery and from the look of Rachel she had more than enough of that already; whatever she might or might not say about Jared Lytton she had feelings for the man, and those feelings were not just of friendship.

'Ellen,' Rachel asked when once more they were sitting together in the small living room, 'what do you think of William?'

Her glance almost startled, Ellen looked quickly away. 'I . . . I . . . he is a good man, Rachel. Don't think I say that simply because he allowed me to stay here with you. He is a good, kind man.'

'But his speech.' Rachel let her own words break the silence that suddenly held the room. 'What do you think of that, or has he not spoken to you?'

'William *has* spoken to me,' Ellen answered softly. 'And his stammer makes no difference. Beneath it he is a man with a heart, and one that is filled with love for you, Rachel.'

Staring into the coals glowing in the grate, she owned the truth of Ellen's words. William did love her, and it was a love that asked nothing of her, demanded no answers. A love such as Jared Lytton could never feel.

'You should set a date for your marriage, Rachel.' Ellen looked earnestly at her. 'William is too fine a man to keep hanging on a string.'

Rachel lifted her glance sharply. 'Is that what I'm doing?'

'Yes, I think you are. William has your promise but will never push you into keeping it, he is not the sort. He will wait, Rachel. However long it takes, he will wait for you to say when the day is to be.'

Yes, Rachel admitted silently. William would wait as he had already waited. Would Jared Lytton have waited had she been promised to him? But she never would be. He was not a man to marry a woman he thought a whore, much less a ragged-arsed miner's daughter.

From a chair opposite, Ellen watched Rachel's thoughts mirrored on her face. She had warned her once before of the heartbreak that marriage to the wrong man would bring but then she had felt only for the girl, for Rachel. Now she felt for another, for the unhappiness and pain such a marriage would bring to William. He loved Rachel, that much was certain, but could such a love stand the anguish of knowing he had a wife who could not return his feelings. That her heart was held by another man?

'Rachel,' Ellen asked gently, 'are you truly sure of your feelings for William? I know it is not his stammer that has kept you from marrying sooner. Had that bothered you, you would not have accepted him in the first place. But is there someone else? If there is, then tell William now. Don't do something that will only haunt you both for the rest of your lives.'

'There is no one else.' Rachel felt the twisting of her stomach as she said it. 'I love William and his stammer is of no consequence to me.' Rising to her feet, she took Ellen's hand, pulling her from the chair. 'Tomorrow I shall follow your advice, Miss Walker, and set a date for my wedding, but now it's bed for both of us. I have a busy time in the brew house in the morning and I am not such a dab hand at the beer as Beulah was.'

Tomorrow she would speak to William, tomorrow they would set a date for their wedding. Rachel slipped a cotton nightgown over her head. 'Is there someone else?' Ellen had asked. Crossing to the small table that held no more than a hairbrush, Rachel drew a long breath, holding back the tears that had already reached her throat. She had answered no but that had not been wholly true. Slowly she pulled the brush through her hair. She loved William, that part had been honest enough, but her denial of any feelings for another – was that as honest?

Laying aside the brush, she walked to the tiny window and stood staring out at the silver line of water that girdled the heath.

'*Never deny the truth, my little love.*' Suddenly Rachel was seeing a small child wearing a dress that looked as though it had been cut from the sky, her silver-gold hair falling beneath a straw bonnet to touch the deeper sapphire of her sash. Her hand was lifted, holding that of a tall, spare-framed man dressed in dark trousers and jacket, his white Sunday shirt open at the neck.

'But he didn't take them, Father, they were given to him. That boy said he didn't want them any more, but when Peter took them home his mother was angry. She said he had taken them from the nest, but he didn't. Peter wouldn't do anything like that.'

Reliving the scene preserved forever in her memory, Rachel saw the tall figure sink to his haunches, hands on the child's shoulders, turning her gently to face him.

'You are sure Peter did not take those eggs from the nest?'

The deep voice acted on her memory, bringing the suppressed tears to her eyes.

'I'm sure, Father.' The bright head nodded vigorously. 'A boy gave them to him.'

'You do know it is wrong to take eggs from a bird's nest?'

''Course I do. *You* told me.'

'Yes, *I* told you.' The man pulled the child to him, placing a kiss on the tip of her nose. 'You did right to tell Peter's mother what really happened. Never deny the truth, my little love, and never betray a friendship.'

A strangled sob breaking from her lips, Rachel swung away from the window, pressing her hands to her face, willing the memories to fade.

Never deny the truth! But how could she admit it? How could she speak what was in her heart . . . her soul?

Never betray a friendship! Her father's words rang in her mind. Was that not exactly what she was doing? William had befriended her and now he loved her, but wasn't she betraying that friendship, that love, by not telling him?

'I can't, Father . . . I can't!'

In the silence of her bedroom the words seemed to hang in the air, waiting for others to dispel them. But Rachel could not say them. Tomorrow she would ask William to set a date, and on that day they would become man and wife. She could not hurt him by telling him the truth, telling him her heart's secret.

She would never tell him she loved Jared Lytton.

Jared stood beside the canal wharf at Dudley Port watching a cargo from his Five Bricks works being transferred to a goods train bound for the west country.

'That be the lot, Mr Lytton, sir. Will you be wanting any other cargo carried?'

'What . . . oh, yes.' Jared pulled his thoughts from fruitless speculation on his last meeting with Rachel Cade, and glanced at the bargee who stood waiting for instructions. 'There is a load of chain at Tipton Green, my manager there has all the particulars. See him and say I told you to collect it.'

'Ar, I'll do that, Mr Lytton.' The bargee touched a finger to his cap. 'Thank you, sir.'

Jared turned, picking his way carefully over the slender steel railway tracks that led through the massive loading sheds to disappear out the other end, their silver lines snaking into the horizon.

Climbing into the trap he had deliberately chosen as his means of travel, he sat with the reins loose in his hand. '*The way I choose to live my life, and with whom I choose to live it, is not your affair . . .*'

The words had slipped back into his mind almost before that bargee had left him. Now they taunted him, as painful as they had been almost every moment since she had spoken them, returning to haunt him as they did each night when he tried to sleep.

'Was there anything else, Mr Lytton?'

A man who had emerged from one of the many port offices was standing watching him.

'No, nothing more.' He flicked the reins, setting the trap in motion.

Driving along Owen Street, he glanced at a woman standing at the edge of the road waiting for the trap to pass before crossing the busy road, but he did not see the black hair peeping from beneath a plum-coloured shawl, nor the grey skirts that brushed the ground. Instead the sun glinted on hair of silver-gold and added depths to deep violet eyes that stared defiantly back at him.

'*Your company is not agreeable to me.*'

Again the words cut deep into him.

He was not agreeable!

The cold anger that had swept over him that afternoon he had spoken to her in Bloomfield High Street, returned like a rising tide.

He was not agreeable? Not agreeable to a ragged-arsed miner's daughter? Not agreeable to a whore!

Guiding the horse left out of Neptune Street, he took the road to Dudley.

'*You be no better than you should be.*'

Words he had banned from his mind were now allowed free rein. Should he ever come across the girl in such a situation again, he would leave her to it. It would be no more than she deserved.

But as he guided the trap into the yard of the limestone quarry, the shadow of Rachel Cade rode with him.

'I've put some men back up on to the second level . . .'

Jared walked with his quarry manager, his mind not yet entirely free from the image of a girl's face staring defiantly into his.

'I'm none too sure of the pillars. The rock is sound enough but I'm worried they might be a bit on the narrow side. It's best to be sure, I'm not too keen on having half of Wren's Nest caving in on us.'

'If there is the slightest doubt, then have the roof shored with timbers.' Jared's mind cleared immediately, tuning in to the manager's hint of possible danger. 'In fact, regardless of what the reports say, I want those pillars reinforced. See it is done without delay!'

The manager nodded, following him into the workings, blinking at the sudden darkness.

'How far in are they?' Nodding his thanks to a workman who handed him a jar that held a lighted candle, Jared held it above his head.

'That bunch be nigh up to the castle mound.' The manager pointed to a black hole chiselled into the rock to his left.

'Then cease mining in that tunnel. I don't want any mining closer to the castle than we are now. After all,' he smiled, 'it has defied all attempts to bring it to the ground since William the Conqueror had it erected in 1087, I should hate to be the one to undermine it.'

'Wouldn't be exactly popular, would we, sir?' The man returned Jared's smile then went on, 'The main workings be a bit further in. If you'll follow me, I'll take you closer.

Only mind your step, sir. The ground isn't what you might call paved.'

Don't I know it? Jared thought, following deeper into the workings. I've fallen flat on my face more than once.

'This is a good quality limestone, Mr Lytton. Mind, we have had to come deep enough down to get it.'

His eyes accustomed now to a blackness relieved only by jaundiced spots of light shed by quarrymen's candles, Jared stared upward. Above him the earlier levels reached like huge domed halls, each separated from the other by pillars of rock, and above them other excavations had gouged great caverns that rose tier on tier through the bowels of the massive limestone hills.

'Will this take another shaft or do you think it is worked out?'

'I don't reckon it to be worked out, Mr Lytton . . .'

The words rose in the cathedral-like caverns, echoing from the limestone walls in a little river of sound. Above Jared a quarryman leaned forward, gazing down to ground level, his own body dimly illuminated by his candle and by the stream of daylight filtering through one of the many air shafts chiselled through the rock to the surface, to feed fresh air into the underground workings.

Jared Lytton. The workman's mouth curled in a hard smile. He had known this quarry was owned by Lytton; that had been his sole reason for taking a job that kept him in the bowels of the earth thirteen hours a day . . . thirteen hours of each day waiting for the man who had sent him down the line. But after today there would be no more quarrying and no more Lytton. Glancing towards the lump of rock he always kept close to hand, he blew out his candle. Moving carefully on the loose chippings that lay beneath his feet, he rose. Leaning forward again to check that the men still stood on the same spot some hundred feet below him, he paused as a trickle of chippings went sliding over the edge.

A few yards from Jared another of the workmen looked up

from loading a bogey with quarried stone. Falling chippings were not uncommon but the man causing them needed to be warned. One fall could lead to another.

The man turned quickly towards the sound, scanning the upper galleries with a sight sharpened by long hours underground.

'Jesus Christ!' He breathed the words as he saw the figure. Etched in black against a canvas of grey light, it stood with arms raised above its head, a large lump of limestone in its hands.

Automatically following the line of descent, the watcher's eyes came to rest on Jared.

'Look out!' His shout rolled round and round the vast workings, echoing eerily in the endless tunnels. At the same moment he launched himself forward, his outstretched hands knocking Jared sideways as the stone fell, followed seconds later by a piercing scream which ricocheted against the walls of the quarry in long, blood-chilling repetitions. The sound accompanied the figure that fell from the upper workings.

'Holy Christ!' Like a man who had woken from a nightmare, the manager felt the trickle of cold sweat against his spine. 'Mr Lytton, Mr Lytton! Are you all right, sir?' Then taking one of the candle jars that had been pushed forward even before he could call for them, he bent over the fallen body of his employer, which was half covered by another.

'Christ, I think this one's done for!' he said, holding the candle jar closer to the figure sprawled across Jared, a gaping wound on the side of his head spilling a crimson trail into the white limestone dust.

Gently, as if handling a child, several quarrymen lifted away the body of the man who had tried to save Jared, carrying him along the dark stretch of tunnel out into the yard.

Removing his coat, the manager covered Jared then held

the light close to his face. 'Mr Lytton,' he urged softly, 'Mr Lytton, are you all right, sir?' Then as Jared made no sound he looked up at the men standing anxiously around him and gave a slow shake of his head.

Chapter Nineteen

'Rachel, please, I want to help. I am perfectly well now and can't go on sitting here while you work yourself to death.'

Placing a gauze over curds she had just pressed into wooden moulds, Rachel smiled. 'I am not working myself to death, Ellen.'

'Well, how long before you do?' she returned crisply. 'You're up at first light and don't go to bed much before midnight. You can't go on like this without making your-self ill.'

'I've finished here now.' She gathered the scoops and sieves she had used, carrying them to the sink for washing. 'How about the two of us having a cup of tea?'

'You will not dismiss the subject of my helping as easily as that, Miss Rachel Cade.' Ellen wagged a finger. 'I have more to say on the subject.'

'Say it over a cup of tea,' Rachel laughed, rinsing the tools she had used to make her cheese.

'Don't think I won't. Two minutes, that's all it takes to brew a pot of tea. Either you are in that kitchen in two minutes or I'll call William and have him carry you in.'

William! Rachel's hands stilled in their task. In a month they would be married. She had asked him three evenings ago as they had stood together in the brew house, William testing the beer that was to be delivered next day to the Fox Inn. He had taught her all he knew about brewing and it seemed

263

he knew as much as his mother for now the inn required even more beer than it had when Beulah made it. He had smiled at her as he'd praised her quickness in learning, and she had asked him then, asked that a date be set for their wedding.

William had taken her in his arms, gently, tenderly, but he had not kissed her; simply holding her, he had replied that any date she wanted was acceptable to him.

Rachel hung sieves and ladles on the various pegs set into the wall. William had held her but in her heart she had felt none of the rapture she'd always thought would accompany such a moment; and he had not kissed her. Was that not strange, was it not usual for men to kiss their intended bride? Would Jared Lytton behave the same way? Yet William had kissed her once, the evening she had agreed to marry him. But Beulah's son was not a demonstrative man. True he talked to her easily now, his stammer almost gone, but it had taken time. Perhaps it would be the same with her marriage? Perhaps it would take time for him to let his true feelings show?

Hanging up the last ladle, Rachel scanned the dairy, checking that all was cleaned and back in place, then turned to leave as Ellen's call drifted in to her.

That had been another strange thing. Beulah had told her he spoke with ease to no one save her but kept his silence with other people – so much so the villagers of Foxley labelled him weak in the head, though William was certainly not that. It had taken some time before he had spoken to Rachel, yet the strange thing was he had spoken almost at once to Ellen, and spoken with only a trace of a stammer.

Crossing the yard to the cottage, Rachel smiled. She was glad Ellen and William were friends, but would he want her friend living so close once he and Rachel were married?

Seated beside the table in a kitchen she had brightened with flowers, and with pretty curtains and covers she had found stored away in a chest, Rachel watched her friend pour tea into delicate cups. Those two cups had been the only thing she had spent money on, buying them soon after Ellen had come here. Somehow platter mugs seemed wrong in Ellen's hands. Though Rachel herself disliked thick heavy china she would have put up with it for herself, but for Ellen she had wanted something nicer. They had cost fourpence each, and carrying them home wrapped in the cloth that had covered her butter and cheese basket she had scolded herself again and again for such waste of hard-earned money. She had bought them with the savings she had wanted to give to Beulah . . .

Rachel took her tea, sipping it repeatedly, trying to drown the mixture of guilt and sorrow that rose in her throat.

'Shall I fill a bottle of tea for William?'

Ellen was looking at her, a question in her grey eyes though it did not concern a drink for William.

'Yes, please.' Rachel nodded, forcing the smile back to her lips. 'I will take it to him when I have finished my tea.'

'I could take it if you like?' Ellen turned quickly towards the scullery where a couple of bottles were kept beside the larger stone jars filled with cider. 'I quite enjoy the walk up to the fields.'

'If you are sure it will not tire you?'

Returning to the kitchen, Ellen set the bottle on the table then fixed Rachel with a firm look. 'I am perfectly well, your care and William's kindness have seen to that. Now you must let me do my share. I want to help with *all* that has to be done, and that includes working alongside you both in the fields. Just making the odd meal is not enough, I feel I have to do more to help towards my keep. You felt the same way when you came to us in Tipton Green, didn't you?'

It was true. Rachel could not sit idly by while the others worked to pay for her food and board. She smiled again, this time more easily. 'Very well. You can do as much as you want, only promise me you will do so in stages? Don't throw yourself in too quickly. Picking the coal heaps was hard work but this is hard too. Don't let it fool you, Ellen, it will often leave you exhausted.'

'That's the way you look every night.' She screwed a piece of clean white cloth into a tightly rolled tube, inserting it in the neck of the filled bottle. 'You cannot keep that pace up, Rachel, I'll not let you. I'll not have you looking like a ghost on your wedding day.'

Her wedding day. Why did the words have so little effect upon her? Why was there only emptiness where there should have been joy? Would it be different if the man she was to marry were Jared Lytton?

The unspoken question bringing colour to her cheeks, Rachel dropped her eyes, unable to hold Ellen's gentle questioning glance.

'We'll neither of us look like ghosts on my wedding day.' She made an excuse of gathering the fragile china cups. But I will feel like one, she thought, carrying the cups and saucers through to wash them in the scullery. I will feel as empty as I feel now. Oh, God, I can't do it, I can't marry William. But with tears rising in her throat, she knew she could not go back on her word. Struggling to regain her composure, she smiled as she re-entered the bright kitchen.

'Will I take a piece of pie along with the tea?'

'No doubt William will be more than pleased if you do.' Rachel saw the hefty wedge of meat and potato pie already wrapped in a cloth. 'He really enjoys your cooking.'

'It was Cora taught me.' Ellen folded the ends of the cloth enclosing the pie. 'I was never allowed into the kitchens at home, my mother . . .'

She broke off, the pain of words she could not bring herself to speak evident in her eyes.

'We both have much to thank Cora for, and Tansy too,' Rachel said. 'They did a great deal for the two of us and we will never forget them. I think we will both love them the rest of our lives.'

'He saw me try to reach them.' Ellen's hands trembled as she reached for the bottle, and she set it back on the table. 'He saw me, Rachel. My father saw me, and he turned away!'

'Ellen!' Stepping quickly to her, Rachel took her in her arms, holding her as she sobbed. 'Ellen, I'm so sorry.'

The grief she had tried so hard to keep at bay swelled sharply. Like a great inrushing tide it engulfed her, sweeping away her defences, breaking down the barriers she had so carefully built, washing away any strength she had left to hold back the tears. She knew what Ellen was feeling, knew what it felt like to lose beloved parents, knew the pain that was ever there, lying just beneath the surface, waiting like some predatory animal to leap on her the moment her guard slipped. 'Father,' she breathed, her sobs mingling with Ellen's in the quiet kitchen, 'Father, where are you? Why don't you come for me? Come for me before it is too late!'

But it was already too late for her. Rachel drew a long ragged breath, trying to find the remnants of her self-control, drawing them about her as she would a shawl. It was too late for Rachel Cade. She was promised to a man she loved only as a brother, but he was a man she would sooner die than hurt. In a month she would become Mrs William Thomas and nothing in the world would change that.

And Ellen?

Instinctively Rachel's arms tightened about the other girl. What of her? Would William allow her to stay . . . could she see her friend sent away?

Oh, God help me! Rachel felt her heart swell again, with fear and helplessness. Help me to know what to do, give me the strength to help Ellen, show me what to do . . . please, show me what to do!

Slowly their tears died away. 'I . . . I cannot take William his tea with a face as blotched as a herring.' Ellen was the first to break free, lifting the corner of the apron that once had belonged to Beulah and wiping away the last of her tears on it.

'He might take a fishing line to you at that.' Rachel smiled damply, knowing her own face must be equally marked by tears. 'Go and wash your face while I make some fresh tea, William isn't too keen on it cold.'

Taking the kettle to the pump, she watched the trickle of water creep gradually up its sides. She had learned so much more about William since Beulah's death. The way he smoked just one pipe of tobacco in the evening, drank only one tankard of beer . . . Did Jared Lytton smoke a pipe, did he take a tankard of beer or did he prefer wine as he had the night he had taken her to the Fox Inn . . .

Suddenly realising the path her thoughts had followed, Rachel felt guilty.

Jared Lytton had no place in her thoughts and no place in her life. She had as yet found no way of repaying the money he had paid for her night's lodging. 'But I will,' she whispered to the glowing coals as she set the kettle over them. 'I will, and then I can forget all about him.'

Turning as Ellen came downstairs, Rachel wondered why her heart laughed, why it called her a fool.

'Your turn.' Ellen smiled, her face restored. 'Go and wash Rachel. I will finish making the tea.'

Upstairs in her own room Rachel splashed cold water over her face. The sting of it cooled her skin but did nothing to revive her spirits.

'Pull yourself together,' she whispered, drying her face on the cloth that hung beside the wash stand. 'You were glad enough to come here and live in this house. You had plenty of chances to leave. You did not have to accept William's proposal, did not have to agree to become his wife.' So why had she? Did she too want jam on both sides of her bread!

Hanging the cloth back in its place, she stared at her reflection in the small mirror. Her hair, caught back in a scrap of ribbon she had found, shone in the daylight as usual but the eyes that stared back at her were dull and dark, embedded in circles that were almost mauve, and her cheekbones stood high beneath skin that remained pale despite hours spent working in the barley fields. Was it tiredness that had her face looking so drawn, or was it the wanting . . . ?

No! Rachel spun around, rejecting the thought rising in her mind. There *was* nothing else. It was helping to harvest the barley along with the many chores of the house, the dairy and the brewing. It *was* tiredness . . . there was nothing else!

There was no other reason for her to look as she did, Rachel repeated to herself as she went downstairs to the kitchen. So why, with every step she took, did she hear that same mocking laughter in her heart?

Jared Lytton fastened the grey silk cravat about his throat, then touched a finger to the partly healed cut on the side of his head. He had been lucky, very lucky, that bloody maniac of a man could have killed him! And for what reason? Slipping on his grey coat, he shrugged his shoulders into it, settling it comfortably. Why had that workman hurled a lump of limestone down on him? Was it that he held a grievance over his wages? Jared smoothed the soft grey material. The overseer at the quarry had said that none had been heard by him, that the man was new on the job and nothing was known about him. And now nothing would be known. The man had slipped, probably on the same loose shale that had alerted his rescuer, and had fallen from the gallery, splitting his skull as he landed.

Thank Heaven that other man had been aware of the first slip of chippings, that his eyes were so accustomed to the perpetual near-blackness he had seen at once the figure holding the rock above his head. Had it not been for him . . .

Jared dismissed the thought. He would not dwell on might have beens. Refusing a hat, taking only a short driving whip, he walked to the stables at the back of the house. Pausing a moment before climbing into the trap his stable hand had ready for him, he stared at the house built by his grandfather and which he had inherited from his father. Even from the rear it was imposing but beautiful. Jared felt love for the house stir inside him, as it always did. Foxley House had an air about it, an air that said: Bring your loved one here, let these stones love her as you love her.

Only there was no loved one. There was no one in his life, no one to share the serenity and peace of this lovely house. He let his gaze travel over the pointed arches of the Gothic-styled windows set deep in the stone walls, at the tall chimneys topped with their coronets of brick, gleaming honey-coloured in the morning light, then down to the high doorway where for one fleeting moment he seemed to see the figure of a young woman – one whose glorious golden hair challenged the sun itself.

Impatient with his own feeling of sadness, he climbed into the trap, taking the reins. He had vowed never to let that girl enter his thoughts again, to wipe her from his memory as a child in school would wipe chalk from a slate. But at every turn she was there, her violet eyes watching him, her lovely mouth parting to speak to him. And when she did it was to say, 'I am going to marry William Thomas.'

But what was that to him? Jared set the horse to a trot, wanting the breeze that ruffled his hair to blow away the thoughts he could not dispel. Why did the fact of that girl marrying the Thomas man, or any other, bother him? The thoughts remained, though. Was she in love with William Thomas or was she simply looking for a home, any man's home? Yes, that must be the truth of it. That girl would take any man who was willing to put a roof over her head, and would take that roof and the bed that went with it without even the benefit of marriage!

But if what she did was of no matter to him, why did the bile of anger rise so quickly in his throat . . . and why did it burn so badly?

*   *   *

Guiding the trap between the high grey stone pillars that flanked the entrance to Dudley Guest Hospital, Jared handed the trap to a porter standing beside the heavy wooden doors that gave on to a small hall.

'Good morning, Mr Lytton.'

A thin, narrow-faced woman spoke. She wore a starched apron reaching to black boots that peeped from beneath the hem of her abundant grey serge skirts, cap starched and set to attention on her once-auburn hair.

'I am happy to see you recovered.'

'Thank you.' Jared made to smile then thought better of it. It seemed the mechanism of producing a smile might well be unknown among this woman's skills. 'I recovered so quickly and so well due to the care I received here.'

He watched as the nursing sister appeared to grow in stature but still allowed no smile to break the thin line of her mouth.

'We do what we can, Mr Lytton,' the nursing sister replied, unsmiling.

'For which I am most grateful.' He continued to pour on the charm. Men literally jumped when he spoke to them but he knew from his days in this hospital that this nurse was afraid of no man, and would brook neither argument nor complaint. 'As, I am sure, is the man who saved my life. May I enquire as to his progress?'

The woman fastened one hand about her wrist, her thin fingers closing over the white heavily starched cuff set about the sleeve of her grey uniform.

'There is little change from your last visit.' The sister was watching a young nurse, a cloth covering the shallow white pottery vessel held in her hands, as she disappeared down a corridor leading off the hall. 'His injuries are responding well to nursing.' She returned her glance to Jared. 'But his mind, I'm afraid, is not so responsive. Memory continues to elude him. He has no recall of what happened in the quarry, and no recollection whatsoever of his life before the unfortunate occurrence.'

'Have you any idea how long it will take for him to recover his memory?'

'That is something no doctor can tell you, Mr Lytton,' the sister said, shaking her head, 'and I most certainly cannot. Such things rest with the mercy of the Almighty, and we must wait on Him. Patience is the key word, patience and care, though how the poor man will fare as to the latter once he has been discharged from this hospital . . .'

'He will be cared for,' Jared promised. 'I shall see to that. Now may I encroach upon your patience, Sister, and ask if I might see him?'

'Well . . .' She consulted the tiny silver fob watch pinned to the left side of her dress. 'It isn't a day for patient visits and the staff are about to serve the midday meal. Just a few minutes, mind!' She let the watch fall as she looked back at him. 'A few minutes is *all* you may have. We are running a hospital here, not a public amusement!'

'How are you feeling today?' Jared asked the patient while accepting a chair brought to him by a young nurse.

'I be well enough, I thank you.'

Jared felt a twinge of pity as he looked into eyes that were vacant and empty. Into a face scarred from his accident and etched with deep lines of worry. This man had given all except his life to save someone else; he had given the loves and maybe the hopes that had been a part of him, the knowledge of any family he might have, though no one enquiring after him had visited the quarry. He had given as much of himself as he had saved of Jared Lytton. True the man ate and slept and breathed, but was that all there was to life? How could those things be balanced against what was lost?

'You saved my life,' Jared told him. 'What you did was a very brave thing.'

'I take your word for that, sir, though I have no memory of what happened.'

'Do you not recall the figure standing in the gallery above us? Or yourself shouting a warning, throwing yourself forward and knocking me out of the way of the rock that was hurled at me?'

'No, sir.' The man propped against the large white pillows shook his head, the movement slow and regular.

'And your family?' Jared persisted, attempting to strike some chord, hoping that somewhere in the darkness of the man's mind he might touch off a spark, kindle a spark however small, that might fan the flame of memory. 'Do you have a family, a wife or children?'

At the last word the man's sight seemed to turn inward, searching deep within himself, probing the deepest reaches of his soul, but when he looked at Jared again his eyes were empty as before and his only reply was another measured shake of his head.

'You will have to leave now, Mr Lytton.'

Her speech as crisp as the apron that covered her skirts, the nursing sister bustled into the ward. The door swung on its hinges behind her, dispersing the still air, sending it in carbolic-laden waves over the long lines of immaculately neat beds, each containing a patient imprisoned in perfectly laundered sheets.

'Mr Lytton!' The man suddenly leaned forward, his hand lifting to Jared, a glimmer of something dawning in his vacant gaze, a tiny flare of understanding that glittered for a moment before falling away into the blackness of oblivion. Then the hand was lowered and he relaxed against the pillows, his eyelids closing over the terrible emptiness that had once more claimed his gaze.

'Mr Lytton!'

The sister stepped forward purposefully as Jared would have lingered. 'You will please be so good as to leave. We must not tire the poor man.'

The last was added as a balm to the sharpness of her tone and Jared reacted to it by nodding.

'You are right, Sister, we must not tire your patient. However, I trust I may visit again?'

'Indeed you may.' She ushered him towards the door. 'But next time, will you please observe the prescribed hour of visiting?'

Jared directed the trap towards the quarry. Away to his left the heights of Wren's Nest rose to the covering sky, the grass and trees on its stopes hiding the fossils that told of the antiquity of the limestone hills. Behind him, on another hill that rose in the distance, the brooding bulwarks of the ruined castle looked out over a landscape dotted with the brick-built shafts of iron works and darkened by the smoke of factories, while wrapped about by the lacework of canals, black holes yawned in the ground where coal was hewn from its innards. Dudley, like Tipton, was built on coal and iron; they were the blood and body of both towns, the heart beat that sustained them.

But that heart had robbed them of the beauty they had once held. Even while giving the towns life, it was draining the green blood of nature from their veins.

And Jared was a part of that process. He continued what his grandfather had begun. He was helping to change the face of the beautiful Midlands, helping to turn them into what was commonly called the Black Country. But would it help if he closed the coal mines and the limestone quarries of which he was now owner? Would it better the situation were he to shut down the chain-making shops and the iron-smelting foundries he had inherited?

No, logic answered. The injury to nature would heal, but what of the injury to men? Where else would they find jobs that would keep family and home together? What else could they do when mining and forge work was all they knew? No, he could not take that from them; he must go on from where his grandfather and father had left off, follow where they had led.

Reaching the quarry where he had nearly met his death, Jared gave the horse and trap into the keeping of the gate man and walked into the office where his overseer was already reaching for the accounts ledger. Waving the book away, Jared strode to the dust-coated window that overlooked the entrance to the workings.

'Have you heard any more of the man who saved me from that falling rock?' he asked.

The overseer returned the heavy volume to its place before answering.

'Not yet, Mr Lytton. I have had enquiries made but no one seems to have any knowledge of him.'

'No one at the quarry knows anything? Where he came from . . . where he lives?'

'No, sir.' The overseer fidgeted from one foot to the other. Jared Lytton could come down heavy on a man he thought negligent in his duties. 'It seems the man was one for keeping himself to himself, didn't mix much with the other men, didn't go to the public house with them in the evening or at weekends. He did his job and left. Seems he was not seen again until he turned up for work next morning. Like I said, Mr Lytton, the man kept himself to himself.'

'Hmmm! Keep the enquiries going then. Set a man to enquire further afield. I want to know if the man had . . . has . . . any family. There could be children dependent upon him.'

'There could be, sir, though I have my doubts about that. If he had a woman and children waiting on his wage, they would surely have known where it was he earned his money, and that being so one or the other would surely have called here before this? They would want to know was he still here or had he done a moonlight flit. That only stands to reason.'

Jared turned restlessly from the window. 'Of course.' He

nodded briefly. 'What you say is correct. Had the man any family they would have done as you said. But nevertheless, I wish every enquiry to be made. Have a report sent to me daily at Foxley House.'

'Yes, Mr Lytton.' The overseer breathed a soundless sigh of relief as his employer strode from the office. 'I will see one is sent as soon as the shift be finished.'

Glancing only once at the gaping mouth of the tunnel through which they had carried him unconscious, Jared climbed into the trap and left the quarry.

'Rachel, we should not be doing this . . .'

Ellen hitched the large bundle wrapped in an old sheet more comfortably in her arms. Beside her Rachel carried a basket in each hand, the weight of them pulling at her shoulders.

'. . . I should have stayed behind to help William.'

'It will do no harm for us to be away for one day.' Rachel was brooking no argument. 'When there was just him and his mother, he had to work without help whenever Beulah took the cheese and butter to market. Today is no different. Besides he does not have to deliver his duck eggs, so in that way at least we are still helping him.'

She had never thought to see William entrust the care of the ducks to any other person, but he had allowed Ellen to feed them and now the eggs had been given to her to deliver. Rachel thought of the smile with which William invariably greeted Ellen, of his readiness to speak to her and the lack of the stammer she knew would still hamper him were his conversation with anyone else. Yes, William and Ellen were easy with each other and she was glad they had become friends. But was it a friendship he would want to continue once he and Rachel were married?

'I was in such a hurry to tidy my hair when you asked me to go with you to market, I forgot to ask where the eggs were to be delivered?' Ellen hitched the ungainly bundle again.

'There are a dozen for the Shrubberies and the other dozen is for Bloomfield House.'

'There are none for Wallbrook?'

Rachel glanced towards her friend walking beside her, and saw the anxiety that had replaced her smile.

'William has no customers for his eggs in Wallbrook, Ellen,' she said, choosing her words with care. 'It was such a way to walk when he could sell every egg he had much nearer home.'

She left the explanation at that, not wishing to embarrass her friend by saying she need not worry about being in the vicinity of her childhood home, of possibly coming face to face with someone from Bayton Hall – that someone being her father or her mother; neither did she want to speak of the fact that the smaller the area he'd covered, the shorter the gauntlet of jibes and taunts William would have suffered.

They walked on in silence, Ellen unconvinced by Rachel's words. Bloomfield was not so very far from Wallbrook, despite Rachel's having said it was, and the journey between the two was simple by carriage. Ellen's hands tightened on the bundle she was carrying. She had often made that journey with her mother to shop for ribbons or to visit her dressmaker, and once her father had taken her to the town by train. She had been so excited she had jumped up and down, her leather boots echoing on the wooden boards of the platform, until her father's hand on her shoulder had stilled her.

He had loved her then. She had been the pride of his life, the joy of his existence. But she had destroyed that love, blotted it out when she had gone with Tom. But I loved him too, Father! The cry rose from the depths of her, leaving her lips in a silent ragged breath. She had loved them both, still loved them both, but her father had refused to listen. The pride of his life . . . the joy of his existence. Ellen felt the cold touch of despair about her heart. Pride and joy . . . one had destroyed the other, and with it the lives of four people.

Crossing beneath the viaduct close by the canal wharf that served the brickworks, they came into Bloomfield Road. Rachel followed it as far as the inn that stood on the corner of the street that gave on to the Butter Cross and the market square now empty of stalls. She had deliberately chosen to come here today, knowing the market was not held on Tuesdays. She did not want Ellen subjected to the calls and jibes of children or the spiteful remarks of the women, which would without doubt have been hurled at them on a market day.

Putting her baskets on the ground, Rachel stretched her aching arms before taking the bundle from Ellen.

'Wait here. I'll not be long.'

'Rachel!' Ellen touched her arm. 'Do you think we should? I mean . . . they did belong to William's mother.'

'Beulah has no further need of them,' Rachel answered firmly, though her own conscience had plagued her over the decision she had made earlier that morning. 'Besides it was William's own request I should get rid of them.'

He had finished the milking of the half-dozen cows and was putting the milk in the dairy when she had asked him what he wanted done with his mother's clothes. She remembered the look that had crossed his face then, of sadness and helplessness.

'I c . . . can't bring myself to throw them out, Rachel,' he had said. 'I know they h . . . have to go, that I should burn them, but somehow I c . . . can't do it.'

'They could just stay there in her cupboard,' Rachel had replied.

'No.' William had shaken his head. 'No, Rachel. It will do no good to h . . . hang on to them. My mother b . . . be gone and holding on to a few clothes will not b . . . bring her back. They need to be got rid of, I know that, but . . .'

'William, would you like me to do it?' she had asked

gently, trying not to heighten the pain she knew he still felt.

'Would you?' Eyes so blue they were almost navy looked gratefully into hers. 'I w . . . would appreciate that.'

She had taken the pails of milk from him then, lifting them to the long wooden bench and covering them with a gauze hung with pottery beads, using the movements to mask a niggle of guilt at the idea she nursed in her mind. But the question had to be asked if she were to do what she planned.

'What would you have me do with them?'

'Burn them!' he had answered quickly, and she had felt her mouth go dry.

'That would be an awful waste, William. They . . . they could prove rather useful. Would you have any objection to my using them?'

He had smiled then, and a little of the sadness had left his eyes. 'My mother would have given you anything, Rachel, and so would I, but you d . . . don't need to wear her clothes. Y . . . you can have money to buy new ones.'

That was when her courage had deserted her. William was so kind, how could she deceive him? How could she let him think she wanted to take his mother's clothes for herself? She had intended to say nothing of the plan she had formulated; now she knew she could not carry it through without telling him and securing his consent.

'I had not thought to wear them, William.' She had seen doubt furrow his brow and rushed on. 'I thought to sell them. The money would be useful. And I know your mother would agree . . .'

'Rachel!' He had taken her hands between his and smiled at her. 'You and m . . . my mother were alike in many ways, she couldn't bear waste of any sort. It d . . . doesn't really matter what happens to those clothes, not to me it doesn't, 'cos I will always have my mother in my heart. B . . . but it does matter to me that you need money an' will not ask for it. I've told you, Rachel, whatever you want, supposing it is mine to give, then you can have it.'

Standing on tiptoe, she had kissed him on the cheek. 'Thank you, William.' Her eyes as she smiled up at him were moist and soft, like morning mist. 'And *you* are very like your mother. You both gave me much more than a home – you gave me friendship and love. I will always be grateful, and always love the two of you.'

Now, hitching the bundle more firmly in her arms, Rachel remembered the way his eyes had clouded slightly on hearing that.

'The money is not for me, it's for Ellen.' She had not expected to see his mouth tighten slightly at her words. Did William resent her wanting to sell his mother's personal belongings in order to give the money to a woman he had only recently come to know? Would he refuse permission now that he did? Perhaps he would but before he did so she had to finish. 'The dress she still wears is the one that was caked in the mud that buried her friends. Whenever we sit together, I see her stare at her skirts and know she is remembering, seeing that sliding mass all over again, reliving the pain of knowing she could not reach them. I thought if we could buy her another dress, maybe the memory would not trouble her so often; that at least in one small way it could take away a little of the pain. But Ellen has her pride. She would not take money, William, not from you. She feels she already owes you more than she could ever repay, but doing it the way I thought to do it, she might agree.'

'Ellen is . . .'

He had paused as if searching for the right words, and Rachel had felt a sharp lurch of her stomach.

'. . . Ellen is welcome to whatever I can give her. Do what you think is best.'

He had squeezed her hands then, a gentle tender pressure, but had not returned her kiss.

Rachel began to cross the busy road, the bundle carried before her.

William had not returned her kiss! And as he had turned to leave the dairy she saw that his eyes were clouded once more.

Chapter Twenty

'I hear there was a bit of a to do up at that quarry of yours a week or so back?'

'An accident!' Jared Lytton looked coolly at the man settling himself uninvited at his table. Isaiah Bedworth was not what one might term attractive in any sense of the word, but at this moment, his puffy cheeks florid from the exertion of walking from the yard where he had left horse and trap, into the dining room of the Brown Lion Hotel, Jared found him even less so.

'Accident, my arse!' Isaiah dropped heavily into a chair, drawing it noisily to the table. 'That were no bloody accident, least not the way I heard it.'

'Then perhaps you heard wrongly?' Jared resumed eating.

'Ar, and p'raps I didn't! P'raps that man intended to kill you when he hurled that lump of limestone at your head.'

'As you say, perhaps. But we shall never know.'

'Ain't likely now, I give you that.' Isaiah glanced at the waiter standing mutely beside him. 'Beef!' he ordered. 'And claret – a bottle of your best.'

The waiter gone he returned his attention to Jared. 'Pity that fellow knocked his brains out afore he could come to court. It would 'ave been a pleasure having him front of the bench.'

'Really?' Jared's voice retained its coldness. 'You surprise me, Bedworth. I thought it was getting your hands on the

women brought before you that gave you the greatest
pleasure?'

Isaiah heard the sarcasm but refused to be put off by it.
Isaiah Bedworth wasn't a man to be put off easily.

'There be pleasure and pleasure,' he answered cryptically. 'Speaking of which, how much of it did that wench
give you?'

Waiting until Isaiah's meal and wine had been set before
him and the waiter had once more departed, Jared asked,
'Wench . . . to which wench do you refer?'

'So! The young lion has a harem.' Isaiah's coarse laughter
rang over the dining room but as suddenly it was gone,
replaced by an almost vulpine note. 'You know very well
which wench I speak of. Richie Cade's daughter: the one you
spoke up for in my courtroom. The one you lied for, Lytton.'

Jared continued with his meal, unconcerned. There was a
line between knowing and proving, a line the magistrate had
made no attempt to cross.

'Lied?' He did not look up. 'Are you accusing me of
perverting the course of justice?'

'I be accusing you of nothing, Lytton, though were it of
enough interest to me to do so, I could doubtless prove my
words.'

'As you proved them once before.' Jared jabbed his fork
into a potato before glancing up from his plate. 'Or shall
we say, as you *tried* to prove them once before, when
you accused my father of mining land that did not belong
to him.'

'Them be sleeping dogs.' Isaiah picked up his glass,
downing the contents in one gulp. 'They be best left lying.'

For fully two minutes the two men ate in silence, each
entertaining his own thoughts.

'So, what did you do with Cade's daughter?' Isaiah broke
the silence first. 'The wench must have been mighty grateful
to you for saving her. She must have shown that gratitude.
How? How did she show it?'

Jared felt the blood quicken in him, bringing anger rising to the surface. Not all of it was due to Bedworth's insinuations; some was directed at himself. He allowed the memory of that girl to impinge too frequently on his thoughts; spent too many nights staring at her image printed on his mind.

'I took her to an inn.' The words left his mouth with the snap of cracking ice. 'And left her there.'

Isaiah laid aside his knife to pick up the glass he had refilled. Slyly, he studied Jared's face.

'Oh, I've no doubt you did . . . eventually.' The flabby lips parted in a lascivious grin stained by the claret. 'Question is, Lytton, how long after . . . how long was it afore you left her, and how often did she show her gratitude?'

Touching his napkin to his mouth, Jared pushed away from the table, the anger he had hoped to contain now visible in his eyes.

'Once, Bedworth!' He flung the square of starched linen onto the table. 'She showed it once, by saying thank you. And unlike you, words were enough for me. I had no desire for anything more.'

'No desire?' Isaiah laughed again. 'You had no desire for anything more! Is that why you be squaring up like a fighting cock? Oh, you've got the desire all right, a man with no eyes could see that . . . you have it bad, Lytton, you have it bad for a miner's brat! What really happened? Did you try and she pushed you away?'

Jared's hands curled into fists. He was itching to punch Bedworth but knew he must not give way to temptation.

'Like she pushed you away?' He kept his voice soft, though the effort cost him. 'Don't think I don't know what you tried, Bedworth. What you try with every reasonable-looking woman who is brought before your bench. Now you are going to answer for your actions, and the man you will answer to is me. Sleeping dogs, you say? Well, a kick in the rear will waken any dog, and here is yours! You will resign from the Bench and from the Board of Governors of the workhouse . . .'

'Hah, like bloody hell I will!' Isaiah's exclamation brought the attention of several diners, some of whom, recognising the antagonists, watched with interest.

'Oh, you will!' Jared's answer was as cold as his eyes. 'And furthermore you will also dispose of the businesses you hold in this town and leave. Take yourself as far away as possible.'

'Or what?' Already flushed from claret, Isaiah's face darkened. 'Who do you think you be ordering, Lytton?'

Jared leaned forward across the table, his voice a soft snarl. 'A bastard! I am ordering a bastard. I give you a week, Bedworth. Either you are gone in one week or I bring charges of libel and attempted illegal appropriation of my father's property. Then I shall follow up with charges of intimidation and rape on women detained and imprisoned by yourself.'

Within the fleshy folds of his face, Isaiah's eyes held a deadly light. 'Try it,' he rasped. 'You'll never make it stick!'

Straightening, Jared stared into his florid face. 'Oh, I will,' he said calmly. 'Believe me, Bedworth, I have more than enough evidence, and you know me well enough to realise I do not make threats lightly.' Jared observed their attentive fellow diners and looked back at Bedworth. 'They are already interested. Think how avidly they will follow a case against a well-known magistrate.'

'It will be my word against yours,' Isaiah flared. 'Cases can be lost as well as won!'

'True.' Jared nodded. 'Very true. But either way *you* lose. If you are not made to answer by a court of law, you will answer to me. For I swear before God, you will lose that which you are so fond of using on helpless women, and then you will lose your useless life! Remember, Bedworth, I *never* say anything I do not mean.'

Watching him leave, Isaiah poured claret into his glass while all around him tongues began to wag.

Isaiah Bedworth was already finished in Tipton.

Outside the hotel, Jared stood breathing deeply to calm himself.

'Carriage, Mr Lytton, sir?'

'No, not just yet,' he answered the doorman, conscious of the tumult inside him. 'I think I will take a walk, help digest that excellent beef.'

He walked away as the doorman lifted his hand to his brow. A walk would help, not to digest his meal but to clear his nostrils of the stink of Bedworth. Just what had he tried with the Cade girl? Jared felt the familiar tightening around his heart. He had tried something, of that he could be sure, and Bedworth had made no attempt to deny the accusation. But how *much* had he tried . . . and how successful had he been?

Mindless of the rattle of a passing steam-tram, or a lad shouting at a dog sniffing about his butcher's wagon, Jared tried to stem the thoughts still racing in his mind. Bedworth could not have achieved what he intended. If he had, if that girl had already been . . . His mind balked at the thought, but something stronger than himself pushed him along. If Bedworth had already taken her, why run away from Potter? Why give up a home and race away to God knew where? Magistrate or coal jagger, where was the difference?

The difference was that girl was no whore! If she had been, she would have . . .

Reaching the end of Brown Lion Lane, Jared stood staring though still unseeing.

She would have what? Offered herself to him . . . was that what he had wanted, *really* wanted? Was that the reason the girl was almost constantly on his mind? Was it true what Bedworth had said? Did he desire that miner's daughter?

'I wouldn't stand there if I was you, guvnor!'

Alerted by the shout of a passing carter Jared stepped back, avoiding the mud sprayed by the heavy cart wheels, and his glance wandered to the other side of the street, to where a flash of silver-gold glinted from a shop doorway.

Silver-gold above a brown dress and an old shawl ... Quickly, without any conscious volition on his part, he took in the details of the figure disappearing into that shop. She was the same height, the same age. But that was not necessarily so! He pulled his thoughts up sharply. He had not seen the woman's face, only the rear view ... she could be any age, anyone. But on how many other women had he seen hair of such a glorious colour?

Jared's thoughts strayed again. She had all but refused his help that night he had brought her to the Fox Inn, staying there just one night. She had refused his offer of a post at Foxley House, one that would have meant she did not have to live with the widow's son. She would not have been taunted and followed by children in the streets and reviled by women in the market, she would have been ...

What? Isaiah Bedworth's flushed face suddenly flashed before him, mouth set in a mocking travesty of a smile. 'She would have been what, Lytton?' the image seemed to ask. 'Safe? Is that what you were about to say ... she would have been safe at Foxley? Or should that be at Foxley she would have been under your eye, been where you could see her every day? Isn't it nearer the truth to say that if you can't have the wench, then no other man in Tipton will?'

No other man! For a brief moment his heart accepted the brilliant, blinding truth of the words, and then he forced them from his mind. But there was the taste of ashes in his mouth. Was that the reason for his contemptuous reaction whenever he thought of the place she lived? Was it because of William Thomas? Was he jealous of the man for having that girl?

The idea was ridiculous! He was envious of no man, and certainly not of one who would marry a ragged-arsed miner's daughter!

Marry ... A feeling of heaviness came over him then as he realised he could no longer deny the truth.

Yet even now he struggled to dismiss it. He had no interest in Cade's daughter. She was a young woman he had tried to help, and who had thrown that help back in his face. With that he had emptied his mind of her.

Only his mind was never empty of her. That pale, beautiful face haunted his every waking moment, and those violet eyes were the last things he saw before he sought the refuge of sleep. No, since that day in Bedworth's courtroom, his mind had never been free of Rachel Cade.

Across the street the shop door opened and the girl herself stepped out. Even from that distance Jared caught the pale, drawn quality of her face, and despite his promises to himself never again to be bothered with her, he stepped into the road.

'Watch out, you damned fool!'

The irate shout of a carriage driver followed him as he skipped clear of the horse's front hooves, avoiding an oncoming tram with inches to spare as he jumped on to the opposite pavement.

What insanity had brought him here? Jared stared at Rachel's upturned face, the lovely questioning eyes.

'Good day, Mr Lytton.' Too tense to smile, she gazed levelly at him. 'Is there something I can do for you?'

'Nothing.' Jared reined in his thoughts, pretending to be unconcerned. 'I saw you from the other side of the street. One should never pass an acquaintance without at least a nod, Miss Cade.'

A nod might have been less risky, Rachel thought, recalling the driver's shout that had drawn her attention.

'I cannot recall offering my condolences for the death of Mrs Thomas the last time we met.' Jared grasped at straws. He needed a reason to speak to her and that would do as well as any. 'I hope you will pardon my thoughtlessness?'

That was the least part of their last encounter that required forgiveness. Rachel averted her eyes, afraid he might read the message in them. 'It was merely an oversight,' she said, trying to still the tremor in her voice. 'No doubt you had other things on your mind.'

Other things on his mind, Jared thought bitterly. Oh, yes! He had other things on his mind, things like her living with William Thomas!

'There can be no excuse for bad manners, Miss Cade. Please accept my apology and be so kind as to extend my condolences to your . . . to Mr Thomas.'

What had he been going to call William? Rachel felt her heart lurch painfully. What awful term had that pause covered. Your landlord . . . your friend? No, neither of these. The word he had hesitated to use was lover.

'Thank you, Mr Lytton.' She lifted her eyes, feeling the lance of emotion strike again as she looked into the face of the man she loved, a man who thought her the mistress of one man and the destitute daughter of another. But destitute she was not, and a mistress she would never be. 'I will tell William what you said.'

She would tell William. Bitterness, jealousy and rage seethed together in Jared's brain until one emotion could no longer be separated from another. Where would she tell him? Beside the fire later that evening . . . or in his arms, in his bed!

'Yes, tell him!' The bronze eyes darkened almost to black and his tone turned suddenly biting.

'And now tell *me*,' he spat. 'Are you living with that man . . . are you living with him as his wife?'

It was as if he had taken her by the shoulders and shaken her. Rachel felt her mind reel. She had been right in her assumption of what he thought of her. Pulling her shawl about her, she clung to the remnants of her pride, fighting the pain of a blow so intense it might have been physical. He had a right to his own thoughts but no right to put those thoughts into words. No right to accuse her . . . or did he think the difference in their station carried with it an automatic right to accuse her of being a whore? Rachel lifted her head, her bitterness matching his own. She had reason to be thankful to this man but not ingratiating. He had bought her a bed for a night, not custody of her life!

A quiet dignity replacing the bitterness, though the wound caused by his words bled into her still, Rachel met his eyes.

'Though it is no place of yours to ask me such a question,' she said steadily, 'nevertheless, since you have been ill mannered enough to ask, I will tell you. My situation has not changed since last we spoke, Mr Lytton. I am living now as I was then.'

Drawing her faded brown skirts close in to her, Rachel made to step around him. From the expression on his face he could easily strike her.

'I *see* nothing has changed!' He stepped sideways, barring her path. 'You have as little regard for your behaviour now as then. You see no wrong in yourself while you are swift at seeing ill manners in another. But you are right . . .' A cynical smile curved his generous mouth while his eyes turned to golden ice. 'I may be guilty of bad manners. But you, Miss Cade, *you* are equally guilty: of inferior judgement and of having the morals of a street walker! But then, perhaps the man is not so weak-minded after all. I wish you joy, Miss Cade. You deserve each other.'

I am not living as William's wife! Rachel wanted to cry out to the figure walking away from her. I am not what you think . . . I never could be . . . never, not even for you! But the words remained silent within her, though the sound of her heart breaking was loud in her ears.

Please don't judge me guilty of that. Sobs shaking her inwardly Rachel leaned against the wall of the pawnshop. Please don't judge me guilty of that! But he *had* judged her. And Jared Lytton had found her guilty. Why did his condemnation matter so much more than that of her father's wife or the women of Bloomfield? Why did his judgement hold more pain for her than any Magistrate Bedworth had been ready to make?

'You know why.' The answer seemed to rise from somewhere deep within, rushing like a flood tide through her veins, sweeping away the feeble attempt at denial. 'You know why.' The words pounded like living things. 'You are in love with Jared Lytton.'

The tinkle of falling coins pulled her slowly back from yawning despair. Rachel bent to pick up the money that had fallen from her hand and when she looked up Jared was gone.

'Rachel . . . Rachel, are you feeling ill?'

Leaving the baskets, Ellen ran the few yards that separated them. She had watched Rachel come towards her but only now did she see how pale her friend was.

'We will find somewhere where you can rest. I will make the deliveries. Just tell me to which houses, I can ask directions.'

'No.' Rachel swallowed the last of her sobs though the pain in her heart did not lessen. 'It . . . it was being in that pawnshop. I have hated going into them since I was a child.' It was a lie. She had never known the misery of some of the women in Horseley, retrieving their bundles of clothing or household linen and utensils on a Saturday, only to pawn them again on Monday morning in order to feed their families for at least part of the week. Hannah Cade was a jealous, spiteful woman, but she had always proved a shrewd housekeeper. She had lied about the pawnshop but she could not face telling what had really happened.

'Why didn't you tell me, Rachel? I could have taken the clothes in there.'

She glanced at the other girl's anxious face and forced a smile to her own. 'Ellen, I can't go through life giving tasks

I dislike to others to do for me. It was just a silly childhood memory, but now it is forgotten.'

Walking to where the baskets stood on the narrow pavement, she wished she could dismiss the memory of that tall angry figure as easily. But as she held out the coins to Ellen she knew he would never leave, either her mind or her heart.

'I got this for Beulah's things.'

Ellen stared at the money held out to her. 'The pawnbroker gave you all that!'

Unable to speak the words that were yet another lie, Rachel nodded. But spoken or not, a lie was a lie. Oh God, when would it all stop? When would she be free from deceit? It was a lie to say she was used to pawnbrokers, a lie to say she wanted to be William's wife, and a lie to let Jared Lytton think that she was sharing his bed; but her love for that man was no lie, and that was why the deceit could never end. She could never own the truth, never to a living soul.

'But that is so much for a bundle of clothes.'

Rachel looked up, only hearing the tail end of Ellen's sentence.

'They were quite good. There was a winter coat and a couple of shawls, besides a good Sunday chapel dress and two skirts, one wool and one bombazine. I never saw Beulah wearing any but the chapel dress, and that was removed the moment she returned home.'

'Even so.' Ellen touched a finger to the silver and bronze coins that lay on Rachel's outstretched palm. 'There is more than I would have expected.'

'Perhaps the pawnbroker was feeling generous.' Rachel's smile hid the sinking feeling inside her, remembering the hard bargain the man had struck. Only half the money she held out had been paid by him, to say he was generous was yet another lie. But what did that matter? It seemed her life was supported by a tissue of lies. He had offered just nine shillings and she had accepted, guessing it would not be added to no matter how she pleaded. The rest of the money was that which she had been going to give to Beulah. She should have paid it instead to William; the money rightly belonged to his mother and as such should have been paid to him. But she had kept it. Not for herself but for Ellen, to replace the dress stained with the memories of that terrible day. But she would pay William, pay him every single penny, that at least would never become a lie.

'It is not really so much.' Rachel almost laughed. Never in her life had she held so much money, not even after selling every ounce of butter and cheese in the market. 'But I hope it will buy you a dress.'

'Buy me . . .' Ellen withdrew her finger as if the coins had suddenly become red hot. 'No, Rachel, I will not take it. It belongs to William!'

Waiting until the noise of a passing steam-tram had faded enough for her to be heard, Rachel grabbed Ellen's hand, pressing the money into it. 'William gave Beulah's things to me, all of them to do with as I liked, but I took only the clothes – clothes that would not fit you or me, things William *asked* me to take away; things he wanted burned and that he *would* have burned given time. This way they are serving a purpose Beulah would have wanted.'

'It does not alter the fact that the money they have fetched belongs to him.'

'No. It belongs to me.'

'Well, make up your mind who it belongs to then shift yourselves so a body can pass by on the footpath!' An elderly woman, shrouded in black skirts and shawl, glared at them from beneath a black straw bonnet. 'You be standing arguing like two babbies over a stick while folk be 'aving to step into the hoss road to go past you.'

'We beg your pardon.' Ellen stepped quickly aside.

'Ar, it be easy to beg.' The woman moved on, her muttering reaching them. 'Easier than using your brain, easier than it be to think of other folk. Young 'uns today . . . Tch! Don't know what be coming of 'em!'

'We'd better move on,' Ellen giggled. 'Before the constable takes us in for loitering.'

Rachel took up the baskets before Ellen could press the money back into her hand. 'It is only sixteen shillings and fourpence.' She glanced back to where Jared Lytton had barred her way, the way she must take to make her deliveries. 'I want you to take it, Ellen, and use it to buy a dress.'

'But, Rachel, I can't!'

'Then do you propose to be my matron of honour in a dress that has more patches than there are days in a week?' Rachel managed a smile though the significance of her words cut like a knife. Soon she would be marrying William, marrying from loyalty not love. 'It will not get you a dress a duchess might envy, but for you to buy one at all will please me very much.'

'But what about you?' Ellen matched her steps to Rachel's. 'What about your wedding dress?'

'I plan to shop for that later. I may go to Dudley . . . or even to Birmingham. William and I want to choose something special, go together.'

'You already have something special, Rachel,' Ellen said softly. 'You have William.'

Yes, I have William, Rachel thought, closing her mind. But even so she did not close it quickly enough to shut out the thought that followed: But William is the wrong man!

Arranging to meet up at the Butter Cross once her deliveries were made, Rachel walked on along Bloomfield Road, the weight of the baskets pulling at her shoulders.

What would Ellen say when she found out there had never been a planned trip to Birmingham or to any other town; that she would not be shopping for a wedding dress? Rachel rested the baskets on the ground, flexing fingers that were numb from strain. There was no way she could earn enough for a dress, especially since she no longer took her two shillings a week wages, leaving that as payment for Ellen's board, and under no circumstances would she take money from William. She would wear the skirt and blouse she had bought with the money Beulah had lent her.

Oh, William would give her money willingly. She picked up the baskets, resuming her walk. As he would refuse to keep the weekly wage she and Beulah had agreed if he knew. But he did not know. Rachel felt the pull on her shoulders and set her teeth against the aching jar of her bones. Beulah had had sole running of the house and finances while William had seen to the livestock and the barley crops. He had been given little opportunity to learn the economics of the property he now owned. He had accepted the money she handed to him after each market day and asked no questions, and she in turn had said nothing concerning her wage.

Standing outside the servants' door at the first of her calls, Rachel waited while the white-aproned cook religiously checked each package of cheese and butter and twice counted the duck eggs.

'You be marryin' Billy Duckegg?' At last the woman began to count coins into her hand.

'No, ma'am.' The counting completed, Rachel closed her fingers over the three silver shillings and nine bronze pennies.

'Well, you be living with him!'

'Mebbe he won't 'ave her.' A maid dressed in frilly cap and apron over a black dress came to stand beside the cook.

''E has already had her, judging by what I 'eard in the market!' a third voice called from the interior of the kitchen, bringing a swift surge of colour to Rachel's cheeks as the cook and the maid joined in the chorus of laughter.

'You be the talk of the place!' the cook said, the smile vanishing from her mouth. 'Don't it worry you none?'

Slipping the money into the pocket of her brown dress, Rachel took the empty basket the maid had dropped at her feet. 'No, ma'am.' She lifted her head proudly, eyes deep wells of violet fire. 'The filth you hear in the market does *not* worry me, it is simply the echo of your own foul mouth. Kindly arrange to purchase your supplies elsewhere from today. Mr and *Mrs* Thomas will no longer call at this house.'

Her body tilted awkwardly by the weight of her one full basket, Rachel walked away. Tears of anger rather than self-pity were stinging her eyes. How dare people use that name for William? People who had no idea of his kind, gentle nature. He had been labelled an idiot, a weak-minded boy with an afflicted tongue, and it seemed that label would stay with him the rest of his life.

And herself? Would the label 'whore' stay with her?

'It does not matter,' she mumbled. But could not forget bronze-coloured eyes staring from a handsome face, a full mouth thinned in anger. And Rachel knew it did matter.

Chapter Twenty-one

'It's a lovely dress, Ellen, such a pretty colour.' Rachel gently touched the pale sprigged muslin.

'It puts me in mind of the first blush on a peach,' William added his own compliment. 'Just like the b . . . blush on your p . . . pretty cheeks.'

'Will it do, Rachel?' Ellen's colour deepened as she caught William's smile and she glanced quickly to her friend.

They had eaten the meal Ellen and Rachel had prepared on returning from Bloomfield and now Ellen was trying on the dress she had bought.

Rachel nodded. 'It will do excellently. It will be the prettiest bridal attendant's dress Foxley village has ever seen, won't it, William?'

'It w . . . will that,' he said softly, but his eyes were not on the dress.

'I got a yard of ribbon just the same colour as the flower sprays.' Ellen spoke quickly as the colour flared higher in her cheeks. 'I thought it would be a good match around a posy.'

'I am sure it will,' Rachel agreed, 'but save some to go in your hair. It will be lovely against your colouring.'

'Not if my cheeks are flaming as they are now.' Ellen laughed, but it was a strained sound that rang hollowly. 'I shall go and take it off before you two make me blush

even more. A woman can only take so much flattery before
it goes to her head.'

'I must go down to Worcester tomorrow, there be such a
call for the beer we need m . . . more hops.'

William's words faltered only once, Rachel noticed as she
gathered up Ellen's worn-out grey dress. Yet a moment ago
his tongue had stumbled as badly as it had when first he
spoke to her so many weeks ago. Was it that he found it
difficult to pay a woman a compliment? It had to be, for
William did not usually stammer in Ellen's presence; he had
been at ease with her from the start.

'Will you and Ellen be able to manage the few days I'll
be gone?'

'Of course.' Rachel held the dress draped over one arm,
her other hand gently touching the fabric as if it were a
well-remembered friend. 'Ellen has taken well to the milking,
you said so yourself, and I can see to the brewing. As for the
dairying, Ellen helps there too.'

'She be a good woman,' William said, his eyes suddenly
holding the lost, almost confused look Rachel had seen in
them on several occasions when they had talked of Ellen.
Was he searching for a way to tell her that her friend
would not be welcome here once he and Rachel were
married?

'She is a woman any man . . . any friend . . . would be
proud to have.'

What *was* he saying? Rachel's hand stilled on the shabby
cloth. *Was* he trying to tell her that Ellen must find somewhere
else to live?

'You will be back before market day?' She substituted the
question for the one she really wanted to ask but lacked the
courage to speak.

William's eyes cleared, but Rachel saw the effort it took.
He, like herself, appeared to want to put off what she knew
must come.

'Yes.' He nodded. 'I'll be back afore then, but the barley

be due to be delivered from the malt house tomorrow. Will you be able to handle that?'

'I don't see it causing any problems, the driver will carry the sacks into the barn.'

'Ar, well, make sure he does.' William smiled, touching his fingers to her cheek. 'You be f . . . far t . . . too pretty t . . . to go carrying sacks of b . . . barley.'

The stammer was back. Rachel smiled. Poor man, paying a woman a compliment tied his tongue as badly as ever.

'William,' she said as he turned to leave for his own cottage, 'will you burn this, please?' She held out the dress, its faded patches looking like scarred flesh newly healed. 'I don't want Ellen to be tempted to wear it again, it will only revive painful memories. I know she will never forget what has happened to Tansy and Cora, but with this dress gone, maybe she will not recall it quite so often. She has had enough unhappiness in life.'

Taking the dress, William walked slowly to the far end of his own small garden and there threw it on to the remains of the bonfire he had lit earlier.

Ellen had had enough unhappiness in her life. The words ran through his mind, and in his mind he answered: We all have, we have all had enough unhappiness, but is it finished or is there a deal yet to come?

Watching from her own doorway as the spiral of smoke rose lazily on the still evening, Rachel thought again of that lost look that had returned to his eyes as she had spoken of Ellen. It was almost as if he felt her sadness. Was it that sadness had held his mind as he had taken Rachel in his arms, held him as once again he turned and left without kissing her?

'Has William left?'

Rachel turned back into the fire-lit kitchen as Ellen came downstairs.

'I wanted to thank him for my clothes.'

'He knows how you feel.' Rachel admired the dark blue

gabardine skirt and pale blue muslin blouse the other girl now wore. 'It might embarrass him to have you say so.'

'As long as he does not think me rude, accepting his money and saying nothing?'

'William will not think anything of the kind.' Rachel set about lighting the lamps. 'Now, let me see how you look. I don't know where you got these but they look very smart.'

'I found a little dressmaker's shop in one of the side streets. I had no intention of buying anything, but I saw the dress and thought it so pretty, I just stared at it.'

Like I stared at a pretty lavender one. Rachel's mind flew back to the day she'd stood outside a dress shop.

'I knew I hadn't enough money to buy it,' Ellen continued, 'and was about to turn away when the shop owner came to the door.'

Did she tell you to move on, that you were blocking the view of her window . . . that you were deterring customers with money to buy? Rachel's thoughts ran on.

'She asked if I would like to view the dress at closer quarters, and though I knew it would simply waste the woman's time, I could not resist. It was even prettier than I thought when she took it from the window, I couldn't help but touch it. It had been ordered for a girl in the town, she told me, but one day the order had been cancelled. No explanation, just cancelled. The dress and these . . .' Ellen ran a hand over the skirt and blouse '. . . were left on her hands. When she said I could have them for sixteen shillings and sixpence, I could have wept.'

Rachel remembered her own feelings, gazing at a dress she could not afford, a dress she could never hope to buy.

By the light of the lamp, Ellen's eyes glowed and her hair gleamed a rich sherry brown. There had been such a change in her since coming to this house, but what further change would there be when she was forced to leave?

Refusing to allow the question to cloud the moment, Rachel

forced it from her mind. She would cross that bridge when she came to it.

'You didn't weep, did you?'

Ellen returned the smile, letting it light her whole face. 'No, Rachel, I did not. I just had to admit I didn't have that much money, that I was tuppence short of what she asked, and when I thanked her for her time she asked if I had a special reason for looking at the dress. Then, when I told her I thought it perfect for a bride's attendant, she said I could have them all for sixteen shillings and fourpence. Oh, Rachel! I was so delighted, I threw my arms about her and hugged her.'

Was that what *he* had expected? Rachel turned to the dresser, reaching down the china cups carefully ranged on the topmost shelf. Had Jared Lytton expected a delighted girl to throw her arms about him and hug him after he had bundled her so unceremoniously into that dress shop? Had he thought she would be so taken with his generosity she would fling herself into his arms? Was that what he'd expected?

'Wasn't it kind of her, Rachel?' Ellen touched a hand to the narrow frill of pale blue lace that ran in a vee from shoulder to waist of the blouse.

'Yes, it was very kind.' Taking a tin of Bourneville cocoa from the larder, Rachel spooned a little into cups that already held a spoonful of sugar. But as she stirred it into a paste with a little of the hot milk that she took from the hob, she saw only a hard, angry face staring back at her. Had Jared acted out of kindness in buying that dress, or had it been his way of slighting the shopkeeper? Adding the rest of the milk to the cups, she stirred, watching the creamy foam form on the surface.

Whatever his motive, kindness or otherwise, he had not been repaid with a grateful hug. Staring into the cups, watching the streaks of chocolate brown amid creamy white, Rachel remembered the bitterness that had risen in her, driving away any feeling of gratitude. She had literally thrown the dress at him and for that she felt no regret. But what of her words, the words that had shot in an angry torrent from her lips? '. . . the only thing I require from you is that you mind your own business and leave me to mine. I do not need your assistance in anything . . .' Rachel heard the words as she had heard them a hundred times in her mind. But now she knew they were not true. She had not wanted his help nor had she wanted his gift, nor had she wanted to fall in love with him. 'I do not need you.' The words came again, cutting through the pain ever ready to engulf her. He would leave her alone; if he thought of her at all, he would continue to detest her as a whore. And she? Her hands trembling, lips holding back the sobs that threatened, Rachel returned the pan to the hob. She would go on as planned; she would become William's wife; she would work beside him and do all she could to make him happy – but her heart would belong forever to Jared Lytton.

The loaded wagon creaked to a stop. Below lay the canal bridge, a short distance from fresh-mown fields and small cottages resting silently beneath a sun dipping towards the horizon.

This was the way the girl with the silver-gold hair had come. Would she be there today or had she merely been passing the day he had seen her? Was she on her way somewhere else? The driver ran his tongue over his twisted mouth. Would he see her when he delivered his load of malted barley? Would the girl be there?

He had been told he could leave this delivery until the morning but had insisted he would be back in Tipton before darkness fell; he had not wanted to lose the chance, *any* chance, of seeing her.

Flicking the reins, he set the wagon in motion again, eyes scanning the fields for the widow's son. The barley was cut. A stab of anger mixed with frustration tightened scarred hands on the leather reins. That meant he would be around until every sack was stacked in the barn, that likely the girl would not show. The lid over the twisted eye twitched uncontrollably. He had waited weeks! Worked his soul out in that malt house, waiting . . . waiting . . . just to deliver here again, waiting to see *her*.

How many days had passed in hope, how many nights in dreaming? The wagon moved down the far side of the bridge, jolting as a wheel rim bumped over a jutting stone. How many hours had been given over to thinking what he would say, and what she would say in reply? But there would be no conversation between them, not with the widow's son at her side.

A slow dribble of saliva spilled from the side of the distorted mouth, running down the deep-etched channel of the terrible scar that twisted through the mutilated flesh, undulating like a living thing the length of a thin, drawn face.

The widow's son! If only he were not there. If only he could be got rid of! The saliva increased its flow, oozing unattended to gather in iridescent globules that clung for desperate seconds to the serrated tip of the scar losing their hold to fall soundless onto the breast of the dark jacket, gathering there like some obscene medal.

Years of making the same journey had the horse drawing into the Thomases' yard without assistance. Wiping a hand across his face, the man in the driving seat dashed away the spittle then pulled the flat cap lower over his brow.

The widow's son had not yet appeared. Wouldn't he have heard the rumble of the cart, even from the fields? The man darted a quick glance towards the sky. The sun was already low, Thomas must think the delivery would not be made today. He could shout, call out, that would bring Thomas, but silence might bring the girl; she might come from the house into the yard, she might even speak, there might be a chance of . . .

The saliva spilled again and once more he dashed it

away with the palm of his hand. If he could just get her alone . . .

'Good afternoon.'

The words coming from behind him set the man grabbing at the front of his jacket, pulling the two lapels closer to his face as if to hide it.

'I heard the wagon from the byre. I wasn't expecting you, I thought it was too late for you to come today.' Rachel moved to the front of the wagon, seeing the well-filled sacks standing shoulder to shoulder in uniform ranks. 'William isn't . . .' She broke off as she saw the face that could not be entirely hidden by jacket and cap, and for a moment revulsion thickened her throat and she wanted to turn away.

'I'm afraid William isn't here.' It took all her composure to speak evenly. The dreadfully scarred features had taken her unawares but she was determined not to let it show. The poor man had suffered enough in acquiring such an awful deformity, she would not add to it by turning away from him. 'William had to go down to Worcester today for more hops, but I will help carry the sacks.'

'They be heavy for a wench!'

Rachel winced at the gravelly whisper. His voice was somehow as frightening as his face. Perhaps whatever had caused the scarring had also affected the man's throat? Without thinking, she glanced at his neck but his throat was covered with a muffler, looped into a knot, the ends tucked beneath his jacket.

'Open the barn.' Voice sounding like the scratching of dry cinders caught beneath a door, the man gave instructions. 'Open them right up and I'll back the wagon up to them.'

So the widow's son was gone to Worcester! The twisted mouth tightened as he watched the girl's slender form walk across to the other side of the yard. That would mean at least three days away from this house, away from the girl. The tip of his tongue flicked to the ragged corner of his mouth, collecting the saliva that began to ooze over his torn lips, drawing it back into his mouth. That meant she was alone here.

Beside the barn door the sun glinted on hair the colour of fresh ripened wheat. He felt rivers of fire in his veins. The girl was here, she was alone!

Jumping from his seat, he took the reins, reassuring the horse as it backed, pushing the wagon until it stood end on to the open barn doors.

'Be the usual place, does it?'

Rachel felt a shiver run through her body as the man's eyes ran over her. There was something about him that frightened her. Oh, not the scar, though that was scaring enough. It was more than that – something in the way he looked at her, the way she felt that at any moment he might reach out for her.

'No, William said the fresh delivery was to be put there.' She half turned, pointing to a corner of the barn that was wreathed in deep shadow.

For a few seconds the misshapen eyelid jerked and the tongue gathered the wandering spittle. The widow's son was gone. He was alone with the girl!

Hoisting a sack from the cart, he slung it on to his shoulders, the weight of it seeming to have no effect on his wiry frame.

'Here.' Rachel snatched at the empty sacks that lay on the floor where the barley was to be stored, dragging them aside as he dropped the full sack from his shoulders. Then she watched him return for a second. She would be glad when he was finished and gone. The man made her flesh crawl.

He could be gone more quickly if she helped. Rachel turned away as the man's eyes swept over her once more, lingering on her face and then her hair. The central line of sacks was almost gone, only one remained at the front of the wagon. Behind her she heard the man's footsteps. Quickly she grabbed the nearest sack, pulling it on to her shoulders, gasping as the weight threatened to send her to her knees.

Staggering across the floor of the barn, Rachel knew she could not carry more grain. The sacks looked deceptively light, she had thought that helping to unload would be no real strain, but she was wrong, they were too heavy for her. She would drop this one and go back to the byre, stay with Ellen until this man left.

Letting the sack drop from her shoulders, she sighed with relief.

'Be too heavy for you, do they? You need to take a rest.'

Behind her a voice rasped, ground from the man's throat like grit beneath a millstone. Rachel's heart jolted. He was too close, she needed to be further away from him. Half turning, she caught sight of his face: the livid, serpentine line of the jagged scar, the eye pulled downward on to the cheek, the mouth deformed and wet with spittle, and the arm raised above his head. Sunlight dimmed by distance reached into the shadows, playing on a hand that was brittle and puckered as a dried leaf – a hand that held a length of wood!

Pulling gently on the reins, Jared drew the trap to a halt. He had been wrong, he should speak to no woman as he had spoken to her. Whatever his opinions he should have kept them to himself; she had been right to tell him that her business was her own, how she chose to live her life was no concern of his.

His gaze travelled over the heath purpling in the final kiss of the setting sun, following a cart that clung precariously to the narrow towpath. He had no interest in the girl. It was of no matter to him that she lived as another man's wife. It was not concern for what she did that had troubled his sleep, so much as his own behaviour. He should not have used the words he did, and should apologise.

Across the heath the cart rounded a bend in the path and was gone from his sight. '*You have the morals of a street walker!*' He winced. Those words should never have been said. *'Judge not, that ye be not judged.'* The words learned in his Sunday Scripture lessons echoed in his brain, but too late. Judgement had been pronounced.

But surely it was not too late to make some reparation? Tomorrow he would call at the cottage and offer his apology. Then he would be free from the guilt that rode him, and from the face that haunted him. After tomorrow he would not waste another thought on Richie Cade's daughter. There were others more deserving of his thoughts and his concern. Others such as the man who lay in that hospital bed, a man who had almost given his own life to save Jared's.

The dying sun seeped trails of scarlet into the darkening sky, turning the distant canal to a ribbon of blood.

Jared thought of the man he had sat with earlier in the day, of the worn, unhappy look that never quite left his face, of the eyes that seemed almost devoid of life. Who was he? Where did he come from? Where were his family? Question crowded on question. He had asked each of them during his several visits but the man had shown no sign of knowing the answers.

But they had to be there! Jared watched the scarlet trails lose their last defiant stand against the oncoming night, fading to rose, then pearl and finally into grey. Somewhere in that man's memory the answers waited to be brought to the surface. He had sought the advice of specialists he had brought from London and Birmingham, doctors eminent in the study of the mind, but they had only repeated what he had already been told. There was no medical treatment would cure the man, no known procedure that would unlock the doors of his closed memory. Patience was the key, patience and nursing.

That the man would have, for the rest of his life if need be. Jared flicked the reins and the horse walked obediently onward. The man would never again work beneath the earth. Arrangements had already been made for a cottage in Foxley village to be prepared for him; yes, the man would be well cared for: just as *she* would have been cared for. She could have come to Foxley House, taken a position that would have provided her with a bed and her keep. She would not have had to pay as she was paying William Thomas, she would not have been required to become Jared's mistress, she would . . .

'No!' He spoke the word into the gathering night and slapped the reins, sending the horse into a swift trot. 'No!' he spat viciously, angry at the ease with which his mind slipped into thoughts of that girl. 'From this moment I will have no more of Rachel Cade. She will get her apology and afterwards . . .'

But life for him after that was too dismal to contemplate.

Rachel opened her eyes, wincing at the sharp pain that lanced through her head, at the same time feeling the bite of the gag over her mouth.

Struggling to sit up, she moaned as she found her wrists bound together. The man who had delivered the barley, the man with that terribly scarred face . . . he had struck her, hit her on the head with that piece of wood!

But why? She tried to move her legs but they too were tied about the ankles. Why should that man want to hurt her . . . and where was he taking her? It could only be him who had gagged and bound her, and the jostle and feel of full sacks against her shoulders, sacks that smelled of malted barley, told her she could only be in his wagon.

The wooden planks that were the bed of the wagon bit through the worn fabric of her dress, rubbing against her skin. Gritting her teeth, Rachel pushed with her heels, forcing herself up to half sit, half lie against the sacks.

He had not stayed to unload them all. Her eyes accustomed now to the semi-darkness, she could see the sacks that held her in a hollow at their centre. He must have placed her on the wagon almost as soon as she fell . . . but why? What did he intend to do with her?

Hitting a stony outcrop the wagon lurched, jolting her hard against the wooden boards, and she cried out soundlessly against the gag.

Perhaps she could use her feet to push one of the sacks off the rear of the cart? It might be seen by someone who would return it, catch up with the wagon and . . . But it was useless. It would be morning before it was spotted, no one would see a sack lying on the ground at night. Deep inside her a fear she knew she must control began to rise. Flaring her nostrils, she drew in deep draughts of air. She must not let fear get the better of her, she had to remain calm. But how? Oh, God, show me how! The prayer rose silently to her captive lips. Please God, show me how!

'I'm bringing her to you.'

In the driving seat the man began to mutter, his words reaching her over the rumbling of the wagon wheels. Her skin prickling with fear, Rachel listened.

'I'm bringing the one you asked for, the one you want. Soon you will be together. You will have her with you for as long as you want.'

The muttering stopped. Only the rumble of the wheels broke the silence of the night. Who had asked for her? Who would she soon be with? Samuel Potter . . . Isaiah Bedworth? It could only be one of those two. Both had tried to . . . Fear becoming dread, Rachel's screams rose silent and useless against the gag.

'They thought to stop me.'

The muttering began again, and she stifled her screams. If she could hear the reason for her abduction maybe when the wagon halted she could reason with him, get him to release her.

'They thought I would forget the promise I made.'

For several long seconds there was silence. It acted like acid on Rachel's raw nerves. Then it began again, the harsh scratching voice, trailing ribbons of ice through her veins.

'But I did not forget. I *wanted* to bring her to you. I

wanted to see you take her in your arms. And I will, very soon I will.'

The voice tailed off to little more than a whisper, but almost at once harsh, grating laughter took its place.

'They thought they had done for me but they were wrong!'

Every nerve in her body taut as a bowstring, Rachel listened as the muttering was resumed.

'I slashed her throat, the bitch that laughed at me! I slashed her proper. She won't laugh again, none of them will, not after what I did. They thought I was dead, left me strung to that beam hanging by the rags they were given to soak their monthly blood, though there were those had no need of it; dried up they were and long past the use of a man or the need for that cloth, but they took it – took it and tied it together to make a rope for my neck. They strung me like a turkey and stood by to watch me die. And I would have if the wardress had not come when she did.'

Laughter rasped again and Rachel jumped at the sound.

'They cut me down,' the voice went on, stringing words and laughter together, 'the wardress and two others. They took me to the infirmary where the matron said I would die. But I didn't. I didn't die but *she* did, later in the fire I set – the fire that burned down that asylum, the fire that took them but not me!'

The wagon bumped again, throwing Rachel against the sacks of grain, but the jarring of her bones was forgotten in the fear that gripped her. The man was speaking of murder, of people he had killed . . . and he was laughing over it. What if he decided against handing her over to whoever it was had sent him to take her, what if he decided to kill her too?

'I was away with no one to see me go. They thought me dead from the fire that took half my face. But I was alive and got away from that hell hole, away from West Bromwich. I came back to you . . . I knew you wanted me, wanted what you asked for. I've found her, I've found the one that took you from me ... soon, my little love, soon ...'

He laughed again, a terrible croaking sound that rasped from his throat. 'He didn't know, the man who hired me, nobody knows. Nobody guessed the scar-faced man took on to work at the malt house be not a man. Nobody guessed it were your mother, my little love, that it be Hannah Cade!'

Hannah? Her father's wife? Rachel's mind reeled from the shock. What had happened at her trial, to what dreadful place had Isaiah Bedworth sent her? An asylum! She had heard the word among the mutterings. Had Hannah been condemned to a life spent locked in an insane asylum? But she had not been mad. Grazed with grief, yes, but surely not mad.

But what of her face, what other torment had she suffered? And was it such as to shatter a mind already dangerously unstable?

It must have been. Panic swelling in her throat, Rachel tried again to scream. This woman thought Rachel had killed her son and now she had her bound and gagged and was taking her ... where? Where was Hannah Cade taking her?

'I'm bringing the one you asked for ... soon you will be together ... soon she will be with you in that dark water ...' Rachel's blood seemed to freeze and her scalp prickled with the fresh onslaught of terror as she heard the words. The woman was taking her to Robbie, Hannah was going to drown her!

Chapter Twenty-two

Bringing the trap to a halt, Jared watched the tiny point of light dance like a jack-o'-lantern, pricking the gathering darkness like a flickering lamp.

If it were an insect hovering out there above the heath, it was unlikely that it would be alone. Where there was one, there would be others. But this light was solitary. Whatever it was it had no fellow.

Uncertain as to why he felt bothered by the flickering yellow dot, Jared sat for several minutes watching it move; it did not seem to follow the haphazard darting path of a firefly but appeared to be moving in a regular pattern.

He watched for several minutes then decided to light the carriage lamps to either side of the trap before moving on. It was doubtful he would meet any other so far from the town and at this time of evening, but it would do no harm to be seen should he do so.

Taking the carton of matches from a box kept beneath the driver's seat, he opened the glass door of the lanterns then held the lighted match to the paraffin candles. Extinguishing the match, he returned to the driving seat and gathered up the reins. It was then he heard the shout.

Faint, and some distance away, but nevertheless a shout. Sitting perfectly still, he listened. Then it came again. A distinct cry followed rapidly by another, and with each cry the tiny point of light bobbed crazily.

Straining to pierce the deep shadows that held the heath, he peered towards the faint light, all the while listening. Perhaps his senses were playing tricks on him?

The light was definitely coming nearer, moving towards him. It was no trickery on the part of his senses. The light was crossing the heath, coming in his direction.

Jared's hand tightened about the driving whip.

'Help!' The cry pierced the stillness, vibrating on the silence, and he felt his body stiffen.

'Help . . . please, help . . . don't go . . . oh, please don't go!'

It was a woman's voice! Throwing aside the whip, he jumped from the trap, moving at a run in the direction of the bobbing light.

The woman half fell against him as he reached her. Taking the candle jar from her, Jared supported her as she struggled to breathe.

'I . . . I saw the lights of . . . of your carriage,' she panted. 'I was afraid you . . . you would drive away before I could reach you.'

Making no attempt to move yet, Jared waited as she sucked deeply at the air.

'I was so glad when I saw your match flare, I was praying there might be somebody on the road.'

Her breathing easier, the woman straightened. In the dim glow cast by the candle, Jared saw a not unattractive face but it was the eyes that held his attention: eyes that were filled with anxiety.

'Is anyone hurt?'

'No, no,' she answered. 'No one is hurt. At least, I hope not.'

Urging her gently towards the carriage, Jared felt her shiver. The woman's arms were covered only by a thin blouse, she must have dashed from her home without stopping even for a shawl.

'Has someone attacked you?' he asked, his tone suddenly hard and flat.

Shaking her head, the woman turned to him. 'Not me, no one has attacked me, but . . . but I am afraid. I can't find her.'

Reaching the trap, Jared helped her into it, setting the candle jar once more in her hand. 'Who can you not find? Is it your daughter you are looking for?'

'No. Please help me to search, help me to look for her!'

'I will give you all the help I can.' He touched a hand to her arm as she made to climb down from the carriage. 'But first tell me who it is you are searching for?'

'It's Rachel. I am looking for Rachel. She isn't anywhere in the cottage or the brew house. I looked everywhere but could not find her. But Rachel would not go out without telling me . . .'

Rachel! Anxiety gripped him. She was searching for a Rachel . . . could it be the same girl? Tension in the set of his jaw, he stared out across the dark heath. 'Rachel?' he asked. 'Who is Rachel?'

It was as if his question suddenly restored the woman to calm, and though her voice and the hand holding the candle jar still shook, she spoke calmly. 'We have to keep on searching. She would not go off without saying. I feel certain something has happened to her.'

'*Who is Rachel?*' It was said slowly, every word crystal clear in the silence around them.

'Rachel Cade. She is my friend.'

The answer slammed against him like a bare-knuckled fist. This woman was searching for Rachel Cade. 'She would not go off without saying,' the woman had said. 'No one has attacked me, but I am afraid . . .' Her words returned to him with sickening clarity. Had Isaiah Bedworth found out where she lived, sent one of his paid thugs to kidnap her and take her back to him?

Jared's heart twisted with a great wrenching pain. He had been going to call on Rachel tomorrow, had wanted to offer an apology; but there was more to it than that. Suddenly the reason for his visiting Bloomfield each market day, or going to the loading wharfs at Tipton so regularly, flooded his mind. It had been a lie when he had told himself the girl did not matter to him; a lie resulting from his pride, his blind, stupid pride. Rachel Cade *did* matter to him, mattered more than anything else in the world! In a blinding moment of enlightenment he suddenly knew the truth. He loved Rachel Cade!

The woman he had helped into the carriage held the makeshift lamp above her head, feeling for the step with one foot. 'I have to go on looking, I have to help her.'

'Well, you won't do it by running about the heath in the dark. You'll only get yourself killed that way!'

He spoke sharply from a need to hit out at someone, anything to evade the painful realisation of the truth. He loved the girl who had thrown the offer of a post in his household back at him, refused any offer of help from him yet gone to live with another man as his wife. Yet how could he be? How could he be in love with such a woman?

But you are, his mind whispered, you are in love with her, you have been from the beginning.

'But what else can I do? I have to find her.'

Grateful for the woman's words, Jared glanced at her, his mind clearing.

'She will be found. But first I must take you home. Where do you live?'

'At William Thomas's cottage, but . . .'

'William Thomas's cottage!' His voice was almost savage. '*You* live there?'

'Yes, now . . .'

'For how long?' Ignoring the exasperation in her voice, Jared asked again: 'How long have you lived there?'

'Since the day Beulah Thomas died. Rachel brought me there from Tipton. I live in the cottage the Thomases built for their son.'

'And Rachel Cade, where does she live?'

Floating in a timeless vacuum, he waited for the answer. An answer he wanted . . . an answer he dreaded.

'Rachel lives in the cottage . . .'

The words seemed to reach him from a world beyond his own as he waited, hardly daring to breathe.

'. . . with me. William lives in the other one.'

William lives in the other one!

The words were a symphony, a soaring burst of music that filled his heart and coursed triumphant along his veins.

William lives in the other one!

She had not shared the same house. She had not shared the bed of the widow's son. A ragged-arsed miner's daughter she might be, but Rachel Cade was not a whore.

'Please, sir, we have to find her!'

Climbing into the driving seat, he took up the reins and set the horse along the track that led to William Thomas's place. Yes, they had to find her. He had something to say to Rachel Cade.

Her bones aching from the continuous onslaught of the lurching wagon, muscles tense from trying to hold herself upright, Rachel glanced at the sky. A brilliant moon rode there like a yellow balloon but she could only guess at what its light shone upon. Hannah was taking her to Robbie, and to Hannah's crazed mind her son's body was still in the lock at Tipton Green.

The wharfs. Rachel felt a moment of hope. They would have to pass the wharfs to reach those locks, that is if Hannah was following the road, but what if she were not? What if she had been crazy enough to follow the towpath? But it would make little difference. The spark of hope died. There would be no men working the wharfs at night. Whichever way Hannah had chosen, there would be no help.

'They didn't stop me, Robbie.'

The muttering began again, and Rachel felt cold with fear.

'I pretended I was over it, pretended I no longer thought of her who robbed me, her who took you from me. But I fooled them, I fooled them all, and now I'm coming, my little love, bringing her to you. She'll keep you company, you won't be alone any more.'

The wagon drew to a halt. Wedged between the barley sacks, Rachel stopped breathing, terror imprisoning the air in her lungs.

A rattling sound told her the tail board of the wagon was being released, then the sack at her feet was dragged away. Rachel heard the heavy thud as it dropped to the ground, then Hannah was in its place, eyes glittering like silver coins.

'We're there.'

Above Rachel's head the twisted mouth curved in a smile that dragged it further out of shape while the broad seam of the hideous scar gleamed serpent-like in the pallid moonlight.

'He asked me to bring you . . . every night he asked me.'

The twisted mouth hovered inches from her face, the torn eye glinting with hatred beneath its jerking lid. Rachel wanted to scream, to try to tell the poor demented woman that she had not killed Robbie, that he had not asked for her, he did not want her to join him. But no sound came from behind the gag.

'They laughed at me, they all laughed at me, they laughed when I talked to my babby, said I was mad. But it was them were mad, not me, not Hannah Cade, and they stopped laughing when I slashed the throat of the bitch who said the lock were the best place for my Robbie.'

Rachel trembled at the laughter that followed: a high-pitched cackling shriek. The laughter of a woman touched by the hand of madness.

'I took the knife from the kitchen. I fooled them into trusting me, letting me help there and in the laundry. I was too clever for them . . . it weren't Hannah Cade who were mad, it were the ones who laughed.'

Reaching forward with hands that had been burned to claws, she grabbed Rachel, hauling her to her feet with unnatural strength.

'He won't be lonely no more, not after tonight. He likes being with you. Oh, I've watched him follow after you. Pulling at your skirts 'till you played with him. Now you will play with him forever!'

Clutching the neck of Rachel's dress, she hauled her forward then with a push shoved her off the end of the wagon.

The force with which she hit the ground knocking her almost senseless, Rachel felt herself being dragged, the rough ground tearing at her clothes then her flesh.

From the corner of her eye she caught the gleam of a lantern in the distance. Maybe someone was coming, maybe they would see Hannah dragging her towards the canal.

Trying to keep her head from hitting the ground as she bounced on her back and shoulders, Rachel strained towards the light. The lantern was not moving, it was hanging on the wall of a building; it was most probably one of the public houses that were built alongside the canal. Hope was awakened in her. Where there was a public house there would be men; perhaps one would come out, see Hannah and . . . But Rachel realised it was useless. Hannah was shrewd enough to listen and to watch, and any man who emerged from that ale house was likely to be too drunk to see anything.

Passing behind a huge lump of rock that screened the ale house from view, Hannah suddenly stopped, her head to one side as if listening.

'Robbie!' she called softly, letting Rachel's feet drop to the ground. 'Robbie, don't cry . . . don't cry, my little love. I'm here . . . Mother is here.'

The rock cutting into her shoulder, Rachel gritted her teeth as she used it to lever herself half upright.

Hannah had run to the lock. In the moonlight Rachel

could see her kneeling beside it, looking over the edge into its depths.

'Don't cry, my little darling . . .'

Hannah leaned forward, both arms held over the black chasm.

'Mother has come, Mother is here. Come, my babby.'

She leaned further.

'Come my precious . . . my son, my babby . . . Mother will get you out of that cold water, Mother will . . .'

The gag holding back a scream that rose from her soul, Rachel watched the kneeling figure reach down then disappear without a sound as it toppled over the edge and into the lock.

'Thank you. You have done as much as can be done. We will resume the search in the morning.'

Jared watched the tired men of Foxley village walk away. They had searched the area around the cottages, the fields and outhouses, but he could not allow them to search the heath in darkness. It would be too easy to fall into the disused shaft of a gin pit. Refusing to admit the possibility that Rachel was already lying in one, injured or maybe dead, he turned to the cottage where a lamp burned brightly through the small window then glanced at the one next door, wreathed in darkness.

He had thought she lived there, sharing house and bed with the widow's son. He had accused her and she had said nothing; she had not denied it. Why . . . why had she not told him she had a separate cottage? Why had she not told him that she shared a house with another woman?

'*What I choose to do or not to do is no concern of yours.*' Jared remembered her words and the way her violet eyes flashed as she faced him.

It had been no concern of his then, but from now on everything she did would be. 'I love you, you stubborn child,' he whispered softly. 'I love you, Miss Rachel Cade.'

'Have they found her?'

Jared shook his head, dropping wearily into a chair in the warm kitchen.

'No, Ellen. They looked everywhere but there is no sign. I have told them to come here in the morning instead of reporting for work. They will resume the search then, so why don't you go and rest? I will stay here so you will not be alone.'

'Do you think she . . .'

'I'm not going to think anything.' Jared took her hands, holding them between his own. 'And you also must try not to think. Doubts and fears have a way of worsening in the small hours. Don't let them become stronger than you. You must believe Rachel is safe . . . we must both believe it.'

'I want to believe it!' Ellen's face crumpled. 'I want to believe it but . . .'

'There must be no buts, Ellen.' He wiped away her tears. 'Nor must there be any weeping.'

Ellen tried to smile but it was gone almost before it appeared. When he again suggested she go and rest, she shook her head vehemently.

'It is kind of you to suggest it, Jared, but I prefer to remain here. And before you say anything about my being alone with you, Rachel and William would both thank you for staying and their opinions are the only ones I care about.'

They sat through the remaining hours of the night and Ellen told her story as she had told it first to Rachel and then to William. Jared listened in silence, and when she had finished felt his dealings with Samuel Potter to be even further vindicated.

'I wasn't sure I should stay here,' Ellen said in conclusion. 'Arriving as we did, to find Mrs Thomas dead in her chair, it seemed to me I was imposing, that I had no place here. But Rachel was determined that if I left, she would go with me.'

'That decided you to stay?'

Ellen shook her head. 'No, I would not have had Rachel give up a decent home on my account, I would have found some way around her argument. But as it happened William found it for me. You see, he pointed out it would be bad for Rachel's reputation to be seen to live here alone with him before they were married. It was he who asked me to stay.'

'But they still thought she was a . . .' Jared caught the word in time.

'I know what people in Foxley and Bloomfield thought.' Ellen stared into the fire. 'They thought of Rachel as my father thought of me, and that was my fault. For weeks after I came here I still could not bring myself to go into the town, and so few people call here. Consequently no one learned of my presence and Rachel is too proud to have answered their filthy accusations. Pride can often be more of a liability than an asset. It can sometimes do more harm than it does good. I sometimes think she has too much of it.'

More harm than good! Jared stared out of the window through which he saw the first promise of dawn. He too had pride. Pray God he had not let it do harm he could not repair.

Standing up, he glanced again at the window. 'It will be dawn soon. I shall leave the trap here in the yard. It will be easier to scour the heath on horseback. The men will be here about six o'clock, they know what to do.'

'Mr Lytton . . . Jared.' Ellen touched a hand to his arm. 'Please find Rachel.'

Watching him ride out of the yard, she knew why the man had refused to return to his own home but had sat the long night in the tiny kitchen. There was a look in Jared Lytton's face when he spoke of Rachel, a look that said she was more to him than a woman in need of help. Perhaps he *had* spoken to her less than half a dozen times as he had said, but it was not always words that captured a heart and Jared Lytton had lost his, of that she was sure.

'Dear Lord, let him find Rachel,' she prayed softly, watching the sky receive the kiss of the sun. 'Let them find each other.'

And if they should, what of William?

It was almost as if fate were reprimanding her. Ellen glanced over to William's cottage, emerging from the night shadows. Rachel was promised to William, he had her promise to marry him. He also had her love, but did he have her heart or was that given somewhere else? Pride and pain, they went together, and William was caught in the middle. Poor William. Ellen turned back to the kitchen. Poor gentle William. His might be the hardest pain of all.

Rachel floated up from the realms of unconsciousness that had claimed her. Opening her eyes, she moaned at the pain in her arms, tied for so long in one position.

Hannah. She tried to mouth the name, remembering the gag only when it bit into the sides of her mouth. Then memory flooded back. Hannah had knelt beside the lock, calling her child. She had leaned over and . . . Rachel closed her eyes again, trying to blot out the awful scene, but still it played out in her mind. Hannah had fallen in the same way Robbie had fallen, headlong into a water-filled grave.

And her father . . . what had happened to him after she had left Horseley? She thought of him every night, prayed she might hear from him, but she had never had the courage to go back. Did he know of Hannah's incarceration in the lunatic asylum? But of course he must know, he would have been present when Magistrate Bedworth passed sentence.

Rachel shivered. It was just the sort of sentence that man would enjoy giving; especially when he had not enjoyed her. Oh, God! Rachel's eyes flew open. Had he inflicted so terrible a punishment because of her, because she had refused his advances? Isaiah Bedworth must have known Hannah was not truly mad, that it was grief which drove her to say the things she did. Yet he had sent her to an insane asylum, only there she had gone truly mad; and through it all Richie had been alone. She, his daughter, to whom he had only ever shown love, a child whose happiness was more to him than his own, had left him to face that dreadful ordeal alone.

Oh, Father, I'm so sorry! Rachel's heart swelled under the misery that engulfed her, while tears soaked into the gag that bound her mouth. Forgive me, Father, please forgive me. I left because I love you so much, I thought it would only cause you more grief if I stayed in Horseley . . . Oh, Father, I'm sorry . . . I'm sorry!

Blackness swirled again in her head and Rachel whimpered as her father took her hand.

I'm sorry, Father. She looked up, so far up, to where a face gazed down at her, a face with eyes the colour of summer skies, eyes filled with love.

'Why be sorry, my little love?' The smile above her deepened and the hand that held hers closed a little tighter. 'You did as I always told you to, you did what you knew was right.'

The hand not closed about hers held out a posy of wild flowers. Rachel exclaimed at the glorious colours that sparkled in the gold of the sun. Taking the flowers, she pulled her hand from the one that held it, feeling the touch of rougher skin drag over her soft child's flesh, then ran to where a woman sat in grass that waved tall wands of green all about her pale yellow hair; a woman whose lovely face welcomed her with a smile, and whose arms were lifted to her.

'There, my little one.' Rachel bent her head to take the flowers that had somehow become a pretty woven circlet. 'A crown for a princess. You are my princess, my little love . . . my little love.'

'Mother!' Rachel's heart cried out as the voice faded, taking her loved ones with it. 'Don't leave me, Mother . . . don't leave me again . . . ! Please don't . . . ! Please, please!'

'Rachel . . . Rachel, it's all right. You are safe, my love, I have you safe.'

'Father!' She wanted to take his hand again, to hold it so he could never be parted from her again. 'Father, I love you both so much, please don't let Mother go away again, please don't let her leave us . . .'

'Rachel, Rachel, you are safe now, it is all over.'

The arms that held her were so strong, Rachel felt she could stay in them forever. She was with her father. Through the pain that screamed in every bone she listened to the voice, a deep voice that throbbed as it told her of his love, a voice that filled her with joy, evoking deep feelings within her, leaving her wanting only to stay in those arms, to listen to that voice as it said he loved her.

But the voice was wrong. Much as she loved it, the voice was wrong. It was not her father's voice!

Every part of her pulsing with pain, she pushed at the body so warm and strong against her own, struggled against the arms that seemed reluctant to release her.

'Father . . .' Her mind still not clear, she looked into a pair of burnished bronze eyes that gazed down lovingly into hers.

'Rachel. Oh, my Rachel . . . my love!'

The handsome face hovering above her was lowered to her own and Rachel moaned softly, lips parting as Jared's mouth closed over hers.

Chapter Twenty-three

'Rachel.'

The voice was soft and caressing. But she had already slipped away into the black chasms that had sheltered her through the night.

'I don't think her will have taken any real harm, though I can't rightly say it will have done the wench any good either.'

The wife of the landlord of The Navigation tavern bustled in to where Jared waited in the tiny private kitchen. 'Poor wench, whatever be the world coming to . . . fetching her out of her rightful home and leaving her out on the heath. And tied as well by the look of her wrists. Whoever done that to her needs a good hoss whip across his back, he does that!'

'Is she conscious?' Jared glanced towards the room where he had carried Rachel after rousing the landlord.

'Yes, sir.' The woman nodded. 'Her came to soon after you brought her in. I got her all wrapped up nice and warm like, and her don't seem too bad now, considering; but I must say I was worried when first I saw her, so pale and cold. I thought her to be a goner for sure. But like I say, her don't be too bad, considering. A drop of warm broth will soon have her perky again. Have you any idea who could have done it, Mr Lytton?'

'No, I have not, not at present. But the culprit will be found.'

'Ar, and when he is, I hope he gets a taste of the cat afore he's sent down, and that for a good long time an' all!'

Jared's mouth, already taut, firmed to a thin line. 'He will get his desserts, you can be very sure of that.'

'Be no more than he deserves if he gets the rope!' The woman crossed to the fire her husband had fanned into life after Jared had wakened them, and stirred the contents of a pan with a large metal spoon. 'This will be a while longer, but I will take a bowl in to her soon as it be ready.'

'Thank you.' Jared glanced at the watch he drew from his pocket. The woman's husband had gone to the cottage to tell the men to bring the trap; it would be an hour at least before they got here. Returning the watch to his pocket, he glanced towards the fireplace. 'Might I have your permission to go into the parlour?'

'Oh, ar, Mr Lytton, sir. O' course you can.' The woman laid the spoon on a plate set on the hob. 'Her might like somebody to sit wi' her after what her's been through. You go right on in, I'll follow you directly.'

Rachel lay propped up on a dark leather sofa, its padded head curving in a graceful sweep to a low wooden rail that served as a back. The room was dim, the fragile morning light no match for the heavy plush curtains that stood sentinel over the cream lace hanging against the glass. But even in the poor light Jared saw the pallor of her face and the frightened way her eyes jerked open as he approached her.

'I have sent for the trap I left at the cottage . . . at your home. We will get you back there and then send for a doctor.'

'I have no need of a doctor, Mr Lytton. I just want to go home.'

'But you might be injured.'

Rachel caught the note in his voice. It could almost have been anxiety in anyone else, but not in Jared Lytton. He would harbour no anxiety for the welfare of a whore.

'I am not injured.' She let her head fall back against

the sofa, hair spread like a silvery veil across its dark surface.

Looking down at her pale face, her lovely eyes smudged with shadows of exhaustion, Jared felt the whole of his being lurch with dread. She might have died out there on that heath, that maniac of a man could so easily have killed her, so easily have . . . he turned to draw up a chair, using the moment to steady himself.

'Then we have heaven to thank for that.' Pulling the chair to the sofa, he sat down. 'But we will still have the opinion of a doctor, even though he be less qualified than the angels.'

He smiled and for a moment Rachel forgot the harshness he had shown on each occasion they had met since he had taken her to the Fox Inn. He had rescued her from the heath that night, and now . . . She frowned, trying to force her memory into obeying her. Now he was here, but how? It had been her father, she had been holding her father's hand . . .

'Rachel!' Seeing the frown, Jared leaned towards her, his own face drawn, the worry of the long night with him still. 'Are you in pain?'

Not the sort of pain I can tell you about, she thought, her confused mind clearing again. How could she tell him *he* was the cause of her pain? That the very thought of him caused her heart to ache, that dreams of him left her not wanting to face up to the days when he would not be there; days of longing yet days also of reliving those awful moments when he had left her in no doubt as to what he thought of her.

'Will I call the landlord's wife?'

She shook her head, not trusting herself not to break down.

'Who . . . who found me?' When at last she spoke her voice was still tremulous and the tears sparkled behind the velvet softness of her eyes.

Fighting a growing urge to take her in his arms, to kiss the tears from her eyes and the fear from her voice, Jared answered: 'I did, I found you.'

'But how did you know?' Rachel heard the tenderness in his voice, saw the warmth that flared in his bronze eyes. She frowned again. Surely her mind was still playing tricks?

'I was on my way home to Foxley.' He still had not straightened but half leaned towards her, and now his hand touched hers where it rested on the blanket that covered her. 'I saw a light on the heath. I thought at first it must be a firefly . . .'

'A jack-o'-lantern,' Rachel interrupted, her smile gentle and expression faraway. 'My father called them jack-o'-lanterns.'

'So did mine.' Jared held the hand that did not pull away. 'But my mother insisted they were fireflies. But whichever name you choose, I thought the light I saw was one of those insects. It was only after watching it for some minutes I realised it could not be. Then I heard a voice calling for help, a woman's voice. It turned out to be Ellen Walker . . . Rachel, in God's name, why didn't you tell me? Why did you not say she had lived in the same house as you since Mrs Thomas died?'

Rachel made no answer. To tell him it was no business of his would mean his hand would drop from hers. He had taken it as he would take a child's, to comfort her, no more than that, but it was all she had, all she would ever have of the man who tormented her waking moments and filled her sleeping ones.

'Ellen told me how you left the byre to speak to the wagoner who was delivering the barley,' Jared continued when Rachel stayed silent, and his hand remained clasped over hers. 'She said she glanced into the yard to see you talking to the man then went back to the milking. When she had finished she could not find you anywhere. You had left the house without a word, and had not taken a shawl. She waited, thinking you might have gone to show the man the road if he was unfamiliar with the area, but when it began to grow dark and you still did not return, she set out to look for you. We organised a search after taking Ellen back to the house . . . but with night well set in we could not search the heath. I sat with her through the night and she told me everything. Rachel – oh, my love!' Suddenly his arms were about her, drawing her to him, his mouth seeking hers. 'Rachel, my darling . . . forgive me, forgive me for the things I said . . .'

The words came intermittently, his lips reluctant to leave hers for longer than it took to breathe, and Rachel lifted her own to them, drowning in their touch until the cold finger of reality tapped and she drew away. He had called her darling . . . but it could not have been meant as a term of endearment. Jared Lytton despised her. What he had said were words of relief at finding her unharmed. And his kiss? But why should he show relief, why show any emotion towards her at all?

'You have no need to apologise, Mr Lytton.' Rachel withdrew her hand, pushing it down under the blanket. 'What you thought of me caused me no concern, and as for the things you said . . . I lost no sleep on account of them.'

Why are you saying these things? her mind cried out. Why add more lies to what has gone before? But she ignored them. 'William knew the truth of things and that can be my only concern. He will harbour no doubts as to the morals of his wife.'

His face hardening, Jared drew back as if she had struck him.

Seeing the warmth of his eyes give way to coldness, Rachel felt her heart turn over. She could have prolonged the moment, held on a little longer to the dream, but dreams had a way of turning into nightmares and her own particular nightmare would return soon enough – the nightmare of a life without Jared Lytton.

'I thank you for searching for me, and I know William will do the same when he returns from Worcester, but how did you know *where* to search?'

She had to return her thoughts to an even keel, to still the wild tumult of her heart. She could not allow him to suspect, could not let him see or even guess what was truly in her heart.

'I remembered seeing a wagon earlier that evening.' He stood up and moved across the room, standing beside an ornate chiffonier set with elaborate figurines. 'I thought it was perhaps delivering ale to one of the canalside ale houses. I thought that if I failed to find you I would ask at each one in the hope of finding out where the wagon came from, that perhaps its driver might remember having seen you as he might if you had followed the canal towpath. Then I saw the wagon abandoned on the heath and I thought . . .' He picked up a figurine, turning it in his hand, examining the gaudily painted ornament. 'I was about to leave, had looked over the wagon and found it without a driver. I thought the man must have got himself drunk and be sleeping it off somewhere. It was then I saw you over against a rock. You were lying half twisted as if you had been thrown there. I thought . . . I thought you were dead!'

He replaced the figurine, his hand resting a long time on its painted head, his own bowed.

Rachel watched him from the sofa. She might almost have imagined it to be the aftermath of fear that held him, but that must be a delusion; it was tiredness that caused his shoulders to droop and bowed his head, only tiredness. To think it could be anything else was merely feeding her own fantasy, her own dreams and desires.

'Then I heard you moan.'

He was not facing her but Rachel did not need to see his face to know the emotion he was experiencing; his voice cracked and he swallowed hard as though to clear some obstruction from his throat. Seeing him lift his head, hearing him draw a long breath as he stared ahead, Rachel's heart cried out to her to take him in her arms, to hold him, to tell him the truth. But she couldn't. She could not say what was deep within her. She could never tell him that she loved him.

'I . . . I carried you here.' He began to speak again, voice thick and punctuated by long breaths as if he had to fight for control. 'Even then I thought . . .'

His head drooped again and he was silent. In the small parlour, stuffed with furniture, a long case clock softly chimed the hour.

Why had he stayed the night in the cottage? Rachel watched the man standing with his back to her. Would it not have been better for both of them to have taken Ellen to Foxley, have her cared for there? Why had he felt he had to search for her at all?

'Rachel, my darling, forgive me.' His words came back to her and the memory of his kiss burned on her lips, and despite knowing it had resulted from nothing more than relief on his part, she trembled.

A short double tap sounded at the door. She glanced towards it, glad of the interruption. But the memory of his kiss remained. It would return, over and over, in the long days and longer nights to come; return to haunt her mind and break her heart.

'Here you be, miss.' The landlady bustled through the door Jared had opened for her, two bowls of steaming soup set on a cloth-draped trolley which she wheeled up to the sofa. 'A nice drop of hot broth. You get that inside you and you'll feel a lot better. I put a bowl for you an' all, Mr Lytton.' She glanced at Jared, gone to stand before the empty grate. 'By the looks of you, you could be doing with something hot. Fair washed out, you look, and no codding.'

The woman was right. Jared gave her a brief smile. It was no lie to say he looked washed out. He felt tired, but it was not a tiredness brought on by missing a few hours' sleep.

'Eh!' The woman folded her hands over the white apron that covered her ample frame. 'Who would have thought such a thing? To tie up a young wench and leave her all night out on that heath. The man must be a stark staring lunatic, he must be mad! 'Tis to be hoped the men catch up wi' him afore the law do. That way he'll find out good and proper what it feels like to be trussed up like an animal and dragged across the heath. Ar, it will be a good thing if the men find him first!' She looked at Rachel. 'I tell you this, me wench. You'll be more than avenged if they do, for there'll not be much left of him when they be finished!'

'Why *did* that man attack you?' Jared waited until they were alone again. 'What could he possibly have against you? He could not have known you, surely? The woman is right. Whoever the man is, he is raving mad and when he is caught must be put away for life. He must never again be given the opportunity to attack a woman!'

Rachel spooned the broth out of the bowl the landlady had placed on a cloth across her lap, eyes following the spoon yet not seeing it. 'Mad, yes,' she said, so softly the words hardly sounded above the ticking of the clock. 'But not unknown to me – and not a man. It was my father's wife.'

'It's all right, Rachel, you are home now.'

She dropped back against the pillows as Ellen gently touched her shoulder.

'Ellen . . .'

'Shhh,' Ellen's quiet voice soothed her. 'There is nothing to frighten you any more, you are safe at home. Jared brought you himself.'

Rachel's head throbbed and for a moment her senses whirled as the blackness that had dropped over her in the parlour of the inn threatened to take her again. He had brought her home. She struggled to remember. Ellen said *he* had brought her to the cottage himself, but where was William, why had William not brought her?

'William has gone to Worcester,' Ellen said as the name dropped from Rachel's lips. 'Don't you remember? He went for hops but will be back soon.'

'Yes, I want him to come back,' Rachel whispered, but it was not William's face she saw when she closed her eyes.

'I will just go tell Jared you are awake, he seemed so worried when he carried you into the house.'

Jared! Rachel's mind wrestled with the shadows flitting in and out of it. Ellen was speaking of that man, the one who accused her of . . . The shadows deepened then receded. Ellen was talking of Mr Lytton but she was using his first name, calling him Jared as though they were friends!

'Mr Lytton?' Rachel pushed herself up on to her pillows, frowning against the sharp stab of pain in her head.

Ellen hovered, anxious she should not move. 'Yes, he found you and brought you back here. Try to rest now. You will remember everything after you have slept. The doctor says you will most probably be yourself in a week or so, he found no broken bones, but he said you must rest. You are bound to be shocked after what happened so rest is imperative.'

'Doctor?'

'Yes.' Ellen smiled as she fussed over the sheet. 'Jared called him, you did not wake. Now try to relax while I go and tell Jared you are awake.'

'Mr Lytton is here?' Rachel opened her eyes.

'Yes. He dismissed the search party but stayed on. He is in the kitchen.'

'Why has he stayed?'

'He was as worried about you as I was,' Ellen answered truthfully, remembering the look that had haunted his face throughout the night. 'He stayed with me until it was light enough to begin a search then went out alone. He would not wait for the men. He is a kind man, Rachel, and cares about what has happened to you. He might not say it but it shows in his face. Jared cares about you, Rachel.'

Jared Lytton cared about her! Rachel laughed then winced at the pain it caused along her temple. Was it caring that had him label her a whore, had him condemn her without bothering to find out the truth? Was it caring to confront her in the street with his accusations? Was it caring that had him call her darling, take her in his arms and kiss her, or was that a way of proving himself correct in his assumptions? That she was ready to take any man who could furnish her with a comfortable living!

Ellen watched the nuances of her emotions flit across Rachel's face, and again the thought came back to her: the pride and the joy. Rachel had her pride, but was the man waiting in their tiny kitchen her joy?

'I should thank him.' Rachel seemed to come back from some distant place. 'Please ask him to wait until I am dressed.'

Ellen straightened, her hands on her slim hips. 'You will do no such thing, Rachel Cade! You are staying in that bed!'

'No, I am getting dressed.' Rachel smiled up into Ellen's indignant face. 'Then I shall come downstairs to thank Mr Lytton, and if you think to have him gone before I get there, then I shall walk to Foxley and thank him there. I will not have that man add the faults of ignorance and bad manners to the list he has already chalked up against me.'

'Rachel, please, you can't . . .'

'But I am, Ellen. It is only right I should thank him.'

'Does it matter what he thinks?' Ellen watched Rachel's pale face, seeing the unhappiness that clouded her eyes.

Rachel swung her legs over the side of the bed, unable to prevent a groan at the ache in her bones. 'What *he* thinks, no.' She could not look at Ellen as she spoke, fearing her expression would betray her. 'What I think of myself, yes, that does matter and I would not think well of myself if I did not give him my thanks.'

'Then you will give them to him from that bed!' Ellen was emphatic. 'Or you will be caught in your bloomers . . . or out of them, for I intend to send him up. Now!'

She was gone before Rachel could reply. There was no way she could be out of her nightgown and into her clothes before he came up the stairs. Resigned to the fact, Rachel swung her legs back into the bed, drawing up the covers over her chest just as Ellen came back with Jared Lytton.

Samuel Potter fingered the coins in his pocket. They were his last. There had been no coal from the pit bank wenches, even as far along as Lea Brook. Samuel Potter was barred from the pits, the days of coal jagging were over for him, Lytton had seen to that.

Swiping the horse's rump with the whip he always carried, he swore beneath his breath. That bloody Lytton with his high-handed ways had put him out of business. When these last few bags of coal were gone so was his living. The horse and cart were already sold, he had their use for this day only.

Ruined! He swiped the horse again, bringing a whinny of protest from the animal. Samuel Potter ruined. And for what? For a couple of pit bank wenches who were no more than trollops!

Just what had been Lytton's interest there? He never had found out. But then he had made no effort in that direction, there were wenches a-plenty where they had come from and a sight more willing besides. Even so, he thought ruefully, the pale-haired one had been pretty; she was enough to tempt any man's palate. Could it be she had tempted Lytton's?

He flicked the reins but the horse did not alter its pace and Samuel ignored it this time.

He had paid that chap who had sat with him in the Fountain Inn, paid him two pounds ten. Two pounds ten shillings! He felt the bile of anger and regret curdle in his throat. Come the next few months he might be in need of money like that, money he had laid out to have Lytton done away with. And what had he seen for it?

'Bugger all!' he muttered beneath his breath. 'Bugger all, that be what I've seen for that money. And where be it now, eh? A bloody fair way from here, I'll be bound. That bloke would be out of the public house faster than a ferret down a rabbit hole and away with my two pounds ten. More bloody fool me!' He flicked the reins again, eliciting the same response. 'I should have had more sense than to pay a penny till I knowed Lytton were dressed in his Sunday suit with a couple of pennies on his eyes!'

But Lytton was not dead, though rumour had it he had run it close. Something about a miner heaving a lump of rock at his head. Quite likely it would have killed him if another man had not thrown himself at Lytton and pushed him clear. Seems the rock hit that one – almost did for him if tales were to be believed. Pity it hadn't! Samuel's thoughts ran on, their bitterness increasing. Pity it hadn't knocked his brains out, bloody interfering bugger! Christ, if he knew who the man was, he would knock 'im out himself! Two pounds ten shillings, that was what he had paid. Two pounds ten and nothing to show for it.

The horse ambled slowly along, needing no guidance from the man who intermittently flicked the reins, following the route it had come to know so well.

'You got a couple of sacks to spare?'

As if understanding the shout directed at his driver, the horse drew to a stop.

'Ar.' Samuel nodded. 'Be ninepence a sack.'

'Ninepence!' The woman tightened her shawl then flapped her hand in a dismissive gesture. 'I can get it from old Bache for sevenpence.'

'You can get coal dust anywhere, missis, and for a lot less than sevenpence a half hundredweight. This be coal I'm hauling, not dust!' Samuel replied, his glare as sour as his words.

The woman stared up at him, undaunted. 'That be right?' she scoffed. 'Then you take your coal and get somebody else to pay you ninepence a bag for it, 'cos I ain't!'

'I ain't taking nowt off the price!' Samuel remained adamant. He had little more than a couple of shillings remaining, but he still was not giving coal away. Sell one bag for less than ninepence and the rest would be asked for at the same price. Lytton had put an end to his business but he wouldn't be given any further reason to laugh. He glared at the woman, venom in his tone as he shouted: 'Ninepence I asked, and ninepence it be. Take it or leave it.'

'I'll be leaving it.' The woman tugged her shawl again. 'And you think on this: the coal be yourn but the money be mine. You be stuck with that coal till you finds somebody daft enough to buy it from you but I can take my money anywhere.' She turned on her way, the last of her words drifting back along the street. 'You can't eat coal, Potter, think on that. You can't eat coal!'

No, he couldn't eat coal. The horse had already moved off by the time Samuel flicked the reins again. But you could do a man a lot of damage with it, and so sure as that one from the Fountain Inn ever showed up again, he would stuff a hundredweight up his arse, kibble by kibble!

Chapter Twenty-four

Jared gazed at the face of the girl in the bed, his heart contracting. She could have been killed, that woman might so easily have killed her.

'I have to thank you, Mr Lytton, for your kindness in searching for me, and for the kindness you showed to Ellen in staying with her.'

'Ellen thanked me herself, and so have you, several times.'

Each referred to the other by their Christian name, Rachel noted as she listened to his answer.

'You must forgive me my repetition, my mind is still a little distracted.'

'Are you in pain?'

Rachel shook her head, confused by the look on his face. He despised her, he had made that very clear, yet the look he wore now spoke only of concern, and almost of fear. Why was he still here? She wanted him to stay but at the same time wanted him to leave. She wanted . . . the wetness of tears rested along her eyelids and her mouth trembled . . . she didn't know what she wanted.

'Rachel!'

He dropped to the bed, sitting beside her, and suddenly she was in his arms and he was murmuring against her mouth, just as on the heath. But it had not been his arms that held her then, his lips against her hair or his voice telling of his love: it had been her father. But where was her father now . . . why was *he* not with her instead of Jared Lytton . . . why did it feel so right to be in this man's arms . . . why did she feel she never wanted to leave them?

Thoughts ran through her mind, twisting and turning, but one thought remained dominant, superseding all others as his mouth came down and she lifted her own to meet it: she never wanted to leave his arms.

'Rachel, my love, I was so afraid . . .'

His lips on her eyes, her temple, her brow, Rachel felt the terror of the night melt away and the unhappiness of the past weeks fade into nothing. It was as if they had never been, a dream his kiss dissolved like the mist of morning, a fantasy the touch of his mouth drove away, a figment of her own imagining . . .

'. . . I dreaded my own actions should you be hurt, the thought of what might happen!' His arms tightened and above her head his voice was strained and tight. 'I could have lost you forever. Rachel, my darling, I love you . . .'

A figment of her own imagination! the thought hammered in her mind. That is what this is, a figment of your own imagination. It is not real, he is not truly saying these things. It is *you*, you yourself. You are taking words and weaving them into the song *you* want to sing, building a dream *you* want to dream. It is all a figment . . . a figment . . .

A figment! Suddenly the bubble of happiness that cocooned her shattered and the cold wind of reality blew into her mind. He had felt a natural concern for Ellen, a woman alone in a house so far from the village. He had promised to join in the search for Ellen's friend and he had kept that promise. His holding her now was no more than a way of comforting a woman he knew had undergone a frightening ordeal. There was no more to his action than that. To pretend even for a moment that there could be, would only add to her future heartache.

Reluctant to break the dream yet knowing she had to,

Rachel pushed at his arms, pressing them away before lying back against the pillows.

'I am perfectly all right now, Mr Lytton.' She kept her eyes deliberately on his, the truth carefully veiled. 'Apart from a little tiredness. Please do not let me detain you any longer. I am sure my fiancé will wish to add his thanks to my own. No doubt he will call at Foxley when he returns.'

'You are not really promised to William Thomas!'

The eyes locked on hers were disbelieving and Jared paused, seeming to wait for her to agree, to tell him she had made no such commitment. Rachel's fingers curled about the edge of the sheet but she made no answer.

Suddenly his eyes darkened. 'You told me that you were to marry the widow's son merely to strike back at me, didn't you?' His stare held but when still she didn't answer there was a subtle change, an indefinable difference, a shadow almost of fear. 'I accused you and you wanted to hit back. That's it, isn't it? But the things I said . . .' he reached for her hands, holding them tightly in his own '. . . I didn't realise at the time why I said them but now I do. I accused you of having the morals of a street walker because I was so eaten up with jealousy. I couldn't accept the idea of your being here when you had refused to come to Foxley. I *knew* you could do no such thing, yet each time I let my own jealousy get the upper hand. Rachel, I'm so sorry for those awful words. Can you believe me when I tell you I love you . . . that I have loved you from seeing you in that courtroom? I love you and want you for my wife!'

The voice on the heath had not been her father's, nor had those words been a figment of her imagination. They were real, she had truly heard them. Jared Lytton loved her, he loved her! Rachel's world suddenly filled with a happiness she could almost touch. He loved her, he wanted her for his wife . . . And as quickly as it came the happiness faded. What of William? She had promised to become his wife.

'Rachel.' The strange look in his eyes sharpened as Jared

watched her, almost as though some sixth sense told him her thoughts. 'Rachel, I love you. I want you for my wife. Will you, my darling? Will you marry me?'

It seemed to Rachel she was struggling up from some great depth, struggling against an unseen force that wanted to pull her back into a world without light.

'I am promised to William,' she whispered.

'You do not love him!' Fear turned his voice razor sharp. 'I know you don't. It was in your kiss, in your touch. I tasted it on your mouth, I felt it tremble in your body as I held you . . . you love *me* . . . you love me as I love you. If you have given any promise to William he will not hold you to it, not when we tell him . . .'

'No!' Rachel pulled her hands free. 'I have given my word to him and I will keep it. I will not have him hurt on my account, William must not know . . . he must never know!'

'But you can't . . .'

'Yes, Mr Lytton, I can.' Rachel felt a tug at her heart but forced her words to come calmly. 'And I will. I have promised to marry William Thomas and that is what I will do. The banns have already been called and in three weeks I shall become his wife.'

Jared rose slowly and stood looking down at her. 'I am not wrong, am I?' he asked quietly. Then, receiving no reply, he walked from the room.

'He sh . . . should have kn . . . known,' William said, anxiety tripping his tongue. 'He should ha . . . have known the m . . . man was no good, not with a f . . . face as scarred as you say. I've a m . . . mind to take my barley some place else for malting.'

'Ernest cannot be blamed, he was not to know, how could he have? And a scarred face does not always indicate a scarred nature.'

William reached for his pipe, agitatedly cramming fresh

shavings of tobacco into the small bowl. 'You c . . . could have been killed!'

'But I wasn't, William, and anyway it is all over now and no harm done.'

'N . . . no thanks to him. The man must be a m . . . maniac, there be no other explanation.'

'You *were* very lucky, Rachel.' Ellen smiled across the table at her. 'I mean, for that man to have left you there on the heath after taking you away. I wonder what made him run off?'

Rachel stared into the fire, watching flames dance blue and gold at its crimson centre. She had pretended tiredness after Jared Lytton had left yesterday and Ellen had left her mostly alone, only coming into her room with meals or a drink and not pressing to be told anything. Rachel had volunteered nothing more of what had happened, and neither it seemed had Jared.

'There is n . . . nothing to say he won't try again. I will go to the malt house tomorrow. Ernest has to be told what k . . . kind of man be working for him. And sh . . . should I seen him afore the constables do, then I'll stretch his neck myself and beat the law to it!'

'You will not need to visit the malt house.' Rachel stared into the dancing flames.

'But, Rachel, you cannot just ignore what happened,' Ellen said quickly. 'What he has done once he can so easily do again. Next time the woman he attacks may not be so fortunate as you. Next time the man might not run away, at least not before . . .'

'Not before he has killed her!' William held a taper to the fire. 'I shall go and see Ernest tomorrow and then I shall see the constable. That man has to be caught before he harms someone else.'

'He will not harm anyone else,' she said softly.

'Rachel, how can you defend him?'

She lifted her gaze from the fire, resting it on Ellen's face and saying softly, 'I am not defending him, Ellen. I am just stating a fact. The one who attacked me will never harm anyone again. That person is dead, drowned in the lock at Tipton Green.'

Knocking the taper against the bars of the grate, extinguishing the glow at its tip, William looked up sharply.

'You saw it! You saw him go in?'

In her lap, Rachel's fingers curled into each other. 'Yes,' she whispered. 'Yes, I saw it, I saw him fall over the edge. Except it was not a him. The person who bound my hands and feet and then intended to drown me was not a man, it was a woman . . . my father's wife.'

Ellen and William sat in silence, listening to the story as it all poured out, watching the sadness shadow Rachel's face, sharing with her the pain of the telling.

'You see,' she finished softly, 'Hannah thought it was Robbie she heard. She thought he was crying, that he was there in the water. She leaned down to get him and fell . . . into that same lock, just as . . .'

'Don't say any more.' Ellen was on her feet, her arms going around Rachel's shoulders. 'You're safe and nothing else matters.'

'Safe, yes.' William made a show of inspecting his pipe but the thickness in his throat owed nothing to tobacco. 'Thanks to Jared Lytton. Lord knows how long you might have lain out on that heath had he not gone in search of you. I'll be going to thank him soon as I can, and for sitting along of Ellen. The man has been more than kind.'

More than kind, Rachel agreed in her heart as Ellen released her, going to swing the kettle over the fire.

'Mr Lytton asked if he could call again in a few days,' Ellen said, reaching for cups. 'I told him I did not think you would object, William.'

'Not at all, I can give him my thanks then.'

Rachel's heart twisted. Jared was coming back to this house! Would he tell William what had passed between them, that she had not denied her love for him? She raised her glance to Ellen, a glance that asked why. But the eyes that returned her look held not penitence but defiance.

The church had already called the banns. Jared guided the carriage between the high stone gate posts of Dudley Guest Hospital. In less than a month Rachel would be William Thomas's wife. But she was not in love with him, not in that sense! He felt the same hopelessness he had on leaving the cottage. He had been such a fool: giving way to thoughts he knew were not true, making accusations that had driven her into the arms of the widow's son.

Leaving the carriage in the care of a thick-set porter, Jared made his way into the grey oppressive-looking building, the words his grandmother was fond of using ringing in his mind. 'You've made your bed, lad, and now you must lie on it. And shaking it every day of your life won't soften it!'

Yes, what had happened was his own fault. He had set that girl against him almost from their first meeting and now he must bear the consequences. Yet what had he expected? Did he think she would break her promise and come rushing into his arms when he told her he loved her?

Jared's boots rang loudly as he entered the hushed building.

Perhaps he had expected that. But the expected had not happened. She had spoken no word to William, had made her intentions perfectly clear: she would marry in less than a month.

But she was not in love with the man!

Jared's troubled gaze swept over the entrance hall. Its walls were bare except for their covering of paint – the top half cream, the lower half green; a table devoid of ornament of any sort was set in one corner; doorways like gaping mouths led on to empty corridors.

She was not in love with William Thomas, she was in love with him. '*You've made your bed, lad* . . .' The thought brought a cynical laugh in its wake. Oh, yes! Jared Lytton had done that all right. He had fallen in love with a girl who was to become another man's wife.

'Mr Lytton.'

Jared turned to face a man of medium height. He had grey hair brushed back from his brow, and a neatly trimmed goatee beard above a perfectly laundered white shirt that glowed against a dark jacket.

'Good evening, Dr Taylor.' Jared extended his hand then nodded to the nursing sister standing impassively at the other man's shoulder.

Leading the way along the corridor, the doctor showed Jared into his office, a room infinitely more agreeable than the hall with deep armchairs set on thick carpet, a mahogany bureau and a desk gleaming from hours of dedicated polishing reflecting the glow of the several lamps.

'Do you have any further information concerning the man you brought here?' The doctor looked at Jared as they each took a chair.

'No, nothing. My enquiries have revealed nothing we did not already know. It is as if he stepped out of nowhere. No one at the quarry knows anything at all about him.'

'Pity!' The doctor remained silent for a moment, then said, 'He is well enough to be discharged, though he will need nursing for a time yet.'

'That is taken care of.' Jared rose. 'There is a cottage on my estate and I have employed a couple who will be responsible for his welfare for as long as is necessary.'

'Then you can do no more, Mr Lytton.' The doctor stood up, offering his hand. 'The man is very fortunate to have you provide for him.'

'*I* am the fortunate one.' Jared shook the proffered hand. 'If that man had not acted as he did, I would most probably be dead. Whatever I can do for him now is nothing in comparison.'

'Quite . . . quite.' The doctor cleared his throat, glancing at the woman standing silently by. 'Have the patient ready for collection by . . .' taking a gold hunter from his waistcoat pocket he flipped open the lid glancing at the dial before returning the watch to his pocket, '. . . shall we say eleven in the morning.'

'Is he well enough to leave now?' Jared glanced from one to the other. 'I have rugs and a closed carriage, and the evening is quite mild.'

'The man is well enough but . . . what of clothes? I mean, the ones he came in . . .'

'The patient has new outdoor clothing, Doctor.' The nursing sister seemed to grudge parting with the words. 'Mr Lytton had them sent in last week.'

The doctor nodded. 'I can see no objection to his leaving in that case. See to it, please, Sister.'

The man had not spoken, but as he had come towards Jared, flanked by two nurses, there had been a flicker in his empty eyes, a tiny fleeting spark of life, and his lips had moved. Then the spark had died.

'There be a hot broth ready and his bed be aired. He'll be well taken care of, Mr Lytton, never you fear.'

A round-faced woman smiled as Jared drew the carriage to a halt outside a small house set back from the track that led to it.

'I've had a fire burning in his room since coming here, just as you said, sir.'

'Thank you, Mrs Jenks.'

The woman's husband stepped forward as Jared opened the carriage door.

A heavy woollen rug about his shoulders, the patient leaned out, his eyes fixed unmistakably on Jared.

'Bastard!'

Though quietly spoken the word was clearly audible and the woman gasped. 'Well, there's gratitude, Mr Lytton, and after all you've done for him, the . . .'

'Shh!' Jared halted her in mid-flow, his tone sharp, eyes fixed on the man in the carriage. 'Who is?' he asked, his voice soft.

'He be a bastard!' His movements stiff and unsure, the man stepped slowly down from the carriage and for one more brief instant a spark flickered in his sad eyes. 'Isaiah Bedworth be a bastard!'

'Rachel, I feel so badly about taking the money for clothes. Had I known you did not intend to buy a wedding dress, I would never have accepted . . .'

'I know you wouldn't.' Rachel glanced up from the large wooden tun to which she had just added hops and barley. 'But there's no reason for you to feel badly about buying that dress. It's very pretty and it suits you.'

'That is all very well, but you . . . you are not really going to wear that skirt and blouse to your wedding?'

'There is nothing wrong with my skirt and blouse.' Rachel lifted a small sack, pouring a stream of sugar into the tun.

'There is nothing wrong with it. But to use it as a wedding dress . . . why, Rachel? You told me that William was to buy you a gown, is there some reason he has not?'

Putting the sack on the floor, she lifted a jar from a shelf set on one wall and emptied yeast mixture into the tun. 'There is no reason, except I have not asked him.'

'But, Rachel . . .'

'No, Ellen.' She turned from the tun. 'I will not spend William's money on a dress I will probably never wear again. The skirt and blouse that Beulah lent me money to buy will do well enough.'

So that was the reason Rachel had not worn the maroon skirt or pretty blouse to market! Ellen had wanted to ask why often enough. Now she knew. 'You could wear my dress and I could take the skirt and blouse . . . we are much the same size.'

'I will not hear of it. You will wear that pretty dress to my wedding or . . .' Rachel smiled '. . . I will refuse to *have* a wedding.'

In the dim light of the brew house Ellen did not smile. It was not normal for a girl to speak so of her forthcoming marriage, to dismiss the subject almost as soon as it arose, to show so little interest in any aspect of it. To behave as though it were not happening to her, as if the whole affair held no happiness. Was that the reason Rachel would not discuss her wedding, nor entertain the idea of a new gown? Was she unhappy at the prospect of marrying William? Certainly she had been even more reticent since Jared Lytton's visit a few days ago.

'Rachel,' said Ellen, 'are you sure of what you are doing? Are you sure William is the man you really love?'

Rachel turned back to the tun but Ellen had already seen the smile fade from her face.

'Don't do the wrong thing, Rachel. Don't be misled into something you may regret for the rest of your life. Grasp the chance of happiness while you can, it may never come again. Take them both, Rachel, the pride and the joy. Take your pride in your hands and tell William what we both know is the truth: that you are in love with Jared Lytton. Then you can take the joy. Without it your life will be as empty as my own.'

Going to her friend, Rachel took her hands, a hint of tears in her voice as she answered. 'It seems we are both to have an empty life, Ellen, but whatever the cost I will not have William hurt. I will make him happy, believe me I will, only he must never know. Promise me you will say nothing, Ellen, promise me!'

Ellen looked sadly into eyes wet with tears. 'Has Jared Lytton made that promise?'

Rachel nodded and Ellen gave her hands a gentle squeeze before releasing them. 'Then I will too,' she said. 'William will never learn the truth from me.' She smiled then. 'And neither will he have his midday meal unless I get a move on and take it to him.'

'You and William get on well together,' Rachel said. 'He liked you from the first day you came here, Ellen.'

'I like him too, Rachel. He is a kind, gentle man who does not deserve to be hurt.'

'I'll never hurt him, Ellen.' Rachel met her eyes. 'That is why . . .'

'That is why, despite being in love with someone else, you are marrying him!'

Ellen's face seemed to register that strange sadness that Rachel had seen play across it so often since she had come to this house. Was she unhappy here, would she rather be somewhere else?

'I hope things will go well, Rachel. I love both of my friends, and would not want to see them unhappy.'

Turning quickly, she left Rachel standing in the dim coolness of the brew house, each of them locked in her own thoughts, each of them staring at her own tragedy.

'Good afternoon.'

Still nervous from her experience on the heath, every unexpected sound a source of fear to her, Rachel swung around to see Jared Lytton. He stood in the doorway, daylight framing his strong figure, emphasising the width of his shoulders, the long line of his legs.

'Good afternoon.' She had to force the words past the lump that suddenly filled her throat. 'I did not hear your carriage.'

'Perhaps that is because you were day dreaming?'

He smiled, a slow lop-sided smile that sent her pulse soaring. Why had he come here? Why could he not leave her alone?

'I don't suppose you were day dreaming about me?'

Rachel blushed, the colour rising to her cheeks. 'You would suppose correctly, Mr Lytton.'

He stepped further into the dimly lit brew house, his smile

fading as he reached her. 'I can always hope, Rachel, and I will go on hoping, right up to the moment that wedding ring is slipped on your finger. I love you and will go on loving you even after you become William Thomas's wife.'

'Please . . . don't! Don't say any more.' Her voice cracking, Rachel made to step away but he caught her arms, preventing her from leaving.

'No, Rachel!' In the shadows his eyes gleamed like molten gold. 'You have refused my love but you *will* hear my words. You may give your body to William Thomas but you can never give him your heart. That is not yours to give, it belongs to me, and will belong to me all the days of your life as mine will belong to you. We have many days before us, Rachel, days that will not relieve the heartache, days in which love and pain will grow in us both, my love, days when all I will have of you is this!'

Loosening her arms his own slid about her, drawing her against the hardness of him, taking her mouth with his own.

'Jared, please . . .' Torn between love and her promise, her strength suddenly deserting her, Rachel lay limply against him. 'It . . . it is difficult enough . . .'

'Then end it, my love,' he murmured, his lips against her temple. 'Let us go to William and tell him. Let us put an end to the lies . . .'

'No!' The words seemed to give her back her strength and Rachel pushed herself free from his arms. 'I will not break my word. I respect William too much to hurt him by breaking our engagement.'

'You respect William?' He wheeled away, kicking against a barrel standing against the wall. 'But you *do not* love him! How can you when you are in love with me? And as for respect . . . what is the respect that would allow you to lie to a man, to marry him when you feel for him only as a friend? What about the hurt there will be for him in that, should he find out?'

'But he will not.' Rachel leaned against the mash tun, eyes closing against the feelings that rocked her. 'He will never find out from me . . .'

'Won't he!' Jared whipped round to face her, his voice raw with anger. 'Won't he, Rachel? He won't feel your body tense when he takes you in his arms? Won't notice there is no fire in your lips when he covers them with his own? Won't wonder why you whisper no words of love to him? You think he will not realise these are all missing from his marriage? For God's sake, Rachel! The man would have to be a complete fool not to know something was amiss. You might fool yourself, you might with luck fool your husband, but not for long . . . no, Rachel, not for long!'

Resisting the urge to return to his arms, to admit to the truth of all he had said, she opened her eyes. When she turned to face him only the sparkle of tears gave any indication of the torment inside her.

'I *will* make him happy, despite all that you say. I will be a true wife to William, and a loving one.'

He laughed at that, a low harsh sound that rasped against her ears.

'A loving wife! Oh, yes, there can be no doubt of that! You will be a loving wife to William Thomas, but not a wife who is *in* love with him. There is a vast difference, Rachel, a gulf you will never cross.'

'Is that why you have come here?' Bitterness her only defence against him, she used it. 'To tell me what a fool I am?'

'No, Rachel.' His eyes cooled and the harshness evaporated from his voice, leaving a gentle softness that scalded her senses even more than the heat of his anger. 'I came to tell you I love you, to try to show you what you are doing to us both, but I see that I have failed. So now I will do the second thing I came to do: I will speak to William.'

Chapter Twenty-five

'Why do you wish to speak to him?' Rachel felt the tension return, holding her body stiff, throwing her into confusion. Was that why he had returned here only days before her wedding? Had he regretted giving his word to say nothing to William of the feelings he held for her, or of hers for him? Was he about to break that word?

'Is William at home?'

Drawing breath, Rachel nodded. 'He . . . he is in the top field, cutting the last of the barley.'

'Would you ask him to spare me a few minutes? Or perhaps you would prefer me to go to him?'

'To tell him what?'

Every trace of passion now skilfully concealed, Jared stared coolly. 'Tell him? Is there anything I should tell him, have you changed your mind?'

'No.' She shook her head.

'Then neither will I. Like you, Rachel, I will keep my promise. What I have to discuss with William has no bearing on our feelings for each other, or on anything that has passed between us. Believe that if you can believe nothing else I have said.'

'I do believe you, thank you.'

Lifting a round wooden cover, she placed it over the tun. Then removing the sack which had protected her worn dress from splashes, and putting it to one side, she led the way to the cottage she shared with Ellen.

'Can I get you something to drink before I fetch William?'

Facing him across the kitchen she had made so pretty with curtains and covers, Rachel fought with the longing that filled her. This was the man who filled her days and nights, the man for whom she yearned but could not marry.

'No, thank you.' Jared moved restlessly to gaze out of the small window. 'If you will tell William?'

His voice was so tight . . . Rachel went to the field where she knew William was reaping the last of the harvest, her own hands tightly clenched. Jared would not break his word to her, that she knew without doubt, but what else did he have to speak to William about? They did not do business together, or none at least that she knew of.

Topping the crest of ground that swelled gently from the rear of the cottages then flattened into a wide band bordering the heath, Rachel shielded her eyes with one hand, her glance sweeping the short stubble of the scythed fields. William and Ellen stood in the far corner of one, their backs towards her, and as she opened her mouth to call to him, William bent to pick up the basket that had held his midday meal. Rachel watched as he held it out to Ellen, seeing his hand rest a few seconds on her arm as she took it.

Thank God those two were friends. Rachel raised a hand as Ellen turned towards her. At least she would still be here after the wedding.

'What does he want with William?' Ellen said as they reached the cottages and watched the two men disappear into William's house.

'He did not say.' Rachel fidgeted nervously with the crockery set on the plain wooden dresser.

'You don't think . . .'

'No,' she answered. 'He will not say anything to William, he assured me of that.'

'Oh, well!' Ellen heaved a deep breath. 'I've no doubt we shall know what it's about in good time. Until then it will do no good to mope, and tomorrow's bread won't make itself.'

Yes, no doubt she would be told in William's own good time. Rachel fetched the white enamelled flour jar from a shelf in the scullery.

But why could Jared not have told her?

'What be fair be fair, and what I don't see as being fair that I won't hold to.'

Rachel went over the conversation in her mind. They had sat, the three of them, in her small kitchen. It was more convenient for William to take his meals with her and Ellen rather than one or the other of them carrying food to his cottage, and it had become a habit of his to stay talking with them before going home to bed.

'But it is fair,' Rachel had contradicted. William had remained adamant.

''T ain't fair for anybody to work for no wage, and that be what both of you have been doing since Ellen come to live here.'

He had spoken without a trace of his impediment. Rachel smiled to herself, glad for William's sake that the stutter seemed to be gone. Her fingers closing about the coin in her pocket, she joined the towpath where it ran before the cottages. It would be pleasant to follow the green ribbon of the canal to Foxley village.

'I had not given a deal of thought to household accounts,' William had said after asking if he could smoke a pipe of shag in her house. 'Mother always had to the seeing of such as that. But when I went over what you had written in the ledger, the amount you got from cheese and butter and the eggs from the ducks, then what you paid out for meat and the like, well, I could tell right away you had taken nothing for your labour, neither you nor Ellen.'

'I had my food and lodging, William,' Ellen told him. 'I did not want anything more.'

'And I d . . . didn't want s . . . slave labour!' William's tone had been sharp, anger tripping his tongue, then Rachel had seen softness leap to his eyes as Ellen's lip had trembled. 'I've no wish to keep anything from you, Ellen.' The words that followed his outburst were as gentle as the look he gave her friend. 'You do far more here than food or lodging pays for, and it be only seemly you should take what be due for it.'

Ahead of her sunlight rippled like sequins of gold on the velvet water and the stillness of the heath was broken only by the call of a bird as it swept low over the coarse bracken.

'Two shillings a week over and above bed and board.' William had turned then to Rachel. 'That were what were agreed between Mother and yourself, so her told me.' Then at Rachel's nod he continued, 'I make that to be twelve shillings owing to each of you.'

'William, I don't want it,' Rachel had protested again. 'It will belong to both of us in three days . . .'

'You'll take it!' He had pushed the six florins across the table, his mouth firm. ''Twere earned by you as a single woman. It be yours to keep, to do with as you will.'

Rachel raised a hand in greeting as a narrow boat laden with coal slid quietly past, the hooves of the great shire thudding on the beaten earth of the towpath, ripples of wake glittering on the dark water as those florins had glittered in the light of the lamp.

She had taken them in her hand. Six round silver coins, the head of Queen Victoria emblazoned on each. She had held them for a moment while memory rushed in on her, then placing one aside she put the remainder in front of William.

'Those are to replace the money Beulah lent me to buy clothes,' she said quietly. 'As her son that money now belongs to you.'

'There be no need . . .'

'There is every need.' Rachel walked on, remembering the frown that had accompanied William's attempt to refuse the coins. 'I vowed I would repay your mother with the first money I earned, now I am doing just that.'

'I'll not accept it!'

William's mouth had set stubbornly but Rachel refused to be put off. 'What be fair be fair,' she quoted as his frown had deepened, drawing his brows together in a line. 'Those were your own words, William, and they are mine too. And what I don't see as being fair, that *I* won't hold to. I do not see it as fair for you to prevent me from repaying a debt that was kindly lent, to prevent me from keeping my word. I would rather begin my married life knowing I had kept my promise to Beulah.'

She had quoted his own words to him and William had conceded, though she could see it went against the grain for him to take back the money. But he had taken them and that had meant one of her debts was paid, one vow had been redeemed. Now she was on her way to fulfil the second.

A rustling in the rough grass distracted her and she smiled at the flash of white tail that was all she saw of a rabbit diving for its burrow.

She had thought William would say nothing of the reason for Jared Lytton's visit of the previous day, but when she had said she was coming to the Fox Inn to see the landlord there, William had asked her to leave word for Jared. The beer he had asked be brewed specially for the party he gave annually for his workers and their families would be seen to.

Rachel fingered the coin in her pocket. Would two shillings be enough to repay her night's lodging at the Fox? What would she do if it were not? She would not ask William for any more. Withdrawing her hand, leaving the coin in her pocket, she pulled her shawl up on to her shoulders. Don't build bridges over dry land, her father had always told her, and don't build them over water till it be too deep to wade across. She would wait and hold her worry until she knew whether or not her money was sufficient to repay her debt.

The sound of men's laughter drifted from the open door of the low bow-fronted building; a wooden sign on which a painted fox held a chicken in its mouth swung on a rusty chain, while beneath it a black and white dog stared sleepily at her from one eye before closing it again.

Rachel hesitated. She had not thought there would be customers in the inn, but then she ought to have remembered that many colliers and quarrymen would call in for a drink before going home at the change of their shift. There were many in Horseley who had practised this, to the dismay of any wife who dared say the meal had gone cold in the waiting.

Shouts of laughter rang out again and Rachel cringed at the thought of going inside, but she had come this far . . .

Pulling her shawl protectively round her, she drew a long breath then stepped through the open doorway.

Light slanting in through the doorway joined that entering timidly through the net curtain but their combined strength was not enough fully to disperse the tobacco-laden shadows of the bar room.

Rachel held the shawl about her. The laughter had ceased the moment she stepped inside the inn and several of the men stared in open criticism.

'Get you wum, woman!'

An older man, with heavy whiskers, slammed his tankard on the long wooden counter of the bar, running a coal-grimed hand across his mouth. Rachel felt a tremor run along her spine as she caught the man's glare. She would go home, but first she would do what she had set out to do.

'Hold up, Jack, mebbe the wench would like a drink . . .'

A stockily built man, moleskin trousers held up by a broad leather belt, muffler tucked inside a shirt that might once have been white, a flat cap drawn down over hair whose colour was lost beneath a layer of coal dust, pushed his way out from a group of colliers standing together about the fireplace.

'You'll take a drink wi' Ben Davis, won't you, me wench?'

Already halfway towards being drunk, the man swayed across to where Rachel was standing. As he bent towards her she drew back from the stench of his beer-laden breath.

''Er don't seem too ready to me, Ben. Seems you'm going to 'ave to make do wi' your old woman!'

The remark coming from the group he had just left caused a fresh burst of laughter but the stocky man was not to be denied his sport.

'You'll take half of best, ain't that right? Then after we can 'ave ourselves an hour on the 'eath.'

His free hand clutched Rachel's arm, jerking her against him. The sour smell of his body and clothing filling her mouth and nostrils, she tried to drag herself free. She was still struggling and the men still laughing when the landlord slapped his palm noisily on the counter.

'Now then, Ben Davis, that'll be enough of that caper!'

The landlord's tone was heavy with unspoken threat. He was a heavy-set man whose twisted nose and bulging muscles told of days spent bare-knuckle fighting. 'I don't keep no bawdy house, as you be knowing well enough. You want that sort of entertainment then you go somewheres else. But you ain't bringing it into the Fox!'

Fastening one massive hand over that of the collier, he lifted it away from Rachel's arm. Then, as the man grumblingly rejoined his fellows, he turned to her.

'You best be off from here, me wench. Ben Davis ain't one to take no for an answer when I don't be behind him. Besides, like you heard me say, I don't have no doxies selling their wares in my house.'

'I am *not* a doxy!' Rachel's head came up. Sliding the shawl from her hair, she raised a face turned scarlet with embarrassment.

'Hold up!' The landlord's eyes half closed and he peered at her. 'I seen you afore. It ain't often we see hair the colour of yourn. You be the same wench as Mr Lytton fetched in some months back. I ain't like to forget as how pretty I thought you then nor how mad Lytton was when he found you stopped here no more'n one night. But I mean what I say nonetheless: this be no place for a young wench like yourself.'

'I only came to ask the price of a night's lodging and breakfast.' Rachel lifted the shawl back to her head, aware of the stares of the inn's customers.

'You means you want to come here, to stay? But the missis reckons you be going to wed with the widow's son, wi' Billy Duckegg . . .' The man's eyes widened to normal but his voice sharpened with an unmistakable inquisitiveness. ''As he changed his mind then, 'as he showed you the door?'

Rachel felt her blood quicken with anger, and when she answered her voice was cold. 'I do not wish to hire a room here, I merely wish to enquire as to the cost of doing so.'

'Well now, a best room such as you had before, together with breakfast, would cost a shilling and sixpence.'

She would have enough! Relief seeping through her, Rachel dipped a hand into the pocket of her brown dress, closing her fingers over the coin. She would be able to repay her debt to Jared Lytton.

'Mr Lytton does sometimes call here?'

'Sometimes.' The landlord's tone was still inquisitive as he replied.

Bringing the coin from her pocket, Rachel laid it on the counter. 'Then might I ask you to return this to him?'

The landlord's glance dropped to the florin gleaming in the dull, smoke-filled light.

'I said I would repay the money my stay here cost him. Perhaps you will be good enough to give it to him when next he calls?' She waited and when the man made no answer, went on: 'There is also a message from Mr William Thomas. He would be obliged if you would pass that also to Mr Lytton – but then, you might prefer him to stammer that out for himself. Perhaps *that* is an entertainment you *do* allow in the Fox.'

'Her had you that time, Three Rounds!'

The call from the fireplace elicited a fresh outburst of laughter. The landlord's eyes showed a rueful appreciation of the courage of her reply.

'Won't take me three rounds to knock you on your back, Davis!' he called. 'So watch your mouth or you'll be needing no more visits to the tooth puller!' Ignoring cries from the men to be as good as his word, the landlord glanced again at the coin, its silver sharp against the mahogany counter. 'You say the widow's son has a message to be passed to Mr Lytton? Then why not give it to him yourself, and this along with it?' Scooping up the coin, he passed it back to Rachel. 'He be here now, in the back parlour.'

Rachel was taken aback. She had not envisaged the possibility of Jared Lytton's being at the Fox Inn. Surely at this hour of the day he should be at one or other of his business premises?

'Mr Lytton had some dealings to go over with me concerning the do he gives every year for his workers here in the Foxyards. He were just about to leave when I heard the ruckus in the bar and come to see the cause of it.'

The landlord was already halfway along the narrow corridor she remembered led to the parlour but Rachel did not move. She did not want to see Jared, wanted only to leave the florin and the message with the landlord and then return to the cottage.

'In here, miss.'

The landlord was facing her, the door to the bar parlour open in his hand.

Blood drumming hard in her veins, Rachel stared at the open doorway then felt her heart lurch as the figure of Jared Lytton came to stand in it.

It seemed he stood there for an eternity, his eyes on her face, then he stepped aside, speaking quietly to the landlord who came towards her.

'Mr Lytton said for you to go in, miss.'

She could turn and leave now. She could tell William the

men drinking in the inn had frightened her – that at least would not be a lie; ask him to return the money on her behalf. William would believe her, believe it was fear of the men that had turned her away when all the time it was fear of meeting Jared. *'Never fear to speak when you know that what you say be all of the truth.'* How often her father had said those words to her. But to tell William the reason she had not delivered his message was because of the colliers would not be all of the truth.

Her tread soft on the quarry tiles that paved the passage-way, Rachel walked slowly into the small room. Behind her the door closed with a soft click.

Ellen took the pails that held the morning's milking and emptied them into the long shallow stone sink. She had watched Rachel out of sight along the towpath that led in the direction of the inn. She was going to return the money that Jared Lytton had paid for her one night of lodging but repaying the money would not rid Rachel of the feeling she carried inside her; it would not erase the love she carried in her heart.

Reaching a jar from an overhead shelf, she poured rennet into the milk and swirled it about with a small wooden paddle before covering the sink with a gauze covered frame.

It was a love Rachel had owned to but one she would not accept. Ellen picked up the empty pails, carrying them, along with the utensils she had used in the dairy, to the scullery for scrubbing. Fetching the kettle that steamed gently on its bracket above the fire, she poured a little of the water into each bucket, scrubbing them all with a brisk thorough motion.

Why did Rachel insist upon going through with her marriage to William? Ellen set the freshly scrubbed milk pails aside, pouring the remainder of the boiling water into a white enamelled bowl and topping it up with cold water from a tall matching jug. Could she not see such a marriage would hold no true happiness for either William or herself? Did she honestly think she could blind herself to the truth of where her real love lay?

And William . . .

Plunging the wooden paddle and ladles into the steaming bowl, Ellen continued to scrub. He was different somehow, in a way she could not explain. He was the same gentle caring man she had known him to be since coming to live in this house yet his manner was not as it was. He no longer laughed so readily, that twisted lop-sided smile that gave him the appeal of a mischievous boy did not come so easily to his lips, and his deep blue eyes no longer held the light they once had. There was a sadness in William, almost an expectancy, as if something he waited for had not yet come.

The scrubbed pails and utensils returned to the dairy, Ellen set about preparing the lunch she would carry to William in the barley field. He had returned from Worcester the day after Jared had brought Rachel home following her abduction, and that night had insisted on sitting with her until the morning. Ellen laid a slice of fresh-baked bread beside the wedge of cheese she had placed in a wicker basket. It had been after that night that a change had taken place in him, and though he never mentioned it, Ellen feared he might have heard something Rachel had murmured in her fretful sleep.

Going back into the scullery, Ellen filled a bottle from the stone cider jar then carried it to the kitchen, setting it beside the cheese and bread in the basket. But if William had heard anything, if he even guessed that Rachel loved another man, would he in his turn remain silent? Or would he too insist on going through with a marriage he must realise could bring no real happiness?

Setting a cloth over the basket, Ellen stared through the window, seeing nothing of the little garden or of the water of the canal that glistened beyond. She had tried to tell Rachel of the unhappiness that could ensue from placing too great an importance on pride; to awaken her to the misery that could follow marriage to a man who held her love but not her heart. But had her attempts been made only on Rachel's behalf? Was it to save her friend's heart from breaking that she had ached, or was it perhaps to save her own?

Picking up the basket, Ellen left the cottage, striking out for the partly harvested field that lay farthest from the two cottages. It was true, her own heart would break the moment Rachel became William's wife. She had loved him almost from the first moment, loved him with a deep quiet love that would outlive eternity, a love that she could never speak of, a love that only she would ever know existed.

Tears slipping slowly down her face, she watched the tall figure bend to the sweep of the scythe. She loved William with a strength that far outweighed the love she had felt for her husband; it was a strength she would have to hold to in the empty years that stretched before her.

'I will not ask what you are doing in this place.' Jared spoke quietly, his eyes on Rachel's face as she stood just inside the door of the bar parlour. 'The landlord has already told me you bring a message from William, but perhaps you will tell me why you choose to deliver it to this inn rather than to Foxley?'

He had made no move to touch her, but his bronze eyes burned into hers and Rachel could see the line of tension about his mouth. *'All of the truth . . .'* The words burned in her brain. There could be no less than that, there must be no more lies between them for the truth was all she would ever be able to give him.

Drawing a deep breath, her own gaze meeting his, she answered. 'I did not call at Foxley House because I thought there would be a possibility of your being at home.'

'By that I take it you have no wish to see me?'

'Jared, please . . .' Suddenly the determination drained from her and she cried out, her hands covering her face.

'Rachel!' With one word he was clear across the room and

she was in his arms, his lips pressing against her tear-wet lids. 'Rachel, my love! Oh, my love!'

He held her for long moments, his lips touching her eyes and temple, one hand stroking her hair, his voice low and tender. For long moments Rachel gave way to the sheer ecstasy of feeling him close against her; of the strength of his arms, the warm male scent that acted like a match to the explosive desire she felt within.

'Rachel . . . oh, my darling, it's not too late.'

Without knowing it, she turned her head, lifting her face to his lips, parting her own to take his kiss.

'We can still tell William . . .'

He kissed her mouth, drawing out her very soul.

'. . . we will go to him together, now. He will under-stand.'

Beneath the intoxication of his mouth, she felt her head swim.

'He will not hold you to a promise given before you realised your love for me.'

'*A promise given* . . .' The words circled her mind, surviving the maelstrom that surged inside her. '*A promise given* . . .' Somewhere in the depth of the passion that held her, Rachel felt the pinprick of guilt. It jolted her, driving a cold wedge into the soft pleasure that tried to suck her back, that tried to tell her that Jared was right, that they should tell William, that he would not be hurt by her breaking her word, but her word had been . . . was . . . a promise given.

'No!' The reality of Jared's words flooding over her, she twisted away. 'I can't . . . I won't. I will not break my promise, I will not hurt William!'

'I see.' The mouth that seconds ago had been soft with love, hardened with the passion of anger. 'You would rather live a lie than tell the truth!'

'Jared, please, try to understand.' Rachel held out a hand but he stepped away, his face closed and cold.

'I understand very well.' He spoke with quiet control

though his eyes seethed. 'This weekend will see you married to William Thomas. He is the man you have chosen. I apologise for having spoken when I gave my solemn oath I would never again mention my feelings for you. It will not happen again.'

Picking up the shawl that had fallen to the floor when she had lifted her arms to return his embrace, Rachel set it about her shoulders, drawing both ends across her breasts. There could be no joy in prolonging this meeting. The sooner she left, the easier it would be for both of them.

'William asked me to tell you the beer you ordered to be brewed will be ready on the day you requested. And . . . and *I* wish to return this.' Drawing the coin from her pocket, she laid it beside his tankard on the table.

Jared glanced at the florin. 'What is that for?'

'The one night I stayed here. A night's lodging you paid for, and I promised to repay it. I asked the landlord if that was enough and he assured me it was.'

Jared's eyes turned back to her and now the coldness that had held them was gone, replaced by a glimmer of amusement. 'You are quite a determined little thing, are you not, Miss Rachel Cade?'

'I have been known to be.' She risked a smile.

'Stubborn too.' Jared's mouth curved, answering her own. 'I shall take your florin, and I shall wear it on my watch chain. It will remind me that some things are worth fighting for . . . even if I do not succeed in getting them.'

Rachel sighed with relief. She had not expected him to take the money without some sort of protest. Turning to leave, she had already seized the handle of the door when he spoke again.

'Rachel . . . I shall always call you that in my heart so allow me to do so during our last time alone . . . do you trust me?'

'Trust you?' She turned a surprised look on him. 'But of course I trust you, why do you ask?'

'Because I want you to come to Foxley with me.'

'Foxley!' Her surprise deepened. 'But for what reason?'

'That I would rather keep to myself until we get there. Will you come?'

She should say no. Every minute spent with him was agony, but they were minutes she would live again and again. 'When?' she asked simply.

'Now.' Jared's reply, equally simple, only added to her surprise. She could not go with him to Foxley without first telling William. And what of Ellen? She would worry if Rachel were late getting home.

Her thoughts were clearly read by Jared. 'I have a carriage outside, it is no more than a fifteen-minute drive, and of course I would see you safely back to your future home.'

Would it be questioning his integrity to ask again his reason for inviting her to his home? Would it be seen as doubting his honour? Then what would William have to say?

Suddenly she knew these questions did not matter. She would go with Jared to Foxley, and if William was half the man she knew him to be, he would understand. She had to show Jared Lytton the trust she had in him, the trust she had in the man she loved with all her heart.

Chapter Twenty-six

Sitting beside him in the trap, Rachel was content to leave the silence that had fallen between them unbroken. To either side of the road the heath stretched away in ragged grandeur, outcrops of grey-white limestone partly clothed in fern and bracken, low-growing gorse bushes, their bright yellow flowers long faded, lifted sturdily above grasses and wild flowers swaying softly in the late-summer breeze.

Jared had helped her into the open carriage that an ostler had brought around to the front of the inn, assuring himself of her comfort before climbing into the driving seat, but although he had glanced at her, he had said nothing as to the purpose of their journey. She had gone over it again and again, searching for a reason, any reason, but had found none.

Turning the carriage left off the road, he followed a narrow track bordered with sycamore and horse chestnut, branches spread widely into an arcade of green through which the sun glittered in broad spangles. Rachel breathed deeply, relishing air heavy with the scent of greenery, and as the carriage drew towards a small cottage set a little way from the track, she murmured appreciatively at its pretty garden. But when the carriage stopped beside the gate, she turned an enquiring look to Jared.

'This is surely not Foxley House?'

'No.' He swung easily from the driving seat, handing the

reins to a middle-aged man who hurried from the rear of the small thatched house.

'But you asked if I would go with you to Foxley!'

'So I did.' Bronze eyes smiled up at her as he held a hand towards her. 'But I do not remember mentioning Foxley House. This . . .' he waved an arm in a wide arc '. . . and all of the land we have driven through since leaving the road, is Foxley, and this is the house I wished you to visit.'

Helping her down from the carriage, Jared turned first to the man who had hurried to greet them. 'Has there been any change?'

'None, Mr Lytton, sir. Just them same words over and over, though he do seem better in hisself.'

'Thanks to the care you and your wife give him.'

Smiling, and obviously pleased with the praise, the man touched a finger to his brow, but the look he swept over Rachel's patched and faded dress held none of the deference he paid Jared.

Allowing her to go before him along the flower-bordered path, Jared touched her arm as they reached the wooden door studded with large round-headed nails and iron hinges that stretched half across its width.

'Rachel.' The smile had left his eyes and now they held a hint of uncertainty. 'I should tell you before you go inside, the man I want you to meet underwent a serious accident in the limestone workings some weeks back. He suffered a blow to the head that caused him to lose all memory of his life before that. As a consequence you may find his vagueness a little disconcerting.'

'How terrible for the poor man.' For a moment the horror of her own abduction and the bouts of black emptiness that came and went in the hours that followed returned to mind with startling vividness, leaving her shaking.

'You do not have to go in. It was perhaps wrong of me to bring you here, there is nothing you can do.'

The grip on her arm tightened and Rachel felt the gentle

pull that began to take her into his arms, then it was gone and his hand fell away.

'A visit from someone new might cheer him if it does nothing else.' Rachel had a sudden vision of a lonely old man cut off from the world because of an accident. 'I would like to meet him.'

The door opened then and a smiling chubby-faced woman, her sparkling white apron covering an ample bosom and full black skirts, greeted Jared politely. Like her husband, she swept a barely concealed look of disparagement over the girl with a ragged shawl draped over a shabby dress.

'He be in the kitchen, Mr Lytton. He seems to prefer being there to sitting in the parlour. 'Pears my bustling and chattering keeps 'im company like.' She stepped back, holding the door wider on its hinges as Jared ushered Rachel inside. 'I be sorry but we didn't know as you would be calling today, it not being your regular time. But if you and the . . . the young lady will take a seat in the parlour, I will bring him to you.'

'Thank you, Mrs Jenks.'

Jared returned the woman's smile but Rachel did not.

This woman was like so many others she had met in Bloomfield and Tipton Green: a smile for those people whose dress denoted money; a frown and a rough word for any who like Rachel wore no fine clothes and whose hands told of working hard for a living.

'I too would prefer the kitchen, if I may,' she bristled. 'I am afraid my dress is unsuited to Mrs Jenks's parlour!'

'The kitchen it is then, Mrs Jenks,' Jared said as the older woman coloured. But when he glanced at Rachel as they followed, the smile had returned to his eyes.

'You 'ave visitors.'

Inside the kitchen a bright fire glowed at the heart of a range blackleaded to burnished silver. Against one wall a dresser was decked with china painted with dark pink peonies. The table that claimed the heart of the room was covered with a cloth of mustard-coloured cotton bordered around with blue, while beneath the window a small table held a brass lamp topped with a blue glass shade.

All of this Rachel took in with one sweeping glance but it was on the figure huddled in a tall-backed wooden chair drawn up to the fire that her glance rested.

The hair was iron-grey, the shoulders slightly stooped and the clothes newer. Newer than what? Rachel's throat tightened and the colour drained from her face. The man's back was turned to her but from somewhere deeper than her soul a memory rose: a memory of golden days on the heath, days when a tall man had taught her songs that named the bridges of Tipton, taught her the names of birds and plants; a man who had laughed with her, played with her and carried her home set high upon his shoulders. A man she had last seen outside her home in the village of Horseley.

'Father!' she whispered, her hands against her mouth as if they would hold back the word. 'Father!'

Beside the fire the man's back stiffened and he hesitated, eyes still probing the glowing coals as though searching for something long lost.

Behind Rachel, Mrs Jenks glanced curiously towards Jared but a slight movement of his hand stayed her question. His eyes never left Rachel.

'Father . . .' she whispered into her hands, taking an involuntary step forward. And then the man turned.

On the mantelshelf above the fireplace a clock ticked. For long seconds they were held by invisible bonds, seconds in which haunted eyes stared at Rachel and a drawn mouth wrestled with unspoken words.

At her back she felt the touch of Jared's hand and his softly spoken, 'Wait!'

Slowly, pain still marking his movements, the man in the chair rose to his feet, and as her stifled sob dropped into the gulf of silence his arms lifted and he cried one word: 'Rachel!'

*　　*　　*

'But why did Jared not tell you he thought the man who saved his life was your father?'

Rachel sipped gratefully at the tea Ellen had made for them all. 'He had no idea the man *was* my father. He knew nothing at all about him: not his name or where he lived or whether he had any family. All he did know was that the man must have had some dealings with Magistrate Bedworth, from words he repeated over and over again.'

'And them dealings none too pleasant, judging by them same words,' said William, holding up his long-stemmed clay pipe for Rachel's nod before setting a taper to the fire.

'Jared . . .' Rachel blushed as the name slipped from her lips '. . . Mr Lytton knew I had been tried before the same magistrate. But he did not recognise him as the same man he saw in the courtroom on that same day.'

'That still don't explain why he took you along to that house without telling you of the man that were living there!' William held the lighted taper to the small white bowl until the shreds of tobacco glowed like miniature coals.

'I asked him that, William, as he drove me back here. It seemed I told him once that I longed to be with my father again, but during a visit to Horseley he learned that my father had left the village the very same day that Magistrate Bedworth sent Hannah to an insane asylum, and no one knew where he had gone. Jar— Mr Lytton did not mention the man who saved his life in case I set too much store on his being my father. He did not want to raise my hopes in case they were dashed.'

William drew on the pipe until he was satisfied the tobacco was truly lit then extinguished the taper before returning it to the pottery jar set in the hearth. 'Ar, I can understand his reasons, he wouldn't want you hurt.' Then, more softly, the words seemingly only for himself, he added: 'Jared Lytton would never hurt you, Rachel.'

'Rachel, I am so very glad for you.' Behind Ellen's grey eyes her own memories brought unshed tears. 'It is wonderful that you and your father can be together again, but why did you not bring him home with you?'

'I could not do that without first asking William's permission. I . . . I was not sure . . .'

'Your father be welcome to a home here, Rachel, welcome as you yourself. You say when it is he is to be brought and I will take the cart along to Foxley and fetch him.'

'Thank you, William, you are very kind.' Leaning forward in her chair, Rachel held out a hand and he took it, pressing it gently with his own. But his eyes as he looked at her held a kind of sadness in their depths.

'Mr Lytton suggested that with the wedding so close, it might be better all round if my father remained where he is for the present.' Rachel withdrew her hand. 'He pointed out that Father is still very weak and all the bustle of a wedding might prove a little too much. He thought it best to leave him in the care of Mrs Jenks and her husband until you and I are settled, and said I was welcome to visit as often as I wished.'

'Jared is a good friend, Rachel,' Ellen said. 'You can trust him to do what is best for you and your father.'

Yes, Jared Lytton was a good friend. Rachel reached again for her tea, hiding her expression by glancing down. But he could never be more to her than that.

'Did you remember my message about the ale?'

It was as if William sensed the grief inside her and tried to change the subject.

'Yes, I mentioned it to the landlord of the Fox Inn and then to Mr Lytton himself, but I did not know you made a special brew for his workers' annual celebration? Beulah never made any mention of it.'

William tapped his pipe gently against the bars of the firegrate. 'No more her would till it were time, but we have brewed for Foxley for years – since the grandfather first built the place, so my mother told me. Seems my granny did the brewing then, though I remember nothing of that, not having been born. And if it's going to get done at all this year, I'll have to get along to the malt house tomorrow and talk to Ernest. They like a pale roast at Foxley.'

'I . . . I had thought to visit Father tomorrow. I did not know you would be going into Tipton Green.'

'It will make no odds.' William stood up, slipping the clay pipe into his pocket. 'The last of the barley be in so I have no need to be in the fields again yet awhile. As for the milking, I'll see to that afore I go.'

'But that means Ellen will be here alone.'

'I know what you are thinking, Rachel,' said Ellen, gathering the used cups, 'but I shall be perfectly safe. That dreadful business with your father's wife is over. The poor woman was mad but her hatred was only for you. She would have hurt no one else here. Anyway, she's no longer able to hurt anyone so you go to Foxley. There is nothing here I can't manage alone.'

'If it will ease you, why not wait until I get back? That way I could drive the pair of you out there on the cart.'

Rachel smiled her thanks as she followed William to the gate of the cottage. He was so very good to her but deep inside she felt a pang of disappointment at his offer. She had looked forward to the walk to Foxley . . . then even as the thought arose she knew it was a lie. It was not the promise of a long walk to the house that had her stomach churning, it was the hope of seeing Jared Lytton again.

They had reached the gate and William had turned to say goodnight. Even under the shadows of evening Rachel knew he saw the colour that thinking of Jared had brought to her cheeks.

'Not much longer, Rachel.' In the half light he stared down at her and his voice held a curious note, almost cautioning her. 'Day after tomorrow we will be man and wife.'

Man and wife! Her heart plummeted like a stone. In two

days' time Jared would be lost to her forever; but he was lost to her now, lost by a promise given.

Facing her in the fading light, William watched the shadows flit across her face and felt a matching sadness in himself. Did this girl who had come into his life from nowhere truly love him? Was it pain he watched flickering across that lovely face or merely the shadows of evening, a trick of the light? It would be so easy to find out, he had only to ask, to put his own fears into words, but he knew he would not; he would never want her to think he was breaking his word to her. She would never know.

'Rachel.' The warning note was gone, replaced by a gentle protective quality that lent a huskiness to his voice as he drew her against him. 'Rachel, I'll take care of you. You will want for nothing my two hands can give you. I will be a good husband to you, and with God's help we will be happy. You mean a great deal to me, Rachel . . . you know that.'

Yes, she knew that. In his arms, she felt that all the sorrow of the ages was walled up inside her; sorrow for Jared, sorrow for herself. But William would know no sorrow because of her. She meant a great deal to him, he had told her, and nothing would be taken from him. She would match his promises. She would be a good wife to him, he would want for nothing that she could give him.

Want for nothing she could give him . . .

Standing there in the circle of his arms Rachel felt the warm touch of tears prick her eyelids.

William would want for nothing . . . except her heart!

Her father had looked so thin and pale, the scar that marked one side of his face still an angry red. But he had smiled on seeing her. Rachel took comfort from the thought. Soon now she would be married, and William she knew would give her father a place in their home.

Their home, hers and Williams! 'I will be a good husband to you.' William's softly spoken words returned to her mind.

Yes, William would be all she could want in a husband, but could she be all he would want in a wife?

'I'll try.' She whispered, tears not far from her eyes. 'I will try, William.'

Beyond the towpath that edged the still waters of the canal the sound of laughter erupted from the Fox Inn. Rachel glanced at the low roofed building suddenly seeing again the half amused smile in Jared Lytton's eyes as she had placed that coin beside his hand on the table. With the paying of it she had kept the promise she had made all those weeks ago, and with that had severed the need to meet with him ever again.

Never to meet him again! The thought as painful as a knife in her heart she drew her shawl more tightly about her as if by doing so she could close herself off from the hurt. But it was a hurt she would always feel.

'It is not too late . . .'

Jared's words shouted in her brain. But for Rachel Cade it *was* too late. She had given her word to William, she would become his wife; nothing would change that.

Samuel Potter blinked as the afternoon sun slanted across his ale blurred eyes. The drink was good and the company much to his taste at the Fox but the money had fast slipped from his pocket and once it were gone so would his chance of a bed, for the landlord had no mind for charity, what you couldn't pay for you didn't get.

'Pah!' He spat onto the dusty ground. They was all the same, take a man's last penny then kick his arse! That were what Lytton had done. He had taken everything, his home, business, the lot; and for what? For a bloody whore, that was for what, a pit bank wench with hair the colour of that one!

Stepping from the doorway of the inn he blinked again, steadying the glance that followed a woman in dark skirts, a woman whose hair shone pale gold in the sunlight.

It were a wench with hair that colour had caused Lytton to do what he had.

Anger that had been soothed with ale flared afresh. It were on account of him wanting the wench for himself that could be the only reason . . . Lytton had ruined him for the sake of a bloody doxy!

Drawing a deep breath, the clean air clearing the fog of ale from his brain Samuel set off across the heath.

She would keep to the towpath. He picked his way over the rough ground, his steps sure as the last of the bar room haze cleared from his head. But by cutting across the heath he could get in front of her and with any luck at all she would not spot him.

It might not be her.

Samuel kept to the cover of the rock outcrops that dotted the heath.

But then again chances were it would be; there were precious few women with hair like silken wheat, and certainly none in Tipton Green except . . .

He smiled, ale tainted spittle oozing from a corner of his mouth.

. . . except the one Jared Lytton had a fancy for.

'Well fair be fair Lytton.' The smile swallowed in a throaty laugh he stood hidden by a large rise of limestone abutting the towpath. 'You took from me, now it be my turn. How badly will you want the pit bank wench once Sam'l Potter be done with 'er?'

Rachel's steps made little sound on the path, but heightened by the thrill of stalking her, Potter's ears told of her approach from yards away.

He would let her pass. Take her from behind. That way she would offer less resistance.

Somewhere within him a pulse beat a rhythm, increasing in intensity as excitement added to lust creating a kind of obscene joy that brought the breath from him in short ragged bursts.

A few more steps, that's all it would take, just a few more steps and then . . . spittle oozed from his lips, dribbling down over his chin, forgotten as the flesh inside his trousers jerked; then he was on the path, one arm thrown about Rachel, lifting her from her feet while the other hand stifled her scream.

'Keep quiet 'less you want to feel the waters of that cut close over your 'ead!'

Throwing her face down behind the clump of rock, Potter knelt over her, one knee pressing into her back.

'Please . . .' Rachel tried to speak against the coarse grass filling her mouth.

'Oh you'll please alright.' Potter chuckled. 'Sam'l Potter will be well pleased.'

Samuel Potter! The realisation of who it was attacking her only added to Rachel's terror. There would be no reasoning with him, no chance of mercy.

'. . . But Lytton won't.' Removing the belt from around his waist Potter snatched her arms roughly across her back, binding her wrists with the rough leather. 'He won't be at all pleased, not when he finds someone else beat him to the cherry.'

Removing his knee he rolled her onto her back then stood up, the smile on his face leering and lascivious.

'Mr Potter, you are wrong.' Rachel held the scream, forcing it to become words instead. 'Mr Lytton does not want . . .'

'I know what Lytton bloody well wants, and he can have it . . . after Sam'l Potter be through with it . . . !'

Hands still ingrained with the dust of coal sacks unbuttoned trousers that clung unaided to the fullness of his body, letting them fall to his ankles. Beneath them long woollen underwear displayed the same tracery of coal dirt as his hands. Rachel felt her throat fill with sickness. How had Potter found her? What had Jared to do with his raping her?

'. . . But I reckon Lytton won't be so full of desire, not once he learns you opened your legs willing and eager, that you give Sam'l Potter all he wanted for a couple of shilling.'

Almost paralysed with fear Rachel saw the woollen pants being pulled aside, saw the bulging flesh beneath, flesh that would soon be pressed against her own, soon be thrust into her body.

'No . . . o . . . o!' Her scream filling her ears she raised both feet, felt them sink into the flabby mound of his stomach; felt them withdraw and strike again, sobbing as Potter fell backward.

Ellen had kept her word. She had said nothing to William of Rachel's stumbling into the house, her wrists bound with a leather belt. The belt had gone into the fire and Rachel had been put to bed with a 'headache'.

She had been terrified of Potter following her to the house, of finding not only her but Ellen also. But Potter had not come. Then William had told of him being found floating in the canal. 'Got himself the worse for drink and while relieving himself had fallen and drowned.'

That had seemed to be the finding of the Court, and Ellen had urged she add no more to it. What was done was done, but it was over. Potter had got nothing he did not deserve . . . and William and Jared need never know.

William had left for Foxley. Rachel glanced to where the maroon skirt and pretty pink blouse she had bought from that pawnshop in Bloomfield lay draped across her bed, and suddenly her mind was filled with a picture of a lavender gown. It would have looked so lovely as a wedding gown, matching ribbons holding her hair high on her head, fellow ones entwined in a posy of flowers . . .

Stop it! She twisted away, pulling the brush through her hair with a savage motion. Thoughts such as that were futile. She was marrying William and a sensible skirt and blouse was all she needed. What was a pretty dress anyway? It would add nothing real to her life, give her no lasting benefit. No, that lavender dress would have given her neither of those things, but then it was not the dress her hidden longings yearned for, but the man who had bought it.

'Are you not dressed yet?'

In the pretty flower-sprigged dress, her rich sherry-coloured hair caught up with peach ribbons, Ellen came into the room.

'You look beautiful!' Rachel caught the other woman's hands, spreading her arms wide as she admired the lovely picture she made. 'And those silk rose-buds in your hair are so pretty . . . you really are clever.'

'Well, let's see if I am clever enough to get you dressed and ready to leave for that church when William gets back with your father, or are you deliberately exercising a bride's prerogative?'

'Prerogative?' Rachel's brow furrowed into the pretence of a frown.

'To be late.' Ellen smiled, freeing her hands and grabbing the hairbrush Rachel had dropped. She knew it would be useless to ask one more time for Rachel to take the pretty flower-sprigged dress instead of the clothes lain across her bed. They had argued long over that last night but Rachel had refused, as she had refused to accept what Ellen had said about her leaving this cottage. Rachel had solidly declared there would be room here for all of them, but should their marriage be blessed with children then William's cottage would not hold them and Rachel's father also. No, she would have to go eventually. It would be far better to do it as soon as the wedding was over. That way would mean less pain at seeing the man she loved be husband to the friend she loved.

Pushing Rachel to the stool that stood before the small dressing table, Ellen worked quickly, her nimble fingers piling the silver-blonde hair high upon Rachel's crown then pinning tiny pink silk rose-buds among the folds before teasing a few curling strands to curl about her ears and touch the nape of her neck.

'There!' She smiled approvingly into the mirror. 'William will think he is marrying an angel from heaven.'

Rachel smiled back. 'Just so long as the angels know how to brew beer and make cheese and butter.'

'That's the wagon.' Ellen listened. 'The groom is back and you not into your clothes. Get a move on or he will think you don't want . . .' She stopped, a stricken look replacing the smile of moments ago. 'Oh, Rachel, I'm sorry! I didn't mean . . .'

'I know you didn't, Ellen.' Rachel's own expression was wan. 'Would you go and see if my father wants anything? I . . . I'll be down in a moment.'

He will think you don't want to marry him! That was what Ellen had been about to say. Rachel reached for the blouse, slipping her arms into it. Ellen had been about to say what she herself should have said to William long since, but she had not wanted to hurt him.

'Is that the truth, Rachel?' she whispered softly to the reflection staring back at her from the mirror. 'Or is it that you lack the courage?'

'Dearly beloved, we are gathered here in the sight of God . . .'

From the back of St Matthew's church Jared Lytton stared at the tiny group standing below the steps of the altar. He had vowed he would not come here today, vowed never again willingly to set eyes on Rachel Cade, yet when the widow's son had collected her father so he could give her away, he had followed.

Give her away! The thought seared his brain, leaving a trail of smouldering bitterness in its wake. The woman he loved was being given in marriage to another man.

She had not seen him as she had arrived on that farm cart. But from the shelter of a huge elm he had watched her walk up the path to the church, dressed simply in a maroon skirt and pink blouse, the tiny posy she carried the only hint that she walked into a new life, and out of his. Now from the backmost pew, hidden among the shadows that cloaked the rear of the church, he watched and listened – listened to words that would forever keep her from him.

Why had he not spoken to William Thomas? Why had he not told him where Rachel's heart lay, why was he letting this happen; letting all that mattered in his life be taken away from him?

'If any man should know of any just cause or impediment . . .'

Jared glanced across to the little group standing before the priest, his white vestments stippled with colour from the sunlight that streamed through the stained glass of the east window, then studied the few villagers who had come merely from curiosity, to see the widow's weak-minded son take himself a wife.

'. . . to this woman being joined to this man . . .' the priest raised his eyes, letting them drift over the puny congregation '. . . let him speak now or forever hold his peace . . .'

Let him speak now! Here was his chance, his one and only chance. From the corner of his eye Jared saw Ellen lift a handkerchief to her lips, saw the villagers exchange glances, then the priest's eyes fixed on him as he started to raise his hand.

He could not do it! Outside in the churchyard Jared leaned his head against the bole of the elm that had shielded him a few minutes before. He had raised his hand as the priest had spoken those words whereby the marriage could have been brought to a halt, but even as the clergyman had looked at him, Jared had lowered it, withdrawn his silent objection, relinquished that most final chance. He could not take Rachel under these circumstances, could not force her this way; she had chosen William Thomas and he must abide by her decision.

Inside the tiny church Ellen stared down at the posy Rachel had passed her to hold. The tears that filled her eyes blurred the delicate little blooms into a cloudy mass as the priest, finding no just cause or impediment, droned on, asking, 'Who giveth this woman to this man?'

'Stop!'

A flurry of hushed words broke out over the pews as startled villagers asked each other the same question, chasing it from mouth to startled mouth. To the right of Rachel her father glanced sharply sideways while Ellen drew in a startled breath. Who had called out, who had interrupted the service?

'Is something wrong?'

Rachel felt the world sway about her. In the pews the onlookers fell silent, listening . . . waiting.

'Rachel Cade will not break her word, so I must break mine.'

A quiet, half-stifled sob escaped Ellen's mouth as she sagged against a pew.

He couldn't! Rachel's mouth moved but no sound came.

'I sat beside her when she was brought in from the heath after her life had been threatened by a madwoman . . .'

The voice went on, strong and even, ignoring the gasps from priest and congregation.

'. . . many times during those long hours she drifted in and out of consciousness and each time she called one name, each time she cried out for one man. It was during those hours I learned the truth, I learned who it was held the love of her heart. Since that night I have waited, waited for her to speak, but the words were never said. To Rachel Cade a promise given is a promise she will keep, though the keeping break her heart. I do not have that strength. She could not find it within herself to hurt the man to whom she gave that promise. I only hope she will forgive me for hurting her now.'

Beside her William took her hand, his blue eyes full of compassion as they looked deep into Rachel's own.

'Forgive me, Rachel,' he said softly, 'but I couldn't let you do it. I can't hold you to your word, knowing you are in love with Jared Lytton.'

Around them whispered comments buzzed like bees in a flower garden, ignoring the angry scolding of the priest. This was an event even the clergy could not prevent their talking of: the widow's son refusing his marriage vows and never a trace of a stutter in the doing of it!

'I know I ought to have spoken long since . . .'

The buzzing died away as the self-invited guests strained to catch the words that would be a talking point in Foxley village for many months to come.

'. . . but I was feared of hurting you, Rachel. I wanted the choice to be yours. I didn't want you to think . . .'

'I . . . I know, William.' Standing on tiptoe, she kissed his cheek. 'I know, and thank you.'

Her glance moving to Ellen, she could not hold back a gasp at what she saw in the other woman's eyes. She was in love with William! In love, yet willing to remain silent, to forego her own happiness for that of a friend. A smile trembling her lips, she murmured, 'Thank you too, Ellen, for what you would have done.'

'I never wanted you to know.' Ellen's own mouth quivered. 'I never said anything to William.'

'Nor me to you,' he broke in, his hand reaching for Ellen's, drawing her to his side, the truth of the love he had held hidden gleaming in his eyes. 'But there is no more need for silence, no need for any of us to hide the truth any longer.'

The smile gentle on his mouth, he turned again to the girl who had come to this church to marry him, to sacrifice her happiness so that his life could be happy. 'Go to Jared, Rachel,' he said quietly, 'tell him of the love you hold for him as I now tell mine to Ellen.'

His hand holding Ellen, drawing her close to him, William touched his lips to her hair. 'I love you, Ellen.' It was no more than a murmur, but it echoed round the hushed church. 'I love you dearly.'

The look in her eyes matching the love in his, Ellen smiled

through a haze of tears. 'I love you too, William, so very, very much.'

His hands bunching into fists, Jared watched the wedding group emerge from the church. It was over, Rachel was married to another man. Every part of him wincing with a pain he knew he would carry with him for the rest of his life, he watched her walk, arm through William's, face wreathed in a radiant smile as she looked up at him. She had made her choice. He turned away to where his carriage stood waiting. It was obvious she was satisfied with it.

'Jared.' He stopped at the sound of his name, then turned to see Rachel coming across the grass towards him. 'Jared, I . . .'

'No!' He stepped back as she stretched out a hand to him, his face drawn as if he had aged overnight, his voice ragged. 'Don't touch me, Rachel, for if you do . . . if once I take you in my arms . . . I swear I'll never let you go.'

'Jared, please . . .'

'It's too late for please.' The words were dragged from him, the pain of every syllable marked in his face, stamped in the shadows that filled his eyes. 'I should have done what I came to do, but I did not and now it's too late for both of us. I came to this church to prevent your marriage to William Thomas. When that priest called for any just cause against it, I raised my hand. I was ready to claim you, Rachel, regardless of the promise I had made; ready to tell the whole damned world that you loved *me*, not the widow's son. Then I looked at you. I could not see your face but I did not need to. Knew I could not hurt you any more, I have done enough of that already.'

His voice softened, and as Rachel caught the vain attempt at a smile, she felt her heart swell. He loved her so much he had come to prevent her marrying someone else then stepped aside, thrown away the last chance of his own happiness so as not to cause her grief.

'Jared . . .' She raised a hand once more and this time he caught her wrist, holding it in a grip of steel.

'I wish you happiness, Rachel, you and William. But before you go to him, I want you to know . . . I want to tell you one last time: I love you, Rachel Cade. I will love you to my life's end.'

For a long moment he stared down at her as if engraving every line of her lovely face on his memory. Yards away the watching group of people seemed to fade from existence, leaving only him and a silver-blonde girl with pink rose-buds in her hair, a girl whose violet eyes shone with a love that tore at his heart. 'Rachel!' he murmured, then almost throwing down her hand he turned away, knowing if he did not go now he never would.

'Jared!' Rachel called as he turned away. 'Jared, if you will not listen to me then, please, look . . . just look!' She ran in front of him, her left hand lifted.

For a moment the significance of her gesture did not penetrate his haze of pain, then he looked at her, his molten copper stare unbelieving . . . questioning.

'It's true, Jared.' Rachel smiled at him. 'I am not Mrs William Thomas. William halted the wedding, he . . .'

But she got no further for she was in his arms and his mouth was already claiming hers.

'Did I ever tell you that I love you, Mr Lytton?' said Rachel, smiling impishly as he released her.

Around them the breeze rustled the leaves of ancient trees which murmured their approval as he caught her close, his whispered words ruffling her hair.

'Only in your sleep, my darling, but we have the rest of our lives for me to teach you better than that.'

If you enjoyed A PROMISE GIVEN, here's a foretaste of Meg Hutchinson's new novel, BITTER SEED:

Chapter One

'Oh, yes, Father, *you* know best! You have always known what was best, both for Mark and myself. It has always been do what *you* say, do things the way *you* think they should be done. No thought to what Mark or I might want, no matter what our feelings . . .'

'Shut your mouth!' Luther Kenton smashed his fist on the table separating him from his daughter. 'I haven't asked for your opinion nor never will, no fear of that. There be nothing inside a woman's head that's worth the enquiry . . . just do what a woman be meant to do: keep your mouth closed!'

'Like my mother did, like she had to do all those years she was married to you, like you have forced Mark to do ever since he became old enough to think for himself!' Isabel Kenton stared into the face of her father, a man she had feared for almost all of her twenty-one years. 'Well, this time there is nothing you can do. For the first time in his life Mark is his own man, he is free of you . . .'

'I said, shut your mouth!' Eyes starting with the anger that raged inside him, Luther jumped to his feet, his heavy-set body leaning across the table, one hand coming close to her face. 'Shut it . . . or you'll feel the back of my hand across it!'

'It would not be the first time, nor would it come as any surprise.' Isabel sat perfectly still. 'After all, that is the only place either of your children has ever felt the touch of your hand. You are a bully and a bigot. You ruled my mother until the day she died, just as you have ruled my brother and me, but your rule is ended, Father. Mark is free of you and from today I will be too . . .'

'I told you to shut your mouth!' Luther Kenton's hand came flashing across the remaining space, smacking hard against her mouth, snapping her head back on her neck. 'You don't have enough sense to learn, you or that bloody brother you be so fond of defending. You will do as I say, the pair of you, and should *you* ever dare back answer me again, girl, it will be more than a smack to the mouth you'll get.'

Blood was oozing from the split in her bottom lip but Isabel made no move to wipe it away. 'I have no doubt of that, Father,' she said quietly. 'That has always been you strategy. If anything gets in your way, destroy it. If anyone opposes you, beat them into submission. Well, you have money enough to achieve the first and the physical strength to accomplish the second, especially where your opponents are your son and daughter. But I tell you this – for all your strength and all your money, you are not nor ever will be half the man your son is!'

Taking in his breath with a soft hiss, Luther stared at her, his hand already raised to strike again.

Across the small space Isabel's hazel eyes held his calmly though her heart thumped with fear. She had never defied him before, never questioned his word, accepting always that as her father she must do what he said no matter what the pain or unhappiness to herself, but feeling that hurt doubled whenever his anger fell on Mark.

'Go ahead, Father,' she said as his hand began its downward swing, 'add one more memory of your spite, one more reason for my remembering you as you are: a man empty of love but filled with ambition. You have already sacrificed your wife to it and would offer your children too. But you will not sacrifice me upon that altar, and when Mark returns I pray God he too will find the courage to throw the business back in your face.'

'Get out!' His raised hand crashed once more on to the table. 'Get out!'

Rising from her chair, she stood looking at the man now hunched over the table, his hands supporting his weight, his chin on his chest.

'That is exactly what I intend to do. This is the last time you will ever have to look on me, or I on you. I wish I could say that causes me sorrow, Father, but it does not. The only sense it gives me is one of joy.'

'You'll leave this house when *I* say.' His voice hard with anger, Luther did not look up. 'And that will be as Jago Timmins's wife.'

Isabel caught the back of the chair from which she had risen, her knuckles showing white. 'No, Father,' she said tightly. 'I will not marry Jago Timmins.'

'You'll do as I bloody well tell you!' Luther straightened up, his face purple with rage, the words exploding from his lips. '*I* be master in this house!'

'You always have been. My mother would testify to that were she still alive, but she is not. She gave up trying to live with your cruelty and meanness, and I will no longer live with them either. Nor do I intend to die because of them.'

Isabel felt a shiver of fear tingling along her spine even as she spoke. Luther Kenton had never before been confronted with the truth in his own house; now it was being thrown at him by the daughter who had always been quietly submissive, and his reaction could only be anticipated.

Across the room an ormolu clock ticked into a silence charged with both fear and rage. Isabel's hands still held on to the chair though she longed to turn and run from the room. But she would not. She had long awaited this day, each of the ones before filled with terror that her father would marry her off to Jago Timmins before she could make good her escape; but now her deliverance was here and nothing would make her consent to marry that man. Breath catching nervously in her lungs, Isabel kept her voice calm.

'I tell you again, I will not marry Jago Timmins and I am leaving this house today.'

The muscles in his neck standing out like thick cords, the left side of his face twitching spasmodically, Luther remained hunched across the table but now his face was lifted to hers. 'You leave this house and you burn your boats. You won't get a brass farthing from me, not so much as a bloody brass farthing! And who do you think will even look at you without it?'

'If you think that causes me worry you are wrong.' Isabel stared into eyes that still seemed cold and dead despite the anger etched clearly on her father's chiselled features. Money is the last thing I ever wanted from you. As for my boats, let them burn. When I come to a river I will swim across or drown in the attempt. Either way I will do it smiling, glad to be free of you.'

'Oh, arrh?' Luther snarled. 'You'll be glad to be gone from me. But how will you feel a few weeks from now? A few weeks of having nothing to eat save what you can beg will have you singing a different song. A month . . . I'll give you a month. But you'll be back long afore that, whining for me to get you out of the mess you'll be in, begging to be given back your home; and him, that brother of yours, he'll be mewling after summat else. Will already have forgotten this latest fad of joining the Army.'

Isabel walked to the door then hesitated, looking back to meet cold eyes that burned like grey ice. 'I cannot speak for Mark.' Blood still oozed from the cut in her lip, trickling down steadily to drip from her chin, but still she did not check it. 'But for myself, I vow that once I have left this house only your death of mine will ever bring me back to it.'

'Arrh, you be right.' Luther's anger flared anew. 'It will be the death of one, but that one won't be me!'

'I said I would not speak for Mark's feelings.' Isabel forced herself to stand firm as her father got to his feet, his face dark with rage. 'And perhaps before *you* do, you should know you can no longer exert any influence over his life. The fad, as you call it, will by now be reality. Mark left for Birmingham on the morning train. He has gone to enlist. And before you speak of buying his release, even should he wish you to do so, you might remember this country is now at war! If Mark has enlisted, and I am positive he will have done so, then there is nothing your money can do. He will be beyond your reach, for at least as long as this war continues, and if God sees fit to return him here then maybe he will continue to follow his own way. Maybe you will no longer dominate him!'

'Mark's gone to enlist?' His voice was thick with rage. 'After what I said to him!'

'Maybe it was *because* of what you said to him. Mark is no longer a child. You cannot go on ordering his every move, making every decision for him. You cannot *demand* he go into the business, he . . .'

'I can't demand?' Luther kicked savagely at the chair he had earlier sat on, sending it crashing sideways against a tall spindle-legged plant stand, toppling the aspidistra that crowned it. 'I can't tell him? I can tell him this: either he comes into the business *now,* or he can kiss goodbye to my money. Like you, he'll not see a penny.'

'Bringing Mark into the business will not be achieved by kicking over a hundred chairs.' Isabel felt her heart jump violently as the china plant pot crashed on to the floor. 'That is a matter you will have to discuss with His Majesty and the Prime Minister. Somehow I feel that given the present situation they will be less than impressed by your temper or your money.'

'Present situation!' Luther said scathingly. 'This war that everybody's going on about – how long do you think it will last? Six months and the Kaiser will be on his knees. By Christmas this war will be over and done with but the country will still need steel.'

'And that is all you care about, isn't it?'

'Arrh, it is all I care about. What else do I have? A daughter – what good be them to any man? – and a son whose bloody head be filled with daft notions. Well, hear this, any man who leaves the employ of Kenton's to go playing bloody soldiers will need to find himself a new place of work when he comes back.

Arrh, and a different home if the one he has belongs to me. And that goes for your brother too. If he has signed on then he be finished. Let the Army find him a place for good. He won't be welcome back here!'

Isabel sat in the small trap outside Wednesbury railway station. Mark would rather he were picked up in one of those racy motor carriages he loved to talk about, the machines their father dismissed as 'useless contraptions that would not last out the decade'. They were noisy, Isabel admitted to herself. At least the one that Joseph Hayden had bought was. It was the only one she had seen in the town so maybe she should not pass judgement, but if they all made as much of a racket as that or smelled so terribly of oil and fumes then she hoped the town would not be blessed, or rather plagued, with more. In this one thing at least she was in accord with her father: motor carriages were definitely no replacement for the horse and trap.

'Train be due shortly, Miss Kenton.' The station master, smart as new paint in his green uniform embellished with brass buttons and gold braid, had come out on one of his two-hourly checks of the exterior of the station, colourful now with the flowers of summer. 'Would you care to sit in the first-class waiting room and I'll 'ave you some tea sent in?'

'No, thank you, Mr Perkins.' Isabel smiled. 'I prefer to wait here and watch the world go by.'

'If Wednesbury be the world then it won't take a deal of passin'.'

'Yes, it is a small town.' Isabel's smile widened as she answered. 'But you know the saying, Mr Perkins: there can be some good stuff in a little bundle.'

Albert Perkins lifted his peaked cap, smoothing one hand across his grey hair before replacing it. 'That be right enough and no mistake, and I reckon old Kaiser Bill will find out just how good when a few of our blokes get set about him. He'll see then just 'ow much of a mistake it is to be at war with England.'

'War is a terrible business.' Isabel's smile faded.

'Now don't you be worryin'.' Across the town the clock of St Bartholomew's chimed four and Albert Perkins checked his pocket watch, giving it a shake and holding it to his ear before replacing it in the pocket of his waistcoat. 'Like I said, this little shindig with the Kaiser will be over afore it starts. We'll soon see 'im off, never fear.'

'I do not doubt that for one minute. It is the thought of the men who might be hurt in the process, maybe even killed . . .' Isabel shuddered. This was why she had tried to talk Mark out of his determination to join the Army . . . what if he were killed?

'Won't be no men killed.' The station master adjusted his cap, this time with an air of confidence as if already having seen off the enemy. 'And only ones to be hurt will be the Germans as they tumble over one another running away. No, Miss Kenton, this little tussle ain't worth getting yourself in a state over. Come Christmas you'll be wondering why you ever felt bothered in the first place.'

Why had she felt bothered in the first place? Isabel watched the station master return to his office as the blast of a steam whistle heralded the arrival of the four o'clock train. Mark, her father, Mr Perkins, everyone she spoke to seemed to think this war was no more than a childish prank, an escapade to be enjoyed. Why then did she feel so differently, why did her heart sink at the very thought of it?

'Hello, Bel!'

Isabel lifted a hand to her twin brother as he strode from the station, coming towards her with all the self-assurance of a man who had achieved what he had set out to do. His mouth was set in a wide happy grin, sand-coloured hair which always resisted every attempt at constraint flopping forward untidily. This was why her heart always sank at the thought of war. Mark, the only thing that mattered in her life, would be a part of it.

'Good of you to come and pick me up.'

'Did you think I would leave my baby brother to find his own way home?'

'Less of the baby!' Reaching up, he pulled her easily from the driving seat of the trap, whirling her around in his arms. 'Or I might have to teach you a lesson in manners, me wench!'

'Mark, put me down!' Isabel tried to sound shocked though the smile that came instantly to her face belied her tone of voice. 'What on earth would Father say?'

'Who cares what that old ogre thinks?' Mark dropped a kiss on her nose before setting her on her feet. 'Nothing he says can affect me, not now.'

Isabel winced as he kissed the side of her face.

'Bel!' Holding her at arm's length, he studied her closely and his smile disappeared. 'Not you too . . . it was him, wasn't it? He did this to you?'

'No, Mark, I . . .'

'Don't lie, Bel, not for him, he's not worth it. Though I must admit I never thought even he would strike a woman . . . But he will pay. As God is my witness, I swear he will pay.'

'Forget it, Mark, there are other things to worry about.'

Isabel settled back into the driving seat, watching her brother walk around to the other side of the smartly painted trap and climb in beside her.

'*You* are my main worry, Sis. Leaving you with that swine while I was away getting an education was bad enough, but now . . . now I know he uses his hand on you the same as on me . . . Oh, Bel! Why didn't you tell me before? Why does it have to be now when it's too late?'

'I said not to worry about me.' Taking up the reins, she urged the mare from the station, into Great Western Street.

'*How?*' Mark asked through clenched teeth. 'How can you expect me not to worry? I know just how easily that man loses his temper, how hard his hands can strike . . . of course I am going to worry for you. Oh, Christ, Bel!' If only I had known yesterday.'

Passing tradesmen's carts on their way to the railway goods depot, Isabel guided the pony trap left into Dudley Street before answering.

'I did not want to tell you yesterday, Mark, because I knew what would happen then. I knew you would forget about joining the Army, and if that had happened you might never have got out from under Father's thumb. He is so determined you should join the business, and I know how much you hate the idea.'

'It isn't that I hate the business so much as I dislike the idea of devoting myself to it, body and soul. Father would allow nothing less. Once I started at the works I would be given time for nothing apart from the factory – and there are so many things life has to offer. Is it wrong to want to live a little before devoting myself to Kenton Engineering Works?'

'No, there's nothing wrong in wanting that.' Isabel smiled at a young boy who trotted alongside the mare, one hand set lovingly on her neck. 'And neither of us *will* be sacrificed to it, not if you have enlisted. Have you, Mark?'

Lifting a hand, he ran it through his sandy hair, a gesture that displayed the worry he was feeling. 'Yes. Yes, I have. I put my name on the dotted line and now I wish to God I hadn't.'

Returning the wave of the lad who reluctantly left the side of the horse, Isabel turned on to the Holyhead Road and glanced at her brother. 'It was what you wanted, Mark?'

'Yes, it was what I wanted.' He dropped his hands, letting them both hang limply as he hunched forward, resting his arms on his knees.

'Then we both have what we wanted.' Isabel smiled, feeling a stinging pain in her lip over the cut. The price of freedom, she thought, was a price well worth the paying.

'How can you say that . . . and how can I believe you want to be marred to Jago Timmins, a man as old as your own father?'

Ahead of them the heath lay to one side and half-mown cornfields to the other. The vaulting sky above changed from blue to scarlet as the furnaces of a myriad distant workshops were opened for the tipping of molten metal and the drawing of bars of steel. Isabel stared at the spectacle, feeling as she always did the awesome, almost frightening, beauty of the sight, knowing the power that lay behind it: a power that would soon be turning raw metal into weapons of war.

'I will not be marrying Jago Timmins,' she said quietly. 'Today I have reached the age of twenty-one. From this day forth Father cannot force me to do anything I do not want to do. I am free of him, Mark, and so must you be. Do not let him bully you into giving up the Army or anything else you want to do. Live your own life, Mark, live it before it is too late.'

'But you will still be here, in his house . . . But it won't be for long, Bel. Four months at the most is all this war will last, everybody says it will be finished by Christmas. Just four months more and I will take you away from here, I promise.'

Her glance still on the scarlet bowl of the sky, Isabel smiled. 'I will not have to wait four months. My belongings are already packed. Once I have delivered my baby brother home, I shall leave. I have already told Father.'

'You have *told* him!' Mark jerked upright, surprise replacing the worry in his face. 'What did he say?'

'What I expected. He used the same weapon he always uses . . .'

'His money?'

'Yes.' Isabel nodded. 'His money. He thought to make me change my mind about leaving the house and refusing to marry Jago Timmins by telling me I would not get one penny . . . or as he put it not a bloody brass farthing . . . from him. But his threats and his bullying did not work. I *will* leave, nothing is going to prevent that.'

'But where will you go, how will you make a living?'

Isabel guided the mare past the fever hospital and along the path worn by miners and laden carts going to and from the Lodge Holes coalmine and which now linked the towns of Wednesbury and Darlaston.

'I have thought of that. I have money I've saved from my quarterly allowance – whatever else Father may be he has never been mean with my dress allowance. I can use that to pay for a room somewhere, and thought that with the war I might be given a job in a hospital. I don't mind if it is only scrubbing floors, at least I will have charge of my own life.'

'There's no need for that, Bel.' A smile breaking across his face, Mark was suddenly the boy she had laughed and played with in those long-gone days before their mother's death. 'I have no money saved, I'm afraid, but I will get my pay from the Army, which should be enough to keep us both. I will find a place and we will share it, you and me together, and Father can keep his money.'

'Then you will not let him talk you out of the Army?'

'There is less chance of that than there is of the Kaiser becoming King of England!' Mark laughed. 'You can pick up your belongings from Woodbank House and when you leave, I leave with you. Flying Office Mark Kenton and his sister Miss Isabel Kenton will begin their new life together.'

'Flying Officer!' Isabel's face took on a puzzled look. 'But you were hoping to be given a place in the regiment of the King's Dragoons.'

'A commission, Bel.' Mark laughed again. 'A man is not "given a place" in the Army, he is given a rank. Either private, non-commissioned officer or officer.'

'Well, whatever!' A frown settled on Isabel's brow. 'The fact is you said you were hoping to join the Army, and not five minutes ago you told me you had, and now you are calling yourself a Flying Officer, whatever that might be. Mark . . .' The frown faded, leaving a hint of concern in her hazel eyes. 'Was there something wrong . . . would the Army not take you?'

Mark's hoot of laughter momentarily drowned the crunching of the gritty coal waste beneath the trap's wheels. He threw an arm about Isabel, drawing her close and hugging her.

'Oh, they took me all right.'

'But how?' Wriggling free from his grasp, she stared at him. 'You called yourself Flying Officer Kenton. You did, Mark, I distinctly heard you say it. But men do not fly to war, at least not in the British Army.'

'They will from now on.' His voice became low and eager.

'Men will fly to war and I will be one of them. Oh, Bel, I can't tell you how I feel. It's all so exciting, so new. It's the start of a wonderful world.'

Was it? Isabel looked at the face of her brother, shining with enthusiasm. Was it the start of a wonderful new world or was it the beginning of the end?

'I can see how exciting it all is.' She forced away the doubts that filled her mind. 'But perhaps, Flying Officer Kenton, you will tell me just what occurred in that recruiting office. Do they have flying officers in the Army, and if so, just what is it they are required to do?'

'They do and they don't. Now don't frown at me like a displeased school mistress – I will explain everything while you coax this old hack into getting us home.'

'Janey is not a hack!' Isabel was suddenly indignant. 'You call her that again and you will find yourself walking to Woodbank.'

'Sorry, Janey. See, she has forgiven me . . . she knows I love her like a sister.' Mark laughed as, hearing her name, the mare's ears flickered. 'Though I wish it were a Bean we were driving in. Now *there* is a motor car a man can feel proud of.'

'Janey and the trap will do for me.' Isabel flicked the reins. 'I am not a lover of those awful motor carriages.'

'You will be, Bel, you take my word for it.'

'Like I took your word you were going to join the Army but you did not?'

'I did, Bel. Look . . .' Mark twisted in his seat, meeting her gaze as he explained himself. 'I was in the recruitment centre. There were queues of men all waiting to sign on . . . I tell you, Bel, the Kaiser is going to get such a belting . . .'

'Mark! Flying Officer?'

'Oh, yes.' The boyish grin widened. 'I had already signed for the Dragoons when in walked Goosey Gandere . . .'

'In walked who?' Isabel shot him an amused look, her indignation at his calling Janey a hack forgiven and forgotten.

'Goosey . . . John Gandere. We are . . . were . . . at Cambridge together. His father bought him a biplane, lucky blighter! He got his pilot's licence then used to take me up at weekends or whenever we could shove off to his parents' place in the country. Needless to say, I got the bug. I spent every moment and every penny I could on flying lessons – that's why I've got no money. But I have got my pilot's licence.

'Well, like I say, Goosey walked in just as I signed. Turns out the man he was with was his uncle, Field Marshal Sir William Gandere. Anyway, Goosey told me he had signed on with the Royal Flying Corps. He was full of it, said they were set to play a pretty active part in the fun to come and that good pilots would be like gold dust. So when he told his uncle I too could fly an aeroplane, the Field Marshal immediately seconded me to the Flying Corps. Hence Mark Kenton, Flying Officer, RFC.'

'Mark, you mean you have been in a flying machine . . . up in the sky!'

'They don't do so well anywhere else, Sis.' He chuckled.

'But you never said.'

'And you know why.' The chuckle ended abruptly. 'Because of what Father would have done. He'd have put the kibosh on my flying straight away.'

'Yes, he would have put a stop to it,' Isabel agreed. 'But I don't know that he'd have been wrong. Flying machines are dangerous Mark.'

'Nonsense.' Mark swivelled around, once more looking to his front. 'They're as safe as riding with old Janey and she wouldn't hurt a fly, would you, old girl?'

The mare's ears flickered again.

'Aeroplanes will not be just a part of fighting this war against Germany. They are the future, Bel. They're here to stay.'

'You said that about the horseless carriage.' She felt the pace of the trap quicken as Janey recognised home ground. 'Surely there will not be the same noisy machines over our heads? They would terrify Janey, not to mention me.'

'You'll get to love them, Sis, despite the noise. This war is going to change a whole lot of things. Aeroplanes being only one of those changes . . .'

Isabel felt a sudden chill down her spine, as though his words were prophetic, speaking not of fun and daring in flying machines, but death and twisted bodies and the weeping of widowed women. Would it be like that? She wondered. Would this war that Mark dismissed so flippantly leave the nation weeping?

'. . . but the first step is to find ourselves a place to live,' he went on as his sister turned the trap into the short drive that led to Woodbank House. 'I'll ask Mrs Bradshaw if she knows of somewhere just for tonight. Even if we drive back to Wednesbury there will be no train until morning. Who knows? Perhaps now we are at war Darlaston might reopen its passenger line. Lord knows, we could do with it.'

Isabel glanced at the house partly screened by tall conifers. She had planned so long, dreamed so often of leaving this place, yet had not thought of finding herself an alternative home. What if her father's housekeeper did not know of rooms she and Mark might rent . . . what if there were nowhere else she could go? How Luther would smirk, how he would revel in making her apologise. What was it he had said? That she would soon be back, begging to be given the shelter of her old home? Glancing again at the house as Mark helped her from the trap, Isabel set her teeth. That was one pleasure her father would never enjoy. He would never hear her beg!